A Call to
ARMS

A CALL TO ARMS

A Novel by William Hammond

- ISBN: 9781612511443
- Era: 19th Century
- Number of Pages: 256
- Subject: Fiction
- Date published: 15 November 2012
- List price: $29.95

Like the previous books in William C. Hammond's award-winning historical fiction series, this fourth novel features the seafaring adventures of the Cutler family of Hingham, Massachusetts, and an expanding cast of characters. Interwoven with his fictional characters are such historical figures as Edward Preble, Stephen Decatur, Richard Somers, Samuel Coleridge, Bashaw Yusuf Qaramanli, and Horatio Nelson, along with such real events as the naval bombardment of Tripoli, the burning of the USS *Philadelphia*, the USS *Intrepid*'s last voyage, and the assault on Derne. Drawing on years of historical research and a lifetime of sailing, Hammond has been lauded for vividly recreating in his Cutler series, a chapter of early American naval history overlooked by most American novelists.

Set primarily in the Mediterranean Sea during the First Barbary War (1801–1805), *A Call to Arms* offers readers intriguing and often startling insights into the young republic's struggle to promote its principles in a world ravaged by wars and piracy. This time, the actions of a few heroic naval officers, the country's fate in a fast-paced plot that moves from New England on to at are the magnificent super footsteps of Richard Cutler and his beloved wife, Katherine. Theirs is a love story for the ages, but one whose future, readers will find, is threatened in a way that Capt. Cutler could not possibly have foreseen as he takes command of the USS *Portsmouth* and sets sail to join the Mediterranean Squadron and his son James, a midshipman on the USS *Constitution*. The author's unique blend of real-life people and events with equally unforgettable fictionalized characters, assures hours of entertaining reading for lovers of rousingly good sea stories.

William C. Hammond is a novelist, literary agent, business consultant, and sailing enthusiast. He lives in Minneapolis, MN, and frequently sails on Lake Superior and off the coast of New England. His first novel in the Cutler chronicles, *A Matter of Honor*, was published in 2007, followed by *For Love of Country* in 2010, and *The Power and the Glory* in 2011.

Praise for *A Call to Arms*~

"Hammond deftly weaves impeccably researched history with the day-to-day lives of the Cutlers. Readers are in the room as Jamie announces his interest in obtaining an appointment as a midshipman under Captain Edward Preble and are on the quarterdeck with Richard as *Portsmouth* sails into the Med and is attacked by Barbary corsairs.

'Hammond's intriguing plot and page-turning prose is a delight for anyone who enjoys a view of history as it happened through the eyes of well-drawn characters. This epic series fills a void in nautical fiction, offering a fresh look the Age of Sail from the American perspective." — *Quarterdeck*, **November 2012**

Praise for the Cutler series~

"I highly recommend this historical fiction series. It's as good as the novels of Patrick O'Brian. Start with the first book and read all three—then wait, as I must, with great anticipation for the release of book IV and other novels in the series. Bill Hammond is a master writer of nautical fiction whose literary gifts are yours to enjoy." —*Good Old Boat Magazine*

Praise for *The Power and the Glory*~

"Two previous books covered the Cutlers' naval service during the American Revolution, but *The Power and the Glory* is a fine stand-alone read. Hammond offers a deft blend of fictional and real characters that range the American coast from Massachusetts to Barbados, as Lt. Richard Cutler rises in the new American Navy. Hammond's meaty tale climaxes in 1800 with a splendid ship duel between the newly built USS *Constellation* and *La Vengeance*. This battle alone is so thrilling that I am now eager to look up Hammond's previous works, and I heartily recommend *The Power and the Glory*."—*The Historical Novels Review*

"As always, the naval, family, and political threads are woven together in an excellent, well-written, and believable narrative by the author as [Hammond] explores the early history of the young nation. I look forward to reading the next in the series. Recommended." — *Historical Naval Fiction Review*

sailors, and Marines determine the ... Tripoli, Malta, Sicily, Alexandria, and Cairo. At the center of all the excitement ... frigates of the fledgling U.S. Navy and a new generation of Cutler sons and daughters eager to follow in the

AT BOOKSTORES, ONLINE, OR DIRECT:

Customer Service
U.S. Naval Institute
291 Wood ...

MEDIA INQUIRES & REVIEW COPIES, CONTACT:

Judy Heise, Publi...

IN ENGLAND AND EUROPE

A Call to
ARMS

A NOVEL BY

WILLIAM C. HAMMOND

NAVAL INSTITUTE PRESS
Annapolis, Maryland

Naval Institute Press
291 Wood Road
Annapolis, MD 21402

Library of Congress Cataloging-in-Publication Data

Hammond, William C., 1947–
    A call to arms : a novel / by William C. Hammond.
      p. cm.
    ISBN 978-1-61251-144-3 (hardcover : alk. paper) —
    ISBN 978-1-61251-145-0 (ebook)   1. United States. Navy—History—18th century—
Fiction. 2. United States--History, Naval—To 1900—Fiction. I. Title.
    PS3608.A69586C35 2012
    813'.6—dc23

                                                                    2012028105

∞ This paper meets the requirements of ANSI/NISO z39.48-1992 (Permanence of Paper).

Printed in the United States of America.

20 19 18 17 16 15 14 13 12   9 8 7 6 5 4 3 2 1
First printing

In loving memory of my sister
DIANA H. O'NEILL

In war there is no substitute for victory.
GEN. DOUGLAS MACARTHUR

Prologue

THE CONVENTION of Morte-fontaine, signed in September 1800, ended the Quasi-War with France. The Caribbean had provided an inspiring testing ground for the infant U.S. Navy, which over the course of two years had proven its mettle against French privateers and heavily armed French frigates. The treaty's terms were generally favorable to the United States and reestablished "inviolable and universal" peace between the two countries.

The dispatches defining the terms of the treaty that reached Washington in early October bolstered the spirits of President John Adams if not his chances for reelection. Each of the sixteen states chose its own election day, and the voting that had begun in April was just wrapping up when the military packet boat arrived from Brest. The campaign had been a bitterly fought affair between two rivals who had once been close friends and colleagues. In the end, by the margin of just one vote in the Electoral College, Thomas Jefferson was elected the nation's third president. Aaron Burr was elected his vice president.

The new president's stance vis-à-vis the military—specifically, the Navy—remained a subject of some concern, especially in the commercially vibrant New England states. Their merchant fleets were the life-blood of the American economy and the British-held West Indian islands. Those fleets were now carrying their trade around the Cape of Good Hope into the Indian Ocean and South China Sea. Enterprising New England shipping families—the Cutlers of Hingham, Massachusetts, among them—had opened the doors to the exotic Spice Islands of the Orient and the riches those lands promised. In these Far Eastern waters, however, lurked pirates eager to seize American cargoes. Would President Jefferson truly cut naval expenditures at a time when America desperately needed a strong navy to protect these vital trade routes? Would he willingly sacrifice the blood of American sailors just to save money, as his new treasury secretary, Albert Gallatin, seemed to be advocating? Most Federalists viewed such a policy as not only penny-wise and pound-foolish, but treasonous and suicidal as well. And it seemed uncharacteristic of Jefferson.

Was he not the man who, fifteen years earlier as minister to France, had angrily proclaimed force to be the only deterrent to terror? Did he not, as vice president under John Adams, argue that maintaining a substantial naval presence would be cheaper and more honorable than kowtowing to Barbary tyrants? On this issue, at least, Jefferson seemed more federalist than the Federalists.

But the facts were indisputable. One of Jefferson's first acts as president was to approve the Peace Establishment Act, which summarily cut the size of the U.S. Navy. USS *Constitution* and other magnificent ships of war were being laid up in ordinary, and officers worthy of promotion following the Quasi-War saw their promotions deferred or denied and found themselves languishing on the beach at half pay.

Navy Secretary Benjamin Stoddert was so frustrated by the president's flip-flopping that he resigned his post and returned to civilian life. So poor were the Navy's prospects that the first four men who were then offered the post declined the honor.

It was not top-level resignations, however, that soon forced the president's hand. It was the Barbary States. For centuries the rulers of the Barbary regencies had relied on piracy, extortion, and bullying to extract annual payments of tribute from European nations whose merchant ships plied the Mediterranean. True, they did not demand such tribute from England, France, or Spain, whose well-armed navies could fight back. But even these maritime powers offered consular gifts of jewels and coin and naval stores to maintain the goodwill of the Barbary rulers—and, not coincidentally, encouraged pirate attacks on ships of lesser nations to cripple commercial competition. The petty despots were only too happy to oblige. The merchant ships of Greece, Denmark, Naples, and other Christian nations continued to find their cargoes appropriated and their crews enslaved until ransoms were paid for their release. And the annual tributes rose ever higher.

American ships suffered in the same way, especially in the late 1790s when the infant U.S. Navy was preoccupied in the Caribbean. More than a hundred American merchant sailors had been seized and imprisoned, some for more than a decade. A peace treaty signed in Algiers in 1796 had proved ephemeral, as peace treaties involving the Barbary States usually did. The rulers of these nations relied on the booty their corsairs brought back not only to enrich themselves, but also to provide the wherewithal to add warships to their fleets and promote their reign of terror on the high seas. All this was justified, in the eyes of man if not of Allah, as a *jihad*, a sacred war against Christian nonbelievers.

Yusuf Karamanli, bashaw of Tripoli, was particularly put out. He felt slighted by the Christian nations, inferior in their eyes to the dey of Algiers, the bey of Tunis, and the sultan of Morocco, and he placed the blame for this squarely on the shoulders of the new American president. Thomas Jefferson had not yet paid the $225,000 Yusuf had demanded to ensure peace between the two nations. Nor had he paid the $25,000 in annual tribute that Yusuf claimed had come due; nor even the paltry sum of $10,000 to console the bashaw for the death of former president George Washington. Compounding the problem, because of a recent treaty with Sweden, Tripoli was now at war with no nation. Tripolitan sea captains and crews were growing restless, a potentially dangerous state of affairs for a despot whose sole source of power lay in his military.

By May 1801 Yusuf Karamanli had had enough. The six-month deadline of the ultimatum he had granted the United States to pay had come and gone. Worse, rumor had it that an American naval squadron was on its way to the Mediterranean to protect American shipping in the region. These upstart Americans had insulted him, his country, and the glory of Allah for the last time. Following a vote in the Divan whose outcome was never in doubt, he ordered his soldiers to march to the American consulate, chop down its flagstaff, and toss the Stars and Stripes over the city walls into the sea.

Tripoli had declared war.

One

Batavia, Dutch East Indies,
May 1801

D ECK, THERE! SAIL HO!"
The cry of alarm came from high above on the mainmast crosstrees. Below on the weather deck, hard by the helm, Agreen Crabtree shielded his eyes and peered up into the fierce equatorial sun. "Deck, aye! What d' you see, Hobbes?"

"Two sets of canvas, sir," the lookout called down. "Lateens."

"Where away?"

"Fine on our larboard beam." The lookout pointed in the general direction and added, "Standing southeast by east on a starboard tack."

"Ensigns? Other identification?"

"None that I can see, sir."

"Very well, Hobbes. Keep me informed."

Agreen cursed under his breath as he glanced down at the rudimentary chart he held in his right hand. Until recently, the waters that defined the gateway to the fabled Spice Islands had been off-limits to American merchantmen, and ship captains of other nations were still reluctant to share information that might aid a competitor. The chart merely indicated that the waters in these western regions of the Sunda Strait were deep, while those off Java, across the strait, offered hazardous shoals and sandbars—and thus, so sea lore cautioned, treacherous tidal currents. Agreen ran his left hand through his shoulder-length, reddish-blond hair as he considered his choices. He quickly concluded that he didn't have any. *Falcon* had sailed too far into the strait to wear ship or take some other evasive action. He had to maintain his present course and try to weather Cape Tua on the southeastern tip of Sumatra before jibing her over to eastward.

The cry from aloft brought Caleb Cutler up to the weather deck through a hatchway amidships. His eyes scoured the ocean to larboard before he strode aft toward Will Cutler standing by the mainmast chainwale. "Good morning, Will," he said somewhat nervously. "What do we have?"

"Good morning, Uncle," Will replied cheerfully, adding in an equally cheerful tone, "Trouble, it would seem."

"What sort of trouble?"

Will deferred to Agreen, whom he and Caleb joined by the helm. "Two vessels are approaching us," Agreen explained. "It's possible they're coastal traders, though I wouldn't bet the farm on it. Wrong rig. And they're on a course of interception . . . there." He pointed ahead to the northern limits of the strait where a mere fifteen miles separated Bakahuni on Sumatra from Merak on Java. "I'd bet a month's pay that we're lookin' at a pirates' reception committee."

"Pirates, you say?" Though no one doubted Caleb's courage, he had good reason to fear pirates.

"Most likely."

"We've seen pirates before," Will scoffed, "and not one of them has been able to catch us. We haven't fired a single shot." Then, hopefully, "Think we will *this* time, Mr. Crabtree?"

Falcon carried six long 9s as armament, though she was not a ship of war. She was a double topmast merchant schooner, the fastest vessel in Cutler & Sons' merchant fleet. But most vessels in these Far Eastern waters, whatever their pedigree, carried guns for protection against freebooters and cutthroats. Despite her new brass guns, *Falcon*'s speed was still the best deterrent to being attacked and boarded.

"Careful what you wish for, Will," Agreen muttered grimly. He wasn't at all surprised that Will Cutler relished the prospect of a fight. Everyone in Hingham, Massachusetts, was familiar with the lad's fiery nature. Agreen sighed and tried to calculate a way out of this mess; he found none. "Our friends out there obviously have an interest in us. And given our circumstances, there's only one way t' discourage that interest." He glanced at Caleb. "With your permission?"

"Of course, Agee," Caleb said. "Do what you think is necessary." Caleb Cutler's family owned *Falcon*, and he managed the wide-ranging commercial interests of Cutler & Sons, but he knew only too well that in a showdown at sea, the power and prestige of his position accounted for naught. "You have command of this vessel."

"Very well." Agreen looked hard at Caleb's nephew. "Will, take the tiller and maintain her present course. Do not—I repeat, *do not*—alter course without a direct order from me or Mr. Weeks. Understood?" Will nodded and took the tiller. Agreen walked forward to where his mate awaited his orders. "Are the guns primed and loaded, Mr. Weeks?"

It was a rhetorical question. Although *Falcon*'s crew had not yet fired the guns in anger, they had drilled with them nearly every day since leaving Boston three months ago.

"They are, Mr. Crabtree."

"Very well. Call out the gun crews, larboard side."

"Aye, aye, sir."

In short order, Peter Weeks had each crew of four men standing by a gun with its lashings cast off, its tampion removed from the muzzle, and its barrel loaded with a cylindrical flannel bag filled with 4½ pounds of powder and a 9-pound ball rammed down the bore to the breech. Assigning men to the guns left only a skeleton crew to sail the schooner, but the wind was blowing fair from the southwest, and the lack of fetch in these sheltered waters churned only a modest chop. Behind each gun, in specially designed rectangular containers, lay additional round shot and chain shot and, for hotter action close in, canister and grape shot. Rammer, sponger, loader, and wormer: each sailor understood his assignment and awaited orders from the gun captain—who, for each gun, was Agreen Crabtree. He had learned his trade while serving as a naval lieutenant with Will's father in *Bonhomme Richard* under Capt. John Paul Jones during the war with England, and, during the war with France, under Capt. Silas Talbot in USS *Constitution*.

The sun was approaching its zenith before the mystery sails closed to within view of those on the schooner's deck. Each man watched in silence as the two vessels—each with the high forecastle, lateen rig, and raked masts favored by local brigands—followed an oblique line of interception slightly ahead of *Falcon* to larboard. Beyond them, the islands of Krakatau, Sebesi, and Sebuku hovered low on the horizon before the lush green mountains of Sumatra.

"Mr. Weeks," Agreen said when the vessels had approached to within two miles, "stand by the helm. At my signal, have Will veer two points off the wind." He had considered sending Will below for his protection and ordering Weeks to take the helm, but that, he knew, would be problematic because the young man would refuse. Nineteen-year-old Will, the future of Cutler & Sons, insisted on taking every risk the crew took. He had made it clear even before the cruise began that he would not accept any sort of special treatment or attention because of his name. While he did not challenge that argument, Agreen realized, as did Caleb, that beneath Will's lofty stance blazed an almost reckless desire to prove his mettle. Both men also understood that if anything were to happen to Will on this cruise, they would have to answer to Will's mother. Katherine Cutler had been none too pleased when she learned that Will would be sailing with Agreen in *Falcon*. She relented, grudgingly, after her husband intervened to explain the business rationale behind the decision.

Standing by the forward larboard gun, Agreen studied the two mystery ships through a long glass. As he had expected, they had not altered course. A swift mental calculation of distance and relative speeds suggested that they would intercept *Falcon* in thirty to forty-five minutes. Speed provided no advantage now. Convergence was inevitable. They had closed to within a half-mile: a daunting distance for most long guns. But a long 9 could be fired with greater accuracy at a greater range than a shorter-barreled, wider-bore gun. Which was why it was so often used as a bow-chaser on large naval warships.

Agreen looked aft and signaled to Weeks. Weeks relayed the order to Will, who slowly coaxed the helm up. *Falcon* veered off the wind to lie on a parallel course with the two other vessels. Agreen knelt low beside the gun and sighted its barrel over the broad stretch of glittering turquoise water. Accuracy was not the aim of this first shot. He was simply sending a message.

He stood up. "Firing!" he shouted. With a yank on the firing mechanism he struck hammer on flint. Sparks sizzled down a quill to the main powder charge in the breech, and an explosion of orange flame and white sparks sent the 2,800-pound gun carriage careening backward and a 9-pound ball streaking forward.

All hands searched for the splash, and there it was—a plume of white water gushing up between the two vessels.

"They're not convinced, Captain," a member of the gun crew commented moments later. "They're maintaining course." As if to underscore that remark, the lead vessel fired a blank charge to windward, an internationally recognized signal of hostile intent.

"Well, then, let's convince 'em." Agreen walked a short way aft to the middle gun, larboard side. He knelt down and peered over the top of the brass barrel until he had the lead vessel wavering in his sights. He shook his head. On the uproll, where he could sight the best, the gun was aimed too high. A hit to her rigging wouldn't account for much. And more likely than not he'd miss her altogether. No, he needed to hit her near where her captain would be stationed. "Pull out the quoin two notches," he ordered a member of the gun crew.

"Better," he said to himself when the gun had been lowered. To Weeks he shouted, "Bring her off a quarter point," motioning with his right hand for emphasis.

Weeks relayed the order aft, and *Falcon* veered further off the wind.

Agreen suddenly held up the flat of his palm. "There! That's it! Hold her steady!" He stood up. "Firing!" he spat out as he yanked the flintlock lanyard. Another explosion. Another squeal of wheels as the red-painted carriage rocketed backward until checked by its breeching ropes. A second 9-pound ball screeched northward.

On the afterdeck, Peter Weeks raised a glass to his eye. Agreen did likewise amidships. Neither glass was necessary. *Falcon*'s entire crew saw the ball strike the railing of the lead vessel halfway between her mainmast and stern. Distant screams of men impaled by shards of jagged wood echoed across the jeweled waters of the strait.

A great cheer resounded through *Falcon*, followed, moments later, by a second great cheer when both vessels suddenly wore ship and made for shelter among the numerous islands dotting the strait's western regions.

"Great jumpin' Jehosephat!" Will exulted as Agreen made his way aft. "What a shot, Mr. Crabtree!" He punched the air with a fist.

"Mind the helm, Will," Agreen cautioned.

"Well done indeed, Agee," Caleb said calmly. "Cutler & Sons is most grateful for your excellent aim." Even the normally staid Caleb could not resist a smile.

Agreen grinned back.

An hour later *Falcon* hauled her wind and set a new course due east toward Cape Pujat. Tonight she would anchor in Peper Bay. Tomorrow morning, God willing, the long outbound leg of her cruise to the East Indies would be over.

VENETIAN MERCHANTS trading with the Muslim sultanates on Java were the first to open Westerners' eyes to the richness of the Spice Islands. What Europeans beheld in the Far East inspired the Age of Exploration, an era during which one maritime power after another sought not to advance the teachings of Christ, but rather to control the lucrative trade routes bearing the cloves, mace, coffee, black pepper, and other luxuries that well-to-do Europeans were keen to purchase. Throughout the 1500s,

Portugal, France, Spain, Britain, and Holland fought fierce campaigns against each other and against local kingdoms to gain control. In the end, the Dutch prevailed.

The Dutch East India Company—Vereenigde Oost-indische Compagnie, in Dutch—was founded in 1602. It became the world's first megacorporation—the first company to issue stock and the only company ever to be granted quasi-governmental powers to wage war, negotiate treaties, coin money, and establish colonies. For almost two centuries the VOC paid an annual dividend of 18 percent on investments. That handsome return encouraged additional investments in VOC and the spice trade, which the Dutch protected with all the means at their disposal. VOC merchant vessels were armed to the teeth with the latest in naval gunnery; on land and at sea VOC military personnel confronted and eliminated any threat to the company's commercial empire. By 1625 Holland held a virtual monopoly on the East Indian spice trade. Such was their resolve to control every source of supply within the 17,500 islands of the East Indian archipelago that the Dutch gave away the island of Manhattan to the English in return for the tiny volcanic island of Run in the Banda Islands where nutmeg was cultivated. The Dutch drove away, starved, or slaughtered the local Bandanese to ensure exclusive Dutch control of the island's plantations.

By the time *Falcon* sailed through a breakwater of small islands protecting the northern approaches to Batavia Bay in 1801, Holland's iron grip on the East Indies had relaxed considerably. VOC, in fact, was bankrupt and had closed the doors to its Far Eastern headquarters several years earlier. A victim of both internal corruption and external pressure exerted by the rival British East India Company and French East India Company, VOC had finally bowed to the inevitable and allowed in the competition.

Dutch influence remained strong, however, especially in Batavia, the old colonial capital on the north coast of western Java. Will Cutler stood as mute and full of wonder as the rest of *Falcon*'s crew as Peter Weeks guided the schooner under reduced sail toward the long commercial wharves near the base of the city wall. He could not see much of the city proper—the smooth, ten-foot stone wall prevented that—so he took in the area around it: a flat, largely treeless area where simple stone huts and makeshift tents seemed to form a separate city; the lush tropical rainforests beyond; and, farther away, jagged volcanic mountains wisping smoke. In the harbor, boats of all descriptions swung at anchor. Many were two-masted, ketchlike vessels with rounded bow and stern; others were larger—brigs, brigantines, and dhows—and several others were larger still. The largest of all looked more like a first-rate ship of the line than a merchant vessel.

It was another vessel, however, that demanded Agreen's attention as *Falcon* glided in toward her anchorage. She was of considerable length— Agreen estimated 150 feet on her weather deck—and displaced 800 or 900 tons. She had graceful lines and a jaunty bow and stern, and she was clearly a naval frigate: her gun port strake was painted pure white, and her sails were furled to their yards in Bristol fashion. Agreen's gaze took in her ensign halyard. There, high up on its peak, stirring to life in the awakening breeze, fluttered the Stars and Stripes.

"Well I'll be goddamned," he muttered under his breath.

"That's *Essex*, Agee," Caleb Cutler confirmed. He had walked forward to stand beside him by the foremast chain-wale. "I don't see *Congress*," referring to the U.S. Navy superfrigate that accompanied *Essex* as they became the first American warships to round the Cape of Good Hope into the Indian Ocean. "Perhaps she's out on patrol, gathering up other merchantmen."

"Stations to drop anchor!" Peter Weeks shouted from the helm. As the schooner slowly turned to the wind, the leeches on her jib and spanker began to shiver and her spanker boom jounced about. "Away anchor!" Weeks ordered when the way came off her. Sailors in the bow let go the anchor holds. The anchor rode rumbled out through the hawser hole, and the great wrought-iron fluke splashed into the harbor. The jib and spanker were quickly doused. For the first time since departing Cape Town, *Falcon* lay peacefully at a port of call.

Her entry into Batavia Bay had been duly noted aboard *Essex*, anchored several hundred feet away. *Falcon*'s anchor had barely touched bottom when the frigate dipped her ensign three times. *Falcon* returned the salute. Within the half-hour a ship's boat glided up alongside the yellow hull of the schooner. An officer dressed in white duck trousers, a loose-fitting white cotton shirt, and a fore-and-aft bicorne hat climbed up the rope ladder and stepped through the larboard entry port.

"I am George Lee, third lieutenant of the United States ship of war *Essex*, at your service." He raised his hat deferentially and bowed as the hot breeze tousled his sandy brown hair. "And you are?"

"*Falcon*, out of Boston," Caleb responded. "My name is Caleb Cutler. I am the proprietor of Cutler & Sons, which, as you may know, is a joint partner with C&E Enterprises based here in Batavia. This gentleman"—indicating Agreen—"is Agreen Crabtree. He is the master of this vessel. This young man is Will Cutler, my nephew. And this"—indicating Weeks—"is Mr. Peter Weeks, the schooner's mate. All sailors aboard are American citizens in the employ of Cutler & Sons."

Lee bowed a second time. "Thank you for the introductions, Mr. Cutler." His eyes scanned the deck. "I bid you all a very good morning and welcome you to Batavia. My captain, Edward Preble, has asked me to determine your business here, but from what you just told me, that hardly seems necessary. That ship you see over there"—he looked admiringly toward the vessel that looked like a ship of the line—"as I am certain you are aware, is *China,* one of your own. She carries thirty-six guns, four more than *Essex,* and a crew of one-hundred-fifty. In two weeks' time we shall be escorting her and a number of other merchant vessels home to Boston. You are most welcome to join us."

Most of *Falcon*'s crew had not, until this day, seen *China,* although everyone knew of her. Not only was she the largest merchant ship in the C&E fleet, she was one of the largest merchant vessels afloat. Her thirty-six 12-pounder guns had been procured by Will's father through his connections with the Cecil Iron Works in Havre de Grace, Maryland, the same foundry that had provided guns for USS *Constellation* in the war with France.

"Or perhaps it's the other way around," Lee commented dryly. "Perhaps it is *China* that will serve as escort. You will still be in Batavia in two weeks?"

"I doubt it," Caleb replied. "Your kind offer is duly noted, Mr. Lee, but we must conclude our business with our agent in Batavia as quickly as possible and return to Boston. Among other reasons, young Mr. Cutler here has a wedding to attend. His own."

George Lee smiled at Will. "Well, Mr. Cutler, I can understand why you wish to return to America with all due haste. Congratulations on your upcoming nuptials and on the success of your family's business. I am honored to have the pride of your merchant fleet with us on our voyage home to Boston. I hail from Manchester on Cape Ann, you see, and I, too, am the scion of a shipping family. I was, if I may be so bold to say it, one of the private citizens who staked the money to have *Essex* built." He grinned. "Perhaps that explains why Captain Preble saw fit to appoint me her third lieutenant."

Caleb reflected that Lee might well be right about that. *Essex* had been built three years ago on Winter Island off Salem, Massachusetts, courtesy of seventy-five thousand dollars in private subscriptions staked by merchants in Salem and elsewhere in Essex County who sought a means of protecting their carrying trade. She was subsequently offered to the fledgling U.S. Navy—which was delighted to receive her.

"A final matter," Lee concluded, "before I must regretfully shove off. Captain Preble has asked me to extend every courtesy to you while you are in Batavia. You will soon receive an invitation to dine with him aboard *Essex*, as your schedule permits. If I am also invited, I shall take pleasure in learning more about your cruise to the East Indies. In the meantime, if there is any service I might perform for you or courtesy I might extend, you know where to find me."

WHEN CALEB AND WILL CUTLER disembarked at the commercial quays and walked through the open gates into the city later that day, they took a few moments to steady legs still anticipating the roll of the deck. It was hotter here away from the gentle breezes of the Java Sea, and the intense humidity made the light cotton of their shirts stick to their skin. As they walked along the raised left bank of the Jacatra River, which bisected the city, each had the thought that they could just as well be in Amsterdam or Rotterdam. The red-brick and gray-stone construction characteristic of Dutch colonial architecture lined straight, wide streets intersected here and there by stinking canals with raised embankments. The center of the city was itself a fortress; nearly everything about this government hub had a military feel to it. Caleb took pleasure in identifying the buildings he had visualized from the descriptions of others. The nearby Koningsplein, a large open square, was surrounded by the three-story mansions of the social elite, each mansion separated from the others by rows of teak, rattan, and pine trees. Gardens full of orchids, sago palms, and flowering shrubs perfumed the air and masked the city's rank odors. On the far side of the square, nestled between two European-style churches, he spotted the Stadhuis—city hall—a substantial gray-stone, red-roofed building with Greek-style columns at the doorway. The attractive two-story building to its right housed the Far Eastern headquarters of C&E Enterprises.

"You haven't said a thing since we left ship, Will," Caleb teased. In truth, he was equally awed by the unexpected dimensions of this exotic city, notwithstanding the many details that Jack Endicott had described to them back in Boston. "What are you thinking?"

"I'm not sure what to think, Uncle," Will replied as he absorbed the city's sights and scents. Caleb had never seen his nephew so subdued. Perhaps he, too, was thinking that this city and others like it in the Far East were the future of Cutler & Sons.

A knock on the front door of C&E Enterprises summoned a servant wearing red-and-white livery and a sugar-white peruke with a black bow attached to the queue at the nape of his neck. He bowed low when Caleb introduced himself and his nephew.

"*Welkom, Herr Cutler. Wij verwachtten u.*" The servant caught himself and straightened. "*Excuseer.* Welcome, Mr. Cutler. We have been expecting you."

"*Dank u.* Is Herr Van der Heyden in residence?"

"He is, Mr. Cutler. If you will follow me, please."

The servant led them down a handsomely appointed hallway floored in black and white tiles. Numerous landscapes and seascapes adorned the wood-paneled walls. Here and there a chair or settee was strategically placed between long, thin, Chippendale-style tables set with blue-and-white porcelain vases full to bursting with fragrant flowers. The high ceiling kept the temperature in the hallway blissfully comfortable.

At the end of the hallway the servant stopped before a door and turned to face the Cutlers. "If you would be so kind as to wait here," he requested politely. He knocked on the door and disappeared inside.

He reemerged in the company of a square-jawed man of medium build with white-blond hair, ice-blue eyes, and a thin mouth. Although the finely attired Dutchman appeared younger than Caleb, Caleb knew him to be in his early forties, the age of his older brother Richard. Caleb also knew that Jan Van der Heyden hailed from Groningen in northeastern Holland but had spent most of his adult life outside Europe in the employ of VOC. Despite his good looks, he was unmarried. He had remarked to Jack Endicott during an initial interview that he was married to his business, and she was a most jealous mistress. That single remark had confirmed for Jack Endicott the wisdom of hiring Van der Heyden to manage the business affairs of C&E Enterprises in the Far East.

"Mr. Cutler, I am so very honored to meet you." He extended his hand and Caleb felt the strong grip as their eyes locked. Van der Heyden's English bore only a trace of a guttural Dutch accent. "And this young man, I must assume, is William Cutler, eldest son of your brother Richard Cutler."

Caleb gave Will a brief nod.

"Yes, Herr Van der Heyden" Will confirmed. "But please call me Will. Everyone does."

"So Mr. Endicott informed me. When he visited here last year, Will, he spent much time telling me about your family. From what he told me, and from what he has written to me since, there is much to admire." His gaze shifted back to Caleb. "Will you join me in my office? It is, after all, *your* office, Mr. Cutler.

Will looked about in appreciation as they entered the well-appointed room. Van der Heyden's office was the size of a living room in a substantial Hingham home. Oriental carpets graced the floor, each carpet supporting either its own cast of sofas, rattan chairs, and tables, or a desk with a straight-backed chair. There were three desks in the room, each of fine wood. The most substantial was near a large mullioned window overlooking a colorful flower garden as well maintained as any English garden in Kent or Hampshire. The walls were replete with tapestries, bookcases neatly filled with leather-bound books, and oil paintings of Dutch statesmen of a bygone era. At Van der Heyden's invitation, the three men settled comfortably on sturdy rattan chairs upholstered in a stylish red-and-yellow fabric.

May I get you anything? Some food or drink, perhaps?"

Caleb looked at Will, who shook his head. "Not at the moment, thank you. But Will and I hope to take supper with you this evening."

Van der Heyden made a small gesture toward the servant, who discreetly took his leave. When the door closed softly behind him, Van der Heyden turned back to his guests. "Mr. Cutler," he said, "not only do I insist that you and your nephew join me for supper this evening, I also insist that you both stay in my home during your time in Batavia. It is near the city square that you passed on your way here. We will have a better opportunity to become acquainted, and a bed with clean sheets in your own rooms must seem a luxury after shipboard accommodations. Am I correct?"

Caleb smiled. "You are. Will and I greatly appreciate your kind hospitality, Herr Van der Heyden."

"Not at all, Mr. Cutler." The Dutchman returned the smile. "It is the least I can do for an employer who agreed to hire me without ever having met me."

"I have great faith in Mr. Endicott's business judgment."

"As do I, sir. As do I."

"So," the Dutchman said, "How do you find Batavia thus far?"

"Will perhaps said it best on our way over here," Caleb replied good-naturedly. "Batavia is not Boston."

Van der Heyden sent Will a humorous glance. "Since I have not had occasion to visit Boston, I cannot make the comparison. Certainly the

climate here is different from yours, yes? This is our dry season; be thank-
ful you did not come here during our wet season, when we have drenching
rains every day. And the humidity! Ach! Such misery!"

Will and Caleb exchanged glances. The humidity could be worse?

To break the ice, or rather to melt it, Van der Heyden said jovially,
"Will, I understand from Mr. Endicott that you are soon to marry his
eldest daughter, yes?" Will nodded. "How delightful. When is the wedding to occur?"

"A year from now, in June."

Van der Heyden beamed. "June is an excellent month for a wedding. I
understand that Adele is a very beautiful young woman, and as intelligent
as she is beautiful. All of which makes you, my dear sir, a most fortunate
young man. I hope someday you will sail with her to Batavia."

"Or you, sir, to Boston," Will countered politely.

"It *will* be a grand affair," Caleb commented, "which is why we must
work diligently during our time here. On our return voyage we plan to
sail across the Pacific and around the Horn—a circumnavigation for
our schooner—and we plan to be back in Boston by early October. Can
we conclude our business within ten days, do you think, Herr Van der
Heyden?"

"We shall make it so, Mr. Cutler. We shall start tomorrow morning by
reviewing the accounts line by line, and we shall continue our work until
you and Will understand every element of our business, from our sources
of supply to the customers we serve in Asia, Europe, and North America.
Once you have mastered the ledgers, we shall visit several plantations on
which we harvest spices. I am not certain which you will find more to your
liking: the exotic plantations out there or the accounting books in here. I
hope you will find enjoyment in both. It is, after all, your future."

Two

Bermuda and Hingham, Massachusetts,
October 1801

H E APPROACHED the open *door cautiously, reluctantly, loath to enter. But he had to go in. He had to come to grips with the harsh reality. His love for his father bade him continue, as much today as it had two weeks ago when he received Katherine's letter at the naval base in Virginia.*

His father lay supine on the bed, propped up by pillows, clean white linen sheets pulled up across his chest. He appeared to be asleep, but it was hard to tell, so drawn and ashen was his face. Richard's two sisters, on deathwatch, sat on chairs near the foot of the bed. They were on their feet the instant Richard entered the room.

Anne was first in his arms. "Thank God," she breathed. "Thank God you have come."

Lavinia, the younger and more emotional of the two, burst into tears when her turn came to embrace him. She tried to speak but choked on her words; she could only clutch her brother tighter, her message as clear to him as if it had been preached from a pulpit. He held her close, comforted her, dabbed at her tears with a handkerchief until her sobs subsided.

"Leave him, Liv," Anne soothed. "He needs to be alone with Father."

"Yes." Lavinia swiped at a tear. "We'll be downstairs helping Katherine with supper," she half-whispered.

As they left the room, Richard drew a deep breath and turned to his father. To his surprise he found him awake with a weak smile of welcome on his chapped lips.

Powerful emotions coursed through him. "Father." He kissed him on the forehead, then knelt down on the floor beside him and clasped his father's left hand between both of his own, as if in prayer. "Father."

"You have come, Richard," Tom Cutler murmured. "I have been praying you would."

"Of course I came, Father. I will always be here when you need me."

Tom Cutler gave Richard's hand a faint squeeze. "You have been a good son, Richard. You have made your mother and me very proud. I will be with her again soon. So please, do not weep for me." Richard had to lean in close to hear. "Time is short, my son, and there are things I must say. Promise me you will think on my words."

"I promise, Father," Richard said, and the tears welled up despite his best efforts to control them.

Fifteen minutes later Richard Cutler, deep in thought and remembrance, walked slowly down the front stairway. His cousin Elizabeth Cutler Crabtree and his daughter, Diana, a precocious thirteen-year-old already showing her mother's grace and beauty, met him at the foot of the stairs.

"Richard?" Lizzy asked tentatively after he had embraced her. Katherine, Anne, and Lavinia joined them in the front hallway.

"He's asleep now," was all Richard could manage. No one pressed him to say more, respecting the tears in his eyes. Not until later that night, when he and Katherine were sitting alone together in the parlor of their home on South Street, did Richard confide in his wife.

"He told me I have his blessing to remain in the Navy. He knows that is where my heart is. Caleb will manage the family business, though I will be involved to the extent I am able. He wants Caleb and me to finalize the partnership with Jack Endicott. He sees that partnership as the future of Cutler & Sons. I'll discuss all this with Caleb tomorrow when he returns from Boston."

"It has long been on his mind," Katherine remarked. "I suspected it was why he needed to speak with you before . . ." She rested her head against his shoulder and began gently kneading the nape of his neck. Despite the intense sorrow of the moment, of so many moments recently, she could not deny her joy at having her husband home again. "So, my darling," she ventured gently, "what do you think?"

Richard put his arm around her, drew her in close, and kissed her forehead. "I think," he replied in a woeful whisper, "that I need your love now more than ever before."

"You have that, my dearest Richard," she replied softly. She kissed him tenderly on the mouth. "You shall have it forever."

• • •

"Captain?"

"Yes, enter." Richard had not been caught daydreaming or catnapping, though someone might have mistakenly drawn that conclusion. He sat fully alert in his after cabin, his brain reenacting a scene of that fateful day a year and a half ago that had brought him to this point in his life.

A young topman edged into the cabin and doffed his cap.

"What is it, Wilkinson?"

"Mr. Wesley sends his respects, Captain, and asks me to inform you that a vessel is approaching us from eastward. She's ship-rigged and looks to be a frigate."

"A British frigate?"

"I believe so, sir. She's flying the Jack, and her lines and rig are Royal Navy. She's a fifth rate, Mr. Wesley says."

"We're flying our ensign?"

"Yes, sir."

"Right. I'll come up and have a look."

When will this ever end? Richard sighed to himself as he prepared to go topside. If it was not England harassing American shipping in the Atlantic, it was France in the Caribbean. If not France in the Caribbean, it was Spain on the Mississippi. Or Algiers or Tripoli or Tunis or Morocco off the Barbary Coast. Or pirates in the Indian Ocean. *When in God's name will this ever end?*

He was well aware that the Royal Navy had spent the last twelve years charting the shoals and reefs off Bermuda, especially those in and around the approaches to its naval base at Hamilton. Since the loss of the American colonies in 1783, the Royal Navy had used Bermuda as a strategic stopover point between its base in Halifax, Nova Scotia, and its bases in the Caribbean. To the best of Richard's knowledge, though, the base at Hamilton was still under construction. So why was a Royal Navy frigate bearing down on them from the direction of Bermuda?

The answer was not long in coming. The British frigate was upon them within the hour, crossing the brig's wake and bringing her under her lee. Soon after emerging on deck and studying the oncoming vessel through a glass, Richard had ordered his crew to heave to and bring *Barbara D* to a standstill on the gently rolling swells. The merchant brig under his command carried only four 6-pounder guns and was no match for a British frigate in either armament or speed. There was nothing for it but to see what His Britannic Majesty wanted.

The frigate sailed up close to windward and feathered in and out of the light westerly breeze before setting her topsails to counteract one another and settling down on a lazy northerly drift on the Gulf Stream. Four oarsmen, a coxswain, seven red-coated Marines, and a blue-coated naval officer scrambled down the frigate's starboard side into a launch.

As the launch glided in alongside *Barbara D*, the forward oarsman on the starboard side shipped his oar, stepped over a thwart to the bow, took aim with a long gafflike pole, and hooked it onto the brig's larboard mainmast chain-wale. He and his mates held the launch steady as the naval officer clambered up the five steps built into the brig's hull. The seven Marines followed.

Richard greeted the British sea officer at the entry port. The short, stocky, red-haired man made a sharp contrast to Richard's lean six-foot frame and Saxon facial features as he scrutinized the deck and the American sailors watching him.

"Good morning, Lieutenant," Richard said pleasantly. "I apologize for not having a side-party assembled to pipe you aboard," he added with evident sarcasm. "This is a most unexpected visit."

The officer doffed his bicorne hat, more out of habit, Richard speculated, than in any show of respect or amity. "I am First Lieutenant Robert MacIntyre," he announced in a high-pitched voice with a trace of Scottish burr that reminded Richard of his former naval commander John Paul Jones. There the comparison ended. "I am on official business of His Majesty's Ship *Temptress*. May I ask, sir, who *you* are?" The man gave him a hard stare.

"You may ask, sir," Richard said, irked by the officer's presumption, "but I am under no obligation to tell you. What right do you have to board my vessel in such a manner? Has England declared war on the United States?"

The British officer sighed audibly. He nodded at the Marine sergeant, who motioned to his men to fan out, three on each side of the lieutenant. "I had hoped you would not resist me, Captain. Indeed, I had rather hoped you would cooperate with me."

"Cooperate in what way? I'm afraid you have me at a disadvantage, Lieutenant."

MacIntyre breathed another heavy and long-suffering sigh, as if he were being forced to explain something childishly simple. "You are an American merchant vessel sailing home from the Indies. Perhaps from a

British-held island such as Jamaica or Saint Kitts or Barbados?" Richard maintained an icy silence. "And you are bound for . . . New York? Boston?"

"Baltimore," Richard lied.

"It matters not. If you are sailing from the Indies, it is quite possible— dare I say, probable—that you have seamen aboard your brig who are British nationals, perhaps even a deserter from the Royal Navy. As a man of your apparent intelligence is no doubt aware, the Admiralty does not take kindly to deserters and mutineers. You have heard of *Hermione*, have you not?"

He was referring to an incident four years earlier when a sadistic captain pushed the crew of the 32-gun frigate *Hermione* to the brink of insanity. During a September night in the Lesser Antilles, mutineers seized control of the ship, sliced up the captain and most of his officers with cutlasses and tomahawks, and tossed them overboard to the sharks before surrendering the ship to Spanish authorities in Havana. To date, thirty-three of the crew had either been apprehended or had given themselves up. Of those, twenty-four were hanged. But more than a hundred remained at large, and the Admiralty suspected that many of them had found their way aboard American naval and merchant vessels cruising the West Indies. The Admiralty had pledged to hunt down every man-jack of *Hermione*'s crew, turning over heaven and earth if necessary to bring every last godforsaken mutineer to justice.

"We have no such seamen aboard this vessel, Lieutenant," Richard said flatly.

"Perhaps. It is easy enough for us to arrive at the truth. I will review the papers of every sailor aboard this vessel. It is a matter of international maritime law, Captain, so resistance is as pointless as it would be futile." He indicated the seven Marines standing at stiff attention, muskets at the ready. "If those papers are all in proper order, we shall be on our way."

"You have no right," Richard protested hotly. "Your interpretation of maritime law is incorrect."

The lieutenant curled his lips. "I not only have the *right*, sir," he sneered, "I have the *might*." As if playing his last and best card, he pointed to larboard where *Temptress* was rolling up and down on the swells, her starboard gun ports open and her guns run out. "Should you choose to resist, you and your crew shall pay the forfeit. Now let us get on with it. You are wearing my patience thin."

He nodded at the Marine sergeant, who motioned two men to go forward and two men aft. The two remaining privates and the sergeant stood guard amidships over Richard Cutler and his mate, John Wesley. Some time later, the two Marines sent forward returned from belowdecks, strong-arming a tow-headed youth dressed in standard slop-chest attire. His eyes bulged with terror and he was sweating profusely. He looked at Richard in supplication.

"This man 'as no papers," one of the Marines reported. "And 'e was 'iding from us down in the 'old."

"What is your name?" MacIntyre demanded. "Look at me when I speak to you!"

The seaman tore his eyes from Richard's.

"Cooper, sir."

"Rank?"

"Able seaman, sir."

"Nationality."

"American, sir."

"Where are your papers?"

"Dunno, sir. I must've lost 'em."

The expression on the lieutenant's face suggested that he did not believe either of the sailor's last two statements. "Why were you hiding in the hold? *Look at me*, damn you!"

Cooper did look at him, then dropped his gaze to the deck. "I panicked, sir, when I saw you come on deck."

"Why would you do that if you have nothing to fear?"

Cooper met his gaze and said, with a trace of confidence at last, "Because I lost me papers, sir."

"What he's saying is true, Lieutenant," Richard cut in. "Two days ago he reported to me that his papers were missing. We searched everywhere but couldn't find them."

"Perhaps that's because he never had them to begin with and you're both lying." MacIntyre's glare extinguished the seaman's brief spark of confidence. "Put him in the boat, Sergeant."

The Marine sergeant snapped a salute. "Sir!"

"Mr. Cutler, sir!" Cooper wailed as two Royal Marines seized him. "Mr. Cutler!"

"Stop!" Richard shouted.

"Yes, Mr. Cutler?" MacIntyre snarled. "I appreciate the introduction, finally. What is it, pray? Have you something to add before we depart?"

Richard tried to think. He had no statement rehearsed, no course of action planned. In such situations he had, for better or worse, learned to rely on his instincts.

"Lieutenant MacIntyre," he said, summoning as much respect and deference to his voice as he could muster, "allow me to introduce myself properly. I am Richard Cutler, cousin to John and Robin Cutler, English planters on the island of Barbados. I am also the brother-in-law of two Royal Navy post captains, one of whom is attached to the Windward Squadron. In my own right I am soon to be appointed to the rank of captain in the United States Navy and given a command of my own. Surely, as men of the sea and as fellow naval officers, we can resolve our differences. I have in my hold hogsheads of sugar, molasses, and rum from my family's plantation on Barbados. You are free to take what you desire from our stores if you will release this man Cooper. He has committed no crime. He is guilty only of losing his papers."

MacIntyre slowly shook his head and allowed a thin smile to spread beneath his bushy mustache. "Do I hear correctly? Are you, Mr. Cutler, a man of such high connections and credentials, attempting to bribe a Royal Navy officer? I should think your esteemed family would be shocked—I repeat, sir, *shocked*—to learn of such an impropriety. Perhaps it is *you* who should be tossed into the brig. Good day to you, sir!" He turned again to the sergeant and said, with regal authority, "Into the boat! *Now!*"

As Cooper was hauled off into the launch, Richard turned on his heel. "Get her under way, Mr. Wesley," he snapped before disappearing below. Moments later, those aft on the weather deck heard the sound of his cabin door slamming shut.

A WEEK LATER, on an invigorating October morning of yellow sunshine dancing off an indigo sea, John Wesley steered *Barbara D* close-hauled under shortened sail through the autumn-tinged islands of Boston Harbor, careful, as always when entering the harbor on a northwesterly breeze, to hug the waters off Deer Island and the Winthrop Peninsula before shooting into the channel between Governor's Island and Castle Island. Every member of the crew save for one, her master, was on station either on deck or in the rigging. The sheer beauty of this homecoming helped to mitigate their collective outrage at having to watch a popular shipmate forcibly taken from them.

Wesley felt those emotions as much as any man, but his immediate concern was for his captain. He had never seen Richard Cutler so despondent for so long a period. The captain clearly blamed himself for what had happened, although there was nothing that he or anyone else could have done to save the man. Cooper understood the risk he was taking. He was, after all, a sailor of British origin. Richard had not delved into the man's background when he signed on with *Barbara D* in Bridgetown, Barbados. The questions he had asked, and Cooper's answers, suggested that Cooper had served as a topman aboard several American merchant vessels. He had demonstrated his skill in his trade, and it was certainly a skill that he could have learned while in the employ of the Royal Navy. But Richard had said nothing beyond stating the risk Cooper was taking. Cooper had signed his name in the muster book nonetheless.

Wesley ordered stations for anchoring and searched for a suitable spot, always a challenge in an expanse of harbor teeming with sailing craft of all sizes and descriptions. Long Wharf—a quarter-mile-long wooden and stone structure thick with countinghouses, storage sheds, coopers, rope walks, smithies, sail lofts, deckhands, riggers, dock workers, casual onlookers, and merchant traders—was their ultimate destination. But they would have to wait their turn to offload. Merchant vessels occupied every spot along the wharf, the bowsprit of one nudging the stern of another, the vessels often nested three or four abreast, their yards a-cockbill to avoid entanglement. Wesley was continuing his search when he noticed the flash of a yellow hull.

"Turner!" he called out to a sailor standing nearby.

A wiry youth with a plaited queue and a gold ring in his right ear lobe hurried over. "Mr. Wesley?" he inquired.

"Go below and report to the captain that *Falcon* lies yonder and I aim to anchor next to her."

Turner instinctively glanced forward. "Yes, sir!" he responded enthusiastically. "Right away, Mr. Wesley!"

Turner's report had the desired effect. Richard Cutler was quickly up on deck and striding forward to the bow. He clenched a forestay in his left hand as he examined the waters ahead. Yes, there she was, her bow facing him as she pulled and pranced against her mooring in the fresh breeze and light chop. Richard slammed his fist into an open palm and glanced aft, grinning. Wesley grinned back. Everyone on deck, to a man, grinned back as well.

All was right with the world again.

More good tidings were to follow. *Barbara D* had hardly secured her anchor in the thick mud of Boston Harbor when Richard spotted his brother Caleb waving from the Cutler & Sons shipping office on the wharf. Geoffrey Hunt, the highly competent administrator of Cutler & Sons who had been with the company since its first day in Boston, was with him. Richard waved back happily, but what truly pleased him was the sight of his son Will making his way through the crowd toward a clutch of boats tied up near the landward end of the wharf, hard by a ship's chandlery. These small boats were public property, there for the use of anyone needing to row out to a merchant vessel anchored in the harbor. Richard watched as his son stepped aboard a clinker-built boat, let fly its tether, took a seat facing aft on the center thwart, and fitted the two oars between their thole-pins. Will back-oared away from the dock, expertly turned the boat around, and began pulling hard.

"Mr. Wesley," Richard said, when his mate walked up beside him, "I'll be going ashore with my son. I am certain Mr. Hunt has already requested that a space be cleared for *Barbara D*. He will pay off the crew once she is warped in and her cargo offloaded. Thank you for your assistance on this cruise. And your wise counsel. Please apologize to the men for my . . . bad mood these past several days. I regret burdening you with that."

"Pay it no mind, Mr. Cutler," Wesley said. "And don't fret a fig about *Barbara D*. She'll be as shipshape as can be before anyone is dismissed."

"Of that I am certain, John." They shook hands.

As Will's boat approached, Richard looked fondly about the harbor, happy at that moment to see even the screaming gulls soaring and wheeling overhead and the tidal flats covered with rotting fish, their stench covered by the clean scent of sea air born aloft by a surprisingly warm southwesterly breeze. Minutes later he was in the small boat shaking hands with his son, who moved to the forward thwart for the row back to the wharf as his father settled on the after thwart.

"I want to hear all about your cruise, Will, " Richard said after they had shoved off from the brig.

"There is much to tell, Father," Will said as he guided the boat shoreward through heavy traffic. "But I am under strict orders not to say anything until this evening. Mr. Hunt has sent word of your arrival to Hingham, and he has a packet standing by to take us home whenever you are ready to leave. Until tonight, mum's the word."

"So be it." As Richard watched his son deftly ply the waters of Boston Harbor, the thought came to him that Will had done some maturing during the past few months at sea.

IT WAS A FAMILY REUNION to remember. These days it was rare to have so many Cutlers assembled in one place at one time. Only Richard's sisters, who lived in Duxbury and Cambridge with their own families, were not present. The family had gathered at the former home of Richard's parents on Main Street, which Richard had conferred on Caleb along with the responsibility of managing Cutler & Sons after their father's death.

Edna Stowe, the housekeeper who had devoted the best part of her adult life in service to the Cutler family, worked her magic in the kitchen with the help of Katherine and Diana Cutler and Lizzy Cutler Crabtree. The feast of roast venison and potatoes, freshly baked breads, fruits and vegetables from the garden, and two silky-crusted grape pies topped any meal ever prepared in that kitchen.

"Caleb," Lizzy said, after they had said grace and were happily eating, "it must be a nice change to have so many of us here tonight. I suppose you're lonely sometimes, living alone in this big house. You need to find yourself a nice woman and get married and fill these rooms with children. Zeke needs playmates." She was referring to her young son, the only child she and Agreen could ever hope to have. She glanced at Katherine and then at Richard, a mischievous twinkle in her eyes.

Richard agreed with her, unaware that he was the pawn in his cousin's game. "I've been saying that for years."

Diana Cutler stifled a giggle.

"Well, my good man," Caleb announced magnanimously, "you need say it no longer. Although I shall miss them dearly, my bachelor days are over. I'm striking my colors."

Richard laid down his fork. "You're getting *married*?" he exclaimed so incredulously that those seated around the table burst into laughter. "*You*? God's mercy, will wonders never cease! Who's the lucky girl?"

"Joan Cabot. From Boston."

"A *Cabot*? From *Boston*? You've gone right to the fount of Boston society, haven't you? Are you trying to best your nephew?" He gave Will a quick grin. "How long have you been seeing her?"

"Oh, off and on for a year or so. Most definitely 'on' in recent months."

A quip came to Richard's mind, which he quickly dismissed as inappropriate for mixed company. "So that's why you've been spending so much time in Boston. I thought you were tending to family business."

Caleb smiled. "I was."

Richard shook his head. "Well that beats all. I suppose this means we'll have to make some changes around here." He lifted his glass and crooked his little finger. "Assume fancier airs. Dress in the latest fashions. Commission a carriage or two with the family seal. Take snuff and wear perfumed wigs. When is this magnificent event to occur?"

"Next September. We don't want to preempt Will's wedding. And don't believe for a moment that Joan is like the other Cabots. She's more like Katherine, who, as you know better than anyone, stooped low from her lofty position in English society when she married a base commoner like you." He smiled at Richard's wife. "You haven't fared too badly, have you, Katherine?"

"That's *Lady* Katherine to you, Caleb," she replied pompously, setting off another round of laughter and clinking wineglasses.

The evening wore on with each family member recounting events of the past six months. Richard was keenly interested in *Falcon*'s cruise to Batavia and his brother's impressions of Jan Van der Heyden. As that was far too comprehensive a subject to cover in an evening, Caleb suggested that he, Agreen, Will, and Richard meet the next morning to review the business opportunities inherent in C&E Enterprises. The mood of the evening remained merry until Richard asked his son Jamie for his update. Jamie had been uncharacteristically quiet through dinner.

The brown-haired seventeen-year-old turned immediately serious at his father's question. As if on cue, the mood of the evening shifted from merriment to solemnity. Puzzled by this turn of events, Richard glanced around the table. Although everyone met his gaze, no one offered an immediate explanation. Agreen finally broke the silence.

"We're at war, Richard," he said. "America is at war."

"At war?" Richard said in disbelief. "With whom?"

"Tripoli."

"Tripoli? The Barbary state? Why, for God's sake?"

"We don't know for certain. Details are slow comin' in. What we *do* know is that Tripoli declared war on us, not the other way 'round. Last May, Richard Dale left for the Mediterranean in *Congress* with a five-ship squadron. His mission was t' protect our merchantmen over there. I suppose that still *is* his mission."

Richard Dale was an old friend: a fellow prisoner with Richard Cutler and Agreen Crabtree in Old Mill Prison during the war with England and subsequently their shipmate in *Bonhomme Richard*. It was Richard Dale who had secured the guns for *Falcon*'s cruise to North Africa fourteen years ago when Caleb and the others of *Eagle*'s crew were being held captive in an Arab prison and Richard Cutler was sent to Algiers to try to negotiate their release. Richard could think of no better man to command a squadron against those same Barbary pirates—except, perhaps, for Thomas Truxtun, his commanding officer in *Constellation* during the war with France. Richard's brain was whirling with the implications when Jamie said, with a sudden burst of pride, "Father, I think I may have secured a midshipman's warrant."

Richard blinked. "What did you say?"

"I think I may have secured a midshipman's warrant," Jamie repeated. He looked to Will for support.

"It's true, Father," Will said. "When we were in Batavia, Uncle Caleb and I met with Captain Edward Preble aboard *Essex*. I told him about Jamie's desire to follow in your footsteps and join the Navy. Captain Preble was impressed, even more so when he found out that Jamie had studied at Governor Dummer Academy, just as he had. So he agreed to meet with Jamie in Boston when *Essex* returned."

"And did he?" Richard asked Jamie.

"Yes, sir. We met six weeks ago in our shipping office. Mr. Hunt was there, too. During our conversation Captain Preble asked me if there was anyone of high office who might recommend me to the Navy. I gave him the names of Mr. Hamilton and Mr. Adams. I am hoping you will write them on my behalf."

"Yes, of course I will, Jamie," his father replied in a faraway tone. "You couldn't have picked two better references." His mind struggled to encompass the evening's many twists and turns. The image of USS *Portsmouth*, his future command, still on her blocks at the Portsmouth Navy Yard in New Hampshire, sprang to mind. How would that piece fit into this puzzle? And Jamie a midshipman! The thought filled him with pride—and with apprehension knowing that war had been declared. But was it truly a war? Tripoli could hardly be conceived as a formidable foe. "Where is Captain Preble now?"

"At his home in Portland. He's recovering from some sort of stomach ailment and is waiting to receive his command. Which Mr. Smith," referring to Robert Smith, recently installed secretary of the Navy, "has told him will likely be *Constitution*. Captain Preble wrote me about that. I have his letter upstairs to show you."

"I see. Well, *Constitution* is a fine ship. She's not called 'the pride of New England' for nothing."

Richard stared down at the table, aware of the eyes watching him, his mind churning. Only when his daughter came over to remove his plate and to kiss him on the cheek did he emerge from his brief reverie. "Thank you, Diana," he said.

"You're welcome, Father. It's wonderful having you home with us."

"It's wonderful to be home," he said to her with feeling. He looked around the table and raised his glass. "To my brother's happiness and to my children's dreams. And to all of you for making this such a remarkable homecoming."

"Here, here!" they replied in unison.

LATER THAT NIGHT, as Richard and Katherine were preparing for bed in the fluttering light of three candles, Katherine said, "That was a lot to spring on you. But think on it: if we had started out with reports of the war, the evening would have gone a lot differently. Caleb was so looking forward to sharing his news with you. And Jamie has been wild to tell you. And now I have one more item of interest to relay."

He was sitting on the edge of the bed watching her undress, a sight that never failed to stir him. She was down to her sheer white linen underclothing, an apparition of the night that inevitably cast away the demons of the day. "Oh? What might that be?" His voice was distant, his thoughts conflicted by the prospect of war and the allure of his wife.

She walked over and tilted his chin upward so that his eyes met hers. "The Endicotts want to meet with us as soon as possible to discuss plans for the wedding. Anne-Marie reminded me that June is not far away, and she was right. Are you willing to meet with them? Jack promised that he will not discuss business with you, at least until later."

"That'll be the day. But of course I'm willing. Are you?"

"Yes, of course."

"So, you and Anne-Marie have become bosom friends during my absence?" His eyes dropped again to admire the form silhouetted against the candlelight.

"I wouldn't put it quite that way." She gazed down at him and tugged on an unruly lock of his blond hair. "I have the sense that you are not paying strict attention to what I'm telling you. What exactly is on your mind, my dear husband?"

"You want to know, exactly?"

"Yes, indeed. Exactly."

He placed his hands on her hips and looked deep into her hazel eyes. "I'm wondering," he confessed quite sincerely, "how I came to be blessed with a wife who is even more beautiful and desirable today than on the day I married her twenty-two years ago."

She tickled his neck with one finger. "You are quite the flatterer, Richard Cutler, a quality I have come to admire in you whenever such flattery relates to me. However," she added, "since you have been away at sea for three months, I suspect that at this moment you would find a female lobster desirable."

"I'm serious, Katherine. Tell me: am I as desirable to you now as I was . . . back then?"

Katherine folded her arms across her chest and cocked her head, as though sizing him up. "You'll do," she pronounced at length, "for tonight. But I have in mind several young men in town whom I have come to fancy. In my experience, younger men have more passion, and more stamina."

"Oh, I see. It's a young stallion you desire tonight." He pulled her in close and squeezed the firm flesh of her buttocks.

"Mmm. Think you're up to it, sailor?"

"We'll soon determine exactly who is up for what." He stood and finished undressing her. "If I were you, my lady, I wouldn't count on getting much sleep tonight."

She backed away to sweep him a deep curtsey. "My lord," she said in coy sixteenth-century fashion. From that low vantage point she looked up at him and smiled. Then she set about undoing the buttons of his trousers.

And the fires of the night blazed on.

Three

Hingham, Boston, and Portland,
November 1801–May 1802

A GREEN WAS CORRECT. Dispatches from across the Atlantic were slow to come in. Once they arrived, however, the national press feasted on them with bold headlines and overblown stories. America's appetite for updates about this sudden and bizarre clash of arms seemed insatiable. American honor had been impugned once too often by the Barbary States, and if European governments were too timid or corrupt to stand up to the pirates, then by God the United States would show the world that at least one country would.

"This plays right into President Jefferson's hands," Richard commented as he sat in the kitchen of Agreen's modest but well-appointed home on Pleasant Street, nodding at the latest issue of the *Boston Traveler* spread out on the table.

"How so?" Agreen inquired.

"In a good way, I mean. I'm as surprised as anyone by the president's strong stand on this war, particularly on why he believes it justifies a strong Navy. Listen to this." Richard read from the article he had been reading. "'The only way to repel force is with force.'" His finger slid down the page. "And here: 'Force is the only antidote to terror.' Think on it, Agee. Is this the same president who not so long ago signed the Peace Establishment Act and seemed poised to abolish the Navy?"

He was referring to an act of legislation that President Adams had initiated and his successor, President Jefferson, had executed soon after the Convention of Mortefontaine ended the war with France. That act had reduced the number of ships in the U.S. Navy to the six original superfrigates and a handful of smaller vessels, and the officer corps to 9 captains, 36 lieutenants, and 150 midshipmen—and most of them had been furloughed. Even those who survived the cuts regarded this legislation as the beginning of the end of the Navy.

"Hell yes, I remember," Agreen groused. "It delayed your promotion and booted me right out of the Navy."

"Only temporarily, it seems. And we have our friend the bashaw to thank for that. His declaration of war has forced the Navy to recall former officers. I'm told that *Portsmouth* should be ready for sea trials come spring, and I have every reason to believe that my request for your promotion will be accepted. A ship's captain has wide latitude in selecting his senior officers. As Captain Truxtun once put it to me, his life may depend on the quality of the officers he selects. So start packing your seabag."

Agreen smiled. "I'll do that, Richard. And I'm mighty grateful t' you."

"Nonsense, Agee. I need the best man for the job, and you're that man, friend or no."

"It's a shame Jamie can't serve with you," Lizzy interjected. She had come into the kitchen a few moments earlier with four-year-old Zeke Crabtree, a rowdy lad with the face of a cherub and a shock of yellow hair, who gave his father a gap-toothed smile. He squealed with glee when his father scooped him up onto his lap and started tickling him.

"Don't get him riled up, Agee," Lizzy admonished. "He needs to settle down for his nap."

"I'll just keep him here a short spell," Agreen assured her. He jabbed a finger close to Zeke's face and then drew it away in a game of catch-me-if-you-can. The next time around, Zeke grabbed the finger in his little hands, put it in his mouth, and bit down hard. His father howled in protest, a piece of play-acting Richard had witnessed many times before. Zeke shrieked with joy.

"*That's* the man you want for your first lieutenant?" Lizzy asked her cousin.

"I'm having second thoughts," Richard said as he watched the scene repeat itself, Agreen protesting ever more loudly and Zeke screeching ever more vociferously. The game went on until Lizzy cast her husband a withering look, at which point it ceased.

"As I was saying," she said when her son's shrieks had subsided to giggles, "it's a shame that Jamie can't serve with you, Richard. You *do* think he'll receive that midshipman's warrant, don't you?"

"I do. But I wouldn't want him serving with me, Liz. A father-son relationship on a warship is not encouraged and rarely approved. I can think of only one example in the last war: Oliver Hazard Perry served as midshipman for his father, Captain Christopher Raymond Perry, aboard *General Greene*. But Jamie will receive the warrant regardless of how many qualified applicants there may be. He's the right age; he's well educated; he has experience at sea; he has excellent sponsors; and, most important, he has the support of his future captain, a man of no small influence. And he's from New England. Most midshipmen hail from the middle Atlantic states, and the Navy desires equal geographical representation of its officer corps, to the extent possible."

"You forgot to mention that he comes from a good family," Lizzy commented.

Richard glanced in Agreen's direction. "Well, yes, he does, except for one member of that family."

Agreen gave his son a woeful look. "Damn me, Zeke," he said. "I do believe your Uncle Richard is referrin' t' you."

Even as Lizzy reproved Agreen for swearing she had to giggle at the blank look Zeke gave them. When Richard scraped back his chair, she put a hand on his shoulder. "Must you go, Richard? Do stay a little longer."

"I'd love to, Liz, but I can't. Katherine and Diana should be getting back soon from their ride out at World's End. This weather can't last forever, and they're making the most of it. Katherine and I are leaving for Boston tomorrow, and we have a lot to do to get ready. We have a wedding to plan, remember. Two weddings, actually."

"When are you comin' back?"

"Probably next Friday, Agee. We'll be staying with Anne and Frederick in Cambridge," referring to his elder sister and her physician husband. "And Caleb will be introducing us to his fiancée on Thursday. We're more than a little curious to meet the woman who sweet-talked Caleb into marriage."

"Don't forget your snuffbox," Agreen reminded him.

RICHARD AND KATHERINE awoke the next morning to decidedly different weather. Gone overnight were the summer-like days of early November that just yesterday had been warm enough to work up a fine lather on the bay hunters Katherine and her daughter had ridden hard together in joyful synchrony. The light blue sky had yielded to a dreary overcast that matched the gloomy gray of skeletal trees that had long since shed their bright autumn foliage. To the west, darker clouds were gathering, summoned forth by cool Canadian air that carried an ominous omen of harsher days to come.

The Cutlers had decided to take an enclosed coach-and-four to Boston rather than a packet boat. It seemed more appropriate under the circumstances, but it was hardly more comfortable. The thickly upholstered interior and the latest in leaf-spring suspension technology did little to cushion the bumps as the hackney coach jounced and juddered along the dirt road winding northwestward through the neighboring villages of Weymouth, Milton, and Dorchester. At a Roxbury crossroads, the coachman took a sharp right onto a better-maintained road that led straight into the heart of Boston along the narrow causeway connecting the shops and stables and single-dwelling homes of Boston Neck to the mainland. The coach finally shivered to a halt at Fourteen Belknap Street, in front of an attractive four-story house perched high atop Beacon Hill that offered a panoramic view of the pastures and walkways of Boston Common and the mast-studded harbor beyond. The three-hour journey had blessedly come to an end.

"We're taking a boat home," Richard grumbled to his wife as the driver stepped down to open the larboard door for his passengers and place a footstool under the three-rung disembarkation ladder. "To hell with formality."

As Richard assisted Katherine down from the coach, the front door swung open and a servant dressed in liveried splendor walked briskly down the short flagstone pathway. When he reached the carriage he bowed low in courtly fashion, his left leg out and his right hand over his heart. "Welcome to Boston, Mr. and Mrs. Cutler. Mr. and Mrs. Endicott are awaiting you inside. May I carry anything for you?"

"No, thank you," Richard said to him. To the coachman: "See to the horses, Robert, and be back here by three o'clock. We'll be departing for Cambridge at that time." He glanced skyward. "Looks like rain. Or sleet or snow if it gets any colder."

The coachman tipped his tricorne hat. "At your service, Mr. Cutler."

After they had stepped inside the freestanding red brick building and the servant had taken their coats, John Endicott appeared from a side room that Richard knew to be a parlor. At least it had once served as a parlor. Soon after the launch of C&E Enterprises, the Endicott residence had been transformed from a fashionable Beacon Hill home into something more like a French château or a British manor house. The furnishings and accoutrements were magnificent—the best that money could buy from the most sought-after designers and manufacturers in Europe.

Richard glanced at his wife, who rolled her eyes at him—whether a reaction to the pompous display of opulence or a signal that she was not entirely comfortable being in the home of his former mistress he could not determine.

"Richard! How very nice to see you! And Katherine! How beautiful you look! Marvelous to see you both!" Endicott's booming voice and the hard soles of his silver-buckled shoes echoed off the diamond-shaped tiles as the stout, balding, ruddy yet not unattractive man bustled up to them. He bowed from the waist before Katherine, then took her right hand and kissed it. "Welcome, my dear," he said, glancing up. "Welcome." He straightened, turned to Richard, and took his hand with a firm grip. Behind his back Katherine rolled her eyes again.

"Good to see you, Jack," Richard said. "You and your family are well?"

"Tiptop, thank you. As you are about to see for yourselves." He gestured down the hallway. "Charles," he said to the servant standing by, "please fetch a bottle of our very best Madeira."

"Right away, Mr. Endicott."

Jack Endicott led the way into a book-lined study graced with camelback sofas, Oriental rugs, stylish wingback chairs, seascapes and European landscapes in oils, and an attractive desk made of East Indian teak. Silver weights held down neat piles of papers stacked on the desk next to two goose quill pens set in decorative glass inkwells. A fire crackled agreeably within a deep marble hearth, beside which stood three women, two of them younger, all three dressed in the fashions of cultured good taste. The dark-haired beauty of the older woman was reflected in almost mirror-like fashion in her elder daughter.

"Richard! Katherine!" Anne-Marie welcomed them, her French accent giving her voice a charming lilt. She gave Katherine a formal embrace, which Katherine returned. Drawing close to Richard, she brought a hand to his left cheek, closed her eyes for a moment, and kissed him tenderly on his right cheek. She then stepped back, smiling at both Cutlers, and motioned to her daughters.

"Adele, Frances, you may greet Mr. and Mrs. Cutler."

Adele and Frances Endicott bent a knee in respect to their mother and stepped forward in unison. They stopped side-by-side before the Cutlers, bowed their heads, and swept graceful curtseys that their biological father, a marquis of the Ancien Régime and the last royal governor of the Bastille, would have applauded. Richard bowed low in response, but as she had done in the past, Katherine cast formality aside. She bade Adele rise and then embraced her warmly. She did the same for Frances.

Both young women responded rather cautiously to the overt display of affection—until they noticed their mother smiling at them.

"We have much to discuss, my dears," Katherine said.

"We do," Adele agreed eagerly.

"Then perhaps we can begin. Will is on Long Wharf but has promised to join us for dinner. He should be here very soon."

"I know," Adele gushed. "Mother and I often walk down to the docks to visit him. I find it so fascinating: the ships and their cargoes and the goings-on. Will even invited me aboard one of your family's merchant vessels. Oh, what a delightful day that was! I do hope that someday he will take me to sea with him!"

"I have no doubt he will, Adele, if you wish it. And it warms my heart to hear you talk so enthusiastically about the family business. You make your fiancé and his parents very proud."

Adele blushed. "Thank you, Mrs. Cutler. I can honestly say that there is nothing about Will or his business that I do not find fascinating."

"My son is a most fortunate young man," Katherine replied, "to have a fiancée of such beauty and charm who understands and appreciates his heritage and can support him in so many important ways."

"Thank you, Mrs. Cutler," Adele said from the heart.

"Is Jamie joining us for dinner too?" Frances asked casually, a bit too casually to Richard's ear. She was a pleasant-looking young woman, although as she matured she had assumed more of her father's traits than those of her mother. Her hair was ginger-colored and lank rather than thick and dark, and her bearing and characteristics were less beguilingly feminine than her older sister's.

"I'm afraid not," Richard put in sympathetically when Katherine hesitated. He was well aware that Frances' interest in his younger son was not—as yet, anyway—reciprocated. "Perhaps he will be able to join us on our next visit."

As the others proceeded to the formal dining area, Anne-Marie drew Katherine aside. "Thank you," she said softly, "for being so affectionate with my daughters. Jack can be . . . well, rather stiff and formal, especially when it comes to Adele and Frances, and I'm afraid I reflect some of that formality. It is, after all, part of my own heritage. But it does Adele a world of good to know that her husband's parents are normal people who care so much about her. You and I may have had our differences, Katherine. But please understand how terribly grateful I am. My daughters mean everything to me. They are my joy, my life." She stepped closer. "And understand this as well: I have never been, nor could I ever be, a threat to you. I love Richard in my own way for my own reasons, and I always will. But *you* are the great love of his life. He told me that himself, years ago, as we were fleeing Paris with Gertrud, God rest her soul. He has told me that many times since. And I have seen with my own eyes how very much you mean to each other. Truly your union is one blessed by God."

It took Katherine several moments to respond. "Thank you, Anne-Marie," she said quietly. "I have to admit, you have caught me a bit off my guard. But I do appreciate your words."

"You are most welcome, my dear. I only wish I had said this years ago. Now, if you will excuse me, I'll go on ahead. That knock we just heard on the front door is no doubt my future son-in-law. Charles will see him in."

RICHARD'S PREDICTION that Jack Endicott would not be able to resist talking of business matters proved incorrect, though he contributed little to the wedding conversation. The discussion that began over dinner continued on into the early afternoon. It was decided, once and for all, that because the Endicotts had only a loose affiliation with King's Chapel in Boston, the Reverend Henry Ware of the First Parish, the Cutler family's church in Hingham, would perform the ceremony. The adults agreed, further, that the wedding banns would be published in both churches for three consecutive Sundays beginning in mid-May, and the ceremony itself was set for 11:00 on the morning of June 24. A reception would follow at the Cutler home on Main Street.

In the midst of the excited chatter, Will leaned over to Adele, who was listening intently to the conversation, and offered a suggestion of his own. "I can't wait until June," he whispered in her ear. "Let's sneak out of here and set sail this afternoon for some deserted island in the Bahamas."

Adele clapped a hand over her mouth. "Will Cutler," she gasped. "For shame!"

She glanced furtively about, fearful that someone had overheard him, her rigid patrician upbringing at odds with some very plebeian desires. "Don't you ever tempt me like that again," she admonished in a stern whisper when she realized there was no cause for alarm. He slid his hand over to hers in apology. She took it in hers and squeezed it tenderly.

It was not until Thursday—the day Richard and Katherine were formally introduced to Joan Cabot in her home on Beacon Street, where Katherine was invited to spend the afternoon getting to know Joan and her family—that Jack Endicott broached the subject of business. He and Richard, together with Caleb and Will and Geoffrey Hunt, were together in the Long Wharf shipping office of Cutler & Sons, which doubled as the North American headquarters of C&E Enterprises. Clerks worked busily at desks set against two windows through which they could see the firms' ships tied up a few feet away, taking precise note of what cargoes were going where and to whom, careful to keep the accounts of the two companies separate. To date, the not-inconsequential earnings posted by the sugar and rum production of Cutler & Sons had been dwarfed by the commercial juggernaut that defined the spice trade of C&E Enterprises. The net earnings due the Cutler family from C&E Enterprises were distributed in equal shares to family members in Massachusetts, England, and Barbados, just as the earnings from Cutler & Sons were distributed. Although C&E comprised a much larger number of shareholders, the Cutler family's 50 percent share of C&E's annual earnings significantly exceeded the annual net earnings of Cutler & Sons.

"What effect do you think the war will have on business?" Endicott asked with concern. "I am referring specifically to the business of C&E Enterprises, although I am mindful of the implications to Cutler & Sons."

"None that I can see, Jack," Caleb replied. "The war, such as it is, is confined to the Mediterranean. Our customers in Europe are not affected. We can still serve them through Antwerp and Rotterdam and London."

"I was actually speaking of the war in Europe," Endicott said brusquely. "It has far greater ramifications for C&E. Bonaparte may decide at any moment to close the Dutch ports. Who's to stop him? The Batavian Republic," referring to the successor to the Republic of the United Netherlands, "is nothing more than a French puppet state. Napoléon could shut down the spice trade at any time, notwithstanding the British victory at Copenhagen."

Vice Admiral Horatio Nelson's victory over a combined Danish and Norwegian fleet at Copenhagen the previous year had effectively destroyed the League of Armed Neutrality engineered by Tsar Alexander I of Russia to enforce free trade with France, and had kept the Baltic Sea open to British ships.

"Why would he do that?" Caleb queried. "What would he gain? The French desire our spices as much as anyone else. And his taxes on those spices are helping the French finance the war in Europe."

"As do British taxes," Endicott countered, "for the British, whenever we ship through London. Which to my mind is why Napoléon may try to close down the spice trade entirely."

"With respect, Mr. Endicott," said Geoffrey Hunt, who often served as the voice of reason in business discussions, "that is something Napoléon cannot do. He may control much of Europe, but the Royal Navy controls the seas, and thus the trade routes to the Orient. If Napoléon were to cut off the spice trade to Europe, he would both enrage his own citizenry and lose the tax revenues generated by those imports. With virtually all trade then going through London, the British Exchequer would receive a bonanza in tax revenues. Napoléon would be cutting off his nose to spite his face."

"And there's talk of peace," Richard added. "Rumor has it that King George is finally willing to concede the British monarchy's claim to the French throne. His government is also prepared to formally recognize the French Republic."

"I concede your points," Endicott grumbled. "But it still troubles me."

CHRISTMAS CAME AND WENT, and the New Year delivered a hammer blow that dumped more than two feet of snow on eastern Massachusetts. After the raging nor'easter had howled its way offshore, it backed around off the southern coast of Nova Scotia, much like a mammoth first-rate wearing ship, and returned to blast the coast of New England with yet another broadside of frothing seas, dangerous winds, and layer upon layer of dry, powdery snow. For several frigid weeks travel by land became impossible and crews could not man their ships. When they were finally able to make it back aboard, they were faced with the laborious task of shoveling snow off decks and chipping away at ice layered thick onto standing rigging. The C&E merchant vessel *China* had departed Boston for the Dutch East Indies the day after Christmas, before the first storm hit. But the Boston-based vessels of Cutler & Sons would not be weighing anchor anytime soon, by order of Caleb Cutler.

Richard Cutler did not need a formal notice from the Portsmouth Navy Yard to know that work on USS *Portsmouth* had come to a virtual halt as a result of the storms. He had seen her only once, and that had been seven months ago, prior to his cruise to Barbados. Her keel had been laid down on blocks and her stem and stern posts had been raised into position. But her ribs still had to be set up, and the various knees and beams and angle pieces needed to support her decks were lacking. Planking along her hull and on her decks remained a distant dream.

"At least she'll be well seasoned," he muttered to no one in particular on a day in late January. He was staring glumly out the parlor window at a winter wonderland. Screaming children were romping about. Several of the older ones were pulling toboggan-like sleds toward the hill on Lafayette Street, recently named in honor of the French marquis who had visited Hingham during the war with England. Their cries of delight when an impromptu snowball fight broke out only intensified Richard's foul mood. His gloom lightened somewhat when he saw his daughter and her best friend approaching from the center of town along South Street.

Katherine glanced up from her book. "What do you mean, Richard?"

He jumped as if snapped out of a trance. "What?"

"You said that someone will be well seasoned. To whom were you referring?"

Richard had to smile. "To *Portsmouth*, my ship. Even if they do have her frame up by now, as well they should, it will be months before her planking goes on."

"Why well seasoned?"

"Leaving a ship's frame exposed to the elements helps to season her timbers. The harsher those elements, so goes the rule of thumb, the more seaworthy she becomes."

"Well, we certainly want that, don't we? But how forgetful of me. I recall you telling me that some time ago. So, when will she be ready for sea?"

"Late this year, I should think. By then this war in the Mediterranean may well be over. Agee and I will have missed the entire affair. Not to mention Jamie."

"Well, we certainly don't want that either, do we?"

He made a face in response.

Just then, Diana Cutler and Mindy Conner walked in the front door, rosy-cheeked from the cold wind. "Hello, everyone," Diana said as she closed the door behind them. She propped one hand on her friend's shoulder and slipped off her snow-caked boots. "Mother, is it all right if Mindy stays for supper? It's all right with her mother. And is there hot chocolate in the kitchen?"

"Yes, to both questions," Katherine replied. She smiled at Diana's friend, a shy, coltish girl with blonde curls. "Hello, Melinda," she said, using the girl's given name. "How are you?"

"I'm well, Mrs. Cutler. Thank you." She saw that Jamie was in the room and blushed.

"How was school today?"

Mindy giggled and glanced at Diana, who remarked with smug satisfaction, "Tommy Preston got his backside paddled good and hard by Mr. Evans. He was so mean to Debbie Patterson that he made her cry. He's always doing that. He hates girls. He had it coming."

"I'm sure he did," Katherine mused, recalling a similar incident when Will first attended the school. Derby Academy, which opened in 1791 as the first coeducational private elementary school in the country, was still very much an experiment. "You girls get some hot chocolate and then come back in and warm up by the fire."

"Thank you, Mrs. Cutler," Mindy sang out as the two laughing girls raced to the kitchen.

Jamie watched them go, then said, "Father, here's a thought." He folded his playing cards on the table; Will followed suit. "You want to sail to Portsmouth to inspect your ship, don't you?" His father nodded. "Well, I want to accept Captain Preble's invitation to visit him in Portland. You read his last letter. He's quite anxious to meet you. Why don't we combine the two trips into one?"

Richard gave that notion only a moment's thought. "That's a capital idea, Jamie. I'll write Captain Preble today and try to arrange a visit for mid-April. This cursed snow should have melted by then, even in Maine."

FEBRUARY AND MARCH crept by at an intolerably slow pace. That naval action was taking place across the Atlantic while he sat shore-bound on the other side was unacceptable to Richard. The Navy Department dispatch that confirmed a midshipman's berth for James Hardcastle Cutler in USS *Constitution* under the command of Capt. Edward Preble was some comfort. The dispatch that confirmed the promotion of Agreen Crabtree to the rank of first lieutenant, to serve in USS *Portsmouth* under the command of Capt. Richard Cutler, actually made him smile.

The Boston newspapers offered some comfort as well. The Federalists were outraged that President Jefferson had allowed American sailors and Marines to sail into harm's way in the Mediterranean without proper support and without the authority to engage an enemy that had declared war on the United States. Commodore Dale's squadron was impotent to do much beyond a halfhearted blockade of Tripoli's harbor. It was, the Boston press jibed, more a "squadron of observation" than a fighting force. Thus far, to what Richard privately confessed to Agreen came as a relief, there had been only one meaningful naval engagement: a single-ship action between Master Commandant Andrew Sterrett, captain of the 12-gun sloop of war *Enterprise*, and a more heavily armed Tripolitan corsair. Sterrett had taken the corsair as a prize, claiming after the fact that he was in compliance with the president's orders to retaliate only if attacked. Dale had refused to convene a court of inquiry to investigate the incident despite a storm of protest raging from the bashaw's castle in Tripoli.

Jefferson, for his part, continued to insist that he had sent Dale's squadron to the Mediterranean to chastise the bashaw of Tripoli, not to bribe him—or any other Barbary ruler who might also have a mind to challenge the United States. He had stated publicly that while America would pay ransom money to free captured American sailors, under no circumstances would the nation pay tribute to any Barbary state. And he was flexing American military muscle strictly on his own authority. Congress had been neither consulted nor informed about any of his decisions.

"Is that legal?" Agreen asked one sunny April day when he and Richard finished reading an editorial on the subject.

Richard folded the paper. "I have no idea, Agee," he replied. "At the moment the answer probably depends on who you ask. I'm no constitutional scholar, but my understanding is that only Congress has the power to declare war. But if we're attacked by some other country, the Constitution authorizes the president to act to protect our national interests. It was the same situation in the Caribbean, remember? President Adams acted entirely on his own accord. Congress never did declare war against France. And I don't recall anyone in Congress protesting after the war was over. So the issue remains open to debate. I suppose it's in the hands of future generations."

THE PICTURESQUE TOWN of Portland, Maine—or Falmouth, as it was originally called—held a special place in Richard's heart. It was where his older brother, Will, had taken his last steps on this earth before being flogged and hanged for striking a king's officer on a Royal Navy frigate into which he had been impressed. It was also where he and Agee had renewed their friendship after the war with England, and where Agee had signed on as *Falcon*'s sailing master for the cruise to Algiers. To Richard, Portland had always seemed like a smaller version of Boston, but with cleaner air and water and an ever-present aroma of pine-scented forests mixed in with heady scents of the sea.

On a day in mid-April, as the Cutler sloop *Elizabeth* sliced through the island-studded waters of Cape Elizabeth and Casco Bay, Richard and his son Jamie stood together on each side of a forestay that they clutched for balance. The air was bitterly cold despite the bright sunshine, and Jamie shivered in his thick woolen sweater and wool-lined sea jacket. But he would not go below and risk losing the exhilaration singing in his veins.

"That's the port dead ahead, isn't it, Father," he said, as a statement more than a question. The contours of the coastline and of the town itself were becoming ever more distinct. Directly ahead they could make out a wharf similar in design, though less imposing in structure, to Long Wharf in Boston, with a multitude of bare masts and yards clustered close by. They could see only one vessel under sail—a brigantine with two square sails on her foremast and a massive fore-and-aft sail on her mainmast—and she was standing to eastward, making for Bath or Castine perhaps, or maybe the Canadian Maritimes.

"It is, Jamie," his father replied. "See that tall, white steeple over there?' He pointed it out. "It's on Congress Street, near where we'll be meeting with Captain Preble. It's an easy walk from the docks. Let's hope he has a fire going."

In fact, Edward Preble had three fires going downstairs in the dwelling he and his wife used whenever they came to Portland from the family farm in rural Capisic. When Mrs. Preble showed the Cutlers into the parlor where her husband held court, Jamie reveled in the delicious warmth.

"May I bring you something hot to drink, gentlemen?" she inquired.

"Tea for us both, thank you, Mrs. Preble," Richard answered.

She turned to her husband. "And your usual, my dear?"

"Yes, please, Mary."

Edward Preble rose from a chair. "Welcome to Portland, Mr. Cutler." He offered his right hand, which Richard took in his. "I am honored to meet you."

"The honor is mine, Captain," Richard said.

"And it's good to see you again, my boy." Preble shook Jamie's hand. "I must say, Captain Cutler," he said as his gaze lingered on Jamie, "your sons are two fine, strapping young men. I imagine they send the young ladies of Boston into quite a tizzy."

"That they do, Captain," Richard confirmed, much to Jamie's embarrassment.

As Preble took stock of Jamie, Richard took stock of Preble. What he saw was a plainly dressed man of about his own height and age with a rather thin face, thin lips, and a tapering chin. He had a prominent nose, and his brown hair was combed forward as if to conceal advancing baldness. Thick sideburns grew down below his ears to a clean-shaven, square jaw. The skin on his face and hands was fair, almost sallow, the mark of a man who had spent too many recent months indoors. But the look about him, as his dark blue eyes swung from Jamie to Richard, bespoke intelligence and experience that served to justify his reputation as a hard-bitten sea officer who demanded the highest levels of loyalty and performance from his officers and crew. "Tough but fair," was how those in the know described him.

"Please, have a seat," he said, adding, after the Cutlers had complied, "You had a swift voyage from Boston. I was not expecting you until tomorrow morning, although you are most welcome here today."

"We had unusually fair winds," Richard acknowledged. "Fifteen-knot westerlies. If this wind holds, we'll have a harder time of it tomorrow beating down to Portsmouth."

"Where is your crew?"

"On our sloop. I brought three men with us. I should say four, since Jamie did much of the sail-handling."

Preble glanced at Jamie. "So you're at home in the high rigging, are you, son?"

"Yes, sir," Jamie said proudly.

"That is to be commended. It's imperative for every midshipman to have that ability and confidence, although many find it difficult." He turned to Richard. "Your crew can spend the night in the sailors' home by the docks, Captain Cutler. It's warm, and there are cots for sleeping. As for you and your son, I hope you will stay here with Mrs. Preble and me."

"That is most kind, Captain."

Mary Preble appeared just then carrying a pewter tray that held two steaming mugs of tea and a glass of white liquid. She gave the glass to her husband and handed the mugs to her guests, then smiled and left the room.

Preble held up the glass. "Warm milk," he explained, "for what ails me." He took a sip. "My diet consists mostly of milk and vegetables. It's a hell of a note, but it's about the only tune I can sing these days." He smiled ruefully at what Richard suspected was an oft-repeated witticism.

"How *is* your health, sir?" Richard inquired. He was aware that Preble suffered from multiple disorders, including typhoid, which he likely contracted while imprisoned aboard the notorious British prison hulk *Jersey* during the war with England.

"Depends on the day. Some days I actually feel like my old self. Then there are days so bad that I want nothing more than to resign my commission and be done with it. I actually did that not long ago, but Secretary Smith refused to accept my resignation. He granted me a furlough instead. In retrospect, I am glad he did. I am feeling better now that spring is in the air, and I long to get back to sea. The Navy lifestyle suits me."

"When might you be coming to Boston, sir?" Jamie asked.

"As soon as I am able. I am informed by my first lieutenant that *Constitution* is in need of major repairs. That should come as no surprise to anyone. She has been laid up in ordinary for years. In the meantime, I intend to man her with a caretaker crew. My first lieutenant is Charles Gordon from Connecticut. He has signed on ten sailors and a boatswain's mate—I should say, kept them on, since they've served as her caretaker crew in recent months. I also want two midshipmen as part of that crew: you, James, and a lad your age named Ralph Izard. He's from South Carolina and comes highly qualified. He'll be joining you in a month or two. Now, I warn you," he added sternly, "you will likely not find the superintendent of the Charlestown Navy Yard very cooperative. His name is Samuel Nicholson, and for a reason that escapes me he holds the rank of captain. I'll stop at saying that he has a rather large chip on his shoulder and an ego that could fill this room."

Richard was not pleased to hear Nicholson's name. He knew the man's reputation. Nicholson was the first commander of USS *Constitution* during the war with France, and Agreen had served under him as third lieutenant. He accomplished nothing of note during his tenure as captain, and Navy Secretary Benjamin Stoddert replaced him with Capt. Silas Talbot. Ignominiously dismissed to shore duty, the embittered Nicholson retained considerable influence among the rich and powerful in Washington nonetheless. And he was the uncle of the wife of Treasury Secretary Albert Gallatin.

"If he makes trouble for you," Preble concluded that topic of conversation, "he will have to answer to me. And I assure you he will not find *that* a pleasant experience. But under no circumstances are *you* to cross him. Leave that to Lieutenant Gordon. He will deal with him until I arrive. Is that understood, James?"

"Yes, sir."

With that, the conversation drifted inevitably toward the war in the Mediterranean. And on that subject Preble had surprising news.

"Commodore Dale's squadron is being recalled," he announced. "A second squadron is now on its way across the Atlantic. It's a more powerful squadron and it most definitely has the authority to wage war. *Chesapeake* is serving as flagship to Commodore Richard Valentine Morris. I don't know much about him. Do you, by chance?"

Richard shook his head. "I've heard of him, sir, but that is all. I believe he served with some success in *Adams* during the war with France. He has a good reputation, as far as I'm aware."

"Yes, well. Apparently that reputation involves an appreciation of the good life, which he is able to maintain due to the 'interest' he commands in Washington. Much like our friend Nicholson, I fear. These days and all days, that's the quickest way up the promotion ladder. So we'll just have to wait and see about the man. By the bye, your former ship *Constellation* is part of that squadron."

Richard had heard rumblings of this but as yet had received no official dispatch from the Navy Department. Preble, apparently, had. The fact that *Constellation* sailed with the squadron inspired a question.

"Was Captain Truxtun offered the post of commodore, sir?"

Preble nodded. "He was, for the second time. But again he declined the honor. He insists that if he is to serve as commodore of a squadron, he must have a captain assigned to his flagship. To allow him to devote full time to a commodore's duties, you understand."

"I so understand, sir, and I agree with him," Richard said.

"Do you? As it turns out, so do I. Tom Truxtun is a dear friend and a damned fine officer. He's the right man for the job, as you have seen at first hand. But while you and I might agree on this, our opinions don't carry much weight in the Navy Department, eh?" For the first time that day he smiled broadly.

"Will *Constitution* and *Portsmouth* be joining Commodore Morris's squadron?"

Preble shrugged. "Any answer to that would be pure speculation at this point, Captain Cutler," he said brusquely, but then added, with a curious glint in his eye and a twist to his mouth, "But I daresay it's a speculation worthy of our mutual attention."

Four

Boston, Massachusetts,
June 1802–July 1803

THE SOCIETY PAGES of Boston's newspapers couldn't say enough about Will Cutler's wedding to Adele Endicott. Among those gracing First Parish Church—in such numbers that not everyone found a seat—were the elite of South Shore society decked out in Sunday finery. Intermingling among them was the more heady cream of Boston society, led in regal procession down Main Street by the Endicott and Cabot families settled imperiously in park drag carriages replete with coachmen, postillions, and footmen in immaculate livery. It was, most agreed, a sight never to be forgotten. Quipped Gen. Benjamin Lincoln, at nearly seventy years of age Hingham's most distinguished citizen and war hero, as he took in the majesty of the occasion from the front steps of the church, "I have never so much as glimpsed royalty—until today."

Will and Adele remained oblivious to the rustling crowd and excited whispers around them as they faced each other at the altar. Adele had eyes only for Will, and Will for Adele, dressed in an elegant lavender taffeta dress with a white fichu and a delicate white lace shawl draped across her shoulders, her long ebony curls tumbling across it down to her waist. As the background rumblings, coughs, and throat-clearings quieted, the Reverend Henry Ware stepped forward and launched into a wedding service that many in attendance could recite by rote. As the questions were put to the bride and groom, and as they answered in firm young voices, Katherine, seated by the end of the front pew next to Lizzy and Agreen, stole a glance across the aisle at the Endicotts. Not to her surprise, she noticed Anne-Marie dabbing at her eyes with a handkerchief. Even Jack Endicott seemed, for once, to be moved by something other than black ink in an account book.

Katherine glanced back to the altar, at her husband standing beside Jamie as attendant to the groom, and at Frances and Diana attending the bride. She gave Richard a brief nod and Richard gave her one in return, those two simple motions acknowledging the twenty years of trials and tribulations and untold joys that defined the unique privilege of raising a son like Will, from the day he was born on the island of Barbados to this sanctified moment.

Soon after Reverend Ware had declared Will and Adele husband and wife in the sight of God, the wedding party proceeded en masse to Caleb's house on Main Street. Tents had been erected on the lawn and pits dug to roast the meats and vegetables comprising a feast of gargantuan proportions, for the entire town had been invited and the entire town had accepted. They came for the food and drink, but mostly to take part in a grand affair hosted by one of Hingham's most beloved families. Men, women, and children participated in the dancing and especially the games: lawn bowling for the seniors; quoits, sticks and hoops, and tag for the younger set.

Will and Adele made the rounds greeting their guests, but they did not linger longer than propriety and etiquette dictated. Nor did anyone expect them to.

"Well done, Will," his father said as the Cutlers and Endicotts gathered by the elegant coach-and-two waiting on Main Street to deliver the bride and groom to the Hingham docks. There they would board a specially reconfigured sloop that featured an expanded galley and, in the after cabin, an accommodation that would please an English lord—a snug room with a large bed with choice linen sheets and goose-down pillows. Four hand-picked sailors, an experienced and discreet ship's master, and a cook in the Endicotts' employ—all hands paid triple wages for the next four weeks—would sail the bride and groom through the wonders of Chesapeake Bay, putting into whatever port and cozy inn the newlyweds might desire to visit. The entire expense, including the purchase and outfitting of the sloop, was Jack and Anne-Marie Endicott's wedding gift.

Before the newlyweds entered the coach, Richard took the bride aside for a warm embrace. "Welcome to our family, Adele. We are so very proud to officially call you our own."

Adele returned his embrace and added a buss on the cheek. "Thank you, Mr. Cutler," she replied. "The pride is mine."

"Thank you for everything, Father," Will said. "And you, Mother." He embraced them both, Katherine holding on, for a precious moment, to a dear life. "I'll check in at our office in Baltimore," he promised as he assisted Adele aboard the carriage, referring to a small shipping office that Cutler & Sons maintained on Fleet Street in Baltimore to facilitate the shipment of sugar and molasses and other produce into the rapidly developing interior of the United States.

"You will do no such thing, Will," his mother-in-law admonished with mock gravity. "You've more important work to attend to." Anne-Marie gave her daughter a final embrace. "Go with God, my dear, dear child," she said softly, reverently. "Go with God and with my love, forever."

"Good-bye, everyone," Will exulted. As the carriage lurched forward, he waved out the window. "It's your turn next, Uncle!" was his parting cry.

Caleb Cutler drew his flaxen-haired intended close to his side. "Indeed it is," he whispered to her. "And I am counting the days."

The wedding party trickled back inside to the festivities and familiarity of neighbors and friends. Except for one, who politely dismissed those around her, including her husband. "It's quite all right," she assured them. "I just need a moment. Please." That moment dragged into many minutes as Anne-Marie stood alone in the silence of her private thoughts, staring down Main Street. The newlyweds' carriage had wheeled through the heart of the village, across South Street and North Street, and was visible on a road in the distance leading to Crow Point. She remained until long after the carriage had disappeared from her view and the dust in its wake had settled.

WITH WILL GONE and Caleb's upcoming wedding in the capable hands and financial resources of the Cabot family, Richard turned his attention to preparations for war. The week after Will and his bride sailed south for the Chesapeake, he and Agreen sailed north to the Portsmouth Navy Yard on Rising Castle Island.

There, to their satisfaction, they found *Portsmouth* fully planked with New Hampshire white oak along her hull, her railing up, and her bowsprit and jib-boom firmly in place. She lay on a cradle, the fine sheer of her hull braced upright by stout beams that looked like giant oars sweeping out from her starboard and larboard sides. Tubs of tallow had been placed nearby. When the time came—and that time had to be soon, else the tubs would not be there—the tallow would grease the ways to ease her slide off the cradle into the deep river water.

Once afloat, she would be brought alongside an old hulk equipped with a sturdy mast and sheer-legs, and the supporting tackle necessary to lift and lower the frigate's three masts down three decks where they would be stepped into locked position on her keelson. Only then would begin the arduous and finely detailed tasks of getting a ship ready for sea, from sending up her upper masts and yards, to roving mile upon mile of running rigging, to installing her ship's bell and brightwork and stove and wheel and binnacle, to furnishing the officers' cabins, and finally, with some fanfare, to hauling aboard her twenty-four 12-pounder long guns, twelve on each side of the gun deck, and twelve 6-pounders on her weather deck, six to a side.

"When do you expect to launch her?"

Richard posed that question to the superintendent of the yard, who, judging by his white hair and beard, wrinkled flesh, and yellow teeth, might have observed the launch of Richard's first ship, *Ranger,* from this very spot twenty-five years ago. The rasp of a two-man saw drew their attention to a large sawpit nearby, where they could see one man standing above a large, thick log; his partner was out of sight below in the pit as they fashioned strakes for the construction of yet another naval vessel. The air about them was rife with the pungent yet pleasing scent of freshly hewn wood.

The superintendent cast an experienced eye on the frigate. "I'd give her a month yet, maybe two," he replied. "We'll need to paint her, and her masts could use a bit more seasoning." He pointed, unnecessarily, to a circular pond in the distance where the resinous ship's spars were seasoned underwater to keep them sound and resilient. "She should be ready for her shakedown cruise, oh, by the beginning of September."

"May my lieutenant and I go aboard?"

The superintendent grinned. "She's your ship, Captain."

"Right, then." He turned to Agreen. "Shall we?"

Richard led the way up a ladder on the frigate's larboard side. When he reached what would soon define the ship's entry port and swung his legs over the still unpolished and unpainted railing, he jumped down onto the weather deck between the slightly raised quarterdeck aft and the more pronounced rise of her forecastle forward. Agreen followed him.

There wasn't much for them to see as they gazed along her 140-foot length and 26-foot beam. Anyone else standing where they stood would see a wooden platform propped up on a cradle on land, the blue of sea visible only in the far distance down the fairway of the Piscataqua River, past the harbor town of Portsmouth on its south bank and the village of Kittery on its north bank. Richard, however, saw his first command as a captain in the United States Navy. This was *his ship*; try as he might, he could not quell the surge of elation cascading through him like a raging springtime river swollen with winter melt.

Agreen watched him with a blend of amusement and understanding. "Are you plannin' t' just stand there and gawk all day?" he asked at length. "Or are we actually goin' t' get somethin' *done?*"

Richard grinned. "Right you are, Lieutenant. Where do you suggest we start?"

"I suggest we take a gander belowdecks, then proceed aft and sit on the deck of your palatial cabin and figure out how in God's name we're goin' t' man and employ this ship. She requires three hundred officers and crew, and so far all we have are her two senior officers and the few sailors from Cutler & Sons."

"At least we have those. Caleb insists he can't spare more than the twenty-five who have volunteered, and I have to agree with him. And remember, Cutler & Sons has pledged to make up the difference in pay for those volunteers. Gallatin's policy of slashing sailors' pay to ten dollars isn't doing us any favors." Richard had been outraged when the treasury secretary had recommended cutting the monthly pay of able-bodied seamen in the Navy from seventeen to ten dollars—a recommendation grudgingly accepted by President Jefferson and Navy Secretary Smith. "Most merchant companies today pay an ordinary seaman more than twice that amount. If you or I were in Gallatin's position, I daresay we could find a better way to manage expenses than by taking it out of the hide of the common sailor. That's just plain stupid. And it makes recruitment that much more difficult. All the Navy can offer is the possibility of prize money," referring to the profits shared among a ship's crew, prorated according to rank, realized from the sale of a captured enemy vessel.

"Gallatin never has supported the Navy," Agreen grumbled. "But at least we can make good use of those twenty-five men. They'll make excellent petty officers and topmen."

"That they will. And George Lee will be our second, assuming his promotion goes through. He liked you and Will when you met in Batavia, and Preble has trained him well. We can use an officer of his quality who's familiar with an *Essex*-class frigate."

"Aye," Agreen agreed. "And he can help with recruitment. He's known and respected in these parts."

"There you go, Lieutenant. You see? Everything is under control. You have nothing to fret about. I have every confidence you'll get the job done with your usual flair for efficiency. Why else would I have requested you as my first officer?"

"For my good looks?"

Richard pretended to ponder that. "No. Lizzy's more interested in that sort of thing than I am." He grinned. "I had other reasons, and I suggest we waste no further time putting those reasons into action."

SEVERAL WEEKS LATER, in Boston, Midn. James Cutler reported aboard *Constitution*. Trouble was, there was no one aboard to report to. The frigate's only commissioned officer other than Captain Preble was 1st Lt. Charles Gordon, and he had come and gone—where and for how long, no one seemed to know. A ragtag band of eleven sailors clad in the castoffs from a slop chest lolled about the deck without much to do and without much enthusiasm for doing anything. Certainly they appeared unimpressed by what Jamie realized must have appeared to them as a young, full-of-himself snotty strutting about the weather deck in the relative resplendency of a midshipman's undress uniform of buff trousers and a coat of indigo blue cloth with short lapels, six gold buttons, and a stand-up collar. 'That one came in through the cabin window,' he could almost hear these sailors whispering about him, 'not through the hawser hole the way less fortunate officers do. They have to *earn* their rank.'

Constitution, Jamie quickly discovered, was a shambles. Since returning to her home port following the conclusion of the war with France, she had been laid up along the banks of the Charles River without even a caretaker crew until the men he saw lazing about on the deck came aboard a couple of months ago—and they took care of her hardly at all. Debris littered her weather deck, and few lengths of running rigging were properly coiled to their belaying pins. Hardly anything Jamie observed met the minimal requirements of naval regulations or seamanship. As bad as it was topside, what he found belowdecks was worse. It was as though a herd of wild beasts had run amok, with no one bothering to pick up the mess they left behind. Only the guns on her gun deck were done up properly, bowsed tight against the starboard and larboard bulkheads. But every gun on that deck cried out for someone to scrape away splotches of orange rust and restore its black gleam.

Following a brief inspection of the two middle decks—he did not bother going down to the orlop deck; the stench wafting up from there turned his stomach—Jamie returned to the gun deck. He folded his arms, leaned against the cascabel of a 24-pounder on the starboard side of the gun deck, and peered out its gun port at the Boston skyline visible across the river. Having no idea what to do next, he thought through what his father had taught him about command. *Command.* He snorted at the word. On his first day as midshipman in "the pride of New England," he found himself, for the moment, the ship's ranking officer. And his crew was clearly indisposed to take orders from an upstart eighteen-year-old boy whose every trait bespoke good breeding and privilege.

After considerable thought, Jamie concluded that he had two choices. He could return topside and inform the men that he was going ashore to report to the superintendent of the Charlestown Navy Yard, the very man Captain Preble had warned him about and the officer who bore primary responsibility for the sorry state of affairs in *Constitution*. That option, to Jamie, seemed cowardly. Or he could do what his father had always encouraged him to do when faced with a tough situation: *Trust your instincts and take action.*

His mind made up, Jamie clambered up the main hatchway ladder. The first sailor he spotted on deck was perhaps twice his age and was wearing a blue-and-white-striped jersey and wide-bottomed white trousers. His hair was bound in a loosely plaited queue, and gold shone from his left earlobe. He was lazily coiling a rope that Jamie suspected had been coiled a hundred times in the past week alone. The sailor hardly glanced up when Jamie emerged from belowdecks and approached him.

"Your name, sailor?"

The man gave him a suspicious look. "Simpson, Your Honor," he mumbled. Jamie caught the sarcasm in his voice.

"Come again? I didn't hear you."

"Simpson," the man repeated in a slightly louder voice. "Alan Simpson."

"Thank you. Your rating, Mr. Simpson?"

A pause, then: "Able-bodied seaman."

"I see. Can you tell me, is there a petty officer aboard?"

Another pause. "Aye, there is." He went back to coiling the rope.

"Would you be so kind as to point him out to me, Mr. Simpson?"

Whether from an inbred reaction to an officer's direct query or in appreciation of the midshipman's unusually respectful tone—no officer had ever addressed him as "mister"—Simpson pointed at a stocky, muscular man with a short-trimmed black beard who was leaning against the mainmast whittling on a block of wood. "His name's Baker. Boatswain's mate."

"Thank you, Mr. Simpson."

As Jamie approached the petty officer, Baker stopped whittling, placed his work on a pinrail, and stood slightly slouched, as though signaling either boredom or resentment of this intrusion on his day. His insolence notwithstanding—or perhaps because of it—Jamie saw a man he would most definitely want on his side during a tavern brawl.

"Are you Boatswain's Mate Baker?" Jamie asked him.

"I reckon I am," the man replied, his southern heritage coming through in his accent.

Jamie bristled at the unmilitary response. "My name is James Cutler," he said. "I have a midshipman's warrant, and I have been ordered by Captain Preble to report for duty at my earliest convenience, which is today. Please assemble the men, Mr. Baker."

Baker narrowed his eyes and advanced one step. "Assemble the men, you say?"

Jamie held his ground. He could feel his heart pumping. He fought to keep his voice calm. "Yes, Mr. Baker. That is what I said. And I would very much appreciate you doing it *now*." Feeling a ripple of fear, Jamie realized he was treading in perilous waters. The next few minutes could decide his future as a naval officer.

Seconds ticked by as the two men—one seasoned by years at sea, the other as yet untested—stood face to face, neither budging. Sailors on the weather deck dropped what they were doing and came together by the mainmast, keen to observe more closely this unexpected and intriguing spectacle.

Baker blinked first, although his tone was hardly conciliatory in defeat. "It seems, Mr. Midshipman Cutler," he sneered, "that the men have already complied with your request."

"I can see that, Mr. Baker. And I appreciate your cooperation." Jamie turned on his heel. In a loud voice he said, pointing to starboard, "Men, please gather over there. That's right, over there by the mainmast chain-wale."

Whether driven by a sense of duty or simple curiosity, all eleven sailors, including Baker, obeyed. When they had formed a semicircle close by the broad, thick plank projecting horizontally from the ship's side, Jamie grabbed hold of a shroud and climbed onto the railing.

"Men," he said in as clear and steady a voice as he could muster, "I am James Cutler. I have in my possession a midshipman's warrant, signed by the secretary of the Navy, to serve aboard *Constitution*. That warrant makes us shipmates. During the next few days I shall come to know each of you and your name and your rating. I look forward to that.

"We have serious work to do. Whatever has happened aboard this ship before today is of no concern to me. I care only about what happens from this day forward. Three months from now, Captain Edward Preble will take command of this vessel. We must have her in fighting shape before he does. You know our captain's reputation. He will not tolerate insubordination or dereliction of duty from any member of his crew— including his officers. Make no mistake, lads, if we don't have *Constitution* shipshape from stem to stern by the time Captain Preble steps aboard, you and I will pay the forfeit. You and I *together.* Lieutenant Gordon is out on a recruiting mission," he added, not certain if that was the truth, "so help is on the way. But we cannot wait for help to arrive. We need to start our work today. We need to start *right now.*"

With that, he jumped down onto the weather deck. After removing his coat and draping it over a belaying pin, he rolled up his sleeves and began gathering the debris that littered the area between the main and mizzen masts on the starboard side of the weather deck. Sailors made way for him as he went about his task. One of them picked up a broom; another grabbed a large gunnysack into which he jammed the litter Jamie had piled up. Within the quarter-hour most of the sailors were pitching in. Within the half-hour every sailor was hard at it, including Boatswain's Mate Baker and the seaman named Simpson.

SUMMER AND EARLY AUTUMN plodded by in naval routine for those aboard *Constitution* and *Portsmouth* as both ships made ready for sea. Exactly when they would sail remained a matter of conjecture to the crews and to the national press.

Captain Preble had suffered another medical setback. According to his doctor, Edward Miller, the setback was not serious and should not delay matters more than a few months, and those being the months of winter. To those serving in *Constitution*, that report presented a not-unwelcome reprieve. In mid-September, just a few weeks before Captain Preble was to take command, Lieutenant Gordon, in company with James Cutler and Ralph Izard, had descended to the depths of her hold beneath the orlop and had poked her bottom in numerous places with boathooks and rakes. What they pulled up, at nearly every poke, was a discouraging blend of sea grass and moss.

"Her copper's broken and full of holes," the lanky, brown-haired lieutenant announced. He yanked a clump of green moss off his rake, examined it, and threw it back disgustedly into the watery hold.

"Which means we'll need to bream her and re-copper her," Izard said confidently. Jamie had developed a great respect for the slim, sinewy midshipman from Charleston, South Carolina, in the weeks since he had stepped aboard and dropped his seabag onto the deck.

"Quite right, Mr. Izard," Gordon responded. "Another damned delay. But there's nothing for it. We'll have to ride out the winter and set her sea trials for early spring. Captain Preble should be in fine fettle by then, so nothing is really lost. For the moment, let's get her moved to Union Wharf and set about careening her." He added sotto voce, "At least at Union Wharf we will be outside Captain Nicholson's jurisdiction. That should expedite things. Among other benefits," he added disdainfully.

NAVAL ROUTINE for both Jamie and his father gave way in late September to Caleb Cutler's long-heralded wedding to Joan Cabot within the magnificent confines of Trinity Church. This regal event was a mostly Bostonian affair; the Cutlers were among the few Hingham families in attendance. With his family's permission, Jamie had invited Ralph Izard and Octavius Paige of Delaware, another of *Constitution*'s midshipmen. As a matter of protocol he had also invited Charles Gordon and Robert Greenleaf, the frigate's recently arrived second lieutenant. Both officers had politely declined. Decked out for the occasion in their full dress uniforms, the three midshipmen looked like miniature versions of Richard Cutler—without the abundant embroidery and lace, longer lapels with nine gold buttons on each breast, four additional buttons on the cuffs and at the pockets, gold epaulet on each shoulder, and rich blue cloth cut to the waist in front and with tails behind that defined a captain's uniform.

Richard Cutler and Peter Cabot, brothers respectively of the groom and bride, took up position behind Caleb at the altar. Katherine Cutler, seated in a front pew with Diana, Caleb's two sisters, and their husbands, looked on wistfully as the ceremony commenced. The Endicott family and Will sat in the pew directly behind them. Jamie, seated across the aisle from the Endicotts, sensed more than observed Frances Endicott's furtive glances in his direction. He made a mental note to introduce her to his two fellow midshipmen at the reception and then make a graceful exit.

The ceremony and reception were everything a grand wedding should be, and the newlyweds left afterward on a brief wedding trip to New

York. For the others, it was back to what passed for normal these days. The war in the Mediterranean was going badly, and the national press was making sure that everyone knew it. To date, Commodore Morris's squadron had accomplished little of note beyond sailing from one to another of the more appealing destinations along the north shore of the Mediterranean, setting a social standard a British admiral might covet. Accompanying Morris in *Chesapeake* were his wife—labeled tongue-in-cheek by the press the "Commodoress"—and their young son. It was the commodore's wife, so the newspapers needled, who had set such high standards of social intercourse with a husband all too eager to satisfy her every desire.

True, there had been some naval action. The frigate *John Adams* had blockaded the 26-gun Moroccan warship *Meshuda* in Gibraltar to prevent her from bringing aid to the sultan's friend and ally, the bashaw of Tripoli. But that blockade had accomplished little beyond roiling waters that hitherto had been calm. In April 1803, James Simpson, the U.S. consul in Tangiers, received notice that Sultan Moulay Suleiman had declared war on the United States. Moroccan warships now threatened American merchantmen in both the Atlantic and the western Mediterranean.

To the east the news was equally disturbing. In direct contravention of President Jefferson's long-standing policy of refusing to pay tribute, Secretary of State James Madison had authorized James Cathcart, the American consul in Tripoli who had been summarily dismissed from the regency when the bashaw declared war on the United States, to offer Yusuf Karamanli $20,000 for a peace settlement plus an annual annuity of $40,000. Yusuf, enraged by the consul's refusal to pay the $225,000 he had demanded and an annual tribute of $25,000, again showed Cathcart the palace door, this time for good. With the basis for war against America now reaffirmed, consulate dispatches from Algiers and Tunis warned that both regencies were reexamining their relationship with the United States.

"Looks like everything's blowing up over there," Richard said to Agreen on a sunny, frosty, April afternoon on Long Wharf. His mood matched the brightness of the day. "According to this dispatch"—he held up an official document delivered several hours earlier—"President Jefferson is soon to recall Commodore Morris and is sending a more powerful squadron to the Mediterranean. Jefferson, Smith, and Madison are none too pleased with Morris. Odds are he'll be facing a court-martial for what Secretary Smith refers to as 'an absence of energy' in his naval operations."

"It couldn't happen to a worse man," Agreen said, grinning at his own turn of phrase. "So Captain, what does all this mean for us? From that giddy look on your face, I reckon we've received orders t' sail with the new squadron."

"You reckon correctly."

"When?"

"In late July or early August. And we are sailing in company with the squadron's flagship."

"Which is?"

"*Constitution*, Jamie's ship."

"*Constitution*? Well, damn me. That means . . ."

Richard nodded. "That means that Captain Preble is commodore of the squadron. Richard Dale was offered the post, but he declined because the Navy wouldn't make him an admiral. The fact that the Navy doesn't confer that rank made no difference to him. Commodore Barry"—referring to the Continental navy hero and the U.S. Navy's first flag officer—"was also considered but is deathly ill in his home in Philadelphia. So the honor has fallen to Captain Preble."

"And I'd wager he's as happy as a clam in the sand at high tide."

"I'd say so. Preble's connections in Washington have apparently paid off. But he's also the best man for the job. Now, finally, we'll get something done over there. Mark my words, Agee: under Preble's command, we'll show the bastards!"

Five

USS *Constitution,*
August–September 1803

"ENLISTING A CREW turned out to be a hell of a mess," commented Agreen Crabtree over supper one evening at the home of Will and Adele Cutler on Ship Street in Hingham. The other guests at the young hosts' table—Richard, Katherine, and Diana Cutler and Agreen's wife, Lizzy—nodded their agreement. Will and Adele had meant to hold a family dinner, but Jamie was unable to join them because *Constitution*'s officers and crew were denied shore leave in anticipation of weighing anchor on Friday, August 12, five days hence. Caleb and Joan were attending a social event in Boston that evening but planned to see Richard and Agreen off from Long Wharf the next day.

"At least *Portsmouth* has her full complement," Agreen concluded. "*Constitution* is still short a few hands, including a midshipman and a fourth lieutenant," he explained to his wife. "Preble will likely have them transferred from another ship in the squadron. And from what Jamie tells us, her crew contains a bucket-full of foreigners. Her officers may be Americans, but her muster book has Spaniards, Dutchmen, Malays— you name it—and a few British tars who don't take kindly t' the Royal Navy and don't trust merchantmen t' protect 'em. Captain Preble will have himself a grand old time with that rabble. He'll be talkin' as much with the whip as with his voice. So you might say, my darlin', that the cat's got his tongue!"

Lizzy did her best to smile at her husband's feeble stab at humor. Yesterday's post had brought devastating news from her brother John Cutler in England. John's letter told her that their father, William Cutler, had suffered a debilitating stroke and would likely have passed away by the time she received the letter. Richard understood and shared Lizzy's pain. His uncle was a much-beloved man who had shaped the lives of many people, including Richard. Lizzy had agreed to accompany Agreen tonight only because two of those present at the table would be gone by noon tomorrow. One of them was the man to whom she had pledged her life, the other a cousin she had held dear since those early days together in England a quarter-century ago.

"Is that why Captain Preble denied shore leave to his crew?" Adele inquired. "To keep everybody aboard, lest anyone has a mind to desert?"

"That's a fair assumption," Richard said, giving her an appreciative smile. Adele was not only a good wife for his son, he thought, she was also an excellent business partner. Her grasp of numbers, on the one hand, and of human nature, on the other, reminded him often of his cousin Robin Cutler in Barbados.

"Where are you sailing first, Father?" Will asked. "I've heard Gibraltar. Is that true?"

"I believe so, Will, although I won't know until I open my orders at sea. Each ship is sailing independently to the Mediterranean rather than as a squadron, as I had expected. Presumably we'll join up at the Royal Navy base at Gibraltar. While I'm there, I intend to visit your uncle Jeremy. And who knows?" he added with an arch look at his wife. "Perhaps I'll find Lord Nelson at Gibraltar as well. He *is* Jeremy's commanding officer."

"Horatio is in the Mediterranean?" Katherine asked.

"In grand style," her husband informed her. "He has been appointed commander-in-chief of British forces there."

Katherine smiled. "Most impressive. And you will see him?"

"That is my devout hope, Katherine. It will depend on circumstances, of course." In years past, an encounter with Vice Admiral Horatio Lord Nelson would not have been Richard's devout hope. But he had finally come to terms with his wife's former betrothal to the man. Left unstated this evening—because it was being discussed ad nauseam in nearly every city, town, and village in the English-speaking world—was Nelson's extramarital love affair with Lady Emma Hamilton, the young and vibrant wife of elderly British diplomat Sir William Hamilton. Sir William had been ambassador to the kingdom of Naples in '01 during the French invasion and the subsequent evacuation by sea of the court of King Ferdinand VI and key British personnel, including the ambassador and his wife. It was aboard Nelson's ship *Agamemnon* that the seed of love between Horatio and Emma, already well rooted, had burst into full blossom.

But while the British press excoriated Nelson for abandoning his wife, Fanny, and for siring a daughter out of wedlock with Lady Hamilton, the British public remained steadfastly loyal to England's foremost naval hero. Nelson's popularity had ballooned after he sailed in and defeated a combined Norwegian and Danish fleet in the Battle of Copenhagen, later claiming he had not seen the signal from his squadron's flagship to withdraw. When it was rumored that Nelson had not seen Admiral Hyde Parker's signal to withdraw because he was holding the spyglass to his blind eye, his fame soared to dizzying heights. Jokes were bandied about—in the press and elsewhere—that the sixty-two-year-old admiral had no desire to withdraw because the old goat had recently married an eighteen-year-old English girl.

"If you do have the good fortune to meet up with Horatio," Katherine said sternly, "you *will* send him my warmest personal regards."

"Of course, my dear. I have been well trained."

IN EARLY JULY *Constitution* was moved from her quay on the Charles River to May's Wharf in Boston for the final stages of her fitting out and provisioning. On August 8 the pride of New England cast loose her moorings to land and was towed to a temporary anchorage in the deep waters off the northern tip of Long Island.

At six bells in the morning watch on Saturday, August 13, Capt. Edward Preble, having deemed the northwesterly breeze sufficient for steerage way and fair for sailing out, ordered his first lieutenant to take her to sea.

Charles Gordon touched his hat. "Aye, aye, Captain!" He brought a speaking trumpet to his mouth. "All hands! Stations for weighing anchor! Up anchor! Man the bars!" Shrill boatswain's whistles relayed his orders. "Sailors aloft! Lay out and loose! Man topsail sheets and halyards! Hands to braces! Stand by . . . Stand by . . . Let fall!" Sailors leapt to their posts, the laggards among them earning a whack on the back from Boatswain John Cannon's rattan cane.

Three great billows of topsails fell like white curtains from their yards, and topgallants rose above them in nearly perfect synchrony, as though a single jack-block hoisted all three. Below and forward, the ship's best-bower was hove short, then raised and fished from the harbor waters and double-catted against the starboard bow. With her afteryards braced for a larboard tack and her headsheets hauled over to larboard, her helm to starboard, the combination of helm and canvas caused her stern to swing around. First gathering sternway, she quickly gathered headway as her helm was righted, her headsheets were hauled over, and her great trapezoidal spanker filled with wind.

Hailed by a thirteen-gun salute from Fort Independence on Castle Island, *Constitution* coasted by Boston Light on Little Brewster Island and shaped a course due eastward on a quartering breeze. She made a grand spectacle to those looking on from shore and from small boats. She was bedecked in multicolored flags and pennants, and forty thousand square feet of pure white canvas billowed like great clouds on her three masts. Her hull glistened a rich black with a wide streak of ochre running nearly two hundred feet along the gun-port strake. By the end of the second dogwatch, at 8:00, the only sign of the Massachusetts coast those aboard her could see was the beacon shining from Cape Cod Light in Truro. Soon that too dipped below the horizon, and *Constitution* sailed on into the dead of night under reduced canvas beneath an overcast, starless sky.

The next evening at 7:30, after inspection of divisions, Edward Preble convened what he announced would be a nightly meeting in his after cabin of his four lieutenants, eight midshipmen, senior warrant officers, and captain of Marines. Only officers in sickbay or assigned to watch duty were exempted, for it was a hard-and-fast rule aboard ship that a lieutenant or the sailing master plus two midshipmen and a quartermaster were to be on the quarterdeck at all hours of the day and night.

The after cabin, which ran the full 43½ feet athwartship and had a 7-foot deckhead, afforded ample space for the gathering. Captain Preble lived in a veritable palace compared with every other officer in the ship, from the first lieutenant's berth a deck lower in the wardroom down another deck to the dank underbelly of the midshipmen's quarters in steerage. The after cabin was actually two cabins: the larger one in which the ship's business was conducted, and a smaller cabin aft that comprised the captain's personal quarters and included a private dining alcove and a sleeping cuddy set between plain-glassed windows at the very stern of the ship.

The main cabin contained a long, rectangular table that accommodated, on three sides, the more senior officers. Midshipmen sat in chairs behind them. On the aft side of the table, Captain Preble stood in full undress uniform. In a wingback chair near to him sat an exquisitely attired civilian who casually stroked his double chin as he met the stares of those watching him.

"Good evening, gentlemen," Preble proclaimed. His sharp tone brought an instant halt to undercurrents of quiet chatter. "I have the distinct honor this evening to introduce our honored guest, Tobias Lear." He nodded toward the civilian. "*Colonel* Tobias Lear. You perhaps noticed him and his wife strolling about the deck during the day and may be wondering why he has joined us on this cruise. I will let him explain the details. But before he does, because he is such a modest individual"—those officers seated closest to Preble detected a rare dance of humor in his eyes—"I will tell you this: Colonel Lear has had a most distinguished career in our diplomatic corps. Not only did he serve as personal secretary to our beloved President Washington, he was at the president's bedside when he died. He subsequently served as President Jefferson's envoy to Saint-Domingue when Napoléon attempted to quell the Negro uprising and restore the colony to France. Because of his accomplishments, President Jefferson has appointed him consul general to the Barbary Coast. He is replacing Consul O'Brien in Algiers and has full authority to superintend all American consular activities in North Africa. His authority, gentlemen, includes the negotiation of a peace treaty with Tripoli when and if that becomes appropriate. He has a unique perspective on the war that I daresay will greatly influence our naval strategy in the Mediterranean and our mission there." With that he turned to the newly appointed consul general. "If you please, Colonel, you have my officers' undivided attention."

As Tobias Lear rose to his feet to shake the captain's hand, Jamie Cutler reflected on what he knew about the man. Lear was the nephew of Hingham's own Gen. Benjamin Lincoln, a relationship so meaningful to Lear that he had named his only son Benjamin Lincoln Lear. It was Lincoln who had recommended Lear to serve as George Washington's personal secretary. Jamie also was aware that Lear had never served in the military and therefore held no official military rank. He had, in fact, entered Harvard in '76 rather than join the Continental army. The aging Washington had bestowed the honorary rank in recognition of Lear's fifteen years of service. Nonetheless, Lear had clung to it, as Agreen had once put it, "like white on rice." Jamie smiled at the recollection.

"Thank you, Captain Preble," Lear said formally before turning to face the officers. "Gentlemen, I am honored to be in your company this evening. As you may be aware, my wife, Frances, and I had originally intended to sail to the Mediterranean aboard *Philadelphia*, but that fine frigate had the good sense to sail without us." That remark prompted a round of polite laughter. "So we were reassigned to *Constitution*, to our great joy and privilege, I must add. No more graceful or powerful a frigate has ever sailed the seven seas."

His audience agreed with smiles and nods.

Lear drew himself up to his full six feet. "Our mission," he went on in a sterner voice, "is to gain nothing short of total capitulation from an enemy who has for too many years violated our neutrality, harassed our merchant vessels, and imprisoned our sailors. Suffer no illusions, gentlemen: our enemy is not just the regency of Tripoli. Our enemy is all four Barbary states. If we are victorious over one, we are victorious over all. These states, every one of them, rely on piracy and extortion to realize their goals. They are ruled by petty tyrants who wrap themselves in the cloak of holy war to justify their atrocities and their demands for tribute from Christian states. But theirs is a house of cards, gentlemen. To the rulers of Barbary, religious dogma and the teachings of Muhammad are always—I repeat, *always*—tempered by economic realities. In negotiating with them, the sticking point is always—I repeat, *always*—money, not theology. In this war we intend to dismantle that house of cards and see it topple over."

He took a sip of water and continued in the same tone. "We can win this war one of two ways: military victory or diplomatic victory. Either way, the house of cards comes down, which is why I will be pushing hard with diplomacy onshore while you gentlemen make a show of power at sea. Yusuf Karamanli cannot survive a diplomatic defeat any more than he can a military defeat. Nor can he back down before a display of naval power. His Divan, his council of Janissaries, would feed him to the dogs regardless of the source of his defeat.

"Lest you think our victory is assured, however, I remind you that two American squadrons"—he held up two fingers for emphasis—"have cruised the Mediterranean during the past two years and accomplished this"—he fashioned a zero with his thumb and forefinger and held it high. "Our lack of success has emboldened Tripoli and the other Barbary states. Their leaders believe, now more than ever, that *they* hold the upper hand. They believe that they are invincible to our naval guns and diplomatic threats. And that makes both my job and yours that much more difficult.

"Gentlemen," he cautioned, "do not make the mistake of underestimating Yusuf Karamanli or Tripoli. I have dealt with Karamanli before. He is as cunning and ruthless a man as exists on this earth. He will stop at nothing to get what he wants. Consider that when his father died, Yusuf was third in line for the throne, after his two older brothers. His father's body was hardly in the grave when he invited his eldest brother to supper with their mother. During the meal he stood up and shot his brother in the chest and then, to make certain he was dead, stabbed him a hundred times with a knife—in front of their own mother! What did Yusuf do next? He seized the wife and three children of his next oldest brother, Hamet, as hostages and banished Hamet from the capital city. Make no mistake, Yusuf is a man completely without principles."

He took another sip of water, then: "Not many of you in this cabin have had occasion to visit Tripoli. I have. It is a veritable fortress. Its shore batteries boast 115 cannon, and its harbor shelters a fleet of warships that includes a 36-gun frigate and a 24-gun sloop—gifts from the Ottoman sultan—plus 11 corsairs and a large number of gunboats. And that harbor is protected not only by the city fortress and its gun batteries but also by rocks and shoals that require the knowledge of a local pilot to pass through. Attacking the capital city thus poses a wealth of logistical problems and challenges. Even if such an attack were successful, it could cost many more lives than the American public is prepared to accept. And that is why our diplomatic efforts are so critical. Those efforts, gentlemen, are *my* responsibility. *Your* responsibility, if I may be so crude, is to scare the living Allah out of these Arabs with your naval presence and blockades. Your naval power and my diplomatic skill will combine to form what our president refers to as our "awe and talk" strategy. Together," he raised a clenched fist, "we can achieve the victory our country expects from us!"

He saluted his audience, turned, and exchanged places with Captain Preble, who said in a much more moderate tone, "Gentlemen, I am certain you have questions. There will be time for Colonel Lear to answer them in the days ahead. For this evening I wish to add just one further comment. Earlier, Colonel Lear made reference to an older brother of Yusuf Karamanli, a brother exiled from the city of Tripoli whose family Yusuf holds hostage in his castle. Our envoy in Tunis, Captain William Eaton, knows Hamet Karamanli and has contacted him informally in Derne, a city in Tripoli's easternmost province of Cyrenaica, where Hamet now serves as royal governor. Suffice it to say, for the moment, that we are being urged to make more formal contact with him. It is possible that Hamet will become an important ally to us. Many Tripolitans consider him their rightful bashaw—which of course he is, legally. Because of the sensitivity and urgency of this matter, I have ordered *Portsmouth* to bypass Gibraltar and sail directly to Malta to confer with several of

Hamet's principals there. As you are aware, *Portsmouth*'s captain is Mr. Richard Cutler, the father of our own Midshipman James Cutler. He has admirable experience in both diplomacy and naval affairs, and I have every confidence that he will provide us with useful information.

"That concludes the evening, gentlemen, with the obvious request that you continue to extend every courtesy to Colonel and Mrs. Lear throughout this cruise. You may now return to duty."

SHIPBOARD LIFE in *Constitution* quickly assumed a daily routine that became as familiar and predictable as the clang of the ship's bell and the quartermaster's call that marked each half-hour throughout the day and night. From the start of the morning watch at 4:00 until near its end at 7:30—when boatswains' whistles ordered hammocks moved up from the berthing deck to the weather deck and stowed in bulwark nettings—barefoot sailors scrubbed and washed down the decks. At 8:00, the start of the forenoon watch, those same whistles summoned the crew to breakfast, after which, until 4:00 in the afternoon, the business of the day progressed unabated except for dinner at noon and a half ration of grog—which, at the instigation of Navy Secretary Smith, consisted of a mixture of bourbon and water to make it more American than the traditional Royal Navy rum and water.

At 4:00, assuming the captain was satisfied with the results of the afternoon's gun and small arms drills, the crew received its second ration of grog. They had time for a quick smoke, perhaps, under the forecastle, or a dance to a fiddle and fife before supper was served to individual messes on the berthing deck. After that the crew was mustered into divisions on the weather deck under the diligent eye of the duty lieutenant, who scrutinized each man for any indication of intoxication or slovenliness. When the lieutenant had confirmed all hands present and accounted for and Captain Preble had conducted his own inspection of the crew, Boatswain Cannon and his mates piped hammocks down and slung below. One watch dispersed to its posts while the other went below to snatch some sleep before answering the next call to duty four hours later.

Three weeks into the cruise, during a night of violent thunder and wild streaks of jagged lightning, Jamie Cutler lay in his hammock with his hands behind his head, staring up at the deckhead. The gentler sway of his hammock indicated that the storm had finally passed over them. He turned his head this way and that, willing sleep to release him but knowing full well it could not. The late hours of a Wednesday night were often this way for him, but this Wednesday night was worse than others.

As bad as it was for him, he knew it was much worse for John Stokes, an English topman whose tips on seamanship had made Jamie a better sea officer.

Why Stokes had done it, Jamie could not fathom. Captain Preble had made it patently clear that he would brook no insolence or drunkenness or petty theft from any man at any time for any reason, no matter the sailor's rank or experience at sea or popularity among the crew. Any such offense would be dealt with harshly—and all hands understood what Preble meant by *that*. Jamie could envision certain other members of the crew committing such infractions regardless of the captain's warnings— indeed, two of them were also due to receive punishment the next morning at 10:00—but good God, not Stokes! Jamie sighed quietly at the mental image of the red-haired tar from Northumberland sitting in chains in the brig forward, fully awake and contemplating his fate.

Jamie checked his watch. The feeble light of the lanterns embedded in the midshipmen's mess table was barely sufficient for him to make out the time: 2:40. Fifty minutes before an attendant assigned to the midshipmen's berth was scheduled to shake him awake. Eighty minutes until the start of his watch as a junior duty officer. With another sigh, louder this time, he slipped out of his hammock and dropped onto the orlop deck.

"What it is, Jamie?" a voice murmured from the hammock next to his. "Can't you sleep either?"

"No, William," Jamie whispered back. Midn. William Lewis had become a favorite of the entire ship's complement because of his skills as a musician. The sweet melodies he drew from his violin evoked power- ful images of home, of a love lost or found, and many a sailor remained spellbound long after he had ceased playing. "I'm going topside."

"Want some company?"

Jamie placed his hand on Lewis' shoulder. "I appreciate that, William, but no. Get some rest. You still have a good forty minutes. I'll see you on deck at eight bells."

Jamie quickly dressed, grabbed his oilskin coat, put on his fore-and- aft cocked hat, and clambered up the dimly lit companionway ladder to the berthing deck. From there he climbed upward to the gun deck, where he returned the salute of a Marine sentry on duty before the captain's cabin. One more flight of steps, up hatch, and he was on the weather deck breathing in the refreshingly cool air.

His surmise about the weather was correct. The sky had cleared to reveal a universe of bright stars and a three-quarters moon. The dreary fog that had hung low over the sea for days had dissipated, and the brisk north-northeasterly breeze that had replaced the sultry, erratic air almost took Jamie's hat when he stepped up through the hatchway. Jamie pulled on his coat for warmth and glanced northward at Polaris shining brightly above *Constitution*'s larboard beam, confirming her easterly course on a broad reach. He turned aft and noticed Midn. Octavius Paige, the current junior duty officer, approaching him.

"Why on deck so early, Jamie?" Paige asked. "Your watch isn't for another hour yet." As if on cue, the ship's bell struck six times in three sets of two clangs. "Six bells in the second watch!" the quartermaster on duty confirmed the time.

"Missed your company, Octopus," Jamie replied with a forced grin. Paige's inevitable nickname had by now become so commonplace aboard ship that 3rd Lt. Samuel Elbert had inadvertently addressed him as "Octopus" during the evening assembly of officers three days ago. Paige's befuddled reaction had set off a round of laughter in which even Captain Preble participated.

The two midshipmen watched in silence as Nate Haraden, the crusty ship's master and senior duty officer, passed by on his way to the helm to scratch his hourly report on a chalkboard attached to the binnacle in front of the helm. Ralph Izard, the other midshipman assigned to the second watch, joined them a few minutes later. Izard's primary duty, with the assistance of the quartermaster of the watch, was to toss overboard the log chip every hour on the hour to determine the ship's speed. He had just calculated nine and a half knots, and Haraden had recorded that welcome piece of information on the chalk slate along with the current wind direction, the ship's heading as confirmed by two compasses mounted in the binnacle, and the time of the report.

"Joy of the morning to you, Jamie," Izard greeted him. His tone contained an edge of sarcasm that Jamie had no trouble grasping.

"Morning, Ralph," Jamie replied. "I have the deck if you or Octi want to go below for some extra sleep.

Izard shook his head. "That's a tempting offer, my friend, but I think we'd best decline." Jamie followed his gaze to the topsails, jib, and single-reefed spanker that defined a ship rigged for night sailing. For the first time in days, he noted the yards braced up and the weather bowlines drawn tight. Beneath them, the deck moved as if the ship were a living being pent up for too long and set free to fly at last. "We've finally got some way on her and I don't want to miss out on the excitement. Besides, I have no wish to kiss the gunner's daughter for being caught napping when I'm supposed to be on duty, even if I have been relieved." A "young gentleman" who broke the ship's rules was bent over a cannon with his pants lowered and had his buttocks lacerated by a boatswain's mate brandishing a rattan cane.

Paige stepped in close. "Preble sure can be one mean son-of-a-bitch," he whispered. "I swear his sickness has gone to his head."

Jamie glanced about the deck. Haraden and the others on duty were well out of earshot. "Have a care, Octi," he cautioned nonetheless, adding, somewhat lamely, "Command is no easy matter. Who knows how you or I would handle it? Besides, he's not doing anything outside Navy regulations."

"Actually, he is," Izard put in. "Stokes is to receive thirty-six lashes, but Navy regulations clearly specify a maximum of twelve."

"Mr. Greenleaf," Jamie said, referring to *Constitution*'s second lieutenant, "explained that to me. Stokes was caught stealing a Spaniard's knife, and he was intoxicated at the time. When the theft was reported to Lieutenant Gordon, and Lieutenant Gordon confronted him, Stokes was insolent in front of the men. Mr. Gordon had no choice. He had to put Stokes on report, even though he believed Stokes when he said that the Spaniard had it in for him and that he didn't intend to steal the knife. Mr. Gordon also realized that it was the liquor doing the talking, not Stokes. Stokes would never say things like that sober. Still, Mr. Gordon had no choice.

"Stokes is a good man and an excellent seaman," Jamie continued. "He's no thief, and he respects the chain of command as much as anyone. I can't imagine why he broke into the liquor rations and acted the way he did. But the facts are what they are and the captain cannot ignore them. Stokes committed three violations: stealing, drunkenness, and insolence to an officer. Three violations times twelve lashes for each offense equals thirty-six lashes. You may not find that sort of math in naval regulations, but you *will* find it in the captain's cabin. On this cruise, that's all that matters."

"Poor bastard," Paige commented.

"Well, my good fellows," Izard said with forced joviality, "I'm off to my rounds. See you at six bells."

At 10:00, six bells in the forenoon watch, boatswains' pipes summoned all hands to witness punishment. *Constitution* continued on her eastward course under reduced sail with only a skeleton crew to handle her.

The commissioned officers took position on the quarterdeck directly behind Preble. They were dressed much like the captain if somewhat less grandly. Farther behind and to Preble's left stood the frigate's eight midshipmen, all in a row and dressed in crisp blue and white. To starboard, John Hall, the hard-bitten captain of the Marine guard, offered for the captain's review the double row of Marines lining the starboard bulwark in spotless blue uniforms, their brightly polished sea-service muskets gleaming in the bright morning sun.

Assembled by divisions from the mainmast almost to the bow, their backs to the larboard railing, was the ship's company, many of them dressed in the widely accepted though not yet officially sanctioned sailor dress code of loose-fitting white trousers, shirt and vest under a short jacket, black neckerchief, and black low-crowned hat.

At a stirring of drums all eyes swung to the forward hatchway. John Burchard, the master-at-arms, summoned four barefoot and shackled prisoners up the ladder from the gun deck. The prisoners appeared stunned by the men arrayed in formal ranks all the way from the ladder to the taffrail at the very stern of the ship. Each man blinked and averted his eyes, whether from the sun's glare or from the sight of his shipmates solemnly watching him. As the Marine drummer continued his mournful tattoo, the four prisoners slowly, reluctantly, shuffled over to the bulwark nettings adjacent to the larboard entry port. John Stokes led the way. Last in line was Anthony Guerrier, a lanky, tow-headed French-Canadian lad of seventeen who was well liked in the forecastle. Guerrier trembled as he shambled along, his gaze held hard to the feet of the Dutchman plodding along in front of him. Now and then he swiped at his eyes with a shackled wrist.

When the prisoners were gathered before the entry port the drumming ceased abruptly. John Stokes was singled out from the others and brought forth to the nettings. At Boatswain Cannon's command, he turned and faced Captain Preble, who was standing rigidly on the quarterdeck.

"Seaman Stokes," Preble proclaimed into the ensuing silence, "do you understand the offenses of which you have been accused and found guilty? And the sections of the *Act for the Better Government of the Navy* into which your offenses fall?"

"I do, Captain." Stokes' reply was so soft that the midshipmen, stationed farthest aft, had to strain to hear him.

Preble then put a question to the quarterdeck. "Does any officer here present wish to speak on behalf of this man?"

It was a traditional yet normally rhetorical question. Few officers ever spoke up at such a moment. Jamie Cutler had nonetheless steeled himself to do just that. He advanced one step in front of the line of midshipmen. "Captain, if you please, I wish to speak."

Preble raised his eyebrows. "Yes, Mr. Cutler?"

Jamie faced his captain. "Sir, Seaman Stokes serves in my division. I have never had occasion to put him on report. To the contrary, he has been an exemplary member of the crew. He has obeyed my every command. Until this unfortunate incident his performance has been a credit to his division and to this ship. I therefore wish to vouch for him, and I request with the utmost respect that he be granted leniency."

Preble's expression remained unchanged. "I see. Are there other such requests?"

To Jamie's surprise, Ralph Izard advanced one step to stand beside him. "I too wish to vouch for Seaman Stokes, Captain."

"And I, Captain," Octavius Paige proclaimed on Jamie's other side.

Preble pondered his response, then: "Thank you for your remarks, gentlemen. Your praise of Seaman Stokes and your loyalty to each other are commendable. Your comments shall be duly recorded in the ship's log." He faced forward. "Mr. Cannon, you may proceed with punishment. Seize the prisoner up!"

"Aye, aye, sir!"

At Cannon's command, two of his mates removed Stokes' shirt and ordered him to turn around. As Stokes' hands were being tied to the bulwark nettings high above him, a third boatswain's mate removed a sinister-looking two-foot length of thick rope from a red baize bag. Dangling down from the end of that rope were nine lengths of thinner cord, each about half a yard long with three knots set in at small intervals near the tail end.

Preble removed his hat.

"Off hats!" Cannon commanded. The entire ship's company complied. Stokes was offered a bullet to bite down on but refused it. "Boatswain's Mate O'Neill, do your duty!"

Nine viper tongues lashed out, striking Stokes with such force that his torso arched forward from the sudden searing pain.

"One!" the master-at-arms cried out.

Lash followed horrific lash. By the tenth wallop, red welts crisscrossed Stokes' naked back, oozing blood as the hard knots on the cords' ends ripped deep into flayed flesh and muscle, each blow sending bits of bloody tissue into the air and onto the deck. At Burchard's cry of "Twelve!"— and again at his cry of "Twenty-four!"—the boatswain's mate on duty was relieved by another boatswain's mate wielding a fresh arm and a fresh cat. Their vicious and violent assaults finally made the flinty, red-haired Englishman scream out in anguish.

Closing his eyes to the screams, Jamie felt the warm flow of vomit rising into his throat. He swallowed hard, forcing it back down, silently commanding himself to stand firm, to think of something, anything, that might see him through this. Who could forget that terrible morning two weeks ago when Thomas Baldwin, at age fourteen the youngest of the midshipmen, vomited onto the deck during a flogging and then collapsed in a dead faint onto his own filth. That sorry incident had not won him respect anywhere in the ship.

At the cry of "Thirty-six!" it was finally over, for Stokes. Released from his bindings, he slumped down and had to be coaxed up by two shipmates who helped him hobble across the weather deck and below to the ministrations of Dr. James Wells, the ship's surgeon. An Irishman took his place at the netting, then a Dutchman, their toughened bodies and hardened psyches taking the prescribed twelve lashes with hardly a whimper. When it came the Canadian's turn, the lad was trembling so hard that he required the steadying hand of a boatswain's mate in order to stand and face his captain.

"Seaman Guerrier," Preble intoned for a fourth time this morning, "do you understand the offense of which you have been accused and found guilty?"

Guerrier stood numb.

"Answer the captain!" Cannon admonished.

Guerrier could not speak. He could only nod.

"Then tell me, son: will you will ever again fall asleep at your post while on duty?" Preble's suddenly kind tone was not only unexpected, it seemed entirely out of character.

Guerrier shook his head no.

"Answer the captain!" Cannon barked a second time.

"No, Cap'm," Guerrier croaked, his eyes pleading for mercy.

Preble stared down into the dark, pleading eyes. "I believe you, lad," he said. "And because I do, I pardon you. You may return to duty." He put on his hat.

"On hats!" Cannon bellowed.

Guerrier's relief was so intense that he fell to his knees with his hands clasped as in prayer. The boatswain's mate had to pry his hands apart to remove the shackles.

FOUR DAYS LATER, as *Constitution* battled light and variable winds off Cape Saint Vincent, Captain Preble learned from the merchant brig *Jack*, homeward bound to Cape Ann, that Capt. William Bainbridge of the frigate *Philadelphia* had arrived in Gibraltar and, after a brief holdover, had sailed on in search of two Tripolitan vessels reported to be cruising near the Spanish port of Alicante. Preble became more anxious than ever to reach Gibraltar when he heard that two enemy vessels had been sighted so close to *Constitution*'s current position. But adverse headwinds and calm seas had set in, and because *Constitution* was built for war, not for speed, it took nearly a week for the frigate to finally draw near the Spanish port of Cádiz.

"On deck!" a lookout cried from the foremast topgallant yard.

"Deck, aye!" William Lewis called up.

"Sails on the horizon!"

"Where away?"

"To the sou'east, sir. She's ship-rigged, just ahead."

Lewis relayed the lookout's observation to Lieutenant Greenleaf, the senior watch officer, standing by the ship's wheel afore the mizzenmast. "Cates has spotted a vessel of size, sir," he said, saluting. "She's not far ahead."

"What exactly does that mean, Mr. Lewis?" Greenleaf fired back. "*How* far ahead? What is her point of sail? How does she shape her course?" The questions came fast and furiously at the startled midshipman.

"The lookouts are trying to determine that, sir. It's hard to make out much of anything in this haze."

"I daresay you're right, Mr. Lewis," the second lieutenant conceded with a frustrated sigh, "but we *must* have answers, and we must have them quickly. Please inform the captain of the sighting."

"Aye, aye, sir."

As Lewis disappeared down the aft companionway ladder, Greenleaf passed word for the boatswain.

"We shall clear for action, Mr. Cannon," Greenleaf directed him. "Advise the gun captains to loose the guns and stand by for further orders."

"Aye, aye, sir!"

Preble appeared moments later as drumrolls echoed across the deck. On the weather deck, Marines were standing by the fourteen 12-pounder long guns. The grinding squeal of wooden wheels sounded from the gun deck as the thirty 24-pounder guns were freed from their lashings and hauled inboard.

Midshipman Lewis approached the helm, touched his hat, and waited.

"What do we have, Mr. Greenleaf?" Preble inquired.

"Good evening, sir. Seaman Cates reports sails of consequence directly ahead of us. As yet we cannot determine either her position or her course."

"How far off is she?"

"We are trying to determine that, too, Captain. This damnable mist had concealed her until just a few minutes ago. I have ordered the guns loosed and await your orders."

"Very well," Preble muttered. He scanned the waters ahead, then looked up at the fast-darkening, overcast sky. He was about to add an observation when a lookout's panicked cry brought him up short. It was followed by another cry from the mainmast, and then another from the mizzen.

"*On deck there! The ship lies directly ahead!* Holy sweet Mother of Jesus, we're practically on top of her!"

"*Helm hard to starboard!*" Preble cried out.

Instantly the two quartermaster's mates at the helm brought the great wheel over. As *Constitution* turned into the fluky wind, the leeches of her topsails began to shudder and her foresails to droop and flap impotently.

"Hold her steady!" Preble ordered. "Mr. Lewis, I will have round shot in the carriage guns and the starboard guns run out. Handsomely, now!"

"Aye, aye, sir." Lewis strode forward to the great rectangular hatchway amidships and shouted down the captain's order.

Preble was considering further evolutions to avoid collision when he realized that such maneuvers had become unnecessary. The captain of the mystery ship, whoever he was, had ordered his vessel to heave to. She rose like a great black mass on the inky sea against a slightly lighter backdrop of darkened sky. Only her canvas sails stood out in contrast, and even those appeared a somber dark gray. Here and there tiny balls of light flickered from a lantern up on deck or through open gun ports below. Her captain, too, had ordered his guns run out.

An eerie silence ensued, as though the two ships, drifting perhaps thirty feet apart, had paused like two dogs cautiously sniffing each other before rearing up and having at it. All eyes on the quarterdeck of the American frigate watched as Preble picked up a speaking trumpet and walked to the mizzen's starboard shrouds.

"What ship is that?" he shouted out.

"What ship is that?" the stranger shouted back.

"This is the United States ship of war *Constitution*. What ship is that?"

"What ship is that?" the same voice inquired anew.

"I have just told you!" Preble snapped. "This is the United States ship of war *Constitution*. Now tell me, sir, for the last time: what ship is *that*?"

Again, from the mystery ship: "What ship is that?"

"Damn you, sir!" Preble yelled through the trumpet. "I am finished playing games! Answer me properly or I shall fire a shot into you."

"Fire a shot into me," the stranger shouted back, "and I shall fire a broadside into you."

"*What ship is that*?" Preble thundered into the night.

Finally, a different voice, one that carried the crisp patrician accent of English nobility, answered: "This is His Britannic Majesty's Ship *Donegal*, eighty-four guns. I am Commodore Sir Richard Strachan. I shall require you to send over your boat."

"Uppity bastard!" Preble growled. His dander up, he scrambled atop the starboard railing. Holding a shroud for support, he shouted through the trumpet in a voice of high dudgeon: "This is the United States ship *Constitution*, forty-four guns. I am Commodore Edward Preble, and I will be damned to hell before I send a boat over to you or to *any* vessel!" To his gun crews he shouted, in a voice for the Atlantic to hear, "Stand by your lanyards, boys, and prepare to fire!"

Another round of eerie silence was broken by the splash of oars, the thud of a ship's boat bumping against the larboard side, and the hail of a man about to climb the thirteen steps built into *Constitution*'s hull. The amber light of lanterns at the entry port revealed a superbly uniformed British sea officer, who, after saluting the quarterdeck, introduced himself to 1st Lt. Charles Gordon as Gorley Putt, first lieutenant of His Majesty's frigate *Maidstone*, 36 guns, under the command of Capt. Stephen Elliot.

"I am the officer with whom you first spoke," Putt explained after saluting Captain Preble, who had approached the entry port. "We sighted your ship an hour or so ago, but we did not realize how close we were to you. Captain Elliot, unconvinced of either your nationality or your size, stalled for time to scare you off, or at least to give you pause whilst we put our gun deck in proper array. He *still* is not entirely convinced of your nationality, although I will put that to rights as soon as I return to my ship. I am certain that he would wish to extend to you every respect and his apology for any misunderstanding."

"Thank you, Lieutenant," Preble said, adding with relish, "Please inform your captain that I accept his apology. I am compelled, however, to warn him, and you, that in the future what you describe as a misunderstanding with an American frigate might find you and your ship blown clean out of the water. A very good night to you, sir." With that, he turned on his heel and stalked away.

Below, on the gun deck, Jamie Cutler glanced about at the other gun captains and their gun crews, who had overheard the entire exchange between the two naval commanders. To a man, they were wide-eyed and rendered speechless by their first inkling of the true nature of their captain.

Six

USS *Portsmouth,*
October 1803

THIRD LT. ERIC MEYERS scampered up the starboard ratlines of the foremast shrouds like a topman, using the frigate's larboard heel to facilitate his ascent. Avoiding the lubber's hole cut through the base of the foretop, he crawled like a spider out onto the thick rope mesh leading from the catharpings up and around the sturdy oaken platform. From the futtock shrouds at the deadeyes of the top, the young officer from the Virginia Capes grabbed hold of the narrower topmast shrouds and climbed up to the horizontal timbers that spread the topgallant shrouds at the crosstrees. *Portsmouth* was lying close to the wind, her square sails braced tight in what felt like a considerably stiffer breeze at a height of eighty feet than it had down on deck. Meyers felt as though he had climbed into a hot, windy tunnel. Strands of his tawny hair whipped free from their queue, and his loose-fitting shirt ruffled and snapped. Above him, the foremast topgallant lay furled to its yard. Below him, the leeches of the jib and flying jib shivered and thrummed.

At the crosstrees Meyers joined Able Seaman Harvey Cole, who was facing into the stiff easterly wind with one arm wrapped around the thin topgallant mast. He offered Meyers a hand up and then, after the lieutenant had secured himself, a spyglass.

Meyers first scanned the rolling seas to starboard with a naked eye. "Point her out to me, Cole," he yelled above the wind. "I don't see her."

Meyers brought the small spyglass up to one eye and followed Cole's pointing finger. "Ah, yes, there she is." He adjusted the focus. "Clear as day, almost. I agree, from the look of her, she's a corsair." His voice was high with nervous anticipation. "You're sure she's Tripolitan?"

"I had a good look at her ensign, sir. She's Tripolitan. I'd stake my life on it."

"No need for that, Cole," Meyers commented wryly as he studied the profile of the Arab warship shaping an opposite course to *Portsmouth*'s, perhaps twelve miles upwind and closing fast. "You've already done that once here in Barbary, and once is enough." Knowing Cole's history, he meant exactly what he said. In 1786, at the age of sixteen the youngest hand aboard the Cutler & Sons merchant brig *Eagle,* Harvey Cole had been taken prisoner by pirate corsairs and had languished in an Algerian prison for ten years. During the entirety of that confinement he had stood as a rock of defiance. He even learned enough of the local language to defy his captors in Arabic. Despite a brush with hell every day, Cole had remained steadfastly loyal to his employer's family, especially to Caleb Cutler, who shared his prison cell. When last year Caleb had asked for volunteers among the Cutler & Sons crew roster to serve in USS *Portsmouth* in the Mediterranean, Cole had stepped forward along with so many others that Caleb had the sailors draw lots to determine the lucky twenty-five.

Meyers handed the glass back to Cole. "Odd, isn't it," he mused, his back to the wind. "We're clearly the more powerful vessel, and surely she has spotted us by now. Yet she's not showing us her heels."

"It is odd, sir," Cole agreed.

"Well, keep an eye on her, Cole," Meyers said as he prepared to descend to the deck, "and report any deviation in her course."

Meyers wrapped his legs around a taut hempen backstay attached to the upper masthead and descended hand under hand to the larboard chain-wale, and from there to the deck. He lost no time making his way along the waist and up the three steps to the raised quarterdeck. At the helm he saluted the captain and first lieutenant, who had gathered there with the ship's master, the captain of Marines, a quartermaster's mate at the wheel, and two midshipmen.

Richard Cutler answered the salute. "What company do we keep, Mr. Meyers?"

"A Tripolitan corsair, Captain. She's lateen-rigged on her main and mizzen, a square sail on her foremast."

Richard made a quick calculation. A corsair with that rig was of reasonable size and tonnage, and likely carried fourteen or sixteen 12-pounder guns."

"You're certain she's Tripolitan?"

"Cole is, sir."

"That's good enough for me. Her course?"

Meyers gave him a meaningful look. "On a reciprocal to ours, sir."

"A course of convergence, then."

"It would seem so, sir."

Richard nodded. "Thank you, Mr. Meyers," he said. "Please go below and take position at the guns with Mr. Lee. And pass word for Mr. Weeks."

As he waited for the boatswain, Richard scanned the waters around him. Ahead to the north, many sea miles beyond their current position, lay the rugged southern coast of Sicily. To the south, near the thumb-shaped Tunisian peninsula of Cape Bon, lay the ruins of ancient Carthage. Closer ahead lay Malta, their destination, an easy day's sail in these stiff, hot, levanter winds.

"What do you make of it, Agee?" he asked his first lieutenant, who stood beside him at the waist railing of the quarterdeck peering through a glass. Any minute now, the enemy vessel would heave into view.

Agreen shook his head. "I can't tell for certain. That corsair may have the same weight of guns as we do, but we must have at least three times her weight of broadside. Yet she's comin' right at us; and what's more, she's not tryin' t' confuse us by flyin' some other country's flag." He thought for a moment. "She knows we can't pursue her without tacking. And if we tack, she'll hold the weather gauge. We'd be on opposite tacks for so long we might never catch her. So maybe she figures t' shadow us, t' see where we're headed."

"That's my thinking too, Lieutenant." Richard brought a glass to his eye and peered through it. "There she lies. I can just barely make out her masts. She's still coming at us."

"Damn it," Agreen groused. "There's our enemy and we can take her. But we can't engage her unless she's a mind t' come in too close for her own damn good. And I doubt she'll do that." He sighed in disgust. "It's like a cat playin' with a frickin' mouse."

Richard suddenly recalled an occasion long ago during the war with England. The Continental sloop *Ranger* was being shadowed by a British warship, and her officers were discussing possible tactics in the captain's cabin. Someone had offered that same analogy in the same tone of voice. "Just remember who plays the role of the cat," John Paul Jones had said at the time, "and who the role of the mouse."

Richard turned to the sailing master standing a short distance away by the helm. As was true of everyone granted access to the quarterdeck,

Josiah Smythe understood that the captain and his first lieutenant often conferred in private on the weather side of the quarterdeck and took no offense; quite the opposite, in fact. Never during his forty years at sea had he witnessed such a close bond between a ship's two senior officers. Nor had he ever witnessed a crew more devoted to a ship's officer corps, or a ship's officer corps more devoted to its captain. Morale aboard *Portsmouth* was sky high, from the wardroom aft to the forecastle forward, and Josiah Smythe knew exactly where to place credit for that.

"Mr. Smythe," Richard said to him, "you have the helm. You, Brown," indicating the quartermaster's mate at the wheel, "are relieved."

Peter Weeks approached the quarterdeck railing. Nothing but the silver boatswain's call looped around his neck with a leather lanyard indicated his rank or his history as a boatswain's mate in USS *President* during the war with France and, after that, as a mate in the Cutler & Sons merchant fleet, including service in *Falcon* during her cruise to the Dutch East Indies. When Weeks had stepped forward to volunteer in *Portsmouth*, Richard had excused him from drawing lots, unwilling to risk losing so valuable a warrant officer to a short straw.

Weeks looked up from the ship's waist and snapped a salute. "You sent for me, sir?"

"Yes, Mr. Weeks. We have spotted an enemy cruiser to larboard and we shall clear for action. Have the men stand by the guns and courses and await further orders. We shall not lower away the boats just yet, but prepare the tackle to do that smartly."

"Aye, aye, sir!"

Boatswain's pipes sent all hands aloft or alow to execute the evolutions for battle that the ship's officers had drilled into them since the day *Portsmouth* departed Boston. Fires were extinguished and cabin bulkheads dismantled, including those defining the captain's cabin beneath the quarterdeck. The gun deck was hosed down and sprinkled with sand for better footing should blood be spilled. Anything wooden and portable that could explode into lethal shards if struck by enemy shot was stowed in the lazaret or the hold under the orlop—or in the ship's boats to be towed astern. When all was ready, the gun deck resembled what it was built to be: a substantial floating battery devoid of everything and everyone not required to work the guns. Topside, sailors stood by to brail up the main and fore courses while Marine gun crews loaded the smaller 6-pounder guns with grape or round shot. Down on the orlop, the ship's surgeon worked side-by-side with his mates and the loblolly boy to push together the midshipmen's sea chests to fashion an operating table, then laid out the flesh saws, bone saws, canvas tourniquets, forceps, and other instruments that to the ship's company represented surgical torture and mayhem.

Weeks was about to inform the captain that the ship was properly cleared when cries erupted from aloft.

"On deck there! She's tacking over! She's coming astern of us!"

Midn. Edward Osborn raced aft from the base of the mainmast, where he had been stationed to relay messages from crosstrees to quarterdeck, and took the steps leading from the waist to the quarterdeck in record time. "Captain," he panted after a hasty salute, "the corsair has changed tack. She's coming astern of us!"

"Yes, thank you, Mr. Osborn. I heard that myself," Richard said dryly. He clapped a firm hand on the boy's shoulder and in a low yet stern voice said," Don't *ever* run on deck again, or it will be the worse for you. It's unbecoming an officer and it looks bad to the men. You should have learned that by now."

"I understand, sir. I do apologize, sir. A quick stride on the weather deck is the limit," Osborn said, reciting the rule of naval regulations too often flouted by young, overzealous midshipmen eager to execute an order or inform a superior officer.

"Good lad. Now, return to station."

To the boatswain: "Mr. Weeks, in a moment we shall come into the wind. I'll have the courses brailed up, but leave them hanging in their gear. And make ready to set the t'gants and lower away all four boats. And you may call down Cole and the other lookouts."

"Aye, aye, sir." Weeks saluted and pivoted. "Hands to lower away the boats! Up clews and buntlines! Stand by the t'gants!" As boatswain's mates piped men to action, Weeks strode to the forecastle, his customary position in battle, to direct the handling of the critical foresails and foremast sails.

As sailors in the waist hauled up the main and fore courses to their yards, Richard said to the sailing master, "Mr. Smythe, bring her into the wind. When the courses are up, bring her back on her current course. When the corsair lies a hundred yards astern of us, you may fall off on a parallel course with her, whatever that course may be. Pull within fifty yards of her, but no closer."

To a midshipman on duty as messenger from quarterdeck to gun deck he said, "Mr. Hardy, go below and advise Lieutenant Lee and Lieutenant Meyers to run out the guns, both sides, and have the crews stand by the larboard guns."

Hardy snapped a salute. "Aye, aye, sir!"

To the captain of Marines: "Mr. Corbett, you may deploy your Marines on the tops and behind the nettings."

Carl Corbett acknowledged and summoned his sergeant of Marines.

To his first lieutenant, Richard said, in a low voice, "Well, Agee, that should about do it. All we can do now is wait."

Agreen seemed unsettled. "Wait for what? For her t' rake us?" He was referring to the most precarious position in which a ship of war could find herself: an enemy directly astern pouring a withering broadside into her defenseless bowels, smashing round shot through her stern glass windows and down the full length of her decks, killing and maiming everyone caught in their path, dismantling the ship's rudder and shattering her steering mechanisms, and leaving her adrift on the sea like a gull with clipped wings to be destroyed or captured at her enemy's pleasure. Many a fierce battle at sea had, against all odds, been either won or fought to a draw by an otherwise doomed ship that had somehow managed to maneuver herself into position to rake her adversary's stern.

"No. Her captain can't believe we'd just sit here and take it. He must have something else in mind."

"What, in God's name?"

"I have no idea, Agee. But I've a sense we're about to find out."

Within the hour the enemy corsair's deck and three pyramids of canvas were clearly visible to those on the weather deck and on the gun deck below watching through open ports. She had her starboard guns run out from behind bulwarks that resembled parapets atop a castle's fortifications; the barrels of her eight black cannon protruded through thick wooden embrasures. When the corsair had advanced to within a hundred yards astern, Josiah Smythe, as ordered, brought *Portsmouth* off the wind on a parallel course. Sailing under a reduced rig of topsails, driver, and jib, *Portsmouth* was quickly overtaken by the Tripolitan sailing under a full press of canvas.

No sooner had the corsair's truncated prow drawn even with the frigate's mainmast than her three forward guns opened fire with round shot. Each shot missed its mark. Within seconds the frigate's larboard stern guns answered; on the weather deck, Marine gun crews opened fire with the smaller guns. From behind the nettings on the quarterdeck and waist, and from up on the fighting tops, other Marines pummeled the corsair's weather deck with swivel gun and musket fire.

It seemed to be no contest. The corsair's guns went quiet as sailors on her top deck frantically began waving their arms in the air. As if to underscore their intent, they made a show of hauling down their ensign.

"Well *that* was easy," Agreen commented as he watched the national flag of Tripoli sliding down its halyard.

"A little too easy, to my mind," Richard muttered. He studied the enemy warship intently. She was moving forward now at less than five knots, her progress slowed by sail hastily reduced. It was as though the Tripolitan captain was making every effort to cooperate in the Americans' victory.

"This is likely their first encounter with an American frigate," Agreen reasoned. "Maybe they weren't expectin' such firepower."

"Maybe."

"Well, whatever the reason, she's surrendered to us," Agreen stated the obvious. "So what now, Captain?"

Richard chewed on his lower lip, mulling over that question and keeping his eyes glued on the enemy vessel. Prior experience in the Navy had taught him how to respond to an enemy defeated in battle and how to respond to an enemy victorious in battle. But it had never taught him how to respond to an enemy who surrendered before a battle had truly begun. "Pass word for Seaman Cole," he said.

Within the minute, Harvey Cole stepped hesitantly onto the quarterdeck. Only once before had he been summoned to such hallowed ground, and he timidly glanced about as he slow-stepped toward his captain. "You sent for me, sir?" he ventured after a salute.

Richard returned the salute. "Yes, Cole, I did. Be at your ease, man. I require your assistance, is all."

"Sir?" Cole's expression remained tense although his body relaxed a little.

"Do I understand correctly that you learned Arabic while in prison in Algiers?"

"I did learn a little, sir," Cole confirmed.

"A little is all I need." He handed Cole a speaking trumpet. "I want you to tell the captain of that corsair to heave to and remain under our lee. I am going to send a boat over and he is to receive it with all honors. Can you do that?"

"I can try, sir."

"Good man."

Cole raised the trumpet to his lips and shouted through it, tentatively at first, then with more authority, conveying the message as much with the motions of his free hand as with his words.

"What's your plan?" Agreen inquired as the awkward dialogue between the two warships progressed.

"My plan is to send Lieutenant Meyers over to her with Boatswain's Mate Clausen and a squad of Marines. Meyers can spike the guns and toss her other armament overboard after he has placed the officers and crew under guard. We'll need a few of those hands to help sail her to Malta. Escorted by us, of course. Have you a better plan to suggest, Lieutenant?"

Agreen shook his head no.

"Well, then, let's get to it."

When both vessels were hove to and lying perhaps twenty-five yards apart, the frigate's cutter was freed from the line of four boats astern and brought forward against her larboard hull. Blue-uniformed Marines armed with muskets and pistols scrambled over the railing and rappelled down the frigate's hull into the boat. They were followed by the coxswain, the boatswain's mate, the sergeant of Marines, and, last of all, in deference to his rank, Lieutenant Eric Meyers.

As Meyers settled in at the stern sheets and the oarsmen prepared to shove off, something on the corsair's deck caught Richard's eye. At first he took scant note of it, thinking it was an illusion—sunlight, perhaps, reflecting off the sparkling sea. But again it caught his attention. On closer inspection it looked like a ball of light, ever so tiny, dancing within the gun embrasure. Now there was another one, a few feet away to the left. And now a third: three little fireflies flitting about behind high bulwarks directly above the enemy's guns.

Then it struck him a sickening blow. "Son of a *bitch*!" he breathed. "*Everyone down!*" he screamed. He ran to the larboard railing and leaned over. "Mr. Meyers! Into the water! *All of you! Into the water, now! They're about to fire on us!*"

Just as those in the cutter heaved themselves over the side, the starboard guns of the corsair erupted in a searing broadside so concentrated and so well synchronized that it shoved the Arab warship back broadside against the Mediterranean. Twelve-pound balls lashed the frigate and shattered the cutter alongside, pulverizing muscle, bone, hemp, and wood in one horrific, blinding sweep. Armed Tripolitans sprang up from behind the bulwarks and fired a broadside of musketry as sailors in the rigging let fly all canvas. The corsair surged forward, fleeing toward the protective shoals and shallows of the Tunisian coast.

After few moments of stunned disbelief, those aboard *Portsmouth* began to gather their wits about them. His ears still ringing from the blast, Richard seized hold of the larboard railing and struggled to his feet. To his intense relief, he found his first lieutenant already up and about. "We're going after them, Agee," he cried. "Those bastards won't get away with this!"

Richard glanced over the side and saw several bodies floating facedown in the water and a few survivors weakly treading water or hanging onto flotsam. One of them, praise God, was Eric Meyers. "Mr. Meyers!" he shouted down. "I'm going to let loose the boats." He walked to the stern, untied the rope that connected the three remaining boats to the mother ship, and yanked them in close. He let go the end of the rope and heard the end splash into the sea below. "Have the men get on or hang on. We'll come back for you. Do you hear me? *We'll come back for you!*"

Meyers acknowledged with a weak wave and started sidestroking toward the nearest boat.

"Mr. Weeks!" Agreen shouted. "Crack on all sail—everything we've got—and get her under way!" He glanced aft at the sailing master, who was limping over to the wheel. A red splotch of blood was clearly visible on his trouser leg. "My. Smythe, are you badly hurt? No? Glad t' hear it. Now chase down that corsair! Take careful note of our new compass bearing. We'll need t' follow a reciprocal course on the way back here."

Tripolitan cruisers were widely recognized for the speed their narrow beam and tall rig could draw from even a modest breeze. Speed lay, after all, at the heart of piracy. But as fast as the corsair might be, a light American frigate straining under a full press of canvas was faster. As the minutes ticked by to a half-hour, *Portsmouth* slowly but surely closed the gap between the two vessels; after an hour she was nudging up on the corsair, a cable's length off to larboard.

As soon as the chase commenced, Richard had ordered the dead and wounded taken below to the ship's surgeon and the weather deck cleared of useless ropes and pieces of wood blasted free during the ambush. Richard's eyes confirmed on the weather deck, and Lieutenant Lee confirmed by messenger from the gun deck, that the damage could have been much worse. Two men lay dead on deck, and several were floating in the water by the boats. And while any shipmate's death was to be lamented, Richard's keen eye and cry of warning had saved many lives. Or so Agreen had consoled him.

Throughout the chase Richard's eyes never wavered from the corsair's stern. He burned with the outrage and blasphemy the pirates had perpetrated. Damn them! *Damn them!* His own brother Caleb had wasted ten years in a stinking hellhole of a North African prison for the crime of being born an American. For wanting to follow in his older brother's footsteps. Heavy on his mind as well was the image of Ashley Bowen, Caleb's cellmate who had risked all to escape the inescapable and return home to his bride of six months. He was caught, inevitably, and dragged back from the desert to the prison. His Muslim captors first tortured him and then impaled him, still alive, on a giant hook attached to the outside of the city walls. His shipmates were forced to listen as his cries for mercy slowly faded to moans of agony and then to whimpers of despair, until at last his spirit was released. Ashley's grieving bride had only now begun rebuilding her life.

And here, today, cutthroats just like them had committed an act so vile, so abhorrent, so utterly beyond any acceptable code of human behavior or rule of war that it defied comprehension. The news that Adam Bright, a Cutler & Sons topman with four years of service, was one of the sailors pronounced dead brought hot tears of rage to Richard's eyes. Barbary pirates had heaped atrocity after atrocity on helpless Americans. By God, it was time to answer their abominations, and he, Richard Cutler, now had the means to do it.

Agreen stepped close. "Our bow-chaser can deliver a warning shot from here, Captain. Shall I send word to Lieutenant Lee?"

"No," Richard said with iron resolve. "The time for warning shots has passed."

A pause. Then: "If we're going to fire on her, I suggest we haul up the courses."

"No," Richard grated. "We shall douse no sail."

Agreen drew a deep breath. He understood as well as anyone the danger of a stray ash wafting up from the gun deck or weather deck and setting fire to a lower sail. Or the damage an enemy shot could inflict on such a sail. But he said nothing. The look on his captain's face did not invite suggestions or recommendations.

Those in the corsair must have sensed the hopelessness of their plight as the distance between the two warships narrowed. The blue-hued coastline of Tunis lay enticingly ahead on the southern horizon, but the distance was too great for the corsair to reach it before being overtaken. Her officers could do the math as accurately as the Americans, and the answer they derived could offer little hope of survival in battle. The corsair had already shown her cards, and the realization that she had overplayed her hand had no doubt already dawned on them.

"She's lowering her ensign," Agreen observed. "She's surrendering . . . again."

"Mr. Roberts," Richard snapped. The midshipman on duty stepped forward and saluted. "Advise Mr. Lee to stand by the larboard battery. Then report back here."

"Aye, aye, sir."

"Mr. Corbett," Richard said, "are your guns loaded with grape? And you have deployed your Marines?"

"Yes, sir."

"Very well. Stand by and await my order. Mr. Smythe," he snapped, "bring her to within fifty yards."

The tables had turned. It was now *Portsmouth* pulling even with the corsair's stern, then with her midships. Those aboard the corsair waved their arms back and forth in the air as they had before, but this time with a great deal more urgency. Two of her crew in the stern unhooked the red, green, and white ensign from its halyard and held it up for those on the frigate to see, as if to convince the Americans that this time they were serious about surrendering.

"Mr. Roberts," Richard said, "you may advise Mr. Lee to commence firing."

Agreen stood stone-faced.

The midshipman saluted. "Aye, aye, sir." He strode briskly forward to the large open rectangular hatchway amidships. "Mr. Lee," he shouted down through cupped hands. "The captain sends his compliments and you may commence firing."

Almost instantly *Portsmouth*'s larboard side erupted in yellow flashes, orange tongues, and a spew of white ashes in a vicious blast that shook the very fabric of the frigate. Above, on the weather deck, smaller guns exploded canisters of grape across the deck of the corsair as swivel guns barked and muskets snapped. *Portsmouth* was sailing fast with all plain sails set to royals, and she swept past the corsair in what seemed an instant, without a single enemy gun fired in reply.

At the taffrail, Richard raised a spyglass to inspect the damage. He could not see much. Thick smoke enveloped the corsair in a grayish shroud. Across the span of turquoise sea they could hear the pitiful moans and screams of men wounded or dying, and Richard watched with satisfaction as her foremast teetered back and forth, back and forth, before toppling over toward her bow. The mast disappeared into the murky smoke, taking with it into the gloom a good slug of the standing rigging. He nodded at Agreen.

"Ready about!" Agreen shouted. "Headsail sheets! Mr. Roberts, you may advise Lieutenant Lee to make ready the starboard battery! Helm a-lee!"

As *Portsmouth* began the evolutions of turning her bow away from the wind and wearing the frigate around on an opposite tack, Agreen stepped close to his captain.

"Sweet Jesus, Richard, are you goin' t' fire another broadside into her?"

Richard did not reply.

"For what purpose?" Agreen pressed. "T' sink her? She's already done for."

Richard looked at him. "No, Agee, not to sink her. To send a message to these bastards they will never forget."

Richard walked to the waist railing of the quarterdeck and stared at the waters ahead. As he had anticipated, the corsair had come off the wind as best she could with her severely damaged rig. *Portsmouth* was sailing full and by, on an angle away from her enemy, unable to give effective chase and deliver another broadside without tacking over. The smoke had cleared away enough to reveal the extent of the corsair's damage. At least two guns had been upended; her rigging was in tatters; her fore-and-aft sails were either torn or holed; her foremast and mizzen topmast had gone by the boards; and staves along her hull had been smashed in and a futtock broken through. Agreen was right. She was done for, a floating wreck. She'd have all she could do just to remain afloat until she reached Tunis, let alone Tripoli. Amidships he saw something he had never thought to see: two sailors tossing their ship's ensign overboard into the sea. Aside from those two, he saw only three men moving about the deck. Others had no doubt taken refuge behind the vessel's wooden embrasures.

Agreen came up beside him. "Don't do it, Richard," he quietly pleaded. "In God's holy name, don't do it. You've sent your message. Fire another broadside into that hulk and your message will never be delivered. And remember, we have shipmates in the water back there."

Richard gripped the railing with both hands, aware of those on the quarterdeck, and those in the waist and in the tops, watching him intently, awaiting his orders. For several moments the only sounds to be heard were the gurgle of seawater sweeping along the frigate's hull and the pleasant hum of wind in the rigging. At length he shook his head, as if to cast out demons demanding unholy vengeance against a defeated, defenseless enemy. "Point taken, Agee," he said softly. "Cease fire."

"Cease fire!" Agreen cried out. His order was quickly relayed along the weather and gun decks.

Portsmouth veered away on a more northerly course, her enemy now a lifeless corpse hobbling southward in the opposite direction under a jury rig of hastily fashioned canvas on her mainmast, the only mast still standing.

Seven

Malta,
October–November 1803

LOCATED AT THE geographical center of the Mediterranean Sea, the island of Malta had for centuries held a strategic importance far greater than its hundred-square-mile area might suggest. Catholic to its core—Saint Paul himself had preached the gospel on the archipelago after being shipwrecked there—Malta had teetered back and forth at the epicenter of the struggle between Europeans and Turks, Muslims and Christians, for control of the Mediterranean. Nor did the treaty between Spain and the Ottoman Empire in the late 1700s bring lasting peace or solace to the long-suffering Maltese people. In 1798, on his voyage to conquer Egypt, Napoléon Bonaparte seized Malta and left behind a sizable garrison under the command of General Vaubois. The general's mission, Bonaparte publicly declared, was to hold at all costs an island so vital to French interests and supply lines that he would rather keep it away from the British than any village in France.

Vaubois' tenure, however, proved brief. Reinforced with weapons and manpower furnished by the kingdom of Sicily, the citizens of Malta, outraged by the French Republic's hostility to Catholic doctrine, rose up in defiance. In support, the Royal Navy blockaded the islands and brought its unique blend of firepower to bear against the French. In 1800, to show their appreciation for Britain's assistance and to deter future invaders, the leaders of Malta formally petitioned the government of King George III to grant their island royal dominion status. Sir Alexander Ball, a former British naval officer much beloved by the Maltese, graciously accepted on behalf of His Britannic Majesty. Soon thereafter, Horatio Lord Nelson, Vice Admiral of the Blue, Viscount Nelson of the Nile and Burnham Thorpe, First Duke of Bronté, Knight of the Bath, and commander-in-chief of British forces in the Mediterranean, declared Grand Harbor at Valletta—one of the finest deep-draft harbors in the world—the new headquarters for the Royal Navy's Mediterranean Fleet.

A HOT OCTOBER SUN cast a golden haze over land and sea as *Portsmouth* hauled her wind and rounded the eastern tip of Malta. Nothing suggested anything but tranquility on the island as the American frigate sailed northwestward on a calm turquoise sea under jibs, topsails, and driver. Buildings began to take distinct form within the ancient city perched high on a broad spit of land. Most were baroque in style, with elements here and there of Greek classicism. Valletta had been reconstructed centuries ago by the Knights of Saint John—later to be known as the Knights of Malta—a quasi-military religious order of chivalry that had taken refuge on Malta in the 1500s after the Muslim Turks had ousted them from the island of Rhodes. To Richard Cutler, it seemed impossible that the serene, sun-drenched island possessed a military pedigree as glaring as the sun reflecting off its white freestone dwellings.

Among the thick forest of masts within the two-mile stretch of Grand Harbor he spotted two British gunboats approaching from beneath the imposing façade of Fort Saint Elmo, a stone fortress located on the seaward shore of the Sciberras Peninsula. The Union Jack fluttered on a flagpole high atop the fort's eastern battlements.

"Now *that's* a sight," Agreen Crabtree said with reverence. He was standing beside Richard on the windward side of the quarterdeck. Along with everyone else on deck and in the rigging, they had been absorbing, each in his own way, the silent approach of history.

Richard nodded his agreement. When he noticed the two gunboats in the distance, he had ordered canvas reduced to working jib, fore and main topsails, and single-reefed driver. In the light breeze *Portsmouth* was now making perhaps two or three knots.

Richard glanced aloft at a telltale quivering spasmodically on the ensign halyard and then turned his gaze dead ahead. "Agee," he said quietly, "I want you to know how much I appreciate you saving me from myself yesterday."

Agreen, too, was staring ahead. "Think nothin' of it, Richard," he said blithely. "That's what you and I have been doin' for each other ever since that day Captain Jones signed us on in *Ranger*. It's your turn t' save me next."

Richard's wry grin was the first indication of his former self that Agreen had seen since Richard had presided over the burial at sea of five shipmates the previous afternoon. "I have always admired your ability to transform tragedy into comedy with a flick of the tongue, Lieutenant."

"That's part of my role as your first," Agreen chuckled, adding, more solemnly, "and as your friend. Those five men meant just as much t' me as they did t' you."

George Lee approached and touched his hat. "Gunboat's signaling, Captain," he reported. "They desire us to heave to."

"Then make it so, Lieutenant. But keep the hands at the braces. We won't be here long."

"Aye, aye, sir." Lee whirled about. "Mr. Weeks!" he shouted. "Stations for heaving to!" *Portsmouth* came to the wind and slowed to a virtual standstill on the placid waters outside the harbor.

As the leading gunboat drew near, a British officer stood up amidships and cupped his hands at his mouth. "Identify your ship, please," he requested crisply.

"USS *Portsmouth*," Agreen hailed back from the quarterdeck. "Captain Richard Cutler. I am Lieutenant Crabtree, his first."

"Thank you, Mr. Crabtree. May I welcome you and your captain to Valletta. I am Lieutenant James Bosworth. Might I ask if you put in to any port of call during your cruise here?

"No. We have come straight from Boston."

"I am glad to hear it. Quarantine shall not be required. Might I inquire your business here?"

"Captain Cutler will explain his business to the governor. Dispatches were sent ahead of us."

"Ah, yes. Indeed they were. And we are holding dispatches for you from your squadron commander. You may proceed and take anchorage off the fortress side of the jetty. You will find fifteen fathoms of water there and a sandy bottom. I shall have boats standing by to take you in tow should the wind die altogether. Do you require any other assistance at the moment?"

"We do, Lieutenant. We have wounded men aboard."

"I am sorry to hear it. How many?"

"Six."

"I see. Are they ambulatory?"

"Two are not."

"In that case, if it is agreeable to your captain, I shall make arrangements for them to be transferred to a naval hospital ashore. They will receive excellent care, I assure you. Is there any other service I might perform on your behalf?"

Agreen glanced at Richard, who said: "Provisions."

"Just one," Agreen shouted down. "We are low on provisions."

"I had anticipated you would be. Once you are at anchor I shall have hoys sent out to you with fresh food and water. Now if there is nothing else, you may proceed. I daresay our sweeps will have us in port before your wind. As soon as I am able, I shall send word to Mr. Morath, the governor's representative in Valletta."

"Thank you, Mr. Bosworth. You have been most helpful."

With a screech of boatswain's whistles *Portsmouth* brought her sails to the breeze and made ready to drop anchor for the first time since leaving Boston almost seven weeks earlier.

AT TWO BELLS in the forenoon watch the following morning, the Marine sentry on duty outside the captain's after cabin knocked on the door. Bidden in, he walked aft to the dining alcove where Richard Cutler was having coffee with his commissioned officers and snapped a crisp salute. He handed Richard Cutler a square white letter that bore his name in elaborate black script on the front. On the back, at the juncture of the folds in the middle, was an official seal embossed within a circle of red wax. Richard broke the wax, unfolded the letter, and read:

> *To the Hon. Capt. Richard Cutler*
> *of the United States Ship Portsmouth*
> *Valletta Harbor*
>
> *Dear Captain Cutler:*
> *You and whichever of your officers you choose are most cordially invited to Fort Saint Elmo at four o'clock this afternoon to confer with me and the royal governor's private secretary in the Blue Room located on the main floor. We have some knowledge of your business in Malta and we are keen to understand how we might assist you further. I regret to inform you that Sir Alexander is unable to join us this afternoon, but he extends his best regards and full cooperation to you and your ship. He is most hopeful that in two weeks' time he shall have the honor of your company at a social occasion, the details of which I shall provide this afternoon.*

Kindly acknowledge receipt of this communication.
I am
Your Most Obedient Servant,
Thomas Quentin Morath
Personal Representative of His Honor
Sir Alexander Ball
28 October 1803

"Is the governor's boat standing by?" Richard asked the Marine.

"It is, sir."

"Please acknowledge receipt of this invitation and accept on behalf of Lieutenant Crabtree and myself."

"Aye, aye, Captain." The Marine saluted and departed the cabin.

"Invitation?" Agreen inquired after the sentry had closed the cabin door.

"Just so. The letter is from the governor's personal representative. You and I have an appointment with him in Fort Saint Elmo at the start of the first dogwatch. I would invite you all," he said, glancing at his other two commissioned officers, "but that might be overdoing it. And it appears we have another invitation to consider, this one from Sir Alexander himself, in two weeks."

"You mean we have to endure this island for two whole *weeks*?" Eric Meyers said with a heavy sigh that did not entirely mask his delight. "That's a mighty stiff sentence, Captain."

"Indeed it is, Mr. Meyers. And I should think you will need every bit of it to recuperate from your ordeal in the water. But don't go getting your hopes up just yet. Our orders are to return to base as soon as conditions permit. In the meantime, you may inform Mr. Weeks that the men are granted shore leave in rotation. And please repeat to Mr. Weeks what I have already said: the women on this island are devout Catholics, they take their religion seriously, and the order is 'hands off.' I am most adamant about this. More to the point, Mr. Meyers," he added tongue-in-cheek, "the ship's officers must also understand this, *you* in particular. Your reputation with the ladies is quite well established."

Meyers gave him a solemn look. "I promise you, sir, that I will do nothing for which I have not prayed devoutly."

"That is precisely what troubles me, Mr. Meyers."

THE KNIGHTS OF SAINT JOHN built Fort Saint Elmo to be the centerpiece of Malta's coastal fortifications. Controlling the entrance to both

Grand Harbor and the neighboring Marsamxett Harbor, its massive walls and gun batteries reinforced the older fortifications of Fort Tigné and the Roman-built Fort Angelo on the opposite side of Grand Harbor. During the Great Siege of 1565 the fort withstood an Ottoman naval bombardment. Under British rule, Fort Tigné had been converted into an army barracks and Fort Saint Angelo clearly held less strategic significance. But star-shaped Fort Saint Elmo retained an imperial presence, and woe to any enemy, thought Richard Cutler as he and Agreen Crabtree approached the heavy wooden doors at its entrance, who dared challenge its authority.

The Blue Room was in keeping with its name: everything in the snug little room, from its window drapes to the cushions and fabrics of its furniture, was a bright robin's-egg blue. Wingback chairs and settees surrounded a low table; on a mantle a pendulum clock ticked agreeably. A large rectangular window cut into the seaward wall was open to the pleasant scent of sea air and the pleasing sound of waves swirling and sucking against a rocky promontory below.

A short, pudgy, balding man projecting a no-nonsense attitude strode into the room. He was superbly dressed from the white silk of his neck stock to the polished shine of his silver-buckled shoes, although Richard noticed that the three lowest buttons of his gold-tasseled waistcoat were left undone to allow room for the consequences of overindulgence. Following obediently behind him was a man who appeared not yet thirty, of slight build with dark, flowing hair and thick eyebrows that nearly met in the middle. In his right hand he clutched a leather satchel.

"Good afternoon, Mr. Cutler," the older man said with an aristocratic drawl. "I am Thomas Morath. On behalf of the royal governor, I welcome you and your ship to Valletta. This is Mr. Crabtree, I presume? I am so very pleased to make your acquaintance, Lieutenant. Please, sit down. Before we begin," he continued, "please allow me to introduce the governor's personal secretary. A fine young man, if I may say so, who holds the additional title of public secretary of Malta, a most prestigious position. His name is Samuel Coleridge. He is a Cambridge man and a very fine poet in his spare time. Indeed, he has already had a book of romantic poems published in England in collaboration with . . . um . . . um . . ." He gave the young man a questioning look.

"William Wordsworth," Coleridge replied. The amused glance he gave the Americans suggested that Thomas Morath, for all his accomplishments, had little knowledge of either romance or poetry.

"Yes, quite. Wordsworth. "Rime of the Ancient Mariner" and all that.

Jolly good show. Highly recommended. Ah, here is tea." After a servant had passed tea and crustless cucumber and parsley sandwiches to the group seated around the table, he continued. "Now then, gentlemen, if we may get down to business. Mr. Coleridge carries a dispatch for you from your squadron commander, Captain Edward Preble. We received it just two days ago. Would you care to read it before we begin? It may have some bearing on our discussions."

Richard nodded. "I would, thank you."

Coleridge withdrew the dispatch from the satchel and handed it over. When Richard had finished reading, he folded it and slid it into a coat pocket. "There is nothing in this dispatch that will affect our discussions, Mr. Morath," he said, "and nothing that is not already known to British intelligence. Commodore Preble informs me that a show of naval power off the coast of Tangiers has convinced the sultan of Morocco to make peace with the United States. He also informs me that the permanent base for our Mediterranean Squadron is Syracuse and I am to report to him there by December first." He left unspoken a third item—that Capt. William Eaton was unavoidably detained in Tunis and would not arrive in Malta on schedule. Richard Cutler was instructed to proceed according to plan and to gather what intelligence he could without him. Nor did he mention a fourth item, in the form of a personal note from Preble stating that he had appointed Richard's son James to the rank of senior midshipman. That appointment meant that Jamie was now first in line to serve as acting lieutenant should the need arise.

Morath's eyebrows shot up. "*Syracuse?* Why in heaven's name would Captain Preble choose Syracuse? We have offered your navy the full complement of our services here in Valletta and in Gibraltar. But *Sicily?* I daresay it's good for nothing except bloody grapes and olives."

Richard patted the side pocket into which he had slid the dispatch. "The short answer is what Preble reports here, that when the squadron assembled in Gibraltar, a number of his crew jumped ship. Since they claimed to be British citizens, the Royal Navy would not give them up—a sort of a reverse impressment, if you will. I suspect that Captain Preble fears the same thing would happen here. And *Constitution* is short-handed as it is."

Morath pursed his lips. "Viewed in that light, I suppose it does make some sort of sense. Might I inquire if you are concerned about your own men?"

"It hadn't crossed my mind," Richard confessed.

"Our crew is entirely American," Agreen explained, "and they are loyal to their captain. Many of them were formerly employed in the Cutler family shipping business, me included. These men sail with us because they choose to, not because they are forced to."

Morath smiled thinly. "How commendable. Perhaps our navy may take a lesson from yours." He continued with forced good cheer. "Well, no point in flogging a dead horse, what? Or flogging a deserter you can't string up." He chuckled at his turn of phrase. When neither American seemed to appreciate his humor, he cleared his throat. "Right. Let us return to the business at hand, shall we?"

For the next thirty minutes Richard Cutler explained the plan hatched by Capt. William Eaton, former consul in Tunis, to lead an army in support of Hamet Karamanli against his brother, Yusuf. Although Eaton would lead this overland expedition, the U.S. government had refused to commit substantial ground forces in its support. Assistance was thus required from foreign sources: Arab soldiers loyal to Hamet, certainly, and European mercenaries, if possible, plus sufficient stores of military supplies and a caravan of camels. Britain could help, Richard suggested, through its vast intelligence network in the Mediterranean and especially in Egypt, where Hamet had taken refuge after abandoning his post as royal governor of Derne. Egypt had been under nominal British rule since Admiral Nelson's victory over the French at the Battle of the Nile. Morath could also help by arranging for him to meet Richard Farquhar, an acquaintance of Hamet Karamanli currently residing in Malta, and Salvatore Busatile, a Hamet intimate authorized to speak on his behalf. Both men were under British protection. Richard ended by stressing the plan's advantages for Britain. Although the war with Tripoli was America's affair, an American victory in the Mediterranean would serve the national interests of all Christian maritime nations, Great Britain first among them.

Morath stroked his chin as Richard spoke, and Coleridge took copious notes. "Most interesting," he said at the conclusion. "Most interesting indeed, Captain Cutler. I daresay you make a strong argument. I must discuss this with Sir Alexander, of course, but I foresee no impediment to arranging the meeting you request. Where would you like it to take place? Here in this room?"

"I would prefer my ship, Mr. Morath. I want my other officers to be present."

"Your other officers are most welcome here."

"I thank you for that. But I would prefer my ship."

"Then your ship it shall be. I shall send word when the meeting is arranged." Morath motioned to Coleridge to gather up his writing tools. "Just one more item if you please, Captain, before we take our leave. As I indicated in my letter to you this morning, there is another occasion for you to meet Sir Alexander, and we hope you will be in a position to take advantage of it. Two weeks from tomorrow—that would be the tenth of November—Sir Alexander is hosting an affair at San Anton Palace. The guest of honor, I am delighted to inform you, is Admiral Horatio Lord Nelson, who is to arrive in Valencia aboard *Victory*." He smiled at Richard's reaction. "Accompanying his lordship to Malta, and to the social affair at San Anton Palace, is his friend Captain Jeremy Hardcastle, who, if British intelligence serves, is your brother-in-law. Admiral Nelson and Captain Hardcastle will both be quite distraught if you are unable to attend. Their business in Malta is rather hush-hush, you see, and this will likely be your only opportunity to see them whilst they're here. The invitation includes you as well, Lieutenant Crabtree. You both will receive formal invitations shortly. I bid you two gentlemen a very good day."

THREE DAYS LATER, Lt Eric Meyers was waiting at the entry port to greet two civilians who arrived aboard a British-manned launch. Richard Cutler received the two men in his after cabin and formally introduced them to his three lieutenants. After seating the visitors on one side of the rectangular table, he asked each to say a few words about his background and his relationship with Hamet Karamanli.

The taller of the two men, dressed in the style of a prosperous European merchant, spoke first in a distinct Highland burr. "This looks to me very much like a court of inquiry," he commented, his dark eyes flashing at the four naval officers sitting across from him in full undress uniform. Behind the officers, visible through stern windows hinged open, the azure waters of Grand Harbor shimmered in the pleasant warmth of the day. Sunlight danced about the cabin and deckhead, reflecting off the glass panes with the small motions of the ship. "Or perhaps a court-martial," the man added.

"Rest assured that neither is the case, Mr. Farquhar," Richard responded. "To the contrary, we are gathered here today to learn how we might serve each other and our national interests. My government has long desired this meeting. It is why my ship was ordered to Malta as her first port of call. Please continue and explain your relationship with Hamet Karamanli and how that relationship came about."

The Scotsman folded his hands before him. "I fear you have been misinformed. My relationship is not with Mr. Karamanli. And as to the matter we are discussing, I am more concerned with the interests of the United States than those of Great Britain. My relationship is with Captain Eaton. It is to him—and thus to the United States government—that I owe my allegiance and my professional services."

"I am aware of your relationship with Captain Eaton, Mr. Farquhar. I had, in fact, expected him to be with us here this morning. Unfortunately, he has been delayed in Tunis. As to the matter at hand, how would you describe your 'professional services'?"

Farquhar shrugged. "I procure things."

"What sorts of things?"

"Whatever my client requires. In this instance, should we agree on terms, I will procure whatever the United States requires for whatever objectives it seeks."

"Please be more specific."

"I procure whatever my client requires," Farquhar repeated more forcefully, as though he were repeating what should by now be blatantly clear. "My specialty is weaponry: guns, cannon, fieldpieces, muskets, whatever is asked of me. I can also supply funds and provisions. And mercenaries from many different countries, should you have need of them. You're a Navy man, Captain. Think of me as a glorified purser for hire."

Richard ignored that. "Might I ask how you procure such items?"

Farquhar gave him a toothy smile. "You may ask, Captain, but I am not obliged to answer. Nor do I intend to, at least not in detail. I do not mean to be uncooperative. I am simply protecting secrets and clients I have no wish to divulge. Quite simply, I serve as an agent between those who want and those who have. Whatever is delivered by those who have is paid for by those who want. And because there is so much 'want' in this world of ours, the rather unique services I offer are much in demand."

"Services for which you receive a handsome cut, I presume," Richard said dryly.

Farquhar held up his hands. "I am a businessman. And as you and your superiors will quickly come to acknowledge, I am very, very good at what I do. Yes, Captain, I earn a handsome cut, and what I do and what I provide are worth every penny of it."

"Of that I have no doubt, Mr. Farquhar." Richard paused to gather his thoughts. "How did you become involved in this . . . initiative?"

Farquhar smiled. "If I am anything, Captain, I am an opportunist. I have a rather impressive network of agents whose job it is to inform me and my son of business opportunities. Incidentally, my son George is a most capable young man. It was he, not I, who first made contact with Captain Eaton. Should we come to terms with the United States, I will assign him to your cause. You will be completely satisfied, I assure you."

"Thank you. Now, if you please, you were explaining how you became involved in this initiative."

"So I was. Well you see, Captain, despite what I suspect are your initial impressions of me, I am a man who decries injustice. Yes, I see that statement surprises you and your officers. Perhaps it even amuses you. But it happens to be true. I am a man who desires to do well whilst doing some good in this world.

"You and I both know that Hamet Karamanli is the rightful bashaw of Tripoli. The throne is his by right of succession. And he is a man I have come to both like and respect. Captain Eaton shares my view. I had the great pleasure of meeting him whilst I was conferring with a client in Tunis. He is a splendid fellow and, I am certain, a very fine officer, too. There's the connection, you see. That is how I became involved. I respect what he does; he respects what I do. We wish to work together in a common cause. If I can help him by helping Hamet succeed, then we all come out ahead, don't we? We will all have found our own form of justice."

"Your ethics are to be admired, Mr. Farquhar," Richard commented with a hint of sarcasm.

Farquhar's eyes flashed. "Whether or not you find my ethics admirable is hardly the point, Captain. I have meaningful connections with kings and queens and governors and sultans throughout the Mediterranean, and suppliers on both sides of it. *That* is the point. These people trust me. They want to do business with me. Why? Because I am honest and discreet. Because I safeguard their interests. And because I provide them with a satisfactory return on their investments. So that's how it goes. You pay me. I pay them. I take my cut and you receive what you require: the wherewithal to march an army across five hundred miles of desert. Have you experienced the desert firsthand, Captain? No? Nor has Captain Eaton. There are adversaries and adversities under every rock and along every step of the way. Those who are not thoroughly prepared do not make it across.

"This I can guarantee: I will make certain that Captain Eaton is as well prepared for his overland march as is humanly possible. How can I make such a guarantee? By assigning my son George not only to the cause but to the expedition, as its quartermaster. I have already discussed this matter with him, and he has agreed. So you see, Captain, you Americans need me in much the same way that the English need me. Perhaps you have wondered why they protect me. It's not because of my Scottish heritage"—he shook his head and chuckled—"rather, it's because I deliver to them, time and time again, whatever it is they require in *their* national interests. Do I make myself clear?"

"Crystal clear, sir. I have no further questions. Perhaps my officers do?" Richard glanced right and left. "Thank you, Mr. Farquhar," he said when no one spoke. "Mr. Busatile?"

Salvatore Busatile introduced himself in broken English as a Sicilian who had become acquainted with Hamet Karamanli by happenstance three years earlier. The two men had quickly formed a bond of friendship and trust that brought Busatile into Hamet's inner circle of advisers. Busatile droned on but added little of substance to the conversation beyond vouching for Hamet's character and popularity as governor of Derne before rumors spread that Yusuf had dispatched assassins to execute his older brother. That threat, Busatile explained, was what had prompted Hamet to flee Tripoli for Egypt. He concluded by stating that his connections in the Arab world—connections both inspired and enhanced by his close ties to Hamet—would enable him, working hand in hand with Farquhar, to field a sizable number of Arab soldiers in Eaton's army.

When Lieutenant Meyers returned to the after cabin from seeing off the two guests, he found *Portsmouth*'s three other senior officers huddled around the table.

"Well, gentlemen, what do you think?" Richard threw out. "Permission to speak freely, of course."

George Lee spoke first. "That was an enlightening exchange, Captain," he said. "I now understand the role these men are to play. But I remain confused. If I might ask, sir, just how likely is it that Captain Eaton will actually lead this so-called expeditionary force against Tripoli?"

"That's a good question, George," Richard replied, "and it goes right to the heart of the matter. Unfortunately, it's a question I cannot answer. I'm as much in the dark about all this as you are. Mr. Jefferson and Mr. Madison are wavering, and it's anyone's guess which way the diplomatic winds are blowing at the moment. Perhaps Captain Preble will have received official word from Washington by the time we arrive in Syracuse."

"Was not Commodore Barron very much in favor of this expedition?"

"He was, Eric. Captain Eaton apparently did a good job of convincing him. And the commodore's enthusiasm gained Jefferson's and Madison's support for the idea at first. They even gave Eaton twenty thousand dollars to begin implementing the plan. But bear in mind that Barron knew that his days as commodore were numbered and had nothing to lose by expressing support for what in his heart he may have believed was a doomed strategy."

"What changed their minds? Jefferson and Madison, I mean."

Richard shrugged. "I'm not sure their minds *have* changed, Agee. But anything I might add at this point would be speculation beyond what is commonly known—that Mr. Lear, our senior diplomatic consul in Barbary, strongly opposes the plan. Why, I cannot say. I understand that he cares for neither Eaton nor his mission. That is the limit of my knowledge. So we'll just have to await those dispatches from Washington."

AGREEN THOUGHT the third overcast day in a row a blessing. The salt-and-peppery altocumulus clouds presaged the transition from hot, dry summer to warm, wet winter, and he was all in favor of that. The full dress uniform he was wearing as the coach-and-four rumbled inland along the well-maintained road from Valetta to Attard made him itchy and raw. He could not imagine the torture of wearing such a rig in the fierce heat of July.

"Jesus, Richard," he muttered, "can't we open the windows a tad more? I feel like a lobster in a pot of boilin' water."

"You look more like a crab, I'd say," Richard jested. He added, more sympathetically, "I'm suffering too, Agee. But if we open the windows any further, we're liable to get road dust on our crisp, tidy uniforms. What would the royal governor think of that? And more to the point, the young ladies who will soon be swooning at your feet?"

"Ha. Very funny," Agreen groused. "Though you're doubtless right about the women."

When Agreen offered no further retort, Richard went back to gazing out the left-side window. Although the pastoral scenery was pleasant enough, he paid scant attention to it. His thoughts dwelt heavily on the brother-in-law he had not seen since *Falcon* dropped anchor off Gibraltar fifteen years ago on her way to Algiers. During that brief stopover Richard had formed an immediate bond with Jeremy Hardcastle that went beyond family obligations, just as he had with Jeremy's younger brother, Hugh, also a senior post captain in the Royal Navy. And because Katherine had kept in close touch over the years with her parents and siblings, Richard had been able to follow with great interest as both brothers-in-law rose through the ranks.

Then there was Horatio Nelson, a naval officer whose unique grasp of strategy combined with an unconventional view of naval tactics had earned him a number of spectacular victories over England's enemies. Richard had first met him on the quays of Barbados when he was a young topman serving in his family's merchant brig *Eagle* and Nelson was a midshipman in HMS *Seahorse*, of the Windward Squadron. Five years later, at the age of twenty, Nelson had been promoted to the rank of post captain, a spectacular achievement for so young a naval officer lacking significant "interest" in Whitehall. By the age of thirty-nine he had achieved the lofty rank of rear admiral. And he had proved many times since to His Majesty King George III and My Lords of the Admiralty, especially to the First Lord, Earl Spencer, that he deserved it. Richard had crossed tacks with Nelson several times in the course of his career, and each time he did, he felt he had gained something important as a result.

"Sweet Jesus on a honey-stick," Agreen muttered some time later, "would you look at that." He touched Richard's arm. "I'm serious, Richard. *Look at that!*" He stabbed his finger forward.

Richard glanced ahead. What he saw beyond the easy lope of the four horses as the coach swayed to the right was something out of a storybook. San Anton was still some distance away, but its splendor was already evident. Built originally in 1623 by the first Grand Master of the Order of Saint John, the estate's imposing centerpiece was a palace of polished stone with Greek columns. Widening steps swept down from a narrow apex like a treasure trove of marble spilling from a giant cornucopia. Ivy and jade brush graced San Anton's façade. Dominating the structure was a square tower accentuated by a cornice, a parapet of balustrades, and carved gargoyles at each corner. Orange groves and white marble statues lined the semicircular pebbled drive set between ornamental ponds in which ducks and swans swam lazily or tipped their tails upright in search of food. Nearer to the ivy-covered walls of the palace, palm and jacaranda trees and exotic flowers of all colors and descriptions lined intimate walkways leading to an array of outbuildings—guest accommodations, most likely—their scent saturating the air with a heady, intoxicating aroma. Not for nothing, Richard thought as he breathed in the heavenly fragrance, was the translation of the Latin motto of the palace, "I perfume the air with my blossoms."

"I sure wouldn't mind spendin' a few days here with Lizzy," Agreen murmured as the carriage slowed and liveried servants stationed at the base of the grand front steps made ready to seize the reins of the two lead horses.

"What about Zeke? Wouldn't you want him here too?"

Agreen considered that. "Yes, of course. But first give me a few days alone with Liz."

Richard grinned. "Understood, Lieutenant."

The carriage shuddered to a halt. A servant opened the starboard-side door, bowed low to the men inside, and then placed a short-legged metal footstool beneath the door. Agreen stepped out, followed by Richard. They barely had time to take in the grandeur of their surroundings before an officious-looking man appeared, noted their names, and invited them up the steps and into the palace.

The interior was even more impressive than the exterior. A number of doorways branched off the grand hallway, at the end of which a sweeping stairway similar in design to the outside front steps led up to God only knew what lap of luxury abided there. A dining room off to the right hosted a long, brightly polished table with numerous place-settings arranged in meticulous fashion before Chippendale chairs. Each setting was a paragon of impeccable good taste in the china, silverware, pyramided salmon pink napkin, and multiple crystal glassware it displayed. Bouquets of freshly cut roses in elegant porcelain and glass vases proceeded in regal procession down the table, which was so long that it seemed to diminish into the distance. Platoons of pantry-boys, cooks, maids, and other domestic staff bustled about to ensure that this affair—as was true, Richard suspected, of every affair hosted by Sir Alexander Ball—rose to the highest levels of social etiquette.

"I'll say one thing for the Brits," Agreen mused privately to Richard as he gazed about the vast chamber. "They sure know how t' throw a party."

"Amen to that, Agee."

"Captain Cutler, I presume?"

Richard turned to find yet another elegantly attired gentleman, this one, he assumed, acting in the more official capacity of *le maître*.

"I am Captain Cutler," he confirmed.

The man showed a leg. "I am honored to make your acquaintance, Captain. And yours, Lieutenant. If you gentlemen will please follow me. Two rather distinguished guests are eagerly awaiting you," he said as he led the way across the broad hallway toward a room on the opposite side.

"Richard, are you *sure* you want me around?" Agreen whispered as they followed behind. "Jeremy is your kin."

"So are you, Agee," Richard whispered back. "Besides, they're expecting you."

Le maître rapped gently on the closed door and then opened it to allow Richard and Agreen to step inside. It closed behind them with a soft click.

"Richard! By Jove, look at you! It's been what, fifteen years? In the future we absolutely must do better with our calendars!" Jeremy Hardcastle smiled with delight as he crossed the carpeted room and took Richard's right hand in both of his. "By God, sir, you look well. Not a day older than when I last saw you. Tell me: how do you keep yourself so fit?"

"Clearly by following your example, Jeremy," Richard quipped. "You look as prime as anyone our age I've ever seen."

"*Our* age? I have a few years on you, old boy, but I'll take that as a compliment." His ice-blue eyes shifted to Agreen. "Welcome, Lieutenant. Now *you* I have seen more recently. You were on your way to Algiers, wasn't it, to bring your shipmates home at last."

Agreen nodded. "That's correct, Captain Hardcastle. I'm honored to see you again, sir."

"The honor is entirely mine. And please do away with the 'sir' business and call me 'Jeremy' in the confines of this room. We're all friends and family here, and men of the sea. Sir Alexander was so kind to allow us this time alone together before *le grand fête*. Once the other guests arrive we shall be hard-pressed to find one another. We shall instead find ourselves shipwrecked on the reefs of idle chatter and silly gossip."

Richard grinned. "Well put, Jeremy." His eyes swung inevitably to the man who had stood when the door was opened but had not yet come forward. Unlike Jeremy, who was clad in a blue cloth jacket with wide white lapels, shiny gold buttons, and a gilt-fringed stand-up collar— much like Richard's own dress uniform but with more accoutrements and gold trim—Horatio Nelson wore a coat of dark blue wool cloth, and only a splash of white showed beneath the black silk stock he wore around his neck. Gold embroidery was readily noticeable in the buttons of his coat, in the epaulette he wore on each shoulder, and in the trim on the crest of his uniform hat, which he had placed on a side table. Pinned to the left breast of his coat was the elaborately decorative silver star of a Knight Commander of the Most Honorable Military Order of the Bath.

When Nelson caught Richard's gaze, he stepped forward and offered Richard his left hand. Richard took it in his own left hand.

"Congratulations on your promotion, Richard," Nelson said with a twinkle in his pewter-gray eyes and a tone of genuine admiration. Richard noted that the British admiral's hair had turned silver, and his five-foot-six frame retained an appearance of frailty that even the splendor of his uniform could not conceal. Yet, here before him stood a legend—a sea officer who had lost sight in his right eye at Calvi and his right arm after an assault on Santa Cruz. Once again Richard had the sense that just being in Nelson's presence was a priceless gift, and that Britain's foremost naval commander was yet willing to sacrifice a great deal more in service to God, country, and duty.

"Congratulations on yours, Horatio," Richard replied with a warm smile of his own. "And congratulations as well on the birth of Horatia. You must be very proud."

"I am indeed," Nelson confirmed.

"Shall we all sit?" Jeremy said. "Richard, Agreen, will you join us in a glass of Madeira? Yes? A wise decision, since I have already poured a glass for each of you." He fetched two glasses half-full of the rich golden liquid from a sideboard. "Agreen," he went on. "I hope you don't mind if Richard supplies a few details of his family. It is, after all, my family as well. Horatio has already graciously agreed."

"Of course," Agreen said, happy to settle back and sip his Madeira before facing the social wolves prowling outside.

For the next half-hour Richard brought Jeremy current with Katherine and the children. Hardcastle and Nelson took particular interest in James Cutler's service aboard *Constitution* and asked numerous questions about him, his frigate, and his commanding officer. When he deemed it appropriate, Richard steered the conversation back to other family matters. "You understand, Horatio," he concluded, "that Katherine has threatened me with public flogging if I fail to deliver her warmest personal regards. She remembers you very fondly. We talk of you often."

"I send Katherine my warmest regards in return," Nelson immediately responded. "And please tell her, for me, that she has done exceptionally well in marriage. As a husband and father, Richard, you are to be commended. Your sons and your daughter are clearly exemplary citizens. As for Katherine, she is as lovely and dear a woman as has ever walked upon this earth. It is her great fortune and her great wisdom in life to have tied her star to yours."

Richard was so moved by that last sentence that he had to fight to find his voice. "Thank you," he said quietly. "Thank you for those very kind words, Horatio. I shall pass them on verbatim to Katherine when I write her tomorrow. She will be as deeply pleased to hear them as I am." He looked to his brother-in-law to help stem the emotion that threatened to undo him. "How are Hugh and Phoebe, Jeremy? And how are your parents?"

Jeremy gave Richard a small nod in appreciation of his questions. "Father, alas, is not well, nor is my mother, although, bless them, they both seem to be hanging on to a decent sort of life. I fear that when one goes, the other will soon follow. They have had their share of squabbles, and you know as well as anyone that Father can be rather headstrong, but despite that, they are as close a couple as ever you will find." He paused before continuing in a more positive tone. "The big news is that Phoebe and Hugh are expecting a child in March. For a reason I do not fully understand, Hugh still threatens to migrate to America. He seems to be under the impression—dare I say, the delusion?—that you are prepared to offer him a rather handsome sum to join your family's merchant company. He talks about it whenever we're together."

"We'll sign him on no matter what it takes," Richard said, adding, with a grin, "The same offer, of course, applies to you and Horatio."

The British officers glanced at each other and chuckled. Jeremy said, "I daresay it's a tempting offer now that your country had doubled in size." He was referring to the much-publicized Louisiana Purchase, in which the French had sold their possessions west of the Appalachian Mountains to the United States for fifteen million dollars that Napoléon desperately needed to wage war in Europe. "That transaction should add a pretty penny to Cutler & Sons' coffers, what? You may actually be able to afford Hugh. And see that he earns his money. Send him off to the frontier to sell your family's firewater to those Indian chaps. See if he comes back with his scalp intact. That should bloody well teach him to abandon His Majesty's service."

"An intriguing notion," Richard said, sharing in the mirth.

As their time together grew short, the conversation veered onto a more serious course.

"How goes the war, Richard?" Jeremy asked. "We hear bits and pieces from our intelligence service, of course, but nothing substantial."

Richard put down his glass. "From what I understand, it's going rather well. Morocco has sued for peace, and the war drums in Tunis have subsided. Tripoli, of course, remains our primary enemy, and no doubt Commodore Preble has a new strategy in mind. I suspect we shall hear about it when we see him in Syracuse in two weeks." He decided not to raise the matter of Eaton's proposed overland assault on Tripoli. The notion still seemed far-fetched to him, and besides, British intelligence probably knew more about it than he did. "My ship *Portsmouth* had a run-in with a Tripolitan corsair last week," he added.

"Do say! May we trouble you for details?"

"Indeed you may, Horatio. I shall ask my first lieutenant to relate them."

After Agreen had summarized the battle, Jeremy said, "We had a rather similar experience not two months ago, although on a somewhat different scale." He glanced at Nelson. "By your leave, Horatio?"

Nelson nodded.

"It started right here off Malta," Jeremy explained. "For no apparent reason two Algerian corsairs attacked one of our sloops of war. The sloop managed to escape into Grand Harbor, and a frigate was dispatched with orders to hunt down the corsairs and sink them. Which she did. The dey of Algiers, a chap named Mustapha, was so enraged that he ordered British citizens in Algiers imprisoned and their property confiscated. When Horatio learned of that, he led *Victory* and a squadron of seven frigates from Toulon to Algiers and immediately started bombarding the city. Within an hour, the dey sent out a boat to the flagship under a white flag. Horatio paid it no mind. He kept his guns hot until the outer wall of Algiers had collapsed and fires were burning within the city. Finally, the dey had himself rowed out to the flagship, pleading to Horatio and Allah for mercy. I can't speak for Allah, but Horatio agreed, on the condition that he release the British citizens from prison, restore their possessions, and compensate them for their trouble. *And* on the condition that Mustapha promise never again to impugn England's honor. Thus far, he has acted every bit the angelic schoolboy bowing and scraping before a stern schoolmaster. Is that a fair summary, Horatio?"

"I daresay it is," Nelson responded.

"And I daresay the dey learned a hard lesson that day," Agreen added, setting off a round of chuckles.

"I agree with you, Agreen," Nelson said gravely, "and I am not trying to be witty in saying that. Mustapha learned the same lesson as your corsair captain. And those with Western minds must learn one as well: that the one thing these Arab thugs seem to understand is brute force. That is the only antidote to their tactics. They use diplomacy as either a tool to gain what they want or as a delaying tactic. That is one reason I would not have an Arab in my fleet, except as a prisoner."

The clicks of hurried footsteps and the muffled voices of arriving guests in the hallway signaled the end to the friends' intimate visit. Richard was engulfed by a wave of regret. Horatio and Jeremy were to leave Malta in the morning to return to station off Toulon, their business on the island, whatever it was, having been concluded.

Nelson surprised Richard with an unexpected comment. "I've heard it bandied about, Richard, that the Mediterranean Sea is proving quite the training ground for your young navy. And that many of your hot-headed compatriots are now itching for another go against England."

The image of Able Seaman Cooper being forcibly removed from *Barbara D* two years earlier off the coast of Bermuda flashed through Richard's mind. Flashing with greater intensity was the still painful image of Midn. James Makepeace Hardcastle, Jeremy's youngest brother, dying in his arms on the deck of HMS *Serapis* in the North Sea in September 1779. "I have heard that said as well," he said soberly. "God forbid, it should ever come to that. If it does, I shall resign my commission. I will never again fight at sea against my own family." He gave Jeremy a meaningful glance, and another to Nelson. "Nor against men like you, Horatio."

Horatio Nelson met Richard's gaze. "I say, Richard," he said in a casual tone of voice as he picked up his uniform hat, "if it should indeed come to war, and you stay out of it, I give England better than even odds of winning this time around." He stood up. "Shall we, Captain?"

Richard rose with the others. "Lead on, Admiral," he said. "I forever follow in your footsteps."

Eight

Syracuse, Sicily,
November 1803–January 1804

NOVEMBER 24 dawned clear, with a brisk northeasterly breeze that during the night had dissipated low-lying rainclouds and summoned warm, dry air to the central regions of the Mediterranean Sea. Stationed amidships in *Constitution*, Midn. James Cutler glanced aloft at the complex network of standing rigging profiled against the brightening sky and then walked aft toward a cluster of sailors who were on their knees scouring the weather deck with holystones. Two others stood by to man the pump and hose, ready to wash down each section of deck with seawater until it glistened. It was backbreaking work, but the end result was what the ship's senior officers—and their division commander—wanted to see: a smooth, blanched deck.

As Jamie approached, the sailor named Simpson whistled softly. His mates ceased work, arose, and stood at attention.

"As you were," Jamie told them. He squatted down, ran his fingers lightly along and across the planks, and then rubbed his thumb and forefinger together. "Well done, lads," he proclaimed, rising to his feet. "Well done indeed. Your work reflects well on you and me and our entire division. For that I thank you." He returned their salutes, then turned to go forward.

"Thank *you*, Mr. Cutler," Alan Simpson shouted out.

"And joy o' the mornin' to ye," another sailor cried.

Jamie gave them a brief wave before continuing on. At the mainmast chain-wale he jumped up on the bulwark, swung himself onto the thick hempen shrouds, and began climbing the ratlines. Halfway to the fighting top he paused to gaze eastward over the shimmering waters of the Ionian Sea, then southward into the vast reaches of the Mediterranean. Finding nothing of consequence in either direction, he started descending to the deck just as a quartermaster's mate struck the ship's bell in three segments of two strikes, followed by a single strike. Almost in perfect synchrony, seven bells chimed in the other vessels of the Mediterranean Squadron: *Argus* and *Syren*, sleek 16-gun brigs of war; *Vixen* and *Nautilus*, 12-gun schooners; and the 12-gun schooner *Enterprise* lying at anchor close to her captured prize, the Tripolitan ketch *Matisco*, renamed *Intrepid*.

Back on the deck, Jamie greeted Henry Wadsworth, a midshipman from Portland, Maine, transferred from the frigate *New York* in August after two of *Constitution*'s midshipmen had fallen from grace, one as the result of a severe illness, the other after taking a foolish risk while skylarking in the rigging. That plunge from the fore course yard while trying to prove his mettle to his shipmates had broken Tom Baldwin's right leg and several of his ribs. He was fortunate to have escaped with his life.

"Any sign of *Portsmouth*?" Wadsworth asked hopefully.

"Not yet," Jamie replied, adding, after a moment, "Why on deck so early, Henry? It's not your watch. Shouldn't you be below writing your latest opus?" Wadsworth's work on a book about his cruise aboard *Constitution* in the Mediterranean, its basis a series of letters he had written home to friends in America, had gained the enthusiastic support of his fellow midshipmen. He had written a similar narrative about his cruise aboard *Chesapeake* with Commodore Barron. Several prominent newspapers in the United States had featured certain of those letters, and Wadsworth was hoping that exposure might persuade a book publisher to have a look at the entire manuscript. Such writing, of course, was in addition to the daily diary every midshipman was required to maintain for the captain's review twice a week.

Wadsworth grinned. "This morning I am seeking inspiration rather than word count. At eight bells, Octopus, Ralph, and I are going ashore at Ortygia"—he indicated a small landmass off the eastern end of Syracuse separated from the mainland by a narrow inlet—"to visit the Fountain of Arethusa. They say that Pindar and Aeschylus often went there for inspiration. If that fountain could inspire a Greek poet and a Greek dramatist to reach the very peak of literary achievement, I should think it could inspire an aspiring American author. Why not join us, Jamie? You're off duty in another twenty minutes. The ladies will be out at this hour," he added temptingly, "giggling and waving handkerchiefs at us. Who knows what might happen?"

"Nothing will happen," Jamie said with conviction. "Every unmarried young woman in Syracuse has five older women and a priest keeping a close eye on her. While ten beggars keep a hopeful eye on us. But you're on," he added, intrigued by the notion of visiting the oldest section of a metropolis once described by Cicero as the greatest city in Magna Grecia and the most beautiful of them all, including Athens. At last, he thought with bittersweet satisfaction, he could find a practical use for the Greek classics he had soldiered through in Mr. Getty's class at Governor Dummer Academy.

Just then, a cry came down from the single lookout perched high aloft on the mainmast crosstrees: "Deck, there!"

Jamie cupped his hands at his mouth. "Deck, aye!"

"Sail to the sou'east," the lookout confirmed. "I can't make her out yet, but she's sailing straight for us with the whole nine yards."

Jamie considered that. A ship-rigged vessel with all three yards on all three masts working was sailing at capacity, under a full press of sail. She was a man-of-war, and she was clearly in a hurry to get to Syracuse.

"Very well, Collins," Jamie shouted up. "I'm standing by. Keep me informed."

"Aye, sir," the faraway voice confirmed.

"*Portsmouth*, you think?" Wadsworth prompted.

"Could be," Jamie mused.

Another half-hour passed before the ship's registry could be determined.

"She's British," Collins called down. "A British frigate. And she's flying signal flags."

"Understood, Collins," Jamie called up. To Midn. William Lewis, the junior officer of the deck, who had joined him at the mainmast: "William, go below and inform Nicholson that he is required on deck *immediately*." Joseph Nicholson was the signal midshipman. Although all American sea officers were required to have a working knowledge of Royal Navy signal flags—the British and American navies shared a similar numeric code system first devised by Admiral Lord Howe of the Royal Navy and subsequently enhanced by Capt. Thomas Truxtun of the American Navy—it was the responsibility of the signal midshipman to be thoroughly acquainted with both signal codes. "And inform Lieutenant Elbert. He has the deck in a few minutes."

A disheveled Joseph Nicholson emerged on deck within two minutes, carrying the book of signal codes under his right arm. His auburn hair was unkempt, and the hem of his white cotton shirt stuck out from his partially buttoned fly, an indication that Nicholson had been forward on the "seat of ease" when he received the urgent summons.

Nicholson laid the signal book carefully on the deck and tucked in his shirt. "Well, Jamie?" he inquired softly. Sailors on the weather deck stopped what they were doing and stared amidships as the squadron sounded eight bells. From the aft companionway Samuel Elbert appeared on deck and strode forward.

"Good morning, Mr. Cutler," he said. "What do we have?"

"Good morning, sir." Jamie relayed what the lookout had seen.

"I see. Your glass, if I may? It's my watch at this point."

Jamie handed his spyglass to the third lieutenant, who raised it to one eye and trained it on the fast-approaching British frigate, now only about four cable lengths away. High up on her leeward signal halyard, four pennants fluttered horizontally in the stiff breeze, the halyard itself forming an arc with the heel of the ship, from the afterdeck to the truck of the mizzen, allowing the flags to reach out beyond the billowing canvas.

Elbert adjusted the focus and saw, on each pennant, a configuration of blue, yellow, and red squares, diagonals, crosses and Xs, the combination of the flags representing a code that in turn represented numbers assigned a particular meaning in the codebook. Elbert called out the combinations as Nicholson, down on one knee and balancing the book on his thigh, flipped through the pages of a signal system containing more than three thousand predefined words and sentences.

"Carrying . . . important . . . dispatch," Nicholson translated.

"You're quite certain of that, are you, Mr. Nicholson?" Elbert said sternly.

Not long ago Nicholson had mistakenly interpreted a signal from another naval vessel. It turned out to be a harmless error, but there was no room for error in signal interpretation, and that single mistake had nearly cost Nicholson the prestigious position of signal midshipman. Elbert himself had convinced an irate Captain Preble to give Nicholson a second chance, placing his own head on the block in doing so.

Nicholson didn't flinch. "Quite certain, sir."

"Very well. I shall inform the captain. And we shall assemble a side party. Please make it so, Mr. Cannon," he directed the boatswain.

Within the hour a Royal Navy officer was rowed over to *Constitution* from the British frigate. After the customary honors of whistles and salutes at the entry port, he introduced himself to Samuel Elbert as First Lieutenant Robert Bowers of His Majesty's Ship *Amazon*. Elbert lost no time ushering him belowdecks to the captain's cabin.

When Bowers departed *Constitution* a half-hour later, again with all honors, word spread through the squadron that Captain Preble required his commanders to assemble in his cabin at six bells, no exceptions.

"Of all the bloody luck," Wadsworth groused to his friends minutes later on the orlop deck. "So much for finding inspiration ashore." He and the other midshipmen were busy preparing themselves for the humbling experience of entering the captain's cabin during the day. Wadsworth had before likened it to a new boy in a boarding school being unexpectedly summoned to the headmaster's office.

"There'll be other occasions to see the fountain, Henry; perhaps even tomorrow," Jamie consoled him as he wound a black cotton neckerchief around his neck and carefully tied the loose ends together at his Adam's apple. His own thoughts had nothing to do with the Fountain of Arethusa. *Amazon* had sailed to Syracuse from the direction of Malta. Could this dispatch have something to do with his father's ship?

Wadsworth was not easily mollified. "Maybe. Maybe not. But I have a strong hunch we're about to find out which."

Six bells in the forenoon watch found *Constitution*'s commissioned officers and midshipmen assembled in the copious confines of the after cabin along with the captains of the squadron's other naval vessels: Master Commandant Isaac Hull, captain of *Argus*; Lt. Charles Stewart, *Syren*; Lt. John Smith, *Vixen;* Lt. Richard Somers, *Nautilus*; and Lt. Stephen Decatur Jr., *Enterprise*. As was the norm, the senior officers sat side-by-side along the inboard side of the long rectangular table—and for this meeting, because of the number present, also at the two ends. *Constitution*'s eight midshipmen sat behind them on a row of Windsor chairs. Everyone present waited in suspenseful silence as Capt. Edward Preble, his back to them, stared out through the stern gallery windows, seemingly absorbed in his own thoughts. Jamie Cutler willed him to get on with it. As the seconds ticked by, he became convinced that the British dispatch contained a dire report that somehow involved his father. Why else would the commodore convene his officers and squadron commanders and keep them on edge this way?

Finally, Preble turned around. He walked slowly to the table, rested his hands on the back of his chair, and scanned the assembled host with grave, sorrowful eyes. When he spoke, his words came out as a gravelly voice of doom. "Gentlemen, we have lost *Philadelphia*."

Stunned silence engulfed the cabin. The assembled officers kept their eyes squarely on Preble, as if willing him to deny what he had just said. Because what he had just said was entirely beyond belief. *Philadelphia*, a 36-gun superfrigate that had distinguished herself as the flagship of the Guadeloupe Station during the war with France after *Constellation* had been relieved, was invincible. She and *Constitution* embodied American power and glory in the Mediterranean. No Barbary state had anything to match her. No Barbary ruler would be fool enough to send any of his warships within range of her guns. *How could she be lost?*

When no immediate explanation was forthcoming, Charles Gordon said, because someone had to say something, "Lost, sir? In what way?"

His first officer's question jolted Preble from wherever it was that he had lost himself. "Lost to the enemy, Mr. Gordon," he replied in a quiet but firm voice. "The dispatch I received contains few details. The information we have comes from the British consul in Tripoli, who forwarded it to *Amazon*'s captain. It seems that Captain Bainbridge was chasing down an enemy corsair off the coast of Tripoli when *Philadelphia* struck a reef and her crew was unable to free her. Captain Bainbridge surrendered the ship when the Tripolitans surrounded her with a squadron of gunboats."

Now the officers *did* exchange glances. What Captain Preble had not said, had only implied, was that *Philadelphia* and her massive armament now lay in the hands of the enemy.

Stephen Decatur asked the necessary question. "Did Captain Bainbridge scuttle her, Captain?"

"He may have tried to, Mr. Decatur. We must assume that he did. But she must have gone hard aground. To our knowledge, she remains on the reef."

"What of Captain Bainbridge and the crew, sir?" Richard Somers inquired. As to be expected, the sandy-haired twenty-five-year-old lieutenant was seated between Stephen Decatur and Charles Stewart. The three officers were fast friends, and had been since growing up together in Philadelphia and studying together at the Episcopal Academy in Merion, Pennsylvania.

"All hands," Preble answered him solemnly, "more than three hundred men, are prisoners of our enemy. Beyond that, I know nothing. I have given you all the details I have at the moment. Needless to say, I require time to determine our response. Expect me to seek your advice on the matter, both individually and as a group."

"*Constitution*'s GIG is coming alongside, Captain."

Richard Cutler returned the salute of the young midshipman on watch duty and glanced at his waistcoat watch. "Thank you, Mr. Osborn. Please inform Captain Eaton that we shove off in five minutes."

"Aye, aye, sir."

Four weeks had passed since HMS *Amazon* had delivered her dispatch. It was now December 19, well past the date Edward Preble had requested *Portsmouth* to join the squadron. But the delay was unavoidable. Preble had ordered Richard to await Capt. William Eaton in Malta and convey him to Syracuse aboard *Portsmouth*. Eaton, as it turned out, had been delayed both in reaching Malta and in departing—for the best of reasons, which Eaton promised to explain to Captain Preble at the earliest opportunity. Within half an hour of dropping anchor in Syracuse Harbor, Richard had informed Commodore Preble of his arrival in a note hand-delivered by Lieutenant Meyers. Preble responded with an invitation for an audience the next morning at two bells in the forenoon watch, informing Meyers that he would send *Constitution*'s gig to convey Captain Cutler and Captain Eaton to the flagship.

At a little after one bell the next morning, Richard settled onto the stern sheets of the gig near the coxswain. Shifting his position to make room for Eaton beside him, he glanced up and touched his hat to Agreen Crabtree and Carl Corbett, captain of Marines, their heads and upper torsos visible above the quarterdeck's larboard hammock netting. As the larboard oars of the gig came horizontal and oarsmen on the starboard side pushed off, Richard swung his gaze to *Constitution*, lying at anchor several hundred yards away. As he had when he first saw her lying at anchor in Carlisle Bay in Barbados back in '99, Richard felt his senses thrill. The flagship lay still on the calm harbor waters, a beauty for the ages from her rounded bow and immense bowsprit and jib-boom to her jaunty stern. Her sails were furled in Bristol fashion, and the rich black paint on her 175-foot hull glistened in the warm morning sun.

A wave of anticipation crested over him as he climbed the built-in steps and passed through the larboard entry port, Eaton following close behind. Richard saluted the quarterdeck and then returned the salutes of the side party gathered amidships to honor him. Last in the line of crisp white and blue uniforms, at stiff attention, stood Midn. James Cutler.

Richard managed a brief nod, father to son, before Charles Gordon stepped forward and touched his hat.

"Captain Cutler, welcome aboard, sir," he said. "Captain Eaton, I am First Lieutenant Gordon. Please, if you will follow me. Captain Preble is expecting you."

Captain Preble wasted little time on small talk. Because it was just the three of them in company with Phillip Darby, the captain's clerk, they gathered in the more intimate confines of the commodore's dining alcove. Formalities dispensed with, Preble invited Richard Cutler to speak first.

"I received word of *Philadelphia*'s misfortune in Malta, sir," Richard said. "Rear Admiral Bickerton, the British naval commander in Valetta, offered me what intelligence he had gathered from Mr. McDonough, the British consul in Tripoli, and from a Mr. Nissen, the Danish consul."

"I see. And where did *their* information originate?"

"In part from Yusuf Karamanli himself, sir. Mr. Nissen is a favorite of his, and the bashaw speaks openly to him. But most of my information comes from Captain Bainbridge, and what he has to say confirms what Mr. Nissen asserts."

"How very interesting. Pray, continue."

"You see, sir, the bashaw has given Captain Bainbridge permission to communicate with the two consuls. His letters are censored, of course, so sensitive information such as *Philadelphia*'s location is written, as prescribed, between the lines." He was referring to a procedure developed by American double agents during the war with England and since adopted by British intelligence that involved writing words in lemon juice between the lines of a letter. The words became visible when the recipient held the letter above a candle's flame. "I have these letters with me. Captain Bainbridge intended them ultimately to reach you."

"I shall review them later. Go on."

"We now know, sir, that the Tripolitans were able to plug the holes that Captain Bainbridge ordered blown through *Philadelphia*'s bottom and managed to work her off the reef. They have also salvaged the guns that Captain Bainbridge jettisoned overboard in his effort to lighten her and pry her off the reef. *Philadelphia* was towed inshore and currently lies at anchor just off Tripoli's main battery on a line halfway between the bashaw's castle on the southeastern wall and a battery on the mole to the northeast. Her current position, which I have been able to approximate on a chart, is well within the string of shoals and reefs that ring the inner harbor and make entry so difficult."

"So cutting her out could prove challenging," Preble mused.

"Extremely so, sir, especially under the circumstances. She has no foremast—Captain Bainbridge ordered it cut down to lift her bow when he tried to kedge her off—and her mainmast is damaged. I understand its t'gant mast is gone. We don't know the condition of her mizzen. I assume it remains intact, since Captain Bainbridge mentioned nothing about it in his letters."

"So to retake her we'll need to tow her out, just as she was towed in."

"That would appear to be our best choice, sir. Unless . . ."

Preble arched his eyebrows. "*Unless*, Mr. Cutler?"

"Unless," Richard said evenly, "we destroy her where she lies."

Preble stared. "To keep her, and her guns, out of the hands of the Tripolitan Navy?"

"Precisely, sir. And I believe we'd have a much better chance of doing that than getting her out of the harbor."

Preble appeared to contemplate that. "A most intriguing notion, Mr. Cutler. I intend to discuss it further with my squadron commanders. You will be interested to learn that Master Commandant Hull and Lieutenant Decatur have reached the same conclusion, and I find myself drawn to it as well. Is there anything else?"

"Just that according to Admiral Bickerton, Captain Bainbridge's surrender was an honorable one. When he found himself surrounded by enemy gunboats, he destroyed the signal book and other sensitive documents, and fired her two remaining guns before surrendering the ship. Apparently, the reef *Philadelphia* struck is not on any chart. And her crew did everything possible to free her."

"There will be a court of inquiry, nonetheless."

"Yes, sir." Richard paused. "I have one final item, sir: *Philadelphia*'s officers and crew have apparently been separated. The officers are being held in the bashaw's castle, I am told in relative comfort. The crew is being held somewhere else within the city, I imagine in somewhat less comfort. Captain Bainbridge does not know where. Nor, so he claims, does Mr. Schembri. He's the—"

"Gaetano Schembri?" Preble snorted. "The Tripolitan consul in Malta?"

"The same. I take it you have made his acquaintance, sir."

"Unfortunately, I have. What did he have to say about this?"

Richard deferred to William Eaton, who was more qualified to answer Preble's question. Richard had come to respect Eaton during their three weeks' acquaintance. Born in 1764 in Connecticut, Eaton had enlisted in the Continental army at the age of fifteen and had quickly climbed the ranks to sergeant major. After the war he attended Dartmouth College and displayed a remarkable aptitude for foreign languages. He reenlisted in the army in 1792 as a captain and served under Maj. Gen. Anthony Wayne during the Indian wars in the Ohio Valley and along the border of Spanish Florida and Georgia. Having acquired a keen interest in the Arab world, he convinced his protégé, Secretary of State Timothy Pickering, to appoint him U.S. consul in Tunis. By that time he had mastered two Indian languages, four Arab dialects, French, Latin, and Greek.

Eaton's pale blue eyes flashed at Preble. "I share your opinion of the man, Commodore," he said with a wry smile, "but I felt it my duty to confer with him so that I could understand, in Mr. Lear's absence, exactly what Yusuf Karamanli has in mind for our captured sailors. It was no easy task to arrange a meeting with Schembri, but through the good auspices of Mr. Morath we were able to do so. It is one reason for *Portsmouth*'s delay in arriving here. It was my doing, not Mr. Cutler's, who was gracious enough to wait for me."

"I see," Preble said. Going straight to the heart of the matter, he asked, "What is the bashaw demanding? I assume that the capture of *Philadelphia* has raised the ante?"

The sarcasm underlying that last question was not lost on Eaton. "It has," he confirmed. "By a rather substantial amount, I'm afraid. The price of peace is now $500 per sailor. Schembri insists, however, that if we show good faith he can persuade the bashaw to decrease his demands, perhaps to a grand total of $100,000."

"That *is* a rather grand total, isn't it?" Preble shook his head. "I assume that amount represents ransom payments only, and not the tribute as well."

"That is correct, Commodore. The bashaw continues to insist that ransom payments to free our sailors be tied to annual payments of tribute. Otherwise, Schembri contends, there can be no peace between our country and Tripoli."

Preble leaned back in his chair and folded his arms across his chest. He waited a moment to allow his clerk to catch up with his notes. When Darby gave him a small nod, Preble said, "Then there shall be no peace. President Jefferson has made it quite clear that the United States will not pay tribute money to any nation under any circumstances. Ransom yes, tribute no. I happen to agree with his stand on the matter."

"As do I, Commodore," Eaton returned. "Be assured of that. Mr. Lear may prefer the president's so-called awe and talk strategy, but I oppose it most strenuously. I have said before what I say to you today: we cannot achieve a meaningful peace in this region by engaging in peace negotiations on land whilst our Navy does nothing but flex its muscles at sea. Yusuf Karamanli is not impressed with our naval power, and why should he be? The United States lacks the resolve to exert that power. We will not win this war simply by blockading Tripoli. Commodore Dale and Commodore Morris did that to little effect. To bring Yusuf to his knees we must attack his seat of power by sea *and* by land."

Eaton rushed on with hardly a breath, delivering his next words as a plea wrapped in a cloak of iron. "You have summoned me here to Syracuse to learn of my intentions, and I have come here of my own accord to discuss them with you. Stated bluntly, I have come to enlist your support. I can assure you that Commodore Morris believed in me, as do President Jefferson and Secretary Madison, at least they did when I sat down with them in Washington and explained my intentions. I pray to God that *you* will believe in me as well.

"I am convinced that victory is not possible in this war if we rely on sea power alone. Tripoli has a sizable navy, but Yusuf Karamanli will not risk losing it in a pitched battle with your squadron. He will use his larger warships as he plans to use *Philadelphia*, primarily to reinforce his shore batteries, and will rely on his gunboats to dissuade your ships from venturing in too close. A naval bombardment of Tripoli may have a brief positive effect, but it alone will not induce Yusuf to surrender. He will remain defiant behind his city walls until the American public loses heart in this struggle and demands our withdrawal from the Mediterranean."

Preble rested his elbows on the arms of his chair and brought his fingers together under his chin to form a steeple as he listened to Eaton's passionate words. His brow furrowed in concentration. He asked, when there came a lull, "What, exactly, do you require of *me*, Captain Eaton?"

"Financial and logistical support," Eaton replied without pause. "I am not asking for significant ground forces. A few Marines is all. Captain Cutler has been most helpful in initial discussions with Mr. Farquhar in Malta. Mr. Farquhar can provide European mercenaries, military supplies, and provisions. Another agent, Mr. Busatile, will aid Hamet Karamanli in raising a force of Egyptian mercenaries, horses, and camels. We expect to pick up additional support from local tribesmen on the march across Cyrenaica."

"Ah." Preble tapped the tips of his fingers together. "A bold plan, Captain Eaton."

"Victory is rarely achieved without a bold plan, Commodore."

"And the payment to these mercenaries? That honor falls to me, I assume?"

"It does, sir, although according to Mr. Busatile, Hamet has pledged personal funds to this initiative as well. Secretary Madison informed me that you carry twenty thousand dollars aboard this ship."

"To be distributed at my discretion."

"With respect, that is not my understanding, Commodore. But I will abide by your discretion. More is at stake here than what is obvious. Should we win this war, Hamet will be installed on the throne of Tripoli. He will be a loyal ally to the United States. Together, the United States and Tripoli will shine a light of hope into the darkness of these backward North African autocracies. In doing that, our young nation will have secured a lasting peace in Barbary and will have earned the respect of the world."

Edward Preble drummed the fingers of his right hand on the table, never taking his eyes off William Eaton. Eaton did not blink. "A fine speech," Preble said at length. "A most inspiring speech that I assure you has not fallen on deaf ears. I agree that a lasting peace can be secured only by a military victory. Come spring or early summer, when winds are fair for a campaign, I intend to sail this squadron across the Mediterranean and introduce the bashaw of Tripoli to American naval gunnery. Mr. de Gregorio, the governor of Syracuse, has arranged with the king to loan us a flotilla of Sicilian gunboats and two bomb ketches. I plan to add these vessels to our squadron. Of equal importance, I have been notified in a dispatch from Secretary Madison that Congress has approved additional funding for our campaign, to be financed by a tax on imports. So it appears that at least for the moment, our country continues to support our mission here."

"That is excellent news, Commodore." Eaton leaned forward, silently asking the question that Preble understood only too well.

"However, Captain," Preble replied to the silent query, "I need time to weigh the pros and cons of your proposed campaign. Mind you, I am not opposed in principle. But my orders from Washington are quite explicit. I am to convoy our merchant ships, blockade the harbor of Tripoli and other Tripolitan ports as advisable, and engage the enemy *where feasible*—which I take to mean where the prospects for victory are not weighted against us. If I am to commit funds that are reserved, in part, to ransom captive American seamen, I must be certain that such funds are not deployed on a half-baked scheme to march across a scorching desert with an army of Christians and Arab soldiers who will inherently dislike each other and who will be inclined to fight *against* each other. For me to do otherwise could have serious ramifications for the future of our country. Not to mention for me personally."

Eaton's face darkened. He opened his mouth as if to protest, but Preble cut him off with a raised hand.

"I am sorry to disappoint you, Captain Eaton," he said, "but this matter is not open to debate. I am in command, and I am responsible for American interests and American personnel in the Mediterranean. I shall inform you of my decision when my decision is made. In the meantime, I have the critical matter of *Philadelphia* to consider. On that matter I *have* made a decision, and I require a private audience with Captain Cutler to discuss it. May I ask that you please excuse us. My coxswain is standing by at your convenience should you wish to go ashore."

THE CREW OF *Constitution* saw shipboard activity increase well beyond normal during the following week. Squadron commanders were piped aboard the flagship, either individually or in pairs, at all hours of the day. Most often observed were Lieutenant Stewart and Lieutenant Decatur, and their purposeful strides across the deck and down the aft companionway fed the speculation rampant among the crew. Even the festivities of Christmas Day—during which every sailor in the squadron was served fresh beef and vegetables and an extra ration of grog—did not interrupt the discussions going on belowdecks in the after cabin. And then there was the matter of *Intrepid*, the 70-ton ketch-rigged Tripolitan vessel recently captured by *Enterprise*. Sailors allowed shore leave reported to their shipmates in the forecastle that she was tied up at the dockyards with hammers and saws hard at work within her interior; but for what purpose remained a matter of conjecture. Every tar seemed to have an opinion, but no one had the facts. Whatever information *Constitution*'s officers possessed on the subject remained behind sealed lips.

On the dawn of the New Year, James Cutler was granted leave to dine alone with his father in *Portsmouth*. Father and son had seen each other often during the preceding twelve days, but rarely for very long or in private. The one exception had been on Christmas Day, but that was before Edward Preble had told Richard that he had approved Jamie's request to join the thirty volunteers going on the raid. Richard understood the mission. He had had a hand in shaping its course. And because he knew it was fraught with danger, Richard had mixed feelings as he sat down with his son in *Portsmouth*'s dining alcove while Sydney Simms, his fussy but highly talented steward, busied himself serving roast mutton, roasted potatoes, fresh beans, and freshly baked bread.

After Simms had poured out two glasses of a local red wine and departed, Richard raised his glass. "To the New Year, Jamie."

Jamie raised his. "To the New Year, Father."

They clinked glasses and each took a sip of the heady Sicilian wine. As Richard glanced over the rim of his glass, he felt a stab of pride at the sight of his son sitting across from him in full undress uniform, his thick chestnut hair parted from right to left across his forehead. About him was a look of unblemished youth and innocence, as though Jamie were merely play-acting the role of a Navy midshipman this evening. As though he remained the sweet, unassuming child who had graced his parents' lives and whom either parent would walk barefoot to the ends of the earth to protect. Yet, the eyes of the child gazing unflinchingly back at his father blazed with the confidence and maturity that come from doing a man's job, and doing it well.

"Have you heard from home?" Richard asked, in part to delay the more sensitive topic of the evening, and in part because he was genuinely interested.

"I have. In the last mail packet I received three letters from Mother, one from Uncle Caleb, and one from Will. Actually, that one was as much from Adele as from Will."

Richard grinned. "Frances is still interested, is she?"

Jamie grimaced. "Perhaps. Adele merely referred to her in passing. "

"Yes, of course." Richard sliced off a forkful of pink-centered mutton steak and held it in midair. "You know, Jamie, you could do a lot worse," he observed before leaning forward and putting the meat in his mouth.

It was Jamie's turn to smile. Instead of responding, he dug into his meal with the relish of a young man whose diet rarely included such succulent fare. Father and son ate together in silence before Jamie said, after a sip of wine, "Mother writes that Diana and Peter are becoming the talk of the town."

Katherine had written much the same thing in several of the letters he had received in that same mail call. Peter Sprague, a popular young man who was currently attending Phillips Exeter Academy and who claimed to have aspirations of becoming a barrister, had taken a singular interest in Diana Cutler—an interest that, according to Katherine, was very definitely reciprocated. Peter was the third son of a respected Hingham family, one with whom Richard was well acquainted. The last time he had seen Peter, however, the boy was chasing grasshoppers, not his daughter.

"They're still very young," he commented.

Jamie's smile returned. "Yes, they are, Father. As I recall, about the same age as you and Mother when you first met."

"You have me there," Richard had to confess. "A brilliant parry, Jamie. You and Will always have stood up for Diana."

"Of course we have. She's our sister. We're born allies."

"Against the most feared and dreaded of all enemies, the parents."

"Who else?"

They laughed together. After the mirth had faded and they had resumed eating, Richard said, when he deemed the moment right, "Captain Preble informs me that you will be taking part in the raid on *Philadelphia*."

"Yes, sir," Jamie replied nonchalantly, as though going on raids was a part of his daily routine. "And as I'm sure he has also informed you, practice drills begin tomorrow. Each man in this mission has an assignment, and each man will practice his assignment aboard *Constitution*."

"So the secret will be out."

"The crew already has a pretty good sense of what we're about. But don't worry. It's likely too late for any would-be informer to leak word to the outside world. Still, for the next four weeks, only commissioned officers are permitted shore leave."

"What is your assignment, Jamie?"

"I am to lead a squad of five men down to the berthing deck forward," Jamie replied in the same matter-of-fact tone. "At Lieutenant Decatur's command, I am to set fire to combustibles we will be carrying with us. Once we've done that," he added with an impish grin, "our assignment is to get back on deck, board *Intrepid*, and get the hell out of there. You needn't worry, Father," he said when Richard didn't smile back. "We'll have the element of surprise on our side. British intelligence confirms that *Philadelphia* has only a caretaker crew. They're not soldiers or marines, just ordinary sailors. They should present no problem to us. If they do, *Syren* will be standing by to help."

Richard tried to smile, to visibly demonstrate his faith in his son's remarks and in the prospects for the mission's success. But try though he might, he found it difficult. He recognized the potential dangers. He had run through them in his mind many times during recent days and nights. *Philadelphia* might have only a skeleton crew aboard, but the American frigate lay at anchor within a cable's length of the Tripolitan Navy and directly beneath the mammoth guns of the fortress city's batteries.

Everything, literally everything, depended on three factors interacting almost miraculously with each other: the element of surprise to get the Americans in; a way to get them out; and the combined benevolence of the Almighty and Lady Luck.

"I understand, Jamie," he said. "And I am very proud of you for volunteering for this mission. Still, if it's all the same to you, I shall refrain from telling your mother anything about it until it's completed and you are safely back aboard *Constitution*."

Jamie lifted his glass in a toast. "I think that would be wise, Father."

Nine

Tripoli Harbor,
February 1804

FOUL WEATHER BEGAN dogging *Intrepid* and *Syren* soon after the two vessels set sail from Syracuse on the evening of February 2. Five days later, though, they stood close enough to Tripoli to make out the city's fortifications against the wooded hills in the background; in the foreground they could see the ravished body of the frigate *Philadelphia*. She was lying at anchor, her foremast cut away and her mizzen and truncated mainmast bereft of yards and canvas. A cluster of smaller vessels—a scattering of brigs and corsairs and an armada of gunboats—swung at anchor between *Philadelphia* and the city walls.

Lt. Stephen Decatur, captain of *Intrepid*, decided not to attempt entry that night. Heavy swells from the northeast swirled dangerous white water over the shoals and reefs at the harbor's entrance. And the wind, a brisk southeasterly during most of the day, had backed to the west and was strengthening. The sailor in him warned that conditions could get worse, and quickly.

The storm hit with such wrenching violence that it carried the ketch and brig eastward, despite their best efforts to battle the fierce headwinds. It was as though the vessels were two pieces of driftwood floating helplessly on a raging, wind-whipped sea. The thirty American volunteers and one Sicilian aboard *Intrepid* huddled together belowdecks, trying to find what comfort they could amid the stench of the vomit that almost covered the deck. The roiled sea crashed and thumped against

Intrepid's hull, flinging foamy water over her railing and throwing spume high into her rigging. Seawater frothed across her weather deck, back and forth, larboard to starboard, stem to stern, much of it cascading out through the lee scuppers but too much of it finding its way below into the hold through chinks in the deckhead. Misery was heaped on misery in the slosh of seawater and bodily fluids. Sailors and Marines stared down at the deck in a semistupor, hardly noticing the squealing rats, up from the swamped bilge, scampering between their feet.

"Is this what we signed up for, Jamie?" Ralph Izard queried in a halfhearted attempt at humor. He was sitting amidships against the damp strakes, his arms clenched tightly around his knees. "I was thinking more of glory than sitting in a stew of other men's vomit."

Jamie's smile in return was equally feeble. His quiet resolve never to display unease in front of the crew had long since gone by the boards. He had puked helplessly along with the rest of them. Beside him, a youthful midshipman from *Enterprise* named Charles Morris suddenly lurched forward and gagged loudly, his stomach long since empty of anything to heave up.

Gradually, blessedly, the fierce winds moderated. The high seas subsided to great rolling swells. The water streaming down from the weather deck shriveled to rivulets, then to occasional drips, then to nothing at all. When at last the two hatchways above were thrown open, clean, warm, delicious air washed down into the hold in company with tentative strands of sunlight piercing through gray clouds that were breaking apart to reveal blue sky. First to clamber down the main hatchway ladder, to no one's surprise, was Stephen Decatur.

He stood amidships between two rows of men struggling to get to their feet. Except for the two midshipmen, a handful of sailors from *Constitution*, and the Sicilian, these sailors and Marines were attached to USS *Enterprise*, Decatur's command. And to a man they respected him for his fair-mindedness, derring-do, and calm under fire—the latter best exemplified, perhaps, by the two duels, neither instigated by him, from which he had emerged the victor.

"As you were, lads," Decatur said. "As you were." He placed his hands on his hips as he surveyed the scene, his dark eyes taking in the blank stares fixed upon him. Until this cruise Jamie Cutler had not had occasion to interact with the young lieutenant, although he had learned much about him from his shipmates. Decatur was Philadelphia born and bred, and he had attended the University of Pennsylvania after graduating from the Episcopal Academy. His father, Stephen Decatur Sr., had served with distinction as a naval captain during the war with England and, later, during the war with France, in *Philadelphia*. Stephen Jr. had served in the Mediterranean since the start of the war, as a lieutenant aboard Commodore Dale's *Essex* in the first squadron, and as a flag lieutenant aboard *New York* in the second squadron under Commo. Richard V. Morris. His exemplary actions and accomplishments on those vessels had gained him, at the youthful age of twenty-five, his first command, *Intrepid*.

"Good Lord," he observed in a loud voice with a slice of humor in it, "are you men ever a sight for sore eyes!" Despite their misery and anxiety the volunteers responded with a low rumble of laughter, in part because Decatur himself posed such a sight. His curly black hair was matted down in clumps, and his long sideburns had dovetailed with an unshaven jawbone. The baggy pants, brightly colored vest, and turban-like hat he was wearing reinforced the impression of an Old Testament prophet.

"Right, lads," he went on more seriously when the rumbling had run its course, "here's where we are. We're going to man the pumps and clean up this stinking mess. And I want you all to eat and drink what you can. If we exhaust our provisions, we'll resupply from *Syren*, who, praise God, lies within sight. You may go topside to take the air and to wash and dry your clothes, but only in groups of five. By my reckoning, the storm drove us about two hundred miles from Tripoli. I'll know for certain after the noon sighting. It will take us a while to get back there even if these quartering winds remain fair. But until our hull touches *Philadelphia*'s, it's imperative that we maintain the appearance of a local Maltese tradesman manned by a small crew. The success of our mission depends on our pulling off this ruse. You understand? The storm hasn't fogged your memory?"

Men chuckled, shook their heads. Decatur went on: "I leave it to you midshipmen to determine who mans the pumps, who goes topside and when, and who has deck-cleaning duty. I have ordered the galley fire lit, so you should have warm food in your bellies before too long. Whatever is served, I want you to eat it. I *order* you to eat it. We must get back our strength, lads. Hot work lies ahead for us."

DURING THE EARLY AFTERNOON of February 16, according to plan, *Syren* dropped out of sight astern of *Intrepid*. Although *Syren* had never sailed along the coast of Tripoli—and therefore was not likely to be recognized—she too had been disguised to look like a local trading vessel. Her topgallant mast had been sent down, her gun ports closed

and painted over, and quarter-cloths had been raised to conceal the nettings on the bulwarks and barricade of her quarterdeck. Nevertheless, the
arrival of two unidentified vessels approaching Tripoli Harbor together
might arouse suspicion. So Decatur had ordered Lieutenant Stewart to
keep his distance until nightfall, when he would approach *Intrepid*, lie to,
and send over boats with additional volunteers.

Ahead, in the far distance, Decatur could see Point Tagiura jutting
out to the east of the city. In the farther distance he could barely make
out, through a spyglass, the crests of white water breaking against the
seaward edges of Kaliuscia and Ra's az Zur reefs—the long chains of
partially submerged rocks that protected the harbor both from fierce
winter gales and from unwary intruders. Salvador Catalano, a native of
Palmero who had navigated these waters dozens of times in the employ of
Richard Farquhar—and who, coincidentally, had been in Tripoli the day
Philadelphia was captured—stood beside Stephen Decatur on *Intrepid*'s
foredeck. With the Sicilian acting as pilot, Decatur hugged the coast
south of the two chains of rocks that lay close under the guns of English
Fort, a freestanding bastion located a mile to the east of the city walls. An
alternative harbor entry, Catalano had explained, was through the oft-
used Western Passage, a narrow but deep waterway snaking through the
rocks and shoals near the opposite end of the harbor up by the Molehead
Battery. But Decatur deemed this and other possible entryways too
dangerous to attempt at night even if the moon were full, which tonight
it was not.

Decatur checked his watch: 5:15. He looked astern and searched for
Syren. No sign of her yet. He glanced aloft at a strip of cloth attached to
the signal halyard and chewed his lower lip. The telltale indicated that the
wind held fast and steady from the east, too strong by half for his liking.
He passed word for James Lawrence, his first lieutenant in *Enterprise* and
his first officer in *Intrepid*.

"We need some sort of drogue, Jim," he said, forgoing naval discipline
in using a first-name address, "anything that will slow her down. We can't
stand off and on. That would be too obvious. Toss out a line and tie on
ladders, extra spars, timbers, whatever you can find."

"Aye, Captain," Lawrence said, adding with a grin, "Might I suggest
some lubberly attention to the sails?"

Decatur nodded. "A capital notion."

With what amounted to a sea anchor checking her speed and her sails
luffing at their leeches, *Intrepid* appeared just as Decatur wanted her to
appear to anyone observing her from shore: a Maltese merchant vessel

struggling to make harbor before nightfall. High on the signal halyard, at its apex, fluttered the British ensign.

Dusk was settling over the Barbary Coast as *Intrepid* sailed within a mile of the eastern end of the chain of rocks. Ahead, to larboard, loomed English Fort, its menacing black cannon protruding through embrasures. It was yet too early to attempt entry; the plan was to wait for dark and for *Syren*. Again Decatur scoured the waters astern. Again he saw empty water. Where was she? Yet another glance aloft at the telltale confirmed that the wind was moderating, as it often did this time of day, and was now blowing in increasingly sporadic directions, as if trying to find its proper direction. Soon they would face the opposite of the problem they had encountered several hours earlier.

"Mr. Cutler?" he said to the young midshipman stationed nearby, one of six crewmembers on deck. Like everyone else, he was dressed in the garb of a local sailor.

"Captain?"

"Mr. Cutler, we shall anchor here temporarily. Keep the anchor rode short, just enough to hold her. Cut loose the drogue and have the sweeps brought up. And I'll have our cutter called out and towed astern. We'll have need of it should we lose this wind altogether."

"Yes, sir," Jamie said. He did not salute. Captain Decatur had long since extinguished all visible signs of naval discipline aboard the ship.

Minutes ticked by into a quarter-hour, then a half-hour, then an hour. Decatur repeatedly checked his watch and peered eastward, the growing darkness gradually obscuring his vision. Time had run out. Decatur had to make a decision. He could no longer remain where he was. Abort or continue the mission? He sensed the tension sprouting along the weather deck, and it took all his discipline as a naval commander to keep his own anxiety in check.

"Mr. Morris," he said to the midshipman from *Enterprise,* "we can delay no further. We shall weigh anchor and proceed on our own."

Charles Morris, acting as boatswain, issued the orders necessary to raise the anchor and set the sails.

Decatur took command of the tiller and summoned Salvatore Catalano to his side. Together they set *Intrepid* on a course south by west, their landmark the lights flickering within English Fort. It took thirty minutes in an increasingly fickle wind to sail within two cable lengths of the fort; from there *Intrepid* assumed a more westerly course, shadowing the low, sandy coastline of Tripoli, careful to keep the dangerous rocks and shoals well off to starboard. Ahead, to larboard, loomed the bashaw's castle, a massive stone edifice that anchored the northeastern corner of the fortress' seaward wall. Following Catalano's counsel, Decatur kept the castle between two and three points to larboard, following a course that would bring them on a direct line to *Philadelphia*. They could not yet see the frigate. She lay a mile or so ahead. So they relied on dead reckoning, their new beacons the lights flickering within the bashaw's castle, which they approached in the eerie glow of a crescent moon.

Slowly, ever so slowly, *Intrepid* ghosted along with a dying wind at her back. It was approaching 11:00 when *Philadelphia*'s profile began to take shape. Four lanterns burned aboard her: one forward near the bow, one at the stern, and one on each side amidships. Decatur scanned the shoreline, settling his gaze on the city wall not six hundred feet away at the water's edge. He saw nothing to arouse concern. He saw no one at all, in fact, either on the walls or aboard the vessels of the Tripolitan Navy clustered together at anchor just east of French Fort, a structure similar to English Fort located at the western perimeter of the city's defenses. *Philadelphia* stood alone, closer to the rocks and shoals than to the city, a deformed and ignored belle of the ball.

Decatur signaled to James Cutler and Charles Morris to start bringing the volunteers from the hold onto the weather deck. Sailors and Marines crept up through the hatchways and lay prone, wriggling and snaking to make room for others, their presence hidden by the sharply rising bulwarks, against which lay eight long wooden sweeps on each side of the deck. Each man carried with him a three-inch piece of sperm candle, its wick soaked in turpentine, along with a tomahawk, dagger, or cutlass. Each of the squad leaders brandished a sword and had a brace of pistols tucked out of sight. Decatur had insisted that pistols be used only as a last resort. The weapon of choice this night was the silent double-edged blade.

As *Intrepid* approached *Philadelphia*, she was hailed from the frigate. "Take the tiller, Mr. Izard," Decatur said to the midshipman, "and keep her off as best you can." He walked forward to join Catalano at the bow. Decatur nodded at him. The Sicilian cupped his hands at his mouth.

"Ahoy," he called out in Arabic. "We have come from Malta to load cattle for the British garrison there. We lost our anchor in the storm. We request permission to make fast to your vessel until morning."

Intrepid's crew, both those visible and those hidden from view, tensed while they waited for a reply. *Intrepid* lay all but adrift twenty yards astern of the frigate on her lee side. The wind had nearly vanished. Her sheets were hauled in tight, their sails useless. Then, a cry from the frigate: "Who is your crew?"

"Three English, four Italians. I am Sicilian. My name is Salvatore Catalano. You may know of me. I have been trading in Tripoli for years."

A second pause, then: "Permission granted. We will send over a boat with a line."

"Thank you. We will also send our boat with a line."

Decatur held his breath for two, six, ten seconds. When the Arabs neither questioned nor challenged that last statement, he exhaled slowly, turned around, and walked aft. The cutter was drawn up amidships, and four oarsmen and a coxswain dropped down onto the thwarts.

As the two ship's boats—the launch from *Philadelphia* and the cutter from *Intrepid*—approached each other, Catalano, standing arms akimbo at the bow of the ketch, continued to complain loudly about the storm, how they were blown off course, the nuisance of losing their anchor, anything that might distract those aboard *Philadelphia* and the approaching launch. No one in the frigate offered a reply. Decatur prayed that Catalano's monotonous chatter was lulling the enemy into apathy. It might just buy them a precious minute or two.

The two ship's boats met halfway across, each dragging a line secured to its mother ship. The coxswain in the cutter motioned to those in the launch to toss over a heaving line. When someone complied, an American sailor in the cutter grabbed the heavy knot at the bitter end and tied the two lines together in a sheet bend. The boats signaled the mother ships that all was ready. Sailors in both ships heaved on the line, which popped out of the water and grew taut. Slowly, hand over hand, they shortened the distance between *Philadelphia* and *Intrepid*. The sailors and Marines lying facedown aboard the ketch gripped their weapons.

Suddenly, a Tripolitan sailor watching the approach of *Intrepid* saw something he didn't like. "Americans!" he shouted. "Americans are aboard!"

The captain of the Tripolitan guard ordered a halt to the proceedings and demanded to know if the ketch carried any Americans as crew.

"Certainly not," Catalano shouted back indignantly in Arabic. "This is a Maltese trader with only English and Italians aboard."

The Tripolitan captain believed him and ordered *Intrepid* to be hauled in closer. The whistle-blower, however, remained adamant.

"They are Americans!" he shouted again, this time almost pleading. "They are Americans, I swear it!"

Whether it was the man's certainty or because his own suspicions had been aroused, the captain of the guard ordered the line cut. Only a few feet of water separated the two vessels.

Catalano, his self-confidence rattled, yelled aft to Decatur, "Board, Captain! Board now!"

Decatur drew his sword and held it high in the air. "Belay that!" he roared. "Obey no order but mine!"

As a Tripolitan sailor raised an ax to slash the towrope, the Americans heaved on the rope one final time, propelling *Intrepid* forward just as the line was severed. Izard swung the tiller over to bring the starboard hull of the ketch gently alongside the larboard hull of the frigate.

Decatur leapt up onto *Intrepid*'s elevated bulwarks and from there onto the frigate's mizzen chain-plates. "*Board!*" he commanded. As he made to jump down, his foot slipped and Midn. Charles Morris sprang past him, the first to set foot on *Philadelphia*'s quarterdeck.

Decatur and the volunteers followed close on Morris' heels while the oarsmen in the cutter quickly overpowered the Arabs in the launch and rowed hard for *Philadelphia*. Four men carried lighted lanterns in double bags joined by a strap passing over one shoulder and connecting under the other arm—leaving both hands free to fight enemies who, stunned by the wave of Americans scrambling over the frigate's larboard railing, had backed up in defensive positions across the deck. Several of them jumped overboard. Others, attempting a rally, called on Allah and charged the Americans, their short, scimitar-like swords held high. One muscular Arab came directly at Jamie Cutler, in the front line of attack, and slashed down violently with his sword. Jamie raised his own sword to defend, but too late. The savage blow knocked the weapon from Jamie's hand and sent it slithering across the deck. Jamie groped for his pistol, but the Arab was too quick for him. He lunged in with his fist, striking Jamie on the jaw and knocking him backward and down. The Arab raised his sword high for the kill, his dark eyes flashing hatred.

Jamie, barely able to focus his eyes, saw a glint of silver to his left as a blade pierced the Arab under his ribs, its sharp point and edges tearing, ripping into vital organs, penetrating ever deeper, all the way to the hilt. The Arab, eyes bulging, arched his back and his sword clattered onto the deck. He fell to his knees, blood dribbling from his mouth, and leaned forward as if in a final prayer to Allah. Seaman John Stokes withdrew his blade from the bloody heap and then, for good measure, ran it through at the base of the Arab's neck, execution-style.

Jamie struggled to his feet. "Thank you, Stokes," he said numbly, his gaze stuck on the Arab's butchered corpse. "Thank you most kindly."

"My honor, Mr. Cutler." Stokes whirled around in search of new prey, crouching low, his left arm out, his sword clutched firmly in his right fist. But he found no one to accommodate him. Five Arabs lay dead on the deck. Others had leapt overboard and were either drowning or swimming for shore. *Philadelphia* was once again under American command.

"Anyone injured?" Decatur shouted to the volunteers gathering around him.

No one was.

"Right. We must move fast, men. You know your orders. Squad leaders, transfer the combustibles from *Intrepid* and proceed below. We meet back here on the gun deck in five minutes. Five minutes! That is all the time you have. Roundly, now!"

As the volunteers sprang to action, Decatur scanned the weather deck. He discovered nothing of note except on the quarterdeck, where he found the 32-pounder carronades, salvaged from the waters where *Philadelphia* had gone aground, loaded with powder and shot. He glanced ashore. No alarm had been raised, either within the city or aboard the Tripolitan warships anchored nearby. Likely, those Arabs who had abandoned *Philadelphia* had not yet made it to shore. He beseeched God for fifteen more minutes.

When Decatur clambered below to the gun deck he confronted a sight more in keeping with a Christmas Eve church service than a desperate raid on a captured warship. Thirty Americans stood silently before him, each man holding a candle lit from one of the four lanterns. The illumination effect was beautiful, magical, ethereal. Even the bowsed-up guns seemed transformed from instruments of destruction into symbols of something sacred. Decatur paused just a moment to take it all in.

"Right, lads," he said quietly, as if unwilling to intrude upon such sanctity. "Squad leaders, repair to stations. Wait for my order."

"Squad One, to me," Jamie Cutler called out. The five men assigned to him, each carrying a candle and combustibles, followed him down the forward companionway one deck below to the berthing deck. At the forward part of the ship, near the manger, they dumped paper, straw, odd scraps of wood and rope, anything and everything that would burn in a conflagration. When the combustibles were gathered in a pile, Jamie sprinkled a container of turpentine onto it and waited . . . and waited . . . until Decatur shouted down through the hatchway above.

"*Fire!*"

Jamie and the men in his squad set their candles against the pile as Decatur ran along the deck above them, shouting the order to the other squads waiting on the berthing deck. One by one, four other piles of combustibles burst into flames.

Jamie grabbed a lantern from a sailor named Freese and hurled it into the blaze. The glass shattered, spilling sperm oil that fueled the flames to greater heights and intensity. By now they almost reached the deckhead. Thick gray smoke curled about the forecastle, a living thing seeking the blessing of oxygen. It found it, through the hatchways.

"Everyone topside!" Jamie cried.

When he followed his squad up the ladder, he found Decatur, Morris, Izard, and Lawrence scrambling up to the gun deck. Decatur made a quick survey. Satisfied by what he saw, he pointed upward. "There's no more for us to do here, lads," he shouted over the crackle and sizzle of hot burning timbers. "It's time to shove off!"

Decatur, bringing up the rear, was followed up the companionway by tongues of flames that hissed up to the lower shrouds, instantly setting them ablaze. Melting tar dripped onto the deck. After a wild last look about the frigate, Decatur ran past the stump of the foremast and leapt aboard *Intrepid*.

"Every man accounted for?" he demanded of James Lawrence.

"Every man, Captain."

"Then douse our sails lest they catch fire. Man the cutter to turn us around."

"I've seen to that, Captain," Lawrence said. "We're turning as we speak."

Ashore and within the warships in the inner harbor, Tripolitans had by now awakened to the disaster unfolding in the harbor. Warning bells clanged furiously, and the shouts and curses of angry men could be heard in the distance. Cannons thundered into the night, sending up plumes of water all about *Philadelphia* and *Intrepid*. Musket balls peppered the sea perilously close by.

Oarsmen in the cutter heaved on their oars. Gradually, as if reluctant to abandon a sister ship in her anguish, *Intrepid* turned northeastward and slid away from *Philadelphia*.

"Run out the sweeps!" Decatur shouted.

At his command, sixteen sweeps, eight to a side, rumbled out of ports on the ketch's weather deck, their wooden blades digging into the water, rising, falling, rising, falling, until *Intrepid* had gathered sufficient way for the oarsmen in the cutter to ditch their little boat and scramble aboard the ketch. One of the last men up, a topman named Edwards, took a hit in the arm from a musket ball, lost his grip, and splashed into the sea.

"Man overboard!" Decatur cried out. "Back oars, you men!"

Even as his captain spoke, Ralph Izard swan-dived into the water and swam over to the struggling topman. He seized Edwards around his upper torso and sidestroked the short distance back to the ketch. Eager hands reached down, took hold, and dragged both men aboard.

Oars dug in and found traction, and *Intrepid* was back under way.

Ignoring the enemy gunfire raging about them, those on the weather deck of *Intrepid* not assigned to the oars crouched down, gazing not ahead to safety but astern, mesmerized by the destruction they had wrought. *Philadelphia* lay engulfed in an inferno, a towering funeral pyre that had reached up to her tops, then to her mizzen masthead, and beyond into the heavens. Tongues of dragon fire darted out from her gun ports and scuppers. When flames consumed the ensign halyard and the flag of Tripoli came undone and fell into the harbor like a kite that had lost its wind, a great cheer went up from the ketch. Several seamen cracked jokes.

"Belay that!" Decatur admonished. "We're not out of this yet!"

Then the impossible happened. In a final act of defiance—perhaps, if one believed in such things, orchestrated by the spirit of John Paul Jones on the quarterdeck—the great guns on *Philadelphia*'s weather and gun decks exploded from the heat, discharging an unholy broadside against the city walls and into Yusuf Karamanli's naval fleet. The damage could not be readily assessed. But to the immense relief of Decatur and every American in *Intrepid*, the enemy cannon fell silent, their gunners apparently stunned to the core by the specter of an American ghost ship firing on them.

Later, after midnight, as *Intrepid* ventured into the Mediterranean under an overcast sky, Decatur peered astern through a spyglass. All he could determine was that *Philadelphia*'s anchor cables had burned through and the furiously burning frigate had drifted into shallow water directly beneath the bashaw's castle.

Later still, after *Intrepid* and *Syren* had reunited and yellow streaks of sun were flirting with the eastern horizon, captains and crews could still observe black smoke rising into the sky above the corpse of *Philadelphia*, now forty miles away to southward.

AFTER *Intrepid* AND *Syren* had stood out from Syracuse Harbor for Tripoli and the violent gale had blasted through the region, Commodore

Preble dispatched his squadron on patrol between Syracuse and Tripoli. Their mission: to intercept enemy shipping and, should the opportunity present itself, act in support of *Intrepid* and *Syren*.

Preble designed a three-sided, viselike strategy that cordoned off the central Mediterranean to enemy vessels. Master Commandant Isaac Hull was ordered to take position off Cape Misurata, 125 miles east of the city of Tripoli. Enemy cruisers and merchantmen attempting to hug the North African coast on their way to or from the eastern Mediterranean would find the 16-gun brig of war *Argus* there to greet them. Lt. John Smith in *Nautilus* and Lt. Richard Somers in *Vixen* cruised between Derne and Benghazi, two key enemy seaports in the eastern provinces of Tripoli. *Portsmouth* was stationed between Cape Bon in Tunisia and the western tip of Sicily.

Portsmouth had been at sea for two weeks when she returned to base in Syracuse to take on fresh food and water. Only the flagship and the schooner *Enterprise* were lying at anchor when she arrived. *Intrepid* and *Syren* were conspicuously absent.

Richard Cutler, his anxiety for his son almost overwhelming, reported to Commodore Preble in the flagship's after cabin and informed him that he had not observed a single enemy cruiser or merchant vessel of consequence while out on patrol, just the usual feluccas, small xebecs, and innocuous fishing craft indigenous to the area. Preble acknowledged and then broached the subject weighing heavily on each man's mind.

"I must inform you, Captain Cutler, that as of yet we have received no word from either *Intrepid* or *Syren*."

"I understand, sir. But it's only been two weeks." Richard realized he was stretching the truth: in fact it was coming up on three weeks since the two vessels had departed Syracuse, longer than a "hit-and-run" raid across the Mediterranean should have required. Left unspoken was his worst fear, that the vicious gale of early February had cast the two vessels onto a lee shore and that all hands had either drowned or been taken prisoner. Preble no doubt harbored similar fears, Richard thought to himself as the two men stared across the table at each other. After several moments of silence, Richard collected his hat and said, in the measured tone of a naval commander, "I shall be returning to station, sir, as soon as *Portsmouth* is resupplied."

To Richard's surprise, Preble stood up, came around the table, and offered Richard his hand. "Give yourself an extra day or two before leaving, Captain," he urged. "And if we receive word after you depart, I will send the swiftest dispatch vessel in my possession to find you."

"Thank you, sir." Richard saluted his commander, who returned the salute smartly.

Two mornings later, as *Portsmouth* was concluding final preparations for sea, the cry came from on high aboard *Constitution*. "Deck, there! Two vessels approaching. One is lateen-rigged . . . *the other is a brig!*" The lookout fairly screamed those last five words.

Agreen Crabtree heard the cry from the quarterdeck of *Portsmouth* and immediately sent a duty midshipman below to inform the captain. But there was no need. Richard Cutler was already scrambling up the aft companionway. He joined Agreen at the starboard railing.

Neither man spoke. There was nothing to say until the two vessels had reached the approaches to the harbor. Every available spyglass in *Portsmouth* was swinging like a pendulum between the oncoming vessels and *Constitution*'s signal halyard.

"There she goes," Eric Meyers, on the quarterdeck, commented as three white balls soared up that halyard and broke into flags at the top.

"Numbers 2 . . . 2 . . . 7," Agreen translated.

"It means," Richard responded distantly, "'have you completed the business you were sent on?'" The eyes of the squadron shifted southward to *Syren*, the lead vessel. As Richard peered through his glass, waiting for the reply, an old scar high on his forehead begin to pulse for the first time in years.

Syren creamed into the outer harbor and hoisted her reply: 2 . . . 3 . . . 2: "Business completed, that I was sent on."

Euphoria erupted everywhere. Sailors in the rigging and on deck cheered and began waving hats and arms in the air. The great guns of *Constitution*, too long silent, erupted in a thirteen-gun salute. The cheers and huzzahs reached their crescendo as the two vessels glided in, rounded up, and dropped anchor.

Richard said nothing, showed no reaction, even as his crew in the waist, forecastle, and rigging continued their wild celebrations. He held his glass steady, sweeping it back and forth, back and forth, across the deck of *Intrepid*. His heart pounded; beads of perspiration prickled under his uniform; he held his lips tightly pressed together until a hand reached out and touched him on his shoulder.

"I see him, Richard," Agreen said, pointing. "He's abaft the mizzen, between Decatur and Izard."

Richard focused his glass. Yes, there he was—his features, his grin, unmistakable. "So he is, Lieutenant," Richard said matter-of-factly. He collapsed his glass. "You have the deck," he added with a quick sideways glance that revealed to Agreen eyes glinting with moisture. A minute later, Agreen heard the Marine sentry on duty belowdecks stamp the butt of his musket on the deck. And then he heard the faint click of the after cabin door closing gently behind his captain.

Ten

Tripoli, Egypt, and Syracuse, March–June 1804

T HE TALL, LANKY man ushered into the captain's cabin bore classic Gallic features: thick, curly black hair; an elongated face ending at a narrow chin; aquiline nose; and round, dark eyes set below bushy black eyebrows. The Marine sentry who had brought him saluted his captain and left the cabin. With the sentry's rap on the door, Edward Preble had turned from his writing desk where, in the company of two others, he had watched through an open gun port as the launch approached *Constitution*, the tricolor of France fluttering above the boat's stern. A five-gun salute had erupted from the starboard battery, followed in short order by a shrill of boatswain's whistles piping the visitor aboard. The launch that had conveyed the French diplomat from the shores of Tripoli now lay bobbing alongside the American frigate, its oars shipped and its bow line secured to the mainmast chain-wale. Standing stone-faced before the American commodore was its sole passenger.

Preble stood up. "*Bonjour,* Monsieur Beaussier," he greeted him cordially. "Welcome aboard *Constitution*."

Bonaventure Beaussier bowed in consular fashion. "*Merci, monsieur. Bonjour à vous aussi.*" He glanced around the cabin and said, in heavily accented English, "The rumors I have heard are true, monsieur. You command a fine ship."

Preble bowed in response. "Please sit down, monsieur. Make yourself comfortable. Before we begin, may I introduce Mr. Charles Gordon, my first lieutenant, and Mr. Phillip Darby, my clerk." The two Americans returned the Frenchman's bow. "Mr. Darby will be taking notes of our meeting. May I offer some refreshment? I have a good Madeira and stores of other spirits; whatever you desire."

"Coffee would be most welcome, *capitaine*, if it's no trouble."

"No trouble at all."

After the captain's steward had served a round of coffee and the customary pleasantries had been exchanged, Preble gave Phillip Darby a small nod, the signal to begin taking notes. "Monsieur Beaussier," he said slowly, his dark blue eyes taking in the impeccably attired Frenchman seated across from him, "let me be certain I understand the nature of your visit here today. At the request of Mr. Robert Livingston, the American consul in Paris, your government has agreed to assist in peace negotiations between the United States and Tripoli. Since you are the *chargé d'affaires* for France in Tripoli, you have been asked to act as the mediator in any such negotiations. Are these facts correct?"

"They are, monsieur."

"And Monsieur Talleyrand," referring to Charles Maurice de Talleyrand-Périgord, the recently reinstalled French foreign minister, "has instructed you to contact Mr. Dghies, Tripoli's foreign secretary. Is that correct?"

"*Oui, monsieur.*"

"Have you done so?"

"I have, *capitaine*."

"And you believe Mr. Dghies encourages such negotiations?"

"He has told me so himself, monsieur," Beaussier averred.

"You trust Mr. Dghies?"

The Frenchman shifted position, apparently caught by surprise by this last question and the tone in which it was delivered. "I have no reason not to trust him," he hedged.

"Perhaps you do not, Monsieur Beaussier. But I most certainly do." Preble leaned forward in his chair and clasped his hands before him. "I believe, in fact, that Mr. Dghies is acting in his own interests. Specifically, I believe he is out to line his own pockets at my country's expense. Are you aware that before *Philadelphia* was burned, Dghies had entered into an agreement to purchase the frigate with funds owed him by the bashaw—his boss, so to speak—and that he planned to sell her back to the United States at a tidy profit for himself?"

"I have heard rumors," Beaussier said cautiously.

"I'm certain you have. And are you aware that Mr. Dghies and Mr. Schembri and others of their ilk are urging the bashaw to negotiate with Mr. Lear, the American consul general in Algiers, in order to secure a quick peace? And that the bashaw will then declare war all over again once the United States Navy has left the Mediterranean? And are you among those who believe the American government lacks the resolve to send its Navy back if that should happen?"

Beaussier stared blankly across the table at Preble, overwhelmed by the crescendo of questions. "If I may, *capitaine*, how do you come by such information?" he asked.

"I have my sources, Monsieur Beaussier. They are reliable sources, so I take this information to be true. I regret having to say this to you, monsieur, but I believe you have been duped. You comprehend the word 'duped'? Yes?" Preble pointed shoreward at the city of Tripoli. "Personally, I am convinced that there is no one in that godforsaken den of iniquity over there whom I can trust. Present company excepted, of course." He smiled, but his eyes remained cold.

Beaussier did not return the smile. "*Capitaine*, I can assure you," he said earnestly, "that Napoléon himself supports this effort. He has no wish to see his American friends and allies at war in North Africa."

"I believe that he has no such wish," Preble stated mildly. "But let us try to understand *why*. A détente now exists between our two countries, and I, for one, welcome it. But tell me, monsieur: what does Napoléon intend to do on behalf of the United States in this matter beyond exerting what little influence he has in North Africa to encourage peace? Is he prepared, if necessary, to commit French ships and soldiers to our cause? I ask again: *why* is he doing this? Is it for the love of his American friends and allies, as you seem to imply? Or is it because France desperately needs American trade in its war against England—a trade that would be greatly enhanced by peace treaties between the United States and the Barbary States? Mind you, I am neither drawing conclusions nor making accusations. I am merely asking the questions."

The Frenchman stiffened. "Are you suggesting, *capitaine*, that you are not willing to negotiate with Tripoli? That you prefer war to peace? Is *this* the message you wish me to deliver to your Mr. Livingston in Paris? And to my superiors? Are you prepared to accept the responsibility for taking such a position?"

Preble's expression revealed little. He folded his arms across his chest and looked to his first lieutenant to ask the inevitable question, "What price peace?" Gordon and Preble both realized that although President

Jefferson and his cabinet preferred a military solution to this war, Tobias Lear had convinced the president to keep open the lines of communication to a negotiated settlement. They also were aware, as was Beaussier, that Portugal had recently paid the dey of Algiers the equivalent of one million American dollars in ransom and tribute to free 374 Portuguese sailors held captive in an Algerian prison. That was approximately the number of Americans held captive in Tripoli.

Beaussier's dark eyes shifted to *Constitution*'s first lieutenant on hearing his question. "What price is your country prepared to pay?"

Gordon deferred back to his captain.

"Whatever that amount may be," Preble stated categorically, "it is for the release of *Philadelphia*'s crew. Nothing else."

"What you are saying then, *capitaine*," Beaussier clarified, "is that the United States will pay no amount in annual tribute."

Preble's tone was emphatic. "None whatsoever, monsieur. Not today, not tomorrow, not the day after. What Mr. Karamanli and his pirate allies refer to as 'tribute' is nothing more than bully-payments. The United States will not be a party to extortion. My government is adamant on this point."

Beaussier slowly shook is head and replied sorrowfully, "With respect, *capitaine*, I do not believe you appreciate the realities involved in this situation. Such insistence will not serve your country or your captured sailors. There can be no negotiations for ransom without negotiations for tribute. The two are . . . how do you say . . . clasped together like your two hands. The bashaw is most adamant on *this* point. He has in fact advised his Jewish bankers in Tripoli that they may expect between $600,000 and $800,000 as the result of a peace settlement with the United States."

Preble laughed out loud. "I scoff at such ridiculous amounts," he declared. "I do understand *this* reality, monsieur, and I ask you to please relay it verbatim to your bosom friend the bashaw at the earliest opportunity: he will put a new slant on things when the United States Navy arrives here in force and reduces his city to rubble."

Beaussier again shook his head. "I cannot speak to that, *capitaine*," he said. "I can only report to you what I have seen for myself, that Mr. Karamanli has invested considerable funds in strengthening the defenses of his city. Should you cause harm to Tripoli, the United States will simply have to pay that much more in ransoms and tribute and damages when the time comes."

"In addition," Preble went on, ignoring what Beaussier had just said, "I have dispatched a ship to Alexandria. Her captain is well versed in North

African diplomacy and has excellent contacts in this area. His orders are to find Hamet Karamanli and to assess his ability to lead an army overland against his brother. Hamet will have American naval support, you understand, and the support of Tripolitans who consider him their rightful leader, which he is. Yusuf is nothing more than a usurper. So please, if you will, report to Yusuf Karamanli that before the year is out he will likely have to look to land *and* to sea to defend against those who oppose him."

"I will tell him," Beaussier promised, looking somewhat pale at the prospect.

"And tell him this as well," Preble concluded. "Tell him that the United States will pay nothing for a peace settlement, *ever*. Nor will the United States pay an annuity of any kind, *ever*. My most fervent wish is to see American prisoners in Tripoli freed from cruel bondage. But I would sacrifice them all, and I would gladly sacrifice myself, before I would agree to terms that are incompatible with the honor and dignity of my country. Is that message clearly understood?"

"It is, *capitaine*." Beaussier scraped back his chair and stood up, ending the meeting.

THE FIRST LANDFALL Richard Cutler was able to make out as he looked shoreward from the weather side of *Portsmouth*'s quarterdeck was not what he had daydreamed as a child of seeing: a limestone lighthouse towering 450 feet above the eastern point of the island of Pharos. It was no longer there, of course; a mammoth earthquake had destroyed it five hundred years ago. As a young boy growing up by the sea in Massachusetts, Richard had often imagined that lighthouse—built in the third century BC during the reigns of Ptolemy I and Ptolemy II—and he had half-expected to find it intact, the vast mirrors and fires at its apex visible to mariners thirty miles out at sea, a beacon to guide them in to safe harbor.

To the right of where the lighthouse once stood, however, other wonders of the ancient world still remained. Richard could see the eighty-foot-tall Roman triumphal column known as "Pompey's Pillar" located near the ancient acropolis and, nearby, two great obelisks of slightly lesser height known as "Cleopatra's Needles"—their name a misnomer, Richard's history lessons had taught him, because the imposing red granite structures had been standing a thousand years by the time the fabled queen ascended to the throne of Egypt. Mixed in with Egyptian artifacts were examples of classic Hellenic architecture, proof positive that this great metropolis founded by Alexander the Great in 331 BC was a historic link between the ancient Greek city-states and the fertile Nile Valley.

As Gordon Smythe brought *Portsmouth* in toward land under reduced sail, those on the quarterdeck noticed what a lookout had already spotted: a small boat approaching from the southeast, its single lateen sail drawn in tight on a close haul before the prevailing northerly breeze.

"There's likely a pilot aboard," Smythe commented, the relief in his voice evident. As ship's master, he was responsible for the proper sailing and navigation of the ship. Charts of these waters warned of the tricky entrance to Grand Harbor caused by continuously shifting silt and ballast dumped overboard by centuries of lazy mariners. By now, the harbor entrance was all but choked off, and the skills of a local pilot were needed to direct a vessel along its one functional channel.

Smith's observation turned out to be correct. As *Portsmouth* followed the pilot boat into the harbor and rounded up to her anchorage close to three snub-bowed Turkish warships, her guns erupted in a seventeen-gun salute to the Turkish flag fluttering high above a harbor fortress. The Turkish garrison returned the salute, gun for gun.

An hour later, a small rowboat approached the American frigate, this one bearing a well-dressed, well-groomed man who introduced himself as Samuel Briggs, the British consul in Alexandria. Eric Meyers greeted him at the entry port and escorted him aft to the quarterdeck, where a circular table sat beneath a makeshift canvas awning fashioned by Sailmaker Larson and his mates. The shade it created was a welcome reprieve from a Mediterranean sun that heated land and sea with a blazing intensity.

"Welcome aboard, Mr. Briggs," Richard greeted him. "I have been expecting you." He introduced the consul to his two other commissioned officers and to his captain of Marines.

Briggs bowed politely to each officer before focusing his full attention on Richard Cutler. In his hand Richard held two letters of introduction: one from Edward Preble, the other from Sir Alexander Ball, governor of Malta. These he handed to Briggs, who gave them a cursory glance before handing them back. "Thank you, Captain Cutler," he said, "but these letters are hardly necessary. I have received correspondence of your pending arrival from Admiral Nelson and Captain Hardcastle. I believe you are acquainted with those two gentlemen?" He smiled.

Richard smiled back. "I am."

"Since they see fit to recommend you, I see no need for further endorsement. I am at your service, Captain, if you will tell me how I may serve you."

Richard had decided not to be coy when asked such a question. He had shared the purpose of his mission in a letter to his brother-in-law. As he expected, Jeremy had shared the details with Horatio Nelson. Since the Royal Navy knew of his mission, so must British intelligence, from the halls of Whitehall in England to the halls of British consular offices in Egypt.

"I am here to confer with Mr. Hamet Karamanli," he replied.

"Yes, quite," Briggs said, as if that statement were a foregone conclusion. "Unfortunately, Mr. Karamanli is not in Alexandria."

"No," Richard agreed. "I understand he is in Cairo."

"Some distance south of Cairo, I believe." Briggs had done his homework. "He has joined up with the Mamelukes, who as you may know comprise a rather powerful fighting force in Egypt." He was referring to a warrior class of former slaves, many of them of Greek and Slavic descent, whom the Turks had converted to Islam in the sixteenth century and trained as an elite fighting force. The Mamelukes eventually grew tired of playing a subservient role and decided to seize control of Egypt for themselves. Since then, they had been battling various factions, particularly the Ottoman Turks, for control of the province. "Our intelligence indicates that Karamanli has fled to Upper Egypt, where the Mamelukes have retired since their defeat by Napoléon." Briggs continued, "Hamet has not fled from the Turks, you understand, but from his brother in Tripoli. There are rumors flying about that Yusuf has sent assassins after him. Mind you, these rumors have not been substantiated. But given the bashaw's reputation when it comes to family, they are probably true."

"Can you contact Hamet?"

"Oh, yes. We can send couriers. But I most strongly advise you not to venture south of Cairo under any circumstances. It is no place for anyone of Western heritage. Egypt has its charm and its history, but it is among the most dangerous places in North Africa, especially the farther south one goes. In Cairo one can find a semblance of civilization, but south of there . . ."

Briggs' hand gesture indicated just how senseless and perilous such a venture would likely be. "South of there, the British government could do naught but pray for your safety. Not that we can do much better elsewhere in Egypt. We have not had a significant military presence here since the army pulled out in '03. Those of us stationed here rely on diplomatic immunity and on our popularity among the Egyptian people. And we follow rule number one: we maintain strict neutrality in Egyptian affairs, whatever the provocation and regardless of who is involved. You would do well to do the same."

Richard inclined his head. "I will, thank you. Would Hamet come to Cairo? And would he be safe if he were to do so?"

"I should think the answer to your first question depends on your reason for wanting him to come—the strength of your message, so to speak—which, as I understand that message, should have its appeal. The answer to your second question depends entirely on Muhammad Ali."

"And he is . . . ?"

"Muhammad Ali Pasha al-Mas'ud ibn Agha, the commander of Turkish troops in Egypt. But in reality he is much more than that." To the attentive Americans, Briggs explained, "Muhammad Ali plays the game by his own rules and for his own purposes. After we defeated the French four years ago and they bid adieu to their brief rule in Egypt, Ali marched in under the banner of Selim III, Grand Sultan of the Ottoman Empire, to reclaim Egypt in his name. Ali is of Albanian descent and his soldiers are mostly Albanians. He consolidated his power by appealing to the Egyptian people. He promised them he would end the civil wars, return law and order to the countryside, and restore the glory of Egypt if they would support him and do his bidding. He proclaimed himself their champion, and his message resonated. Today, Ali is the most powerful and feared military commander in Egypt. He is the self-proclaimed khedive of the province, and he is more feared than the viceroy appointed by the grand sultan. More powerful, in Egypt, than Selim himself."

Richard offered a small grunt of acknowledgment. "Can we convince Muhammad Ali not to oppose Hamet's visiting me in Cairo?"

"I believe we can. Major Edward Missett, our acting consul in Cairo, has already informed him of your intentions. By the bye, you will be meeting with Major Missett south of Rosetta. He will accompany you to Cairo. You will appreciate his company. Major Misset is an army officer of impeccable credentials and a jolly good fellow besides. As I told you, the Egyptian people respect our flag. Since they do, Ali does. And Ali very much appreciates England's withdrawal after defeating the French, allowing him to march in and take over. So he is inclined to cooperate with us when it serves his interests. Still, there are bandits and cutthroats everywhere you go in Egypt. So you must never let your guard down. How many men do you propose to take with you to Cairo?"

Richard indicated his first lieutenant and his captain of Marines. "We'll also have with us a midshipman and six Marines."

"That should suffice. Just make certain you and your men are well armed. I cannot stress that enough. However, I must again invoke rule number one. Be absolutely certain to inform your men that their weapons are to be used only in self-defense. I cannot stress *that* enough either."

THE MARINE CORPORAL on duty outside the captain's cabin snapped a salute as Agreen Crabtree approached. Agreen returned the salute, knocked on the door, and stepped inside. When it came to the first lieutenant, naval regulations dictating that only the captain's steward had unrestricted access to the captain's cabin did not apply.

Agreen found Richard sitting at his writing desk, quill in hand. The larger table at the center of the midships cabin bore an assortment of pistols, ammunition boxes, and a gilt-hafted saber lying in its sheath. Like Agreen—like every officer and Marine assigned to the shore party—Richard was clad in full undress uniform. Whether drawing attention to themselves in such a manner would prove an advantage or a disadvantage remained to be seen. So he had ordered every man to carry with him a less formal ensemble more in keeping with local fashions.

"Mornin', Richard," Agreen greeted him.

"Morning, Agee," Richard said without looking up. "I'll be with you in a brace of shakes. I'm just putting the finishing touches on these orders for Lieutenant Lee."

Agreen walked over to a starboard gun port and peered out at the odd-looking three-masted vessel that would convey them sixty-five miles eastward to the seaside port of Rosetta, a long-favored embarkation point for those traveling south into Egypt because it was located at the mouth of one of the Nile's two great distributaries.

"There," Richard said with finality. "It's done." He blew on the ink to dry it and then folded the document into a rectangle, sealing it where the four corners met before slipping it into a top drawer in the desk. "Let's hope that Mr. Lee does not find himself compelled to execute these orders," he added lightly.

"Execute?" Agreen snorted as he walked toward the central table. "Jesus, Richard, you sure know how t' pick a word! And you sure know how t' motivate a fellow. If George has to *execute* his orders, then that means that you and I are stranded in some bone-dry desert hellhole with camels for company and a swarm of hairy Arabs tryin' t' do us in. I'm a sow in heat I'm so excited."

Richard grinned. "Do you know why sows get so roused up when they're in heat?"

Agreen gave him a bewildered look. "I haven't given it much thought. Why?"

"They say it's because a boar has a corkscrew-shaped penis."

Agreen roared with laughter. "Now *that's* funny."

Richard clipped his sword onto his belt, then picked up a snub-barreled pistol, checked the frizzen for powder, and slid it into an inside pocket of his uniform coat. Longer-barreled pistols he stowed in a heavy canvas seabag along with a change of clothes and extra shot and powder. "Everyone's ready?" he asked, his smile fading.

"Ready as we'll ever be."

"And the gear . . . ?"

". . . is stowed in the launch."

"It's time, then." As they made for the door, Richard said, his tone again lighthearted, "Haven't you always said you wanted to see the Nile, Agee?"

"Sure," Agreen bantered back, "in picture-books."

On the weather deck they found a side party dressed in spotless blue and white, the two other commissioned officers, the ship's master, and a clutch of midshipmen. Richard returned their salutes just as Boatswain Weeks signaled the side party to launch into its ceremonial cadence.

"The ship is yours, Mr. Lee," Richard said to his second lieutenant, raising his voice to be heard over the chorus of drums and whistles. "Your orders are in the top drawer of my desk. Pray, carry them out to the letter."

"You may rely on me, Captain."

"I always have, Mr. Lee. Good luck to you. And to you, Mr. Meyers," he said to his third lieutenant, now acting as first lieutenant. They exchanged final salutes before Richard and Agreen climbed down into the launch.

The six oarsmen shoved off from the frigate and the coxswain steered toward the vessel that would transport them to Rosetta. Richard sat in silence, nodding once to acknowledge Carl Corbett, captain of Marines, and once at Edward Osborn, senior midshipman, who sat side-by-side directly before him, facing aft. Behind them, also facing aft, sat three groups of two Marines: a sergeant, a corporal, and four privates, each man hand-picked by Captain Corbett in consultation with his sergeant, Robert Mills.

Once aboard the shallow-draft vessel and under way eastward, Richard stood at the taffrail and gazed astern at a city that was only a shadow of its former self. This sad reality had settled in during the previous three days as he and his officers explored city streets and canals that had once been the site of the glorious baths built by Cleopatra, the Great Caesareum of Rome, and magnificent Greek Orthodox churches intermingling comfortably with grand Muslim mosques and Jewish temples. At the height of its glory, Alexandria had housed a million souls, including, in its northeast sector, the largest Jewish population in the world. But time had been cruel to the legendary city. Invaders and locals alike had pillaged its riches and antiquities, and their desecrations had exacted a terrible toll. Today, even the city's ruins lay in ruins.

The opposite held true in Rosetta, a bustling seaside town of attractive Ottoman architecture, cultivated gardens, and air heavy with the scent of orange and lemon trees. The Americans did not linger there, however. After spending a night in a Turkish inn they were up early the next morning in search of transportation southward beyond the bar of the Nile, where they were to meet up with Major Misset. It took some haggling before Richard managed to hire a local guide and a vessel for him to pilot: a 40-foot felucca with a towering single mast stepped at the foredeck and a small cabin built onto the afterdeck. The small but swift vessel carried them southward through the lagoons and lakes and wetlands of the 150-mile-wide coastal delta, past sand dunes along the shore and clay and silt islands in the river, until the vivid blue waters of the Mediterranean had yielded to a more reddish hue, the salty brine of the coast had yielded to a lush agricultural interior, and they were sailing on the Nile River.

Locating Major Misset was not difficult. Just south of a small riverside village five miles upstream from where the felucca broke free of the wetlands, they came upon a sturdy barge flying an oversized British ensign at the stern and a smaller one on the jack-staff at the stubby bow. She was armed with swivel guns, three on each side, mounted on top of the bulwarks with a Y-bracket.

The felucca nosed in fifty feet astern of the barge and dropped her sail. Midshipman Osborn and three Marines jumped ashore and secured the bow and stern to bollards set into the sandy embankment. Richard paid the pilot, who set off to round up a crew to take back to Rosetta. As Richard walked down a short plank and onto the thin strip of white sandy beach, an officer decked out in the regimental red and white of the British Army did likewise. The two officers met halfway between the two vessels.

"Major Misset?" Richard inquired. When the British officer nodded, Richard offered a salute, which was answered.

"Captain Cutler, may I presume?"

"You may, Major."

The two officers shook hands. The short, sinewy, rather sallow-faced bespectacled man transmitted strength and energy through his grip, and Richard was immediately drawn to him.

"How was your journey here, Captain?"

"Uneventful. Therefore pleasant."

"That's probably better put than you realize, sir. These days in Egypt, one's satisfaction is normally measured by the absence of pain or peril rather than by any real pleasure."

"So Mr. Briggs informed me."

"And you still wish to proceed to Cairo?"

"Those are my orders, Major."

"Yes, quite. I still had to inquire, Captain."

Richard glanced to his right and noted two women toiling in an adjacent field under the hot sun, cutting and gathering a crop he could not identify. What struck him was not the nature of their work but rather what they were wearing. Their faces were largely covered, in Muslim tradition, but their head-to-toe garments with long narrow slits for the arms left their breasts fully exposed.

Misset noticed his surprise and grinned. "That's Egyptian women for you," he commented dryly. "Cover your face from the eyes of Allah but leave your teats open to view. Allah may not approve of the fashion, but I daresay their men-folk do."

"It's a good thing my third lieutenant isn't with us on this expedition," Richard quipped. "Else we'd never leave here."

Misset chuckled. "There's plenty more of that where we're heading," he said, adding in a more official tone, "We shall depart in a few minutes. Cairo is a hundred miles upriver, and it's a gambler's bet how long it will take us to get there. We'll be fighting the current, which as you'll discover is not terribly strong. The prevailing winds are in our favor, and if they hold, we should arrive in three days. If we encounter strong headwinds, though, we shall have to put in to shore and muck around until the wind shifts back to the north. We cannot fight wind *and* current. How long do you expect to remain in Egypt, Captain?"

"If I'm not back aboard my ship in two weeks, my first lieutenant has orders to return to station off the coast of Cyrenaica."

"I say! I mean no disrespect, Captain, but why would you order your ship to sail without you?"

"Because I know my officers, Major. And I know my crew. If we're not back in the allotted time, without orders to the contrary they would come ashore searching for us. That is the *last* thing I want. If we encounter trouble, we'll deal with it on our own. Of course, if we're delayed for a good reason, I am hopeful I may rely on you to send a messenger ahead to delay her departure."

"You may indeed, Captain. And I must say, that is most noble of you, looking out for your crew that way."

"It's hardly noble, Major. It's merely practical. I don't see what is gained by endangering the lives of good men in what would surely become a wild goose chase in hostile territory."

"Hmm, I see your point. You do understand, of course, that whilst you are in Cairo you will be under British protection."

"I am most grateful for your protection, Major. But with respect, British protection in Egypt can only go so far."

Misset's heavy sigh acknowledged the flaw within the omnipotent British Empire. "Unfortunately, Captain, I cannot disagree with that statement. But we will do whatever we can for you. We have already sent three couriers south of Cairo to locate Hamet Karamanli. Surely one of them will succeed."

"Let's hope so."

With that, the Americans boarded the British barge. In total, the party sailing south numbered twenty-two men and included seven British Army personnel serving as a personal bodyguard to Major Misset, plus four sailors whose job was to maneuver the barge.

On its slow slog southward against a current that reminded Richard of the Gulf Stream, the barge passed by agrarian scenes that he suspected had changed little since the dawn of Man. Egypt was a paradox—an immense desert with some of the most fertile soil on earth. Each year, during the rainy season, the Nile overflowed its banks and deposited rich black mud that remained when the waters receded. In that soil grew rice and fruit trees and wheat and melons and vegetables of all descriptions. Whether it was Allah who sent these life-saving floodwaters each year to the grateful Egyptians or the Christian God or perhaps Hapi, the ancient Nile god, they were heaven-sent, regardless.

"I have t' admit," Agreen confessed as he watched the timeless spectacle pass by on both sides of the barge, "I never expected t' find anything quite like this." He and Richard were standing on the larboard side, forward between the substantial foremast and stubby bowsprit. Although the other Americans were equally engrossed in the view, most of the British personnel sat propped up against the bulwarks. Several of them were napping; they had seen it before.

Richard grinned. "What are you referring to, Agee? The bare-chested ladies?"

"Of course. What else?" Agreen shielded his eyes from the searing desert sun and looked eastward. In the far hazy distance he saw camels rise up like a mirage atop a gleaming sand dune. "Where are the Pyramids?"

"Near Cairo. Maybe we can manage a visit while we're there."

"That'd be something to write home about."

"It would. Just leave out the part about the bare-chested ladies. Lizzy would be offended. And peeved."

"Yes, she would, but not as peeved as Katherine after I tell her just what you *did* with those bare-chested ladies."

"Touché, Lieutenant."

The waters of the Nile and the sand along its banks shimmered in the blistering noontime sun, its crushing heat blurring both vision and mental acuity. Richard pulled the front of his wide-brimmed straw hat lower over his brow, crossed his arms, and leaned back comfortably against the foremast. His eyelids grew heavy; he felt himself succumbing to the inevitable. Just for a moment, he promised himself, a moment; and then he drifted into the abyss of deep sleep. Some time later he felt Agreen nudging him.

"Sorry t' wake you, Captain," he said in a low voice, "but we've got company. Have a gander."

"What?" Richard mumbled, his senses muddled and confused. In his dream he was home in Hingham, laughing at something Katherine had said and sweeping her into his embrace. It took him a moment to pull himself back to North Africa. "What did you say, Agee? Company? Where?"

"There." Agreen pointed abeam to larboard. Richard blinked. He shook his head, ousting the last vestiges of sleep, and looked again. A squad of men a-horse in flowing white garb was galloping in the direction of the river toward a small village that lay perhaps a quarter-mile ahead.

"I don't think those gents are herdsmen," Agreen remarked.

Richard squinted. "Your eyes are better than mine, Agee." He glanced at the midshipman standing nearby. He, too, had seen the horsemen and had cautiously approached his commanding officers. "Mr. Osborn," Richard said to him, "please fetch me a long glass from Major Misset."

"Aye, aye, Captain."

Richard raised the glass and brought into focus what appeared to be a cavalry charge against an unsuspecting enemy. He counted eleven . . . twelve . . . fourteen men galloping pell-mell toward the cluster of modest, mud-roofed homes. The harsh brilliance of the savage sun reflected off steel blades held high in the air.

"Major Misset!" Richard cried out. His shout brought everyone alert.

Misset strode forward. "What is it, Captain?"

"*That!*" Richard gave him the glass with his left hand and pointed ahead with his right.

Misset took a look. "*Shit!*" he muttered under his breath. "Brace yourselves, gentlemen," he shouted out. "This will not be pleasant."

The men in the barge watched in horror as the horsemen swept down on the village in a thunder of hooves. Villagers dashed from their homes and fields, darting this way and that, offering no resistance, just running. One man, slowed by age, stumbled and fell. As he struggled to get up, a horseman streaked past him, his scimitar flashing. In one flick of the rider's wrist the razor-sharp blade sliced through the man's neck as though it were a carrot top. Blood spurted into the air for a split second before the headless corpse collapsed in a heap.

"Who are those bastards?" Richard cried.

"Bedouins," Misset answered him, his voice steady. "Or Albanian deserters. Or some local tribesmen. Who knows? Egypt is full of such renegades."

"Can't we do somethin' t' help those poor people?" Agreen pleaded.

"We can do nothing!" Misset hissed gruffly, although he did order his bodyguard to man the larboard swivel guns—as a defensive measure only, he insisted. But even that action did nothing to dissuade the attackers. They paid no mind to the British flag. It was as though the barge wasn't there.

As the barge drew parallel to the village, half of the raiders began herding off the village cattle and water buffalo. The other half dispatched with brutal efficiency everyone who remained alive, including the women, some of whom, unlike their men, did offer resistance, verbally if not with weapons. One woman ran at a horse, seized the reins, and jerked them hard, throwing the rider off. When he hit the ground, she started beating him with a stick. Dazed from the fall, the black-bearded Arab curled himself into a fetal position, cowering before the blows. Another rider came in, dismounted, and unsheathed his sword. When the woman turned to face him, he ran the blade clean through her abdomen. She fell, writhing in pain. The Arab she had unhorsed got to his feet, found his scimitar, and slashed down at her again and again, like a butcher cutting meat from a bone, until her screams subsided and she lay dead still.

"Jesus Christ Almighty," Richard breathed. Instinctively he called for a musket. When Sergeant Mills handed him one, he took aim at the first Arab he found in his sights and began to squeeze the trigger. Before he could fire, he felt the barrel of his musket being forced down.

"Stand down," Misset said quietly, his hand on the barrel. "Please, Captain, stand down and leave it be. There is nothing we can do for these people. Our intervention here would only serve to complicate our mission. And *your* mission, Captain."

With a reluctance born of utter disgust, Richard handed the musket back to the Marine sergeant. As the barge sailed on past the carnage, he crossed to the starboard side and leaned over. For long moments he stared down into the murky water, unable to abide the horrific sights and sounds of the slaughter on the shore.

THE WINDS, at least, remained fair. Brisk northerly breezes filled the barge's two luglike sails and pushed the vessel hard to southward against the weaker northerly flow of the Nile. In just two and a half days they arrived at Bulac, the port city of Cairo, and left the barge behind.

The dusty road leading from the docks to the British consulate was thronged with Egyptian men sitting astride donkeys so diminutive that the riders' sandaled feet nearly touched the ground. Made skittish by what they had observed on the Nile, the Americans avoided eye contact as they marched along. They either stared ahead at the British contingent leading the way or looked at the buildings of the city that during the Middle Ages had played a central role in a highly lucrative Oriental spice trade. Major Misset explained that the wealth flowing to Arab merchants from caravan routes streaming through Cairo from Red Sea ports began to dry up in 1497 when the Portuguese explorer Vasco da Gama discovered a more profitable ocean route to the Orient around the southern tip of Africa.

To Richard, Cairo looked more like Algiers than like Alexandria or Rosetta. Here there was no Greek influence. Islamic architecture dominated; above the center of the city towered the Cairo Citadel, a twelfth-century bastion that reminded him of the kasbahs he had seen in Algiers and other North African cities. Most buildings were two- or three-story affairs that shone blindingly white in the sun. Low-growing date palms and other attractive flora shaded the narrow streets. Veering off from these better-traveled streets were narrower alleyways that seemed ideal for the purposes of thieves and cutthroats lurking in the shadows.

At the front door to the consulate, which was located on an attractive thoroughfare within a compound of other foreign consulates packed tightly together, Major Misset returned the stiff salutes of two armed sentries. The sentries parted to allow Misset, Richard, and Agreen to enter. Just inside the door an Egyptian wearing a loose-fitting robe, short jacket, and white *taqiyah* on his head bowed before them.

"This servant will show you to your quarters," Missett advised Richard and Agreen. "We shall prepare accommodation for Mr. Corbett and Mr. Osborn, as well. Your Marines may bivouac, so to speak, in the barracks behind this building. There is plenty of room in there, and it's really quite comfortable. Are such accommodations acceptable?"

"Quite acceptable, Major," Richard replied.

There was little for the Americans to do but wait during the days that followed. So wait they did, in ever-deepening impatience and anxiety as day after day accumulated into a week without any word from Hamet or any of the three couriers sent to find him. They walked about occasionally simply to have something to do, always alert for trouble and always keeping within sight of the consulate. No one had much appetite for sightseeing; the subject of the Pyramids or the Sphinx or other Egyptian landmarks was rarely broached.

"How long can we just sit here, Richard?" Agreen asked as the first week since leaving Alexandria became the second. They were lounging on a bench beneath the welcome shade of a broad banyan tree. Three Marines leaned against its trunks, their pistols and knives concealed within the robes they were wearing. "Reckon it's time t' send a messenger t' *Portsmouth*?"

Richard used one hand to hold back his thick blond hair while he wiped his brow with his sleeve. Soon after arriving in Cairo they had changed into less formal garb to blend in with the locals. It was far more comfortable in this dry heat than a tight-fitting naval uniform. Even so, their height and European features set them clearly apart from the local population; curious onlookers regarded them warily, and beggars followed them wherever they went.

"Let's give it two more days, Agee. If we've heard nothing by then, I'll ask the major to dispatch a messenger to Alexandria. If another week goes by and we still have no word, we'll rejoin the ship."

"Can't happen soon enough for me. This place makes me miss home and family all the more."

"I'm with you on that, Agee. I have no more love for this place than you do. And there's nothing worse than sitting around all day doing nothing, no matter where you are. But remember, I have a somewhat different perspective on all this. I'm the one who has to report to Captain Preble."

"Hell's bells, Richard, Preble can't fault you. We've given this mission everything we had, and then some. I'll stand beside you a hundred times over."

"I know you will, but that's not the point. This is likely our only opportunity to meet with Hamet. So much is riding on it, yet we're powerless to make it happen. We have to rely entirely on others. *Damn*, it's frustrating."

"Can't Ali help?" Agreen probed. According to the British, Muhammad Ali had promised Hamet Karamanli safe passage should he venture to Cairo. He was pleased to do so, he announced, since whatever Hamet might discuss with the Americans would likely mean the Tripolitan's departure from Egypt.

"I doubt it. I don't know how far we can push Ali, and I don't know how much we can trust him either. Major Misset advised me not to make contact with him. That should tell you something."

Agreen contemplated that, then said, "Hell, Richard, for all we know, Hamet may be dead, sprawled out in some dark alley with his throat slashed."

"For all we know," Richard had to agree.

Five days later, three days after a messenger had been dispatched north to Alexandria with orders to Lieutenant Lee to delay *Portsmouth*'s departure, a small entourage appeared before the two sentries at the front steps of the British consulate. There was nothing unusual about that. Unexpected visitors appeared at the consulate at all hours of the day and night seeking personal or political favors. But these three men were ushered inside without the usual protocol, and their introduction to the majordomo ignited a flurry of activity among the consulate staff.

Richard heard the quick step of feet on the stairs leading up to his room on the second floor, followed by a firm rap on the door. He looked up from the daily journal he was keeping. "Enter."

An Egyptian staff member opened the door. "You have visitors, Captain Cutler," he announced in well-practiced English.

Richard's senses came alert. "Mr. Karamanli?" he asked.

"I believe so, sir."

Richard put down his pen. "Inform Mr. Crabtree," he said. "Tell him, dress uniform." As quickly as the process allowed, he changed into his own uniform, draped at the ready over a nearby chair. After a careful self-examination before a mirror and a quick adjustment to his black neck stock, he walked out of his room and down the stairway, forcing himself to move slowly, deliberately, as though he were attending to a routine matter.

In a large, well-appointed room immediately to the right of the front hallway Richard found Major Misset along with three men dressed alike in loose-fitting shirts, baggy pants, and yellow slippers. Each of the three men wore a turban-like headdress, and each had the hawklike features typical of North Africans, although one had darker skin. At first, Richard could not identify the prince among them. No one stood out as such. It was not until Major Missett made the introduction that Richard realized that the darker-skinned man was Hamet Karamanli.

At first blush he was not impressed. Hamet was tall but slightly built. His face was long and narrow with sunken cheeks and thin lips largely hidden by his ebony mustache and short-cropped beard. Hamet acknowledged the introduction to Richard Cutler with a polite bow but remained beside his two companions—bodyguards, Richard surmised—who stood mutely alert with arms folded.

Richard returned Hamet's bow. "Your Excellency," he said, "I am, as you have heard from Major Misset, a captain in the United States Navy. I am here as a personal representative of my country." After several moments of awkward silence, during which time Agreen Crabtree entered the room, Richard added, "My first lieutenant and I"—he motioned toward Agreen—"are informed that you have a certain command of the English language. Would it please Your Excellency to discuss the matter before us in English?" Hamet nodded. "In that case, you will understand me when I say that my president, Mr. Thomas Jefferson, sends you his respects and the respects of the American people. We as a united country wish to see you restored to the throne of Tripoli. It is your rightful place."

Hamet bowed in response. "Thank you, Captain Cutler," he said in clear but heavily accented English. "May I ask, where is Captain Eaton? I expected to see him here today."

"I understand, Your Excellency. Captain Eaton sends you his respects as well. At the moment he is in Washington conferring with Mr. Jefferson. He will soon be returning to the Mediterranean. When he does, he will contact you directly."

"I see," Hamet said. Then, wasting no words, "Does Mr. Jefferson remain committed to my cause?"

Richard was not caught unaware by the question, but he was surprised that it was raised so quickly and in so curt a tone. No diplomatic niceties for this prince of Tripoli, he thought to himself. He was grateful when Major Misset bade everyone sit down—which everyone did save for the two Mamelukes—and offered refreshments. Hamet politely declined, and the Americans followed suit. The major bowed and left the room, closing the twin doors behind him.

Rather than answer Hamet's question directly, Richard steered around it by first asking Hamet about his affairs in Egypt, hoping to understand the man before trying to assess his leadership qualities. Hamet answered Richard's questions but offered few details. He displayed no emotion until the subject of his wife and children arose. Of all the reasons Hamet Karamanli had for hating his brother Yusuf, Richard quickly surmised, the upstart ruler's treatment of his family was first among them. Richard spoke briefly about his own wife and children, underscoring his love for them and swearing that he would move heaven and earth, if necessary, to free them from bondage. Hamet's stern face softened. He even offered a faint smile, a signal of solidarity between two men who despite vast differences in pedigree and lifestyle were husbands and parents first, and warriors second.

"I wish to know, Captain Cutler," Hamet reiterated when Richard's questions had run their course, "the answer to my initial query. Does your country still support my cause? Or does it not?" This time he posed the question in a less strident tone.

"I am not in a position to answer you, Your Excellency," Richard replied forthrightly. "It is not my place to speak for my president on such matters. Captain Eaton is more informed on that subject, and I am certain he will answer your question immediately upon his return to the Mediterranean."

"Then can you tell me, Captain, what *is* your place, exactly? Why did you and your lieutenant wish to speak with me today?"

Richard did not hesitate. "To understand, Your Excellency, if *you* are committed to your cause."

To Richard's surprise, Hamet laughed out loud. "That was nicely put, Captain Cutler, I must say! Nicely put indeed!" With those words the dove became an eagle. Hamet's mild voice hardened into the tones of a military commander. "Since you are honest with me, Captain," he said, "I can be honest with you. I am not the only one committed to my cause. Others, many thousands of others, will fight for me. And I do not count among them the legions of my countrymen who will rise to my banner when I cross from Egypt into Cyrenaica. Greek mercenaries skilled with cannon are prepared to do battle for me. And many others will swell my ranks. Mr. Farquhar informs me that once we are assured of your government's support, no one will be able to stop us."

Richard winced at the mention of Farquhar. The Scotsman was already hard at work.

"You say you wish to see me restored to the throne of Tripoli? Let me assure you, Captain: your president has the power to make that happen. And once I am restored, I pledge that peace and friendship shall exist between our two countries for generations to come. The United States will never again go to war in the Mediterranean."

Richard shot Agreen a glance and received a small nod in reply. The fundamental question of the day had just been answered to their mutual satisfaction.

As the Americans were leaving Cairo for Alexandria, Edward Preble in Syracuse received a dispatch from Navy Secretary Robert Smith. A fourth squadron, Smith advised, was gathering in Hampton Roads. The frigates *Congress*, *Essex*, and *John Adams* were preparing to sail from Virginia for the Mediterranean in late June. *President* and two brigs of war would follow two weeks later. Preble was at first elated, thinking that these ships were the reinforcements he had most earnestly requested from headquarters. But as he read on, his mood darkened.

USS *President*, the dispatch continued, would convey Capt. Samuel Barron to the Mediterranean. Preble knew Barron—and his reputation as a sea officer who never questioned orders on his steady rise up the promotion ladder. And he had seniority over Preble. Upon his arrival at Syracuse, Smith confirmed, Captain Barron would assume command of the Mediterranean Squadron.

Smith's dispatch included words of high praise for Preble's service to his country. Smith even quoted Admiral Lord Nelson's widely publicized remark that the burning of USS *Philadelphia* was "the most bold and daring act of the age." But the American people had reached the limits of their tolerance for this war, Smith continued; and the president, the president's cabinet, and Congress viewed the current expansion of naval forces in the Mediterranean as a final initiative by the United States to force Yusuf to the bargaining table. If this initiative failed, the communiqué concluded, Consul General Tobias Lear was instructed to offer Tripoli twenty thousand dollars for making peace, plus five hundred dollars per man for *Philadelphia*'s officers and crew, plus ten thousand dollars in annual tribute. Preble bristled on reading those ludicrous terms. Had President Jefferson allowed political expediency to trump his oft-stated principles? Was the U.S. government now prepared to pay an annual tribute to Tripoli in addition to agreeing to crippling peace terms? Preble could not believe it.

But as he reread the dispatch, his lips creased in a tight smile. He felt his mood brightening, the anger lifting. He was still commodore of this squadron, by God, and he would be for at least two more months—perhaps three, God willing. That was all the time he needed. His squadron was ready. He had even received, at long last, the six gunboats and two mortar boats promised by Sir John Acton, the prime minister of the kingdom of Sicily. Every ship in his squadron except *Portsmouth* was standing by. For a fleeting moment Preble thought to recall her from blockade duty in the Gulf of Sidra. He could surely use her guns in the assault. But he pushed away that notion. Her mission was critical, and besides, Preble could not wait for her to return. Circumstances had forced him to act, to move up his timetable. He had to strike, and he had to strike *now*.

Eleven

Off the City of Tripoli,
August 1804

AUGUST 3 DAWNED bright and sunny. The calm seas with long, rolling swells were a welcome relief after the fierce northwesterly gales that had plagued the fifteen-ship American squadron for more than a week. Commo. Edward Preble strolled the windward side of his flush quarterdeck in the early afternoon in a casual fashion meant to inspire confidence in his officers and crew that he was at peace with himself and with his God, a naval commander of resolve with whom they could trust their lives without question or regret. *Constitution* stood two miles off the coast and was approaching Tripoli under reduced sail on a south-southwesterly course. A glance at the telltale high on a mizzen shroud confirmed that the northeasterly breeze was holding steady, perhaps even freshening a bit. *A good omen,* Preble told himself. A glance to larboard revealed six flat-bottomed, 60-foot, lateen-rigged gunboats, each towed by one of the squadron's two brigs and three schooners, with the brig of war *Argus* towing two. Directly aft he could see the two bomb ketches also on loan from the king of Sicily that his own flagship was towing. Following farther behind was the squadron's store-ship carrying extra ordnance and provisions.

It was what lay directly ahead, however, that demanded Preble's attention. Nineteen enemy gunboats had emerged through the Western Passage between Kaliuscia and Ra's az Zur reefs and had dropped anchor in a battle formation running east to west in a line between Molehead Battery, located at the head of the mole where the treacherous outcroppings of the two reefs began, and French Fort to the southwest. These two batteries formed the western edge of the city's seaward defenses. Behind the reefs, near the base of the city walls, three small cruisers rode at anchor, each with a spring line made fast to her anchor cable to allow her guns to be maneuvered into position to cover the main passageways through the chain of rocks. A sweep of the spyglass farther to eastward revealed the bashaw's castle at the northeast corner of the city and, farther still, the English Fort. Within those batteries, Preble had been informed, were 115 cannon aimed out to sea—at his squadron. And unlike the American naval guns, these cannon were mounted on stable platforms and protected by stonework fortifications.

Preble smirked as he again raised the glass and peered at the city of Tripoli. The citizens who had taken to the rooftops and upper terraces clearly entertained no doubts about the outcome of the upcoming battle. They appeared in a festive mood. Some waved small Tripolitan flags while others pumped fists up and down in the air, all clearly anticipating the thrashing the upstart Americans were about to receive.

"Signal the squadron to come within hailing distance," Preble said to his first lieutenant. "Then wear her around on a starboard tack and back the main tops'l. And Mr. Gordon, you may clear for action."

Charles Gordon touched his hat. He repeated the first order to Joseph Nicholson, the signal midshipman standing by. The second order he repeated to Nate Haraden, the ship's master, who repeated it to Boatswain John Cannon and the two quartermasters at the helm. The third order was his to deliver.

"Beat to quarters! Clear for action!"

The commands ignited a flurry of staccato tattoos from Marine drummers that sent men scurrying to battle stations. On the weather and gun decks, sailors removed and stowed cabin partitions, chests, paintings, tables, everything and anything portable that might shatter and explode into shards of lethal spears if struck by enemy shot. Others distributed kegs of water throughout the ship to put out fires set off by hot shot launched from the enemy batteries ashore. Still others strewed wet sand about the gun deck to ensure better footing in the slurry of spilt blood.

As the flagship prepared for battle, officers, sailors, and Marines on the smaller American brigs and schooners stepped aboard the gunboats to which they had been assigned, joining the Sicilian and Neapolitan crews charged with sailing each vessel. Lt. Richard Somers in gunboat 1 commanded the First Division, which also comprised gunboat 2, captained by Lt. James Decatur, and gunboat 3, captained by Lt. Joshua

Blake. Lt. Stephen Decatur in gunboat 4 commanded the Second Division, which also included gunboat 5, captained by Lt. Joseph Bainbridge, and gunboat 6, captained by Lt. John Trippe. A junior officer assumed first-officer rank aboard each vessel.

As the brigs and schooners with their charges in tow came to within hailing distance of the flagship, Commodore Preble repeated his orders to each captain in turn. His battle strategy was as simple in objective as it was flexible in implementation. American gunboats would stand in toward the reefs and attack the Tripolitan flotilla while the two bomb ketches lobbed mortar shells over the city walls. *Constitution* and the squadron would join the fray as conditions warranted.

At 2:00 *Constitution* hoisted the signal for "Cast off all boats and follow my maneuvers." Sailing under reduced canvas to allow the heavyset gunboats to proceed on ahead of the flagship, she shaped a southwesterly course for Tripoli. *Syren*, *Enterprise*, *Argus*, and *Vixen* cast loose their towing cables and fanned out to eastward of her. The two bomb ketches, cast loose from *Constitution*, followed a course parallel to the flagship's. For reasons unknown, *Nautilus* sailed out ahead alone, farther to westward, with gunboat 1 still in tow.

At 2:30 Preble ordered a blue flag hoisted up the signal halyard, followed by a yellow flag and another blue flag. It was signal 170: "Commence battle."

Aboard gunboat 4, Midn. James Cutler pointed westward and said to his commanding officer, "Sir, *Nautilus* has fallen off to leeward. She's cast off her boat, but in these conditions Lieutenant Somers will be hard-pressed beating back to us."

Stephen Decatur was already aware of what, in effect, had forced the commander of the First Division out of the battle plan. The gunboat's lateen rig was too slight, her construction too bulky and beamy, for her to tack or row upwind. She was built primarily for harbor defense, not as an attack vessel. "Unfortunately, Mr. Cutler," he said stiffly, "there is not much we can do about that. I suggest we attend to our own business. Is the gun loaded with case shot?" He was referring to the 24-pounder gun mounted at the bow of the boat. The gun could pivot slightly to the right or left, but for all intents and purposes it shot in the direction the bow pointed.

The first chore Jamie had assigned himself on boarding the gunboat was to ensure that her lone gun was properly loaded with a canister of four hundred small iron balls crammed inside a cylindrical tin case, and that additional case, grape, and round shot were secured aft of the gun in specially designed racks alongside neatly stacked piles of flannel powder bags. Each gunboat was, in effect, a floating bomb set to explode should its stack of munitions suffer a direct hit.

"Yes, sir. Loaded and primed."

"Very well. Serve out a musket to every man and await my order."

"Aye, aye, sir."

Jamie Cutler followed his captain's glance to starboard. Gunboat 2 was making toward them, its captain, Decatur's brother James, apparently having drawn a similar conclusion about gunboat 1. Lieutenant Blake in gunboat 3 followed too far behind and to the east to join them. Stephen Decatur now found himself in command of a squadron of five—effectively, four—gunboats.

At 2:45 Lt. Thomas Robinson in bomb ketch 1 opened fire. Bomb ketch 2, Lt. John Dent in command, followed suit almost at once. Lobbed high into the air, the two 27-inch mortar shells seemed to hesitate at their apex before screeching down onto the enemy positions below. One shell exploded near the Molehead Battery. The other shrieked over the city wall.

Enemy cannon, silent up to now, opened fire with stentorian blasts that rippled harbor waters from English Fort to French Fort. They aimed not at the six American gunboats—Tripoli had nineteen gunboats prepared to deal with them—but at the American squadron a mile offshore.

The American flotilla led by gunboat 4 bore down on the east wing of the enemy gunboats, the wind at its back. When gunboat 4 had closed unchallenged to within fifty yards, Decatur gave the command for its 24-pounder to open fire, the effect of a massive blunderbuss fired at nearly point-blank range. The three gunboats fanned out behind number 4 unleashed their own blasts of grape, case, or round shot. Crews quickly reloaded and fired a second round of hot iron before the enemy could respond.

One Tripolitan gunboat exploded. Others on the east wing suffered a withering broadside from the larboard batteries of *Constitution* and her consorts. In the time it took for the smoke to clear, enemy gunboats in the east and center of the defensive formation, stunned by tactics they had not anticipated, had severed their anchor cables and were retreating back into the harbor through the Western Passage.

The more substantial west wing of the enemy flotilla remained to be dealt with. From what Decatur could discern, the enemy gunboats in that wing were not about to cut and run. He signaled his boats to sail directly at them. As the two opposing forces converged, the squadron's big guns fell silent.

The Tripolitans' west wing, eleven boats strong, opened fire too early, before the Americans were in "dead-on" range. The salvo chewed up railings and bulwarks and bits of masts on the American boats, but claimed neither loss of life nor serious damage except to gunboat 5, which saw the upper end of its lateen yard severed. Americans who had crouched low when the onslaught began sprang to their feet and fired a "boarding dose" of canister, grape, and heavy musketry that temporarily cleared enemy decks and allowed their boats to sail in and smack hard against the Tripolitan boats.

Stephen Decatur, his sword drawn, leapt aboard a Tripolitan gunboat. Jamie Cutler landed on deck behind him, a pistol in each hand and two others tied to a lanyard looped around his neck.

"*To me!*" Decatur cried out. Seventeen Americans brandishing boarding pikes, tomahawks, belaying pins, cutlasses, and pistols swarmed onto the enemy boat's deck. Opposing them were three dozen Tripolitans gathered in close array. A volley of pistol shot from the Americans quickly evened the odds.

Side-by-side, Decatur and Cutler fought off five Arabs lunging in at them. Steel clashed and clanged against steel. The enemy gunboat's commander, a massive hulk of a man with bare rippling biceps, apparently identified Decatur as the American commander and came at him with vengeance in his eyes. Decatur parried his first thrust, then his second, but on the third surge the Tripolitan caught Decatur off guard and slashed down hard with his scimitar, breaking the cutlass at the haft. Decatur tossed aside the useless weapon and charged the Arab, tackling him around the waist and throwing him backward onto the deck. He whacked the Arab's bearded face with one fist, then with the other. But the Arab, bigger and stronger, grabbed Decatur's wrist and slowly, gradually, by sheer strength of arm muscle, forced Decatur up and back, pinning him against the gunwale. His left forearm was clamped hard against Decatur's throat, blocking his windpipe; in his right hand he raised a single-edged, bayonet-style knife. Just as the man was about to slice down with the yataghan, Decatur found his pistol. Mustering his last ounce of strength, he thrust the short barrel against the Arab's ribs and squeezed the trigger. The ball searing through the Arab's kidneys was greeted on the other side by James Cutler's blade. A savage blow to the back of the head by a

Marine's tomahawk shattered his skull, and the Arab slumped over, dead, into the ever-expanding pools of blood overwashing the deck.

Jamie dropped to a knee beside his commander, who lay supine, gasping for air. He searched Decatur's body for wounds but found none, just heavy bruises on his neck and face, including an ugly black eye. "Are you all right, sir?" he asked.

"I'll manage, thank you, Mr. Cutler," Decatur wheezed, his lungs still wild for air. "Pray, give me a moment. And a hand, if you would." He was trying to raise himself to a sitting position against the gunwale so that he could take stock of the battle while he caught his breath. Jamie helped him up. Decatur nodded his appreciation. "What's our situation?" he demanded.

"We've taken the boat, Captain."

"I can see that. Casualties?"

"One dead. Three wounded."

"Enemy casualties?"

"We have a handful of prisoners. The rest are either dead or wounded."

"What of the other boats?"

"Uncertain. My apologies, sir, but my attention was drawn to you once Daniels"—he gestured toward the Marine private who had wielded the tomahawk—"and I were able to fight our way over."

Decatur summoned a weak smile. "Under the circumstances, Mr. Cutler, no apology is required." He made to rise. "Help me up, please. I'm feeling a lot better."

On his feet and gripping the starboard gunwale for balance, Decatur, with Jamie beside him, surveyed the arena of battle, a series of close-action boarding engagements stretching perhaps a quarter-mile along the outer edge of the two reefs. The Tripolitan batteries ashore posed no threat for now. Their cannon were mounted too high to bring to bear. A quick scan of the harbor confirmed that at least one cruiser, a galliot judging by her two-masted rig, was preparing to make sail and join the fray.

"Look, sir," Jamie said in delight.

Decatur looked in the direction Jamie was pointing. Preble had also noted the enemy cruiser's intention. *Enterprise* and *Argus* were sailing on a course of interception.

Decatur swung his gaze back to the battle at hand. It was nearing a successful conclusion, notwithstanding the odds against them. Lieutenant Trippe in gunboat 6 had captured not one but two enemy vessels, each mounting a bright, brass, 24-pounder howitzer. Another enemy boat, seemingly without a crew, was drifting away from gunboat 5 toward the rocks beneath the Molehead Battery. Suddenly that boat exploded in a flash of yellow-orange flame.

"Lieutenant Bainbridge must have set a charge on her before cutting her loose," Jamie commented.

"Well done," Decatur said softly. In a much louder voice, with his hands cupped at his mouth, he shouted out at the bashaw's castle, "I hope you are watching your brother in action, William!" He was calling to William Bainbridge, *Philadelphia*'s captain, held prisoner in that castle.

Decatur swung his glass over to where his own brother was exchanging fierce musket and blunderbuss fire with the second enemy gunboat in line. He held his breath as he watched the enemy gunboat under attack being reinforced by the Tripolitan boat third in line, its crew jumping from one boat to the other until they had joined forces with their comrades and were preparing to board gunboat 2. Suddenly, the 24-pounder on the American gunboat spewed orange flame and white sparks. A steel fist of grapeshot punched across the decks of both enemy vessels, killing or maiming everyone in its path, taking the lifeblood and the fight out of the enemy. The handful of Arabs left standing threw down their weapons as their captain, another burly slab of a man with a wide face and short-cropped black beard, ordered the flag of Tripoli hauled down.

"Well, that's that," Stephen Decatur commented.

To the east, behind them, the galliot that had boldly beaten out around the eastern edge of the reefs had come under fire. A well-aimed shot hurled from one of the two American warships had slammed into the galliot's mainmast, tearing out a sizable chunk of wood. Crippled, her mainmast teetering, the galliot turned and limped back into the harbor without having fired a shot.

On the western side of the mole, Lieutenant Somers in gunboat 1, having failed in his effort to sail upwind to join the battle before the reefs, came off the wind to southward toward five enemy gunboats that had come around the mole to attack him. The Molehead Battery did not join fire; mortar shells continued to streak in and explode near the fort and inside the city. One shell fell directly in front of the five enemy gunboats. Its backwash surged over them, capsizing the lead vessel, heavily laden with enemy personnel, and swamping the second. As the three remaining enemy gunboats struggled in the confusion of roiled waters, Lieutenant Somers gave them a healthy dose of grapeshot followed by a dose of canister shot. Somers came off the wind and beat northward toward *Vixen,* which was sailing in fast to the rescue.

"Well, Mr. Cutler," Decatur said as he surveyed what was left to survey, "it seems we have won the day. Assuming, of course, we can figure out how to get back to the squadron!"

"Captain," Jamie gasped. Something he had seen through his glass made his blood run cold and his intestines twist. "*Captain*!" he shouted in a voice thick with despair.

Decatur focused his glass on gunboat 2. The enemy gunboat had surrendered, yes, but its captain and remaining crew had leapt aboard another Tripolitan gunboat and were making sail toward the Western Passage a hundred yards away. He scoured the deck of gunboat 2 with the glass. "Where's James?" he demanded.

"He's been shot, sir," Jamie said softly.

"*Shot?*"

"Yes, sir. He was boarding the Tripolitan to take her as a prize when her captain, the one who surrendered, shot him in the head."

"*Jesus Christ*!" What Decatur observed through the lens of his glass confirmed the horrible truth of Jamie's words. Midn. Octavius Paige, second in command, was supervising the gunboat's crew as they hauled the limp body of James Decatur from the water.

Stephen Decatur collapsed his glass with a snap. He pointed at the fleeing enemy gunboat. "Cut that bastard off!" he bellowed. "Cut him off! Bring up the goddamn sweeps and set every shred of canvas we have! I'll pursue that whore's son through the gates of hell if I have to. I *will* avenge my brother!"

Out at sea, *Constitution* hoisted the signal for "Cover the boats." As the squadron stood in close to unleash its guns at a cluster of Tripolitan gunboats emerging through the Western Passage, gunboat 4 took off in hot pursuit of the enemy boat fleeing toward that passage. Batteries ashore returned fire. Plumes of white water shot into the air and rained down on the American gunboat while round shot and bar-shot screamed and whined back and forth overhead like some ghastly battle between prehistoric birds. One shot, of friend or foe, lashed the sea to larboard of gunboat 4 and a massive column of seawater soaked the deck with spray, its backwash carrying the boat forward in its clutch like a sled out of control on a steep, slippery hill and threatening to bring it down pell-mell against the larboard quarter of the fleeing enemy boat.

"Brace for impact!" Decatur shouted.

Jamie seized hold of the larboard gunwale and spread his legs. "Let fly the sheets!" he cried. "Stand by to heave grappling hooks!"

The helmsman wrenched the tiller to windward. Sailors heaved small grappling hooks at the fast-approaching enemy vessel. Others released the sheets, spilling the wind from the lateen sail. Then everyone hung on to something for dear life. Seconds later there was a blinding crash.

"*Board!*" Decatur cried the instant the two gunboats were lashed fast together.

Decatur leapt aboard the enemy boat and swiped his sword against the mainsheet, severing the rope and rendering the sail impotent, taking the way off the vessel. Ahead, in the passage, Tripolitan gunboats were buckling under the withering broadsides of the American squadron coming at them in line-of-battle array. *Constitution* was in the van; *Vixen*, *Syren*, *Argus*, *Nautilus*, and *Enterprise* followed in her wake. Overhead, two mortar shells shrieked unholy terror as they streaked down over the walls of Tripoli. One shell exploded inside the city.

Decatur had no trouble identifying the enemy captain. He crouched amidships, a scimitar in his left hand and a raised pistol in his right. Decatur dropped to the deck a split second before the man fired, and the shot hit a Marine directly behind him. The Arab threw his pistol at Decatur, missed, and then charged him, his scimitar raised for battle.

Outnumbered three to one, the Americans fought like demons, taking their cue from their commanding officer, who, possessed by fiery rage, had sliced open two Arabs with his sword before taking on the Tripolitan captain. Steel blades lunged and parried, lunged and parried, Decatur seeking to find and control the flow of the fight, to seize advantage of a sudden opening. Finally he found it. As the Arab took hold of his sword with both hands and raised his arms for one great defining swing of the blade, Decatur lunged in and stabbed him in the stomach. Thrusting his weight forward, he drove the blade in deeper, burying it almost to the haft. The Arab's scimitar slid from his grip. For several moments he stared down at his red-soaked shirt, then lifted dimming eyes to stare at Decatur, his mouth opening as if to ask a question, before he slumped over, dead. Decatur withdrew his sword and wiped the bloody blade on the Arab's baggy trousers.

"You fight like a woman!" he spat down at him.

"The boat is ours, Captain," Jamie Cutler informed him. "The enemy has surrendered."

Decatur blinked. "You're wounded, Mr. Cutler." He took Jamie's right arm in both his hands and examined a deep gash oozing blood.

"It's just a scratch, sir."

"It's rather more than a scratch," Decatur said. He called to a sailor standing by. "See to Mr. Cutler. Do not leave his side until he is back aboard *Constitution* and in the care of Dr. Wells."

"Aye, aye, sir," the sailor said.

Decatur glared darkly at the Arab sailors who had dropped their weapons on the deck and now stood with heads bowed, avoiding the sight of their butchered commander, fearful, no doubt, of what the wild-eyed American commander might have in store for them.

"Tie them up," Decatur snarled. "Tie up every God-cursed one of them and get them out of my sight!" He turned away and glanced northward to where an armada of launches, gigs, and barges was fast approaching the American gunboats to help get them and their prizes out of harm's way.

THE NEXT MORNING, as *Constitution* stood six miles off the coast, Samuel Elbert spotted a small two-masted vessel approaching the flagship from the direction of Tripoli. "Mr. Wadsworth," the third lieutenant said to his junior duty officer, "light below and advise the captain that we have a visitor."

Midn. Henry Wadsworth saluted. "Aye, aye, sir."

Edward Preble came on deck and watched in silence as the small rig hove to a short distance from the flagship and lowered away a boat. Four oarsmen and a coxswain climbed down into the boat, followed by a burly, informally dressed man sporting a chest-length red-copper beard.

"Shall I order boarding honors, sir?" Elbert inquired.

"No," was Preble's prompt reply, and he said nothing further until the bearded man had clambered up the flagship's built-in steps.

The visitor looked about with an appreciative eye as he was escorted to the quarterdeck. He bowed when introduced to Edward Preble. "*Bonjour, capitaine. Je m'appelle . . .*" He switched to English when Preble frowned at the use of French aboard his ship. "I am Pierre Mercellise," he said. "I am master of *le vaisseau*"—he pointed to starboard—"*Le Ruse*."

"An apt name, I am sure." The irony in Preble's reply was lost on the Frenchman, although it made Elbert smile.

"You are a privateer," Preble stated. He had noticed the vessel's four guns mounted two to a side.

"*Oui, monsieur, un corsaire*," Mercellise acknowledged. "But fear not," he added with an ingratiating smile. "I have not come to do battle with your *frégate*." His smile quickly faded when Preble remained stone-faced. Earlier that morning, Preble had buried at sea six of his command, one of whom was Lt. James Decatur, and he was in no mood for frivolity.

"Monsieur," the Frenchman said, his tone turning deferential, "I have come to give you this." He withdrew a sealed letter from an inside vest pocket and handed it to Preble.

"It is from Monsieur Beaussier, *l'émissaire français en Tripoli*," he explained as Preble broke the wax seal and unfolded the paper. The commodore's brow creased and his eyes narrowed as he read down the page. When he had finished reading, he handed the letter to his first lieutenant to read, saying quietly, "More French bullshit."

"*Il y aura une réponse?*" the Frenchman asked hopefully, slipping into his native tongue after too many minutes had elapsed with Preble absorbed in thought. "*Monsieur Beaussier espère très beaucoup que vous répondrez à lui.*" He cleared his throat and translated. "Mr. Beaussier hopes very much that you will respond to him, *capitaine.*"

"I have no response, Monsieur Mercellise," Preble announced. "And there will be no boat tomorrow afternoon. Thank you for your time and trouble in this matter. It is appreciated. Mr. Wadsworth, please see this gentleman off. Please send with him the most seriously wounded of our prisoners."

Preble turned on his heel and disappeared belowdecks to his after cabin. It was not until that evening, during the 7:00 meeting, that he informed his officers of what had transpired on deck that morning.

"Yusuf Karamanli," Preble told them, holding high the French consul's letter, "would apparently prefer to bury himself under the ruins of his capital city than accept humiliating terms of peace. He has sent women and children into the countryside and has vowed to keep his men at their posts day and night, to fight us to their last breath if necessary. However, if I, Commodore Preble, truly desire peace, and agree to a ransom of five hundred dollars per man for the release of *Philadelphia*'s crew, plus twenty thousand for making peace, plus a paltry ten thousand in annual tribute, then I am to send a boat to the Western Passage at eight bells tomorrow afternoon under a white flag of truce." Preble ripped the letter in half. "Beaussier strongly recommends that I accept these terms on behalf of our government. They are, he claims, the same terms that Secretary Madison has authorized Tobias Lear to offer the bashaw. Oh, I should add that Monsieur Beaussier will personally guarantee the safety of those I send ashore in the boat. That is reason enough to reject this offer."

Preble balled up the two halves of the letter, walked over to a basket, and dropped them in. Then he turned to face his officers, his face taut with anger. "I have a different plan," he announced. "Tripoli has seen a significant number of its gunboats destroyed or captured as a result of recent action. One of its cruisers is severely damaged. Parts of the city are still ablaze from our mortar fire, and we have inflicted considerable damage to the westward defenses. What's more, we have thirty of the enemy as prisoners—less the four we sent ashore this morning with the Frenchman—and we have sent dozens more to the grave. Gentlemen, if one strike from our squadron has induced Mr. Karamanli to so urgently seek peace with us, might not a second strike heat things up a bit more? And make our peace terms seem more reasonable to the bashaw?"

These were rhetorical questions. No one was expected to respond, and no one did.

Twelve

Off the City of Tripoli,
September 1804

C APTAIN PREBLE WAS tired,
cranky, and worried. He couldn't
remember his last decent night's
sleep. The bravado and swagger he had exhibited after the first attack on
Tripoli had largely gone by the boards. Subsequent forays had proven to
be inconclusive, including the bold attack on August 7 led by Lt. Charles
Stewart. During that assault, American bomb ketches and gunboats had
crept into the bay on the westward side of the mole, the same spot where
Lieutenant Somers had found himself during the battle on August 3. From
there, Stewart and Somers had convinced their commanding officer, they
could bombard the city almost at will because the cannon in Molehead
Battery and French Fort were trained out to sea, not at the bay behind
them. And if vessels of the Tripolitan Navy dared to sail out and challenge the Americans, the squadron's brigs and schooners could sweep in
to engage them.

It seemed a perfect battle plan, except for two unanticipated factors.
Beneath the placid surface waters of the inner bay ran strong westbound
currents and undertows that made the clumsy Sicilian gunboats difficult
to maneuver. In addition, as if reading the mind of the American
commodore, Yusuf Karamanli had ordered two additional batteries
erected on the mole to cover the bay: one of five cannon, the other—
dubbed the Vixen Battery by the Americans—of eight cannon. Both
positions had been blasted out of action on August 7, but the squadron
had accomplished little else of note. Most mortar shells that fell into the

city, according to accounts delivered to *Constitution* from the French and Danish consuls, had fallen in the Jewish Quarter. The damage wrought might have some psychological value, but it had no significant military value. Worse, many of those mortar shells had failed to explode. The most probable reason for that, Preble mused, was because no American sea officer in his squadron had managed to master the requisite artillery skills. In Syracuse he had retained the services of renowned Neapolitan bombardier Don Antonio Massi to instruct his officers in the art of artillery and mortar fire. But Massi's instruction, as sound as it was in theory, was of a classroom variety lacking any sort of live combat experience. Worse still, those mortar shells that had exploded within the city and might have ignited a conflagration had fallen on buildings constructed of stone and dried mud.

But the most distressing news of all had arrived three weeks ago on an American naval vessel. Master Commandant Isaac Chauncey, captain of the frigate *John Adams*, had sailed to Tripoli carrying three dispatches for Commodore Preble from Navy Secretary Robert Smith and Secretary of State James Madison. The fourth squadron was under way, Smith reported, and should be in the Mediterranean by mid-September. Capt. Samuel Barron in USS *President* would assume command of the squadron immediately upon his arrival in Syracuse. Although Smith praised Preble's performance, the cold reality was that his command of the Mediterranean Squadron could now be measured in days—perhaps a week at best.

The sands in the hourglass were running out. If Preble were to contribute in a meaningful fashion to the outcome of this war—and be judged favorably by his superiors and by history—he had to act soon. After mulling over his options, Preble decided on a strategy that no one could have anticipated, not even his squadron commanders.

Peace negotiations with Karamanli and Foreign Secretary Dghies were dead. It galled Preble to admit that Beaussier was right, but just as the French consul had predicted, his failure to strike a crippling blow against Tripoli during the previous two months had raised both enemy morale and the price of peace. Under no conditions would Preble hazard his reputation by agreeing to pay an amount for ransom and tribute that ran contrary to both government policy and his own sense of ethics. To his mind, a military solution still provided the only viable gateway to peace with honor.

Preble had a plan. Some people, he readily acknowledged to himself, would consider it a plan born of desperation. But few, he was equally convinced, would deem it reckless. Indeed, he had been considering this option for months. He had even written Secretary Smith about it back in March, and last week he had discussed it, in the strictest confidence, with his three commissioned officers. In his considered judgment—and in the judgment of his officers—it had a better than even chance of success. And success might end the war overnight, or at least open wide the door to negotiations for the new commodore. Either way, the credit would go to Preble and to the young men whom he had come to refer to affectionately in his log as "my boys."

Tonight, in his after cabin, he faced his "boys": the officers of his flagship and the commanding officers of the brigs and schooners in his squadron. Every officer in that cabin was considerably younger than he; many were young enough to be his sons. But as was his wont, it was he, Preble, who remained standing while his officers sat.

"Gentlemen," he said to the men seated at the rectangular table and on chairs placed behind, "I bid you welcome. You are, of course, aware of current circumstances. For better or for worse, I am soon to be replaced"— he held up a hand to quell a rumbling of discontent—"and as this will be among our last evenings together as officers of the Mediterranean Squadron, I have instructed my steward to open my personal stores of spirits so that we may raise a glass to one final initiative I have in mind for our Arab friends in Tripoli."

The words "final initiative" and the jovial resolve with which they were spoken seized everyone's attention. Some officers instinctively leaned forward, as though by drawing closer they would receive Preble's information more quickly. Jamie Cutler and Ralph Izard, seated behind them, locked eyes.

"What's he talking about?" Izard whispered to Jamie. He, like the other officers, had assumed that the squadron would now return to Syracuse and mark time awaiting the new commodore. Preble had just implied something quite different. He had infused them with hope. Not an officer in that cabin had anything but the deepest affection and respect for Preble, despite his quirky ways.

"I haven't a clue," Jamie whispered in reply.

Preble cleared his throat, and all eyes turned forward to him. "We are all aware of our situation," he said. "We have discussed it during the course of many evenings. Nevertheless, let me say again—because it bears repeating—that our failure thus far to bring our enemy to his knees is not through any lack of valor or dereliction of duty on the part of anyone in this cabin. I in fact commend each and every one of you for your actions this summer. My service as commodore of this squadron shall be the capstone of my life—my greatest honor as a man and my greatest privilege as a naval officer. Rest assured that whenever I write to the navy secretary or to the president, I shall sing your praises."

He shook his head. "No, the reason we have not, as yet, achieved our primary objective is due, I am sorry to say, to our government's dilly-dallying. Many months ago I was promised, as reinforcements, four additional frigates and a number of gunboats. Thus far, only *John Adams* has materialized, and her I had to dispatch to Syracuse for repairs and outfitting. Had the guns of four frigates been added to our squadron, victory would have been ours by now and we would be home with our wives and sweethearts.

"As for the gunboats we have in our possession," he continued, "we must return them to the king of Sicily, as we agreed to do. Excluding, of course, dear old number nine."

The men all chuckled at that. Preble was referring to an incident three weeks ago in which a captured Tripolitan gunboat, converted to an American gunboat and dubbed gunboat 9, had suffered a direct hit during an assault. The boat had exploded, leaving only its forward half floating amid the flotsam of boat and body parts. As the bow of the gunboat settled slowly into the sea, three survivors managed to reload the gun in a valiant attempt to set off one final round against the enemy. Their attempt failed—the Mediterranean swirled in on them too quickly—but as the bow slipped beneath the waves, the three men held their fists in the air and shouted out three bold huzzahs in defiance. A jolly boat had rushed in to pick them up.

"What we know for certain," Preble went on, " is courtesy of recent night reconnaissance by Lieutenant Decatur and Lieutenant Chauncey. The Tripolitans moor their thirteen remaining gunboats tightly against each other near the city wall with their bows pointing east in a line abreast extending from the Molehead Battery to the bashaw's castle. The larger vessels are anchored in deeper water closer to the reefs.

"My aim," he said after a pause for emphasis, "is to sail a vessel into the harbor between the gunboats and larger vessels, light a fuse, and destroy the Tripolitan Navy where it lies in one fell swoop. With good placement, good timing, and good luck, the explosion should cause severe damage not only to the enemy's ships, but also to Tripoli's shore batteries and to the castle."

Preble stared at his silent officer corps until Stephen Decatur spoke up. "A fire-ship, sir?"

Preble smiled. "Technically, yes, Mr. Decatur. But I prefer to think of her as something rather more than a ketch set ablaze and rammed into enemy vessels. She will be carrying much of the ordnance that remains aboard this squadron."

More silence followed until Master Commandant Isaac Hull of *Argus* asked, tentatively, "Which vessel, Captain? Which vessel will carry that ordnance?"

"*Intrepid*," Preble answered him. "She has already proven her mettle in the attack on *Philadelphia*, and she has only recently rejoined our squadron. Her Mediterranean rig may yet again fool our enemy into believing she is one of theirs, if only for a few minutes. Those few minutes could determine success or failure."

Lt. John Smith, *Vixen*'s captain, asked, "Who will have the honor of commanding this expedition, sir?"

Preble nodded. He had anticipated that question. He knew that to these officers it was the most important question of all. And he knew, without question, that there was not a single man among them who would not beg for the honor.

"I have officers in mind," he acknowledged, "but I would prefer to talk with each of them in private before I decide. This mission, however glorious it may appear, is fraught with risk and peril. It will therefore be strictly a volunteer mission. I will not think any less of a man who declines the opportunity . . . Other questions?" When no one spoke, Preble said, "Excellent. And as I see my steward making his way toward us, I suggest we adjourn our meeting. Drink heartily, my boys. You have earned the right."

THE MARINE PRIVATE on duty outside the captain's day cabin stiffened to attention as Midn. James Cutler stepped down the companionway located amidships at the corner of the lattice-covered main hatch and strode down the gun deck toward him. At the cabin door, Jamie acknowledged the private's salute. "I am here at the commodore's request."

"Aye, Mr. Cutler. He is expecting you, sir. If you will allow me . . ." The Marine pivoted smartly and rapped gently on the door.

"Yes?" a voice inquired from inside.

The Marine opened the door ajar. "Midshipman Cutler to see you, sir."

"Then show the officer in, Private," the gruff voice said.

"Aye, aye, sir."

The Marine gave Jamie a quick grin before he opened the door wide and invited him inside.

Edward Preble welcomed Jamie Cutler into his day cabin and then led the way aft through a second door into his personal quarters, a snug space of comfortable chairs and a settee—good, solid American furniture, none of those spindly European pieces—along with a writing desk, several chests of drawers, and a stately mahogany sideboard. Oil paintings of ships and seascapes graced the bulkheads above shelves specially designed to hold in their leather-bound books. To starboard, the dining alcove; to larboard, the captain's sleeping cuddy.

Jamie had been in these personal chambers before, but on rare occasions and only in the company of more senior officers. To be invited here alone was a singular privilege for a midshipman.

"Please sit down, Mr. Cutler," Preble said, adding, after a pause, "and please relax. You look like you are standing at attention even as you are sitting." His smile was reassuring, in keeping with his voice. "I realize it is early afternoon, but may I offer you a spot of Madeira? I would enjoy sharing a glass with you."

"With pleasure, Captain," Jamie replied. Not normally one to imbibe at this hour of the day, to refuse such an offer from his commanding officer was unthinkable.

"Good, good." Preble ambled over to the sideboard and opened its twin doors. From inside he withdrew a plain glass decanter half-filled with a clear golden liquid. "You and your fellow officers seriously depleted my stores the other night, but *this* excellent Madeira"—he triumphantly held up the decanter for Jamie to see—"I keep safely tucked away, locked up and out of reach." He chuckled as he poured out two glasses. After handing one to Jamie, he sat down on a blue satin–covered settee across from Jamie's chair and crossed one leg over the other. "Cheers," he said, lifting his glass.

"Cheers, Captain," Jamie said, lifting his. He took a sip of the fortified Portuguese wine and felt its exquisite texture course down his throat into his stomach. Never had he tasted a wine so delectable. As if to keep temptation at bay, he placed the glass on a side table. "It *is* delicious, sir. I can appreciate why you have kept it well hidden."

"It *is* frightfully expensive," the captain returned with a smile. "'Waste not, want not' is my motto, especially when it comes to an outstanding

Madeira." After a pause, he said: "We've come a long way, haven't we, since that day you and your father visited me in Maine. On the one hand, it seems as though only a few months have passed. On the other, it seems an eternity. It's been, what, two years?"

"A bit more than that, sir," Jamie replied distractedly. "It was back in April of '02." He had not anticipated this sort of chitchat and was anxious to learn the real reason he had been invited to the captain's inner sanctuary.

"You have been a fine officer," Preble said quite unexpectedly. "You have served me and this ship with distinction and with the highest level of competence. As you have often heard me say, a superior naval commander is distinguished by his ability to *lead*, his ability to *inspire*, and his ability to *anticipate*. From what I have observed, you possess all three qualities. I see something very special in you, James. I see a great future awaiting you in the Navy."

"Thank you, sir," Jamie said quietly.

"Which is why," Preble continued, "upon my return to Washington I intend to recommend to my superiors that you be promoted to the rank of lieutenant. A captaincy should not be far behind."

"Thank you, sir," Jamie repeated, nearly speechless from pride and flushed with embarrassment. Preble was not a man to suffer fools gladly; nor was he lavish with his praise. What lay behind this praise, Jamie was now convinced, was the reason for his summons today. "If I may be so bold, Captain," he pressed on eagerly, "am I to understand that I have been selected to serve under Mr. Somers in *Intrepid*?"

"Is that your wish?"

"Indeed it is, sir."

Preble smiled wistfully. "I admire your enthusiasm, Mr. Cutler. I had expected nothing less from you." He shifted his position on the settee. "However, it would appear that your ability to *anticipate* has temporarily abandoned you." He took a sip of Madeira. "Midshipman Wadsworth will be serving as second in command. Midshipman Israel," referring to Joseph Israel, a midshipman from Annapolis serving in *Constitution* who was widely rumored to be a protégé of Navy Secretary Robert Smith, "will serve as third officer. To date, he has seen no action. It's his turn as well."

Jamie slumped slightly in his chair. He immediately corrected himself. "I see," he said. "Those are excellent choices, Captain." He reached for his glass of Madeira. "I must offer a toast of congratulations to Mr.

Wadsworth and to Mr. Israel. And, of course, to Mr. Somers and to the success of the mission." He raised his glass and drank.

"Oh come now, James," Preble said, in the tones of a father admonishing a petulant son. However fleeting it may have been, he had read the disappointment on Jamie's face as though it were etched in stone. "You have had your chances at glory in this campaign, and you have taken full advantage of them. Mr. Wadsworth has not. Granted, the poor boy was in sickbay when *Philadelphia* burned, and he has himself to blame for that. Syphilis has a way of providing its own unique form of punishment. But he is on the mend and he is eager for his own shot at glory. Besides," he added, eyeing Jamie's bandaged right arm, "your wound has not completely healed. Dr. Wells tells me that you are most fortunate to still have use of that arm."

"Yes, sir," Jamie had to agree. He looked hard at this captain. "Sir, if I may—and I ask this with the utmost respect—why was I summoned to your cabin this afternoon? I thought . . ."

"I know what you *thought*, Mr. Cutler," Preble interrupted, sounding like an annoyed schoolmaster. "I summoned you here to inform you that you are being relieved as midshipman in *Constitution*."

Jamie's jaw dropped. "*Relieved*, sir?"

"Yes. So you might serve aboard *Argus* under Master Commandant Hull."

"But . . . but sir, *why*?"

Preble drained his Madeira and set the empty glass gently on the table. "For a very good reason, if you will just calm yourself and hear me out. As you are aware, Mr. Tobias Lear, our consul general in Algiers, is accompanying Commodore Barron aboard *President* on her cruise to the Mediterranean. Mr. Lear is authorized to conduct and conclude peace negotiations with Tripoli as soon as such negotiations become warranted. At the same time, Captain Eaton, our naval agent for the Barbary States, is sailing with the squadron aboard *Constellation*, your father's former ship. One of the dispatches I received from Secretary Smith contained a letter from Secretary of State Madison telling me that President Jefferson has approved in principle Captain Eaton's plan to cross the desert and attack Tripoli by land. But he is leaving it to the Navy to make final recommendations and arrangements." He laughed shortly. "Yes, I can see you are as confused as I am. War or peace: which is it to be?

"There is more. Communications I have received from your father confirm that Hamet Karamanli is assembling a considerable force of

Arab cavalry to the west of Alexandria—Egyptian mercenaries who are being reinforced by a hodgepodge of Europeans procured, at considerable expense, I might add, by Mr. Richard Farquhar and his son George. I needn't explain to you who they are.

"As plans stand, *Argus* will convey Captain Eaton to Alexandria, where he will assume command of the expedition. Seven Marines will join him on the march. They are to be led by Lt. Presley O'Bannon, an officer I greatly admire, and two midshipmen. As perhaps you have *anticipated*, this force will require the services of an American naval officer to act as liaison between the army on land and our Navy at sea. Because I believe you to be the right officer for that position, I have recommended you to Captain Hull. I shall similarly recommend you to Commodore Barron and to Captain Eaton upon their arrival. And, of course, to your father, whose ship will play a key role with *Argus* in this expedition."

Jamie's keen disappointment was tempered somewhat by the prospect of serving with his father. "Thank you, Commodore. I am honored by your trust. But sir, if I may, once *Intrepid* succeeds in her mission, will this expeditionary force even be necessary?"

"You raise a fair question, Mr. Cutler. Several weeks ago, a month ago, I would not have thought so. But today I do. Yusuf Karamanli is a tough and mean-spirited old bird, much like me. He may see his navy blown to bits, but I have reluctantly come to accept what Captain Eaton and Consul Beaussier have been saying all along: Whatever the circumstances at sea, Yusuf will never accept unconditional surrender without at least the threat of a land assault on his city, especially one led by his deposed brother.

"Captain Eaton and the others might be wrong, of course. It could be that the destruction of his navy will convince Yusuf that further resistance is futile. But I have been instructed by my superiors to continue preparations for the land assault, and that is exactly what I intend to do."

THE MORNING AFTER Commodore Preble had consumed a round of toasts with his officers, every carpenter in the squadron was put to work converting *Intrepid* into what Preble came to refer to as a "floating volcano." Her magazine in the hold was planked up and stacked tight with five tons of powder in five hundred barrels. On the deck directly above the magazine, one hundred 13-inch shells and fifty 9-inch shells were carefully placed in a wooden bin specifically built for that purpose. Under the watchful eye of Preble and Somers and other squadron commanders, carpenters drilled two holes amidships into the bulkhead of the magazine.

Into these holes they inserted gun barrels stuffed with fuses that were connected to a main fuse at the end. These two main fuses were connected on the outside to a shallow trough of powder that ran the length of the ketch on the starboard side forward to a scuttle near her bow and aft to her companionway.

The trail of powder, Preble had explained, allowed the charge to be ignited from either the bow or the stern of the ketch. The length of the two main fuses was set to burn for eleven minutes before the main fuses set off the smaller fuses packed inside the gun barrels. The smaller fuses were timed to burn for four minutes before they detonated the powder in the magazine. Once the train of powder was lit, from either the bow or the stern, the thirteen Americans had fifteen minutes to get off *Intrepid* and into one of the two ship's boats that would be towed behind the ketch. Then they would row for their lives back out through the Western Passage to where *Nautilus*, escorted by *Vixen* and *Syren*, would be waiting to pick them up and convey them back to the flagship.

Richard Somers proposed one modification. Fill a small cabin aft with wood chips and splinters, he suggested, and set that heap ablaze as soon as *Intrepid* reached her target. This blaze would ensure that the fuses would eventually be lit even if the main charge failed. Further, it would discourage anyone from boarding the ketch after the Americans left.

Preble nodded his approval. "Make it so, Mr. Pryor," he ordered *Constitution*'s carpenter, the warrant officer in charge of the refit. Pryor enthusiastically set himself and his mates to the task.

SEPTEMBER 3 broke warm and sunny with a lamb's-wool sky and a pleasant breeze from the northeast. During the previous three days, while Pryor and his mates pounded nails aboard *Intrepid* and Gunnery Officer Simmons collected powder and shells from the squadron's magazines, American gunboats had launched several forays against Tripolitan gunboats poking their bows out through the reefs. The raids accomplished nothing of consequence, but that did not concern Preble. They were diversionary tactics meant to lull the enemy into believing that nothing unusual was afoot and that perhaps the American squadron was winding down its operations against Tripoli. For the first time in weeks, American warships and gunboats had not ventured in close to enemy shore batteries.

Halfway through the first dogwatch on September 3, Jamie Cutler, Ralph Izard, and Henry Wadsworth sat together in the midshipmen's mess on the flagship's dank orlop deck. All of *Constitution*'s other midshipmen not on watch duty were also there, making for cramped

.quarters. The three of them sat off by themselves as best they could, and for the most part they were left alone.

"So, Henry," Izard commented good-naturedly as he stabbed his fork into a slab of salt pork and sliced off a mouthful with his knife, "bound for glory tonight, are we?"

"I should think so," Wadsworth replied. His own tin plate was piled with pork mixed with beans and rice, but he was only picking at his meal. "By tomorrow at this time I should finally have something of consequence to write home about. Perhaps even to write a book about."

"Perhaps you should consider writing a book about how you got syphilis instead," Jamie ribbed.

Wadsworth shook his head. "It's an oft-told tale of woe," he sighed in mock dismay. "I doubt a book like that has much of an audience."

"Depends on who writes it," Izard quipped. "A man skilled with his pen can always find willing women—uh, readers."

"Touché, Ralph." Wadsworth's countenance brightened. He took a small bite of pork and washed it down with a swig from the one glass of wine he was permitted this evening. "As a skilled penman," he added cheerfully, "I must agree."

"So, Henry," Jamie said in a more serious tone, "what do you think will happen tonight?"

Wadsworth contemplated his answer as he moved his fork aimlessly about his plate. "Have you heard," he said quietly, avoiding eye contact, "that when Mr. Somers assembled his ship's company, explained his mission and the risks involved, and called for volunteers, every man-jack aboard *Nautilus* stepped forward? Including the cabin boy?"

Both Jamie Cutler and Ralph Izard nodded. They had indeed heard that. They had, in fact, seen something similar occur aboard *Constitution*. Forced to handpick a crew of ten from the hundred able seamen who volunteered, Preble and Somers were satisfied that the six sailors from *Constitution* and four from *Nautilus* they chose were among the elite of the squadron when it came to experience at sea and constancy aboard ship. All ten were American-born.

"I am honored to sail with such men on such a mission," Wadsworth said with a resolution and finality that closed the door to further discussion on the topic. Left unspoken was what Richard Somers had said in the officers' meeting the previous evening: that he would blow up *Intrepid* himself if that meant keeping five tons of precious gunpowder out of enemy hands. Nor was surrender a possibility. Somers had made it clear that he preferred death a hundred times over to the humiliation of capture and enslavement, and he assumed that every man of honor felt the same.

At 7:30, with the thin cloak of dusk yielding gradually to the thicker mantle of night, Henry Wadsworth shook hands with Jamie Cutler and Ralph Izard at *Constitution*'s larboard entry port. Aft of them, Stephen Decatur and Isaac Hull stood side-by-side on the quarterdeck alongside Edward Preble watching the ship's cutter row Richard Somers, Joseph Israel, and five of the handpicked sailors over to *Intrepid*, lying at anchor two hundred yards off. Lt. Charles Stewart was already aboard *Syren,* and Lt. John Smith aboard *Vixen*. It occurred to Jamie Cutler that Somers, Decatur, and Stewart had passed an evening similar to that of the three midshipmen, one deck up from them in the wardroom.

"Good luck, Henry," Jamie said to Wadsworth as the midshipman made ready to step down into the pinnace. Five volunteers awaited him there, four at the oars, one at the tiller. "Your mother insists you be back aboard and tucked in no later than midnight."

Wadsworth grinned. "Then I mustn't give her cause for alarm or anger. But before I retire tonight, I plan on sharing a bottle with you two."

"You're on, as long as it's from your store of wine. It's of a higher quality than ours."

"Godspeed, Henry," Izard said, squeezing his friend's arm.

Wadsworth did an about-face, grabbed the hempen handholds on each side of the steps, gave his shipmates a brief nod, and climbed down into the pinnace. After he had picked his way astern and was settled in the stern sheets, the starboard oarsmen pushed off, the oars dipped, and the little boat started gliding away from *Constitution*. Wadsworth turned once to look back. When he lifted his hat and waved it in the air, those watching him on the flagship waved back.

"Godspeed, Henry," Izard repeated quietly, as if bestowing a benediction.

At 8:00, the start of the first watch, *Intrepid* raised a jib forward and the lateen sail on her mainmast, slipped her anchor cable, and shaped a course for the Western Passage. As if ordained by Providence, the moon that night was in its first phase. The dazzling canopy of stars shining in the cloudless sky provided barely enough light to see what lay ahead, and scarcely enough for a sentry posted ashore to distinguish much more than the dark outline of a Mediterranean-rigged vessel approaching the Western Passage. The northeasterly breeze, which had held steady for much of the day, allowed *Intrepid* to sail southward on a broad reach, her fastest point of sail. Tonight, however, she was sailing under mainsail and jib only, to slow her progress and to allow lookouts and sounders in the bow to safely guide her through the narrow passage. Trailing far behind, the brig of war *Syren* and the schooner *Vixen* kept pace under double-reefed canvas. Somers' ship *Nautilus*, under the temporary command of Lt. George Washington Reed, ventured on ahead. As instructed, Reed hove to a hundred yards short of the reefs.

Shortly after 9:00 *Intrepid* approached the Western Passage. All eyes in the squadron were riveted on her, though those standing on the weather deck of *Constitution*, resting at anchor five miles out, could see very little at that distance. Jamie Cutler strode aft to near the raised skylight on the quarterdeck where Captain Preble had gathered with his three commissioned officers and the ship's master. He touched his hat and stood quietly awaiting recognition.

"Yes, Mr. Cutler?" Preble asked.

"Sir," Jamie said, "Mr. Izard and I request permission to climb to the maintop. I am officially on watch duty, so I—"

"Permission granted, Mr. Cutler. Tonight, the entire ship's company is on watch duty."

"Yes, sir. Thank you, sir."

Jamie slung the lanyard of his glass over his shoulder and climbed up the ratlines, through the lubber's hole, to the semicircular platform at the maintop. He gave Izard a hand up, and together they searched to southward. Not satisfied with the view, Izard pointed upward to the horizontal cross-timbers that spread the narrower shrouds leading up to the juncture of the topmast and topgallant mast.

"I'm right behind you," Jamie said.

When they had secured themselves in the rope network attached to the crosstrees, the two midshipmen trained their glasses on the tiny lights flickering along the walls of Tripoli and within the bashaw's castle.

Jamie took out his waistcoat watch and held it up close: 9:25. He put the watch back in the fold of his waistcoat. "See anything?" he asked Izard. "They should be through the passage by now."

"Nothing," Izard said.

Seconds ticked by and became minutes. Still nothing.

"Any moment now, Ralph," Jamie said, peering intently though his glass. He could as much hear as feel his heart thumping. "Any moment now . . ."

Two warning shots erupted from a shore battery, and then, suddenly, there came a shock of light so intense, even five miles away, that it temporarily blinded those watching. There was no yellow in the fire, only a dazzling white that for several eerie moments lit up the vast menacing contours of Fortress Tripoli in the background and, in the foreground, the tiny silhouette of the schooner *Nautilus* hove to before the reefs. The flash of flame was quickly followed by a blast so deafening that sailors aboard *Constitution* instinctively ducked and clapped their hands over their ears.

"Jamie, what in God's name?" Izard was pointing in stupefaction at a sight Jamie's mind could hardly take in: a giant rocket-like structure rose from the deck of *Intrepid* and shot high into the sky, trailing a fireball of flames from hell itself. The rocket hesitated at its apex, turned on its side, and came crashing down in a burning heap into the harbor waters as shells streaked and zigzagged through the air like a fiendish July Fourth celebration gone mad.

"I believe that was her mainmast," Jamie said quietly.

Moments of shocked silence followed the explosion. It was as though heaven and earth stood stock still, watching, waiting, stunned to their very cores by the dazzling display of violence. Then cheers resounded through the squadron.

"They've done it, Jamie!" Izard exulted. "They've done it!"

Jamie peered through the glass. "Do you see the flare, Ralph? The blue flare? They're supposed to fire a blue flare."

He was referring to the prearranged signal from Captain Somers to the squadron that *Intrepid*'s crew were aboard the two small boats and had made it back through the Western Passage.

Izard shook his head. "No, but what of it? More than likely they haven't made it through the reefs yet. Give Captain Somers another minute or two."

Jamie strained to see anything that might provide some sort of clue. He saw nothing to comfort him beyond two lanterns perched high on each of *Nautilus'* two masts, raised as beacons to the oncoming boats. Tripolitans ashore had noted those beacons as well. Cannon blasts shattered the eerie silence as *Nautilus* came under heavy fire from all along the enemy battlements. She stood firm, waiting for the thirteen Americans.

"I can't see much anymore," Izard commented minutes later. Waves of anxiety were beginning to wash over the two midshipmen. By any man's calculation, more than enough time had elapsed since the explosion for the pinnace and cutter to have reached *Nautilus*, and for *Nautilus* to be beating back to the flagship. But the sporadic light provided by enemy cannon fire showed *Nautilus* still hove to like a sitting duck. "Let's get back down on deck. Maybe Captain Preble has heard something."

What Preble might have heard, Jamie could not fathom. Nonetheless, he grabbed hold of a backstay, wrapped his legs around it, and quickly descended, hand under hand, to the deck. Izard followed close behind.

"Anything to report, Mr. Cutler?" Preble asked when Jamie approached the quarterdeck. Preble's voice was calm, although even the feeble light of the deck lanterns showed the intense strain on his face.

"Only that *Nautilus* remains on station, sir," Jamie replied.

Preble nodded in acknowledgment. "I have ordered our guns fired at ten-minute intervals, and a rocket launched every ten minutes, until everyone is safely back aboard."

"Understood, sir."

They waited. And they waited—throughout the long night until dawn broke to reveal an overcast sky and a somber, lifeless sea. Quirky breezes wafted in from the east. Even in the light of day, *Constitution*'s guns and rockets continued to go off like clockwork. At two bells in the forenoon watch, Preble ordered the guns silenced and the signal hoisted: "*Nautilus*, join company as soon as possible."

When the schooner had pulled close to *Constitution* and was feathering into the wind, Edward Preble hailed her captain. "Captain Reed, have you sustained damage?" he shouted through a speaking trumpet. "And what can you tell us of *Intrepid*?"

Reed raised a trumpet from the larboard railing of the schooner. "No serious damage sustained, sir," he reported. Before answering the second question, he paused and lowered his trumpet a moment, then raised it again to his lips.

"We followed *Intrepid* until two or three minutes before the explosion, sir," he shouted over. His words then came out ever more cautiously, ever more sporadically, as though he were loath to utter them. "We thought she had reached her target . . . but . . . alas . . . she had not. From what we observed this morning . . . there has been little damage . . . either to Tripoli or to its boats. And sir . . . it is my sad duty to report . . . that Captain Somers and every member of his crew . . . have vanished."

"Repeat that, Lieutenant. And speak up, man! *Vanished*, you say?"

"Yes, sir," Reed replied more distinctly. "Vanished. I'm sorry, sir, but there is no other way to put it. I have seen no sign of any of the crew or either of the two boats. And sir, we never did notice the after cabin set ablaze."

"So, what you are telling me, Mr. Reed, is that the crew of *Intrepid* has either perished or been taken prisoner."

"Yes, sir. We . . . I fear so, sir."

"Dear God. Henry . . ." Izard whispered to himself, staring blankly at the spot where *Intrepid* had exploded. Jamie put a hand on his shoulder, as much to console himself as his friend. Both midshipmen realized, as well as anyone, that no American sailor had been taken alive after that cataclysmic explosion. Jamie felt tears well in his eyes.

"Very well, Mr. Reed," Preble shouted through the trumpet. "Please advise Mr. Smith and Mr. Stewart that they may rejoin the squadron. You may continue to stand off and on the reefs, but stay well out of range of the shore batteries. We shall have no further casualties this day."

"Aye, aye, Captain."

It was, ironically, that very afternoon, as the squadron struggled to come to terms with an almost incomprehensible loss, that the topgallants of USS *President* and USS *Constellation* were sighted bearing down from the north. The Mediterranean campaign of Commo. Edward Preble, once so full of promise, had come to an end.

Thirteen

Cyrenaica, Tripoli,
Winter–Spring 1805

O FF AND ON SINCE LAST July, *Portsmouth* had patrolled the Gulf of Sidra on an approximate line of latitude between the port of Surt on its western shore and the larger port of Benghazi two hundred miles to the east. Although blockade duty was rarely the first choice of a naval commander, Richard Cutler appreciated the vital role it played in this war. The American frigate had chased down three heavily armed Tripolitan cruisers since coming on station, sinking one and reducing another to matchwood. And she had captured or destroyed a number of enemy merchant vessels and turned away, under threat of seizure, merchant vessels and fishing boats of neighboring states seeking to resupply the besieged capital city. It was no secret that food supplies in Tripoli were wearing thin, along with the patience of its citizens. Military men on both sides understood that empty stomachs of a restless public were as much a threat to Yusuf Karamanli as the guns of a naval squadron.

When relieved of duty in the gulf, *Portsmouth* sailed to Alexandria, where Richard Cutler and his commissioned officers met with Hamet Karamanli. Their task was to monitor, for the benefit of Commo. Samuel Barron in Syracuse, the recruitment efforts for Hamet's self-described Allah's Legion. Richard remained unimpressed by the army and its officers. And even by its commander. However decent and principled a man the dethroned bashaw might be, Richard entertained serious reservations about his ability to lead men into battle, particularly the two Egyptian sheiks who were fielding the bulk of the Arab cavalry—at America's expense. The soldiers under them appeared slovenly and undisciplined as they roamed about the makeshift desert campsite dressed in flowing white robes.

"I hear tell," Agreen Crabtree remarked one day in early January as he and Eric Meyers stood watching the activity in the compound outside the village of Marabout, two miles west of Alexandria, "that our Arab friends use those *barracan* things as a blanket at night and they wear nothin' beneath—no shirt, no underwear, no nothin'. Is that a fact, d' you think?" Certainly the long robes, which looped around the body and fastened at the left shoulder, looked more like blankets than military uniforms.

"I don't know," Meyers commented dryly, "and I have no wish to find out."

Agreen raised his eyebrows and leered. "I could pull rank and order you t' find out."

Meyers didn't blink. "I'd rather face a firing squad," he replied.

Matters changed dramatically a week later when the brig of war *Argus* sailed into Alexandria Harbor bearing Capt. William Eaton, Lt. Presley O'Bannon, the seven Marines under his command, and the two midshipmen attached to the expedition. That evening, Richard invited Eaton and O'Bannon to dine with him aboard *Portsmouth* along with Isaac Hull, the captain of *Argus* and a personal friend with whom Richard had served briefly aboard *Constitution* during the war with France. Earlier in the afternoon, amid all the hustle and bustle generated by the long-expected arrival of *Argus*, he managed to squeeze in a few minutes alone with his son in *Portsmouth*'s after cabin.

After the usual exchanges between a father and son who had not seen each other in almost seven months, Richard asked the inevitable question: "Jamie, what happened to *Intrepid*?"

Jamie pursed his lips. "What do you already know, Father?"

"Only what Captain Preble wrote in his last dispatch, that *Intrepid* blew up before reaching her target, with the apparent loss of all hands."

Jamie paused for a moment, the weight of sad remembrance still heavy on his mind. "I'm afraid I can't add much to that. Nobody knows for certain what happened. She may have been struck by a chance shot from a shore battery. Or a stray spark may have set off the explosives prematurely."

"What do *you* think happened?"

Jamie looked hard at his father seated across from him. "I believe she was approached by enemy vessels as she entered the harbor and that

Captain Somers blew her up himself to deny the enemy her powder. He had said he would do that. In any event, he and his crew are dead. There is no possibility that any man was taken alive."

"No," his father agreed, saddened by the sorrow in Jamie's voice and the pain sketched vividly on his face; nevertheless, the parent in him compelled him to make one final comment before changing the subject. "Thank God you were not on that mission, Jamie."

Jamie said nothing in reply.

In a less somber tone Richard asked, "What is your impression of the new commodore? Permission to speak freely, of course."

Jamie shrugged his shoulders. "He's no Captain Preble, Father. My impression, and the impression of nearly everyone I talk to, is that he got where he is today by doing what he was told, avoiding controversy, and relying on seniority to eventually bob him to the top. He's ill much of the time. Of what, I'm not certain. Rumor has it that he will step down soon and be replaced by Commodore Rodgers."

Richard was not surprised by such speculation. He and John Rodgers had served together aboard *Constellation* during the war with France, Rodgers as her first lieutenant and Richard as her second. Until Barron's arrival, Rodgers had been the senior Navy officer in the Mediterranean, senior even to Edward Preble. That had contributed to a serious rift between him and Preble. Secretary Smith resolved the issue by giving Rodgers command of a three-ship squadron based in Gibraltar and bestowing on him the rank of commodore. Rodgers' orders were to keep a sharp eye on Morocco, always a threat to the United States, and to hamper enemy shipping in the western Mediterranean. The two co-commodores had rarely communicated.

"Does Barron support Eaton's expedition?"

"From what I hear, Commodore Barron supports whatever his superiors in Washington support. Therein lies the problem, you see. No one seems to know to what extent President Jefferson and his cabinet will support Captain Eaton. Secretary Smith apparently favors the expedition, although the American consul general in North Africa, Colonel Lear, considers it a waste of time and money. And since Mr. Lear now has authority to open negotiations with Tripoli if and when conditions warrant, I suspect he is already hard at work trying to create those conditions."

"A covert mission? To force his agenda?"

"Something like that."

"Even if that means compromising Eaton's expedition?"

Jamie nodded.

"Do *you* consider the expedition a waste of time and money?" Richard asked.

Jamie shook his head. "No, Father, I don't. I believe that if we are to realize long-term benefits from fighting this war, the solution to it must be a military solution. I well remember the day several years ago when you told Will and me about the raid on Whitehaven during the war with England. Many of your shipmates, including *Ranger*'s two senior lieutenants, thought that a one-ship invasion force was a ridiculous idea. But you, as a midshipman, supported it. Why? Because as you told Captain Jones, the raid didn't rely on success. American Marines landing on English soil would have its effect whatever the outcome. Well, we have the same situation here, don't we? An assault on Derne will have its effect, whatever the outcome. The mere threat of a follow-up attack on Benghazi and Tripoli may be enough to convince the bashaw to sue for peace."

As Richard Cutler listened to his son, it was all he could do to refrain from walking over and embracing him. Instead, he maintained a poker face. When Jamie had finished, he asked, "And you believe Captain Eaton is up to the task?"

"I believe he is, Father."

AN INFLUX of more than one hundred Christian mercenaries from Europe, in addition to an encouraging number of Muslim warriors riding in from Cyrenaica, the easternmost province of Tripoli, swelled the ranks of the allied army in Marabout to five hundred strong. Richard Cutler had ample opportunity to assess the character and skill-sets of William Eaton as he waited for the operation to begin. The more he observed, the more impressed he became. Eaton had all the markings of a born leader: courage, discipline, and protocol; his enthusiasm for the project was matched only by his resolve to see it succeed. Among his first actions after disembarking in Egypt was to fashion a formal agreement with Hamet Karamanli in which he pledged the blood and treasure of the United States to restore Hamet to the throne of Tripoli. In return, Hamet pledged to repay the United States by consigning to it the annual tributes of Sweden, Denmark, and the Batavian Republic once he was restored to the throne. In that same document Eaton designated himself "general and commander-in-chief" of the expedition. After Hamet signed his agreement, Eaton countersigned it, using his self-proclaimed rank, and sent it off to Secretary of State James Madison in Washington.

"Is that legal, Richard?" Agreen asked that evening in the privacy of *Portsmouth*'s dining alcove. "Is Eaton authorized t' do such a thing?"

Richard chuckled. "Your guess is as good as mine, Agee. But from what I've observed of the man, it doesn't matter. If either the president or Congress has the gall to challenge him, I daresay Eaton will convince Mr. Marshall," referring to John Marshall, the Chief Justice of the Supreme Court, "to declare it a legally binding document, at the point of a sword if necessary."

Agreen chuckled in turn. "Hand me a piece of paper, would you, Richard? I've a mind t' declare myself an admiral. From here on, you're takin' orders from me."

On the morning of March 6, the expedition was prepared to march. George Farquhar, son of Richard Farquhar and quartermaster of the expedition, announced that a four-week supply of provisions had been secured on the baggage train, which consisted of 107 camels. Hamet similarly confirmed that his 350 Arab horsemen were mounted and assembled behind Sheik Mahomet and Sheik el Tahib, who were resplendent in baggy pants, turbans, and brightly colored vests. In lock formation nearby, 70 well-groomed Christian mercenaries presented a curious blend of French, Neapolitan, Maltese, and Tyrolean soldiers-for-hire beside a separate group of 38 brightly uniformed Greeks led by two Greek officers. Standing at stiff attention in front of them all were Lieutenant O'Bannon, a Marine sergeant named Campbell, five Marine privates, and a Marine drummer boy. Each Marine was dressed in a blue uniform with scarlet facings—except for O'Bannon, whose uniform coat with two long, vertical rows of polished brass buttons identified him as an officer.

A drum roll sounded. Jamie Cutler saluted his father and mounted his horse. What needed to be said between father and son had been said the night before.

Under a cloudless sky, the expedition set off westward through the desert for Cyrenaica. Eaton led the procession on a grand white Barbary horse. Hamet, the two sheiks, the two midshipmen, and the Arab cavalry rode behind him. Behind them, afoot, marched the Marines and European mercenaries, with the camel drivers and baggage train bringing up the rear of the caravan. The question probing Richard Cutler's mind as he and Agreen watched the procession file past was whether General Eaton could impose military discipline long enough and effectively enough to see the allied army to the Bay of Bomba 450 miles to the east, the army's first rendezvous point with American naval forces. From there it was less than 50 miles to their first military objective: the provincial capital city of Derne, where Hamet had once ruled as governor and where it was assumed he retained strong support for his claim to the throne of Tripoli.

THE TROUBLES BEGAN two days later, only forty miles into the journey. At first, it seemed nothing more than a petty nuisance. The camel drivers suddenly stopped in their tracks and demanded more money than their agreed-upon fee, threatening to return to Alexandria if it were not paid immediately. It took some doing, but eventually Hamet Karamanli was able to persuade the camel drivers that they would be paid in full what they had been promised, plus a little extra, once they reached their destination. If they turned back now, they would receive nothing but the curse of Allah.

"It's an old trick," Hamet explained somewhat sheepishly to the Christian officers as the white-robed, black-bearded camel drivers shuffled back to their stations. "They wait until the caravan is on the march and then demand higher wages."

Eaton turned away in disgust.

Each day blended depressingly into the next. A drumroll at daybreak, a quick breakfast of biscuits and rice, and march until sunset. An earlier than usual outbreak of hot desert winds from the southern Sahara swept across the region and hampered their progress. The wind whipped up fierce sandstorms that inundated Christians and Muslims alike with stinging grit that played havoc with eyes and mouths and nostrils and just about everything else, including morale.

Slowly, although ever more assuredly as one day dragged into another, the army's food supplies dwindled, augmented only occasionally by the slaughter of a camel, the purchase of sheep and ostriches from local tribesmen, and, on one occasion, the killing of a wildcat by a well-aimed shot from the musket of Marine sergeant Campbell.

Worse, their water supply was running out. The camels could get by with very little, but the blistering desert sun inspired a continuous and voracious thirst among the Europeans. Most days, Eaton called a temporary halt to allow his soldiers to search for cisterns of fresh water amid fissures of rocks carved out by the brute force of Nature or by the skill of Roman engineers who had passed by centuries ago. Occasionally they stumbled on a deep cistern, and when they did, they drank their fill and squirreled away as much as they could. Most days, when they did not, water was rationed. And so on they marched, at the discouragingly slow rate of fifteen to twenty miles per day, less than half the distance General

Eaton had originally predicted and on which the army's food supply was calculated.

Each day, the march ended in the cool of dusk. Each evening, by unspoken agreement, Muslims and Christians pitched their tents apart from each other. Most of the men sat quietly before going to sleep, listening to the dulcet tunes of Lieutenant O'Bannon's fiddle and thinking of hearth and home—and, in Jamie's case, his friend William Lewis in *Constitution*, who possessed similar talents with the violin.

"How far d' you reckon we've come, Jamie?" Pascal Peck, the other midshipman on the expedition, asked one evening in front of the tent they shared. The army had encamped on a high, rocky plain overlooking the Mediterranean near the ruins of a Roman mansion. Behind their tent, their tethered horses grazed on grasswort and wild fennel. A short distance away a Marine private named Owens was stirring a thin gruel of rice, water, and bits of camel flesh in a cauldron hanging from a metal rod set atop a fire between two columns of rocks.

Jamie grinned. "And how far do you reckon we have to go?" he said, voicing the flip side of a question forever at the tip of every man's tongue.

"I dunno," Peck said quite seriously. "We must be at least halfway."

"A bit more than that, according to Sheik Mahomet. He's been through this area once or twice, so he at least has some idea of where we are. Besides, we've been at it for nearly three weeks. Do the math."

Peck sighed out loud. "Lord, I'm sick of this place. And I'm sick of rice and beans and stale biscuits. And I'm sick to death of kowtowing to these hot-headed Arabs. Allies? Ha! Any one of them would slit my throat to steal my belt." He sighed again. "I'd give up sex for life if only I could wake up tomorrow morning to the sound of surf on a New Jersey beach."

Jamie grinned. "So this nice Tripolitan beach just won't do, huh?"

"There aren't any beaches around here, least none that I've seen. Just the rocks and cliffs along the shore." In a happier tone he broached another popular subject. "The good news is, this war can't last much longer. I give it three months, tops. So we should be going home soon, assuming General Eaton can keep these turd-sucking Arabs in line."

"That's a big assumption," Jamie said.

The troubles worsened the following morning. Again the camel drivers refused to march, insisting this time that they had contracted with Hamet to go only this far. Sheik el Tahib confirmed to Eaton that the camel drivers spoke the truth and that it would require a minimum of $750 in immediate cash to convince them to proceed. If Eaton refused, the camel drivers would pack up and leave.

His dander up, Eaton summoned Hamet to his tent and demanded an explanation. None was forthcoming, at least none that satisfied either Eaton or the camel drivers. Desperate to continue the march, Eaton reached deep into his pockets and placed $540 on a table, the last of his cash reserves. "Help me out, would you?" he asked of his officers. A hat passed among the men yielded another $140. As Jamie gave up what he had, Hamet stepped forward, put down the Egyptian equivalent of $100, and promised to do what he could to convince the camel drivers that they would receive a bonus when they arrived at the Bay of Bomba, from funds he understood were being held aboard U.S. Navy vessels for Eaton's discretionary use.

"Is such an arrangement acceptable to you?" he asked Eaton.

Eaton grudgingly agreed to yet another example of what he saw as Arab duplicity and extortion.

Just as Hamet was about to set off to mollify the camel drivers, a scout galloped into camp with electrifying news. Many Arabs within the province of Cyrenaica were aware of Hamet's initiative, he reported, and were arming themselves in his name. He also informed the allied commanders that Mustafa Bey, the royal governor of Derne, had barricaded himself inside his palace and was refusing to come out. Best of all, powerful Bedouin tribes camped to the west were preparing to send men to join Eaton's army.

The scout's report elicited shouts of jubilation among Hamet's soldiers. Many fired off a *feu de joie* in celebration. The outbursts of joy, however, were quickly tempered by a further report that a considerable force loyal to Yusuf Karamanli had been spotted riding east toward Derne from Benghazi. He did not know their exact number. Perhaps seven or eight hundred men, the scout ventured.

A hundred yards away, at the rear of the caravan, camel drivers heard the musket shots and mistook them for a Bedouin attack on the column or, worse, the massacre of their Muslim brethren by Christian soldiers. Riled to near panic, they seized several Christians and threatened to kill them with knives and scimitars. Only when Hamet Karamanli came running in, waving cash in both hands, did their blood-curdling screams cease, to be replaced by salaams and praise of Allah once the cash was distributed and Hamet had explained the terms of the expanded contract.

Hours later, during the dark of night, the bulk of the camel drivers took the money and seventy camels and stole off eastward into the desert gloom. The next morning, the few camel drivers who remained refused to budge. Sheik el Tahib haughtily informed Eaton that he would not order his cavalry forward with what was now a seriously depleted food supply.

"Bastards, all of them," O'Bannon snarled when he and his fellow officers received word some time later that an Arab council, to which Eaton had not been invited, had decreed that the Arabs would stay put until riders were sent two hundred miles to the Bay of Bomba to verify that American naval ships were, in fact, there. "It will take a rider a week to get there and back," he added with disgust. "In another week our provisions will be consumed. What do these Arabs think we'll live on then?"

Eaton had an answer. "Mr. Cutler, come with me," he said, his voice as serious as the stern expression on his face. He gave orders to Lieutenant O'Bannon and then stormed into the tent where the Arab council had just ended. "Sit back down, all of you," he demanded, "and listen carefully to what I have to say." He spoke directly to Hamet, who dutifully translated his words into Arabic for the benefit of council members who spoke no English. "From this moment on, American Marines will stand guard over our rations and munitions. Starting at dawn tomorrow, I shall suspend rations for anyone who refuses to march. No Arab shall have access to these supplies. And that includes you, Hamet." He shifted his gaze to the two sheiks sitting side-by-side on a blanket. "Sheik el Tahib and Sheik Mahomet," he scowled, pointing in outrage at the two heavily bearded men, "if you possess a shred of honor, I call on you to chase down the camel drivers who so shamefully deserted this army last night. You may leave immediately."

Jamie Cutler realized at that instant that the Arabs could change the dynamics of this showdown in a blink of an eye if they wished to do so. They outnumbered the Europeans four to one. He forced himself to reveal none of his anxiety as he watched the Arab leaders peer past him through the open flaps of the tent at O'Bannon, Campbell, and the five Marine privates standing guard before the last of the provisions.

Within the hour the two sheiks were galloping eastward.

Late that evening, sixty camels and their drivers returned to camp.

At daybreak the next morning, the Marine drummer boy summoned soldiers to rank and file.

PROVIDENCE SEEMED finally to be smiling on what had become—to the extent possible in this forbidding land of arid plains and sand-filled valleys—a forced march. Jamie Cutler and Pascal Peck clawed their way up a steep, rocky ridge that Sheik Mahomet had told them commanded a sweeping view of a vast valley in the distance, a valley more fertile than any they had come across thus far. When the two midshipmen had grunted and sweated their way to the peak, they stood up and gazed westward. What they beheld was so astounding, so unexpected, that they temporarily forgot their raging hunger and thirst. Stretched out below them was a scene out of the Old Testament: a virtual city of white tents set up in orderly array. Herds of sheep, camels, goats, and horses roamed and grazed the outlying areas. Men and women dressed in flowing white robes tended the herds or prepared food while children darted this way and that, playing games and annoying the animals in the way that young children have done for ages.

"Great God in heaven," Peck breathed in awe. "There must be three or four thousand people down there."

"At least," Jamie said, as enthralled as his shipmate.

"Who *are* they?" Peck asked.

"They are the Eu ed Alli," Mahomet told them and the other Christian officers after the two midshipmen had climbed down and delivered their astonishing report. "This is their land. At least they claim it to be."

"The 'you et alley'?" O'Bannon inquired, struggling with pronunciation. "Is that good or bad?" His questions brought rare smiles to both Eaton and Mahomet.

"It is good, my friend," the sheik replied. "It is very, very good. This is the Bedouin tribe the scout spoke of two days past. It is the most powerful tribe in all of Cyrenaica. They are great warriors, and they hate Yusuf Karamanli and his tax collectors. Come, you will see. They will welcome you with open arms and open hearts."

Open their hearts they did. The starving, dirty, discouraged Christians felt as though they had been transported from fiery hell to the lush Garden of Eden. Here there was food and water a-plenty—due, apparently, to the blessing of an underground river—and the Bedouins were pleased to share their bounty with Hamet Karamanli and his Western allies. How to fairly compensate the Bedouins for their generosity became an issue. The only cash in the caravan was in the pockets of the camel drivers, and they were not about to give it up. The matter was settled when the women of the tribe took a fancy to the brass buttons on the officers' uniforms, and tribal elders agreed that these buttons represented fair compensation for goods received. As a black-haired beauty, her face unveiled, carefully cut away the buttons on Jamie Cutler's coat, the coy looks and brief smiles she gave him whenever their eyes met conveyed a sense of frustration that Islamic law prevented her from offering him something a bit more personal for his buttons.

Although they all hated to leave Eden, General Eaton insisted they press on, his ranks now augmented by 150 mounted Bedouins, each brandishing a musket. These new recruits, Eaton did not fail to remind the Arab officers, had signed on as volunteers. They would be paid nothing, unlike any of the others who marched on this expedition. Except for the five Marine privates who continued to receive their monthly wage of six dollars, a laughable amount, Eaton emphasized, compared with what the lowliest camel driver was now being paid. And unlike the Arabs, Eaton did not fail to add, these Marines had no personal stake in the future of Tripoli. They were doing their duty because their country and their commanding officers expected it of them.

Not long after departing paradise the caravan was once again trudging through hell's fiery pits. Two days later, during the evening of March 26, another scout galloped in to report that an enemy force had been sighted only a day or two away from Derne and would arrive there before Eaton's army. The scout pegged this enemy force at a thousand men.

"God *damn* it!" Eaton cursed, unable to swallow such a bitter pill.

Reaction to the report among the Arabs was as swift as it was adamant. Sheik el Tahib stormed in to where Eaton was conferring with his European officers and informed him in hard language that not only would his cavalry not proceed farther, they would be returning to Egypt. This time, he said, he meant it. This time there would be no Arab council; the matter was settled. And this time, he sniffed, Hamet Karamanli agreed with him.

When he heard that, Eaton's long-suppressed wrath exploded. "You are a liar and a cheat and a coward!" he shouted at el Tahib. "Go, then! Return to Egypt! And take your worthless cavalry with you! I am glad to be rid of you all! I will march on with my foot-soldiers and the Bedouins to Derne!"

Sheik el Tahib, his blood up, ordered his Muslim soldiers to advance on the supply tent.

"*Beat to arms!*" Eaton commanded the Marine drummer.

At the first roll of the staccato tattoo, European soldiers seized their weapons, formed in ranks by companies, and stood at ramrod attention.

"*Officers, to me!*" Eaton shouted. Lieutenant O'Bannon, the European officers, and the two midshipmen rushed to stand beside him. Directly behind them, Sergeant Campbell and his five Marine privates formed a second line before the entrance to the supply tent.

"You may leave whenever you wish," Eaton informed el Tahib. "But you shall take no provisions with you."

The sheik hesitated at the prospect of desert travel without food or water, and without the possibility of pay for services rendered to date. He glanced at Sheik Mahomet standing on one side of him, and then at Hamet Karamanli on the other. Neither man returned his gaze. Seconds ticked by. Deep within a gap in time fraught with indecision, Eaton suddenly blurted out, "Lieutenant O'Bannon!"

"Sir!" the Marine replied.

"The manual exercise, if you please!"

"Yes, sir!"

O'Bannon about-faced. "Sergeant, you may drill the men in the manual of arms!"

"Yes, sir!"

To Jamie's surprise, and to the consternation of the Arabs, Sergeant Campbell put his Marines and the European soldiers through the exercise of presenting and shouldering arms. When the soldiers began twirling their muskets, the Arabs ran for their horses, screaming to Allah that they had been betrayed and were about to be slaughtered. Two hundred Arab horsemen armed with scimitars and muskets advanced toward the Europeans standing at attention, muskets held firmly at their sides. The Bedouins looked on, bewildered by this turn of events.

The vanguard of Muslim cavalry reined in close before the Christians' formation and leveled their muskets at its officers.

"I could shoot you down like a dog," el Tahib sneered down at Eaton.

Eaton kept his lips sealed and his eyes front and center.

"*Do you hear me, Eaton?*" the sheik shrieked.

It was then that Lt. Presley O'Bannon advanced two steps, wheeled smartly to his left, strode in precise parade-ground fashion another six steps, then wheeled to his right and stopped, his sword tip pointing at the ground. He had placed himself between William Eaton and Sheik el Tahib, a human shield before the American general.

"Shoot me first," he said.

El Tahib's jaw dropped. "You would sacrifice yourself for such a man," he asked incredulously.

O'Bannon stood his ground. "Shoot me first," he repeated.

Whether inspired by what they were witnessing or by their reluctance to see the popular Marine lieutenant harmed, one by one the Arabs lifted the barrels of their muskets until they pointed skyward. El Tahib reluctantly followed suit.

"Allah be praised," Sheik Mahomet proclaimed for all to hear. "These Christians are not our enemies. They are our friends. They fight with us. They risk their lives for us, and for what? What do we give them in return? Only complaints and trouble and further demands."

Hamet Karamanli dismounted, walked over to O'Bannon, and embraced him like a brother. "You are a very brave man, Lieutenant," he told him. "And you have shamed us." As if to underscore his words, he withdrew his Mameluke sword from its sheath, held it out horizontally in both hands, and offered it to O'Bannon. "Accept this sword," he said, "from the hands of a grateful prince." To Eaton: "I pledge to you, my general, that you shall have no more difficulties with us. We are your loyal soldiers."

Eaton bowed in response. During supper that evening he ordered Jamie Cutler to make all haste for the Bay of Bomba at the first blush of dawn the next morning.

THE SUN WAS not yet up when Jamie rode west with William Whittier, a bull of a Marine from Kentucky and the most skilled horseman among the Americans. Jamie rode his own horse; Whittier rode Peck's. They carried with them two days' rations of food and what little water George Farquhar could spare.

They estimated they had somewhere between 130 and 150 miles to cover. If they went all-out during the daylight hours, and Fortune smiled upon them, they could expect to reach their destination by late the next afternoon. They would have to stop to rest along the way and search for water among the outcroppings. But the need to push on was paramount. Already the expedition was two weeks behind schedule. Jamie's mind buzzed with questions. How long would the Navy wait for them at the Bay of Bomba? If the ships had left, would that scuttle the expedition? How could Derne be assaulted without naval support? There was no backup plan. It was Eaton's plan or nothing.

"If I may speak freely, sir?"

It was their first night out, and Jamie and Whittier had camped within the protection of a fortlike structure of great boulders that shielded them from the cool breeze wafting off the sea. The route they followed necessarily hugged the coastline, since that was their sole point of reference. The amber glow of a three-quarters moon sparkled off the waters of the Mediterranean, reflecting as glittering jewels far to the north, east, and west. It was a panorama of seaside majesty that the two Americans all but ignored. Too exhausted to gather fuel to light a fire, they were suffering through another meager meal of dry rice, a few beans, and a stale biscuit washed down with half a cup of water.

"Of course, Whittier. What's on your mind?"

Whittier scratched the nape of his neck with an index finger. "Well, sir," he said, "what I can't figure is, why didn't the Navy resupply us earlier? Along the coast somewhere, at some beach closer to Alexandria than Bomba? And why did Captain Eaton wait until now to send us to Bomba?"

Jamie had asked himself that last question many times. The first two questions he had asked his father in Alexandria. The fact that Whittier raised them now did not surprise him. Throughout the expedition, but especially during the past twelve hours, he had come to admire the breadth and depth of the young man's intellect, as well as his physical brawn. It was why, he suspected, Sergeant Campbell had recommended Whittier to accompany him on this ride.

"I can answer your first questions better than the last. The fact is, no one, not even Hamet or the sheiks, knew exactly which route we would follow to the Bay of Bomba. The sheiks are from Egypt, remember, not Cyrenaica. Mahomet has been here before, but only a couple of times. And while Hamet may have been governor of Derne, by his own admission he rarely traveled east of there—in other words, on the land that we've been traveling since leaving Alexandria. So it was anyone's guess how we would get to the Bay of Bomba. We just knew it was to Bomba that we had to get. It's easily identifiable and, according to my father, has one of the few suitable beaches anywhere along the coast of Tripoli. He has been cruising up and down this coast for months and knows it well.

"Our problem is not the rendezvous point. We'd have to march over this land to get to Derne no matter what. No, the problem is the lack of discipline among our Arab allies and the shortage of provisions. General Eaton was convinced the march would take no more than four weeks. So we brought a four-week supply of food that could have been stretched further had not those damn camp followers," referring to the ragtag swarm of Arab freeloaders who had followed the caravan during the early days until the Marines finally drove them off, "pilfered so much of it. Does that answer your question?"

"It does, sir. Thank you, sir. I wish someone could have explained all this to me and my mates. We've been in the dark, so to speak."

Jamie managed a laugh. "Welcome to the Navy, Whittier."

Whittier nodded. "Yes, sir. And as for my second question, sir? Why we weren't ordered to Bomba earlier?"

Jamie shrugged. "You'll have to ask General Eaton that. Perhaps, until now, he assumed we were too far away to do much about it even if our ships were there. But I believe that *someone* should have been at Bomba at the appointed time, whatever it took. I felt it my duty as naval liaison to offer my opinion to General Eaton. And so I did. Not that it did much good."

"Thank you, sir. Again, I appreciate the explanation."

"Such as it is." Jamie began stowing away the few items they had taken off the horses. "Now I have a question for you, Whittier."

"Ask away, sir."

Jamie looked at the young Marine private. "What in heaven's name compelled an intelligent fellow like you from the land-locked state of Kentucky to enlist in the Marine Corps? What did you do? Dilly up some girl?"

Whittier grinned. "Nothing like that, sir. I joined the Marines to see the world. To visit exotic places."

"Like this."

"Oh yes, sir. Exactly like this."

"You're joking."

"Not in the least, sir. I've never been more serious." He stretched out his arms to encompass his surroundings. "Just look around you, sir."

Jamie laughed out loud. "Jesus Christ Almighty, Whittier. Go to sleep, would you? We have an early day tomorrow."

"Aye, aye, sir."

As dawn streaked across the eastern sky they set off again, alternating between an easy canter and a hard lope to pace the horses. The farther west they rode, the firmer the ground became along an increasingly hilly and well-traveled pathway. Always on the alert for ambush, they kept their weapons within easy reach. But the few local citizens they encountered fled before the two Americans, an apparition of an apocalypse, perhaps, to Muslims who had never before laid eyes on a Christian.

At noon they dismounted in a small valley supporting the barest of vegetation. Jamie and Whittier searched for water while the horses nibbled on what sustenance they could find. After half an hour they came upon a deep shaft cut into a pile of large boulders. Jamie dropped a stone down the shaft. After several moments he heard a dull, pleasing splash. "Lower away," he said to Whittier.

Whittier lowered a goatskin bucket down the shaft. When he heard it plop into water, he let the bucket lie on its side long enough to allow it to fill and then carefully hauled it up. He set the bucket on a smooth sweep of rock and scooped his palm into the liquid. He brought it to his mouth and took a sip. Immediately he spat it out.

"Rancid," he exclaimed with disgust.

So they rode on without water, their throats so parched they could not swallow a last ration of rice and biscuit.

"Try not to think about it," Jamie said as much to himself as to Whittier when they took ten minutes in midafternoon in what they hoped was their last rest break before arriving at the Bay of Bomba. "Easier said than done, sir," Whittier replied. Just as he said that they both spotted a large, low-lying rock formation with a flat, indented top shaped like the crown of a volcano. The same notion flashed into both minds at once, and they scrambled to their feet and raced over. There was not much water, but to the two parched Americans it seemed a king's ransom.

Jamie dipped his hand into the warm liquid and savored the feel of it in his mouth before he swallowed. A smile creased his lips as he looked at Whittier, watching him anxiously. "Not bad," he announced, and they eagerly scooped up handfuls. "Save some for the horses," Jamie warned. "And some for us, later."

Revived in body and spirit, they rode on at a gallop. The sun was low on its downward arc when a protected body of water perhaps a mile wide loomed below them. The bay was surrounded by high bluffs on its east and south sides, more severe scarps to the west, and was almost perfectly U-shaped with a sandy beach at its base. The middle of the gulf was deep azure blue, the same color as the Mediterranean that fed it, suggesting that the water there was deep. It shelved rapidly closer to shore; great rollers broke fifty yards out and raced in creamy foam with ever-diminishing force until they purled gently onto the sand.

"Now I understand why Father recommended this place," Jamie said. "It's perfect." He withdrew a small spyglass and began searching, moving the glass from side to side.

"See anything, sir?" Whittier inquired anxiously.

Jamie swung the glass again. "Nothing," he said, trying, without success, to keep disappointment from his voice. "Nothing, Whittier, I'm sorry to say."

"What do we do now, sir?"

Jamie swung a leg over and dismounted. "We do what we said we'd do. We wait."

"For how long, sir?"

"For as long as it takes, Whittier. We can't go back to the caravan empty-handed. At the very least it would mean the end of the expedition. Besides, we wouldn't make it back without food or water."

"True, sir," Whittier acknowledged.

"First thing," Jamie said, after tethering his horse and scanning the barren landscape, "is to find anything we might use to light a signal fire tonight."

There was nothing: no wood or grass or anything at all beyond rocks, sand, and a few sprigs of prickly desert plants that even the horses found unappetizing. That evening they consumed the last of their rations and most of their water.

The next day was no better. The hot sun sucked away their energy, and there was no shade on the bluff to escape it. Whittier suggested climbing down to the beach where they could find shade and cool off in the sea, but Jamie rejected the notion. The urge to drink seawater might prove too tempting, he said; and if they did that, it would drive them mad before killing them. Besides, he reasoned, at sea level they would have nowhere near the range of vision they had on the bluff. Every half-hour Jamie brought out his glass and searched the blue expanse. And saw nothing, nothing at all, as morning inched into afternoon, afternoon into evening, and evening into ominous black night.

Jamie was awake early the next morning, unable to sleep beyond a fitful hour or two. His stomach felt twisted in knots, so intense was his hunger, and it was painful to swallow, so fierce was his thirst. He glanced over at Whittier, lying dead asleep on his bedroll, and wondered if they could survive another day here. Perhaps, he thought, they should backtrack, find food and water, and then return to the bay. But there *was* no food or water in that direction, his brain reminded him. Going west toward Derne would be even more foolish. They would find food and water there, but they would also find enemy soldiers who would hardly be inclined to do anything for them beyond throwing them in prison—or worse. Going south into the desert seemed the worst choice of all. It would take them away from the coastline, and the odds of getting lost in the desert and eventually becoming scrap meat for vultures and other scavengers were depressingly high.

He rose to his feet, stretched, and walked toward the edge of the bluff. He listened to the sound of rollers hissing onto the beach below until the sky lightened and he could as much see as hear the slosh of waves. He glanced seaward into the spreading daylight. Something caught his eye and he looked again. He closed his eyes and rubbed them, as if the image might abide in there and not out at sea. But when he opened them again, it remained.

Jamie ran to his bedroll and withdrew the spyglass and a magnifying glass. Racing back to the edge of the bluff, he focused the lens of the spyglass on the image and kept it there, holding his breath until he could hold it no longer, then exhaling and inhaling and holding it again. Slowly, slowly, the image began to assume a solid form, from the billow of white topgallants that Jamie had first noticed down to a hull rising up on the horizon. His heart pounding, he waited . . . and waited . . . until he was absolutely certain. When he glimpsed the American ensign fluttering high above a frigate's profile he had come to know by heart, he picked up the magnifying glass. Fumbling it, almost dropping it in his jittery excitement, he held it up and reflected the sun's rays off the glass toward the ship. When the ship responded in kind, Jamie threw his strict officer's training to the wind and let out a wild whoop of joy.

Racing back to the campsite, he dropped to his knees and shook Whittier hard. The exhausted Marine instinctively flailed about with his arms. One blow caught Jamie on the chest, knocking him backward.

"William, wake up!" Jamie cried out, undaunted. "Wake up, man!"

That command brought Whittier fully awake. He sat up, blinked, and, realizing what he had just done, scooted on his rump away from Jamie, fear of the consequences of striking an officer sketched vividly on his unshaved and sunburned face. "Sir, I'm so terribly sorry, sir," he said, glancing desperately here and there as if in search of a path of retreat. "I didn't mean to hit you, sir. Upon my honor I didn't. I was dreaming. I—"

"William, you big bumbling boob, look at me!"

Whittier did. What he saw there was hardly anger. The grin Jamie was giving him was so delighted, so impish, that the bewildered Marine found himself grinning back.

"William, the United States Navy has arrived. *Portsmouth* is about to enter the bay and she has signaled us. I daresay we'll be dining aboard within the hour!"

Fourteen

Hingham, Massachusetts,
April 1805

KATHERINE CUTLER awoke as the first light of dawn filtered through the bedroom's two large, east-facing windows. She had not bothered to draw together the dark blue window curtains before retiring the previous night. She knew there was no point in trying to block out the morning sun. She would be up early after a fitful night's sleep, as she had been nearly every morning in recent weeks.

She tossed aside the light blanket and reached for the robe folded over a chair adjacent to the bed. Drawing it tight around her, she walked over to a window and gazed out on the neighborhood she and Richard had come to cherish during their twenty-five years together in this clapboard house. It was neither the grandest house in her immediate view nor one that might be considered a fashionable Hingham residence. But it was their home, their sanctuary. They had raised three children here, children who had grown up forever romping and laughing together. Or so it seemed to Katherine as her gaze took in the familiar landmarks visible through the window.

There had been opportunities over the years to move into a larger house, including the family home on Main Street where Caleb and Joan now stayed whenever they came down from Boston—which was more frequently now that Joan was heavy with child, praise be. Certainly they could afford a larger dwelling. Both Cutler & Sons and C&E Enterprises were flourishing, and Caleb and others had urged

Richard to purchase one of the newer seaside residences out toward Crow Point or World's End. Jack and Anne-Marie Endicott had chimed in on that chorus of voices. Such a residence, they claimed, would provide the Cutlers more comfort and privacy and would be more in keeping with the family's social status. But Richard had always demurred, and Katherine had always understood why. Yes, they could afford something more. But no other house, they both agreed, could ever hold the cherished family memories locked within every nook and cranny of this modest home on South Street.

Richard . . . The thought of him saying that very thing brought an image to Katherine's mind and a smile to her lips. Then that same image pulled her from the past to the present, and to the future she prayed they still had together.

She turned from the window and padded down the back stairs into the kitchen. In days gone by she would have found Edna Stowe there, working the culinary magic that had made her a legend in Hingham. These days, with advancing age slowing her step, Edna typically did not emerge from her bedroom until later in the morning. Katherine had urged her housekeeper to remain abed, pointing out that since she could prepare Diana's breakfast and there wasn't much else to do in the early morning, there was no need for Edna to be up early. In truth, Katherine wanted those early hours for herself, to be alone with her private thoughts. And later, as pink dawn bloomed into the full blush of morning, to have breakfast alone with her daughter, always a highlight of the day.

Katherine drifted through the morning, doing her normal housework but clearly preoccupied, until 11:00, when a gentle knock sounded at the front door.

"I'll get it," Diana warbled from the parlor, the joy in her voice and the bounce in her rapid footsteps summoning a smile from Katherine. Just so had it been years ago, in the Hardcastle residence in Fareham, England, whenever Richard, usually in company with his brother Will, arrived from his uncle's home several miles away to visit with Katherine and her younger brother Jamie. Her heart had raced whenever she heard the clop of hooves and saw the Cutler carriage approaching on the pebbled drive, bringing him ever closer to her.

Diana opened the door to a sturdy, well-proportioned young man of eighteen years whose finely chiseled face and cleft chin suggested family roots in English aristocracy. His wavy brown hair was clipped neatly at his jaw line. He was dressed in loose-fitting buff trousers and waistcoat, and the olive green of his shirt matched the color of the eyes that gazed affectionately at Diana Cutler. He removed his tricorne hat with a flourish and bowed low, as to a highborn lady.

"Hello, Peter," she greeted him, the thick-lashed hazel eyes that were perfect replicas of her mother's dancing with delight.

"Hello, Diana," he said. "You look lovely. Are you ready to go?"

"I am!"

Katherine walked up behind Diana just then, carrying the basket of food she and Diana had prepared that morning. "Good morning, Peter," she said as she handed him the basket. "It's always a pleasure to see you."

"It's always an honor to see you, Mrs. Cutler," he replied correctly. He took the basket from her. "Thank you for preparing this picnic for us."

"Diana had more of a hand in it than I," Katherine smiled. "Now you *will* take a coat, won't you? It may be unseasonably warm today, but the harbor waters are still cold. And a breeze might pick up this afternoon."

Peter nodded. "I've put everything we need in the boat," he assured her, "including an extra coat for Diana and some blankets. Will and Adele are meeting us at the boatyard. And it's a quick row out to Grape Island, Mrs. Cutler, so if the weather does kick up, we can be back ashore as quick as you please."

"So you see, Mother," Diana teased in mock reproach, "everything is in proper order and properly chaperoned."

Katherine Cutler smiled inwardly, wondering just what sort of chaperones Will and Adele might make. An incident that occurred two weeks ago suggested that they might be rather lenient ones. She had purchased a flounder from a local fisherman and thought to make a present of it to her older son and his wife. Carrying the newspaper-wrapped fish, she had walked the short distance from the docks to her son's home on Ship Street. When a knock on the front door produced no response, she had tried the back door, with the same result. Assuming that Will and Adele were out, and planning to leave the flounder on the kitchen table for their supper, she had quietly opened the door and walked in. She found no one in the kitchen, but coming from upstairs were the telltale sounds of low masculine grunts coupled with higher-pitched feminine moans. Quickly she retraced her steps, taking the flounder with her.

"Yes, I do see, Diana," she said in an equally teasing tone. "Be off now, you two. And *please* be careful."

"We will, Mrs. Cutler. You have my word on it."

"Will you be going riding with Aunt Lizzy this afternoon?" Diana asked as they were leaving.

"Perhaps. We'll see."

"You should, you know," Diana replied happily. "It's a heavenly day for it, and the horses need the exercise. Tomorrow we'll go riding together, Mother, shall we?"

"Yes, Diana. Off with you now. Go!" She shooed them away with flicks of her hands.

Stifling sadness born, in part, from watching her rapidly maturing daughter setting off beside her beau, Katherine smoothed her hair, took a coat from the closet, and left the house as well, heading toward Pleasant Street to visit with Lizzy Cutler Crabtree, her lifelong friend. Lizzy met her at the door and ushered her inside.

"How's Zeke?" Katherine asked as she removed her light woolen coat in the hallway.

"He's fine," Lizzy answered. She took the coat and hung it from a peg. "He's in his room playing with Will's old soldier set. I just looked in on him. He has a fierce battle raging up there, so he should be set for a while. Can I get you anything?"

"A glass of wine would be nice."

Lizzy could not conceal her surprise. Never had she known Katherine Cutler to request or accept a glass of spirits of any kind except at the dining room table, and certainly not in the morning. Katherine met her puzzled look steadily.

"Of course," Lizzy managed after a pause. She gave her friend a meaningful look. "Should I pour one for myself?"

"That might be a good idea."

"Right, then. I'll be back with a bottle."

Lizzy returned with a tray holding an opened bottle of claret and two glasses. She set the tray on a side table and poured out two glasses, offering one to Katherine and keeping the other for herself. She sat down beside Katherine on the sofa and looked closely at the woman who had been like a sister since childhood. "Well, this is unusual," she said.

"Yes, it is," Katherine agreed.

"What's the occasion?" Lizzy asked cautiously. "When I saw you at the market yesterday and you told me you wanted to come by today, you seemed so distant, almost as if you wished to avoid me, even though we haven't seen each other for a while. That isn't like you."

"True," Katherine acknowledged.

"Well, then," Lizzy ventured, "what is it? What's troubling you, Katherine?"

When Katherine did not immediately respond, Lizzy put down her glass and clasped Katherine's left hand in both of hers, waiting until Katherine met her eyes.

"What is it, Katherine?" she pleaded, near tears now. "Please tell me. You know you can tell me *anything*."

Katherine nodded. "I do know that. It's why I'm here."

"And . . . ?"

Katherine took a healthy swallow of wine, set down the glass, and placed her right hand over Lizzy's hands. "I have not been avoiding you, Lizzy. Please understand that I could never, ever do that. But I *have* been avoiding something else, a secret I have not dared to share with anyone."

"Including Richard?"

"Especially Richard."

"For God's sake, Katherine, tell me. Let me help you."

Katherine blinked. "I have a cancer, Lizzy."

Instinctively Lizzy tightened her grip on Katherine's hand. For several moments she could not speak. She just looked beseechingly at Katherine, willing her dearest friend in life to deny what she had just said. "You have a *what*?" she finally mustered.

"I have a cancer," Katherine repeated matter-of-factly. "I have a lump on my breast. I've known about it for some time. I've tried denying it, but that hasn't done much good." She gave Lizzy a rueful smile.

"But . . ." Lizzy fumbled for words. "But from what I understand, a lump on the breast doesn't necessarily mean cancer."

"That's true. But in my case, it does."

"How can you be so certain?"

Katherine shrugged. "I just know."

"Have you seen a doctor?"

"No. I can't bring myself to do it. I want to wait until Richard comes home. It won't be long now. He wrote in his last letter that the war is nearly over. Perhaps it's already over and *Portsmouth* is sailing home to us. When he comes home, we'll decide what to do. We have always decided important matters together."

Lizzy took Katherine's hands in both of hers. "Katherine, listen to me," she said sternly. "If this is a cancer, it cannot wait. You must see Dr. Prescott, and you must see him soon. It will only get worse if you wait. Please. I beg you. You know he is an excellent physician. A man we can trust. He has cared for our families for years. He'll know what to do. We can go together, Katherine, right now. I'll stay with you every second."

Katherine shook her head ever so slightly although her voice was emphatic. "It will do no good for me to see Dr. Prescott. I know the treatment for this sort of thing. We both know what happened to President Adams' daughter. I will *not* have my breast removed. I will *not* have Richard returning home from war to a mangled wife!"

Fifteen

Derne, Tripoli,
April–May 1805

RICHARD CUTLER WAS awake in his sleeping cuddy when he heard *Portsmouth*'s bell struck one time. By the time it was struck two times a half-hour later he had washed his hands and face from a tin basin filled with fresh water and had shaved with soap and razor. When his steward, coffee pot in hand, entered the cabin to wake Richard at the appointed hour of 5:30, he found him seated at his desk.

"Good morning, Captain," Simms greeted him cordially. "I see that you have once again denied me the opportunity to intrude upon your dreams. It's becoming a habit."

"Good morning, Sydney," Richard replied. He sketched a grin to camouflage the real reason he had arisen so early in recent days—ever since his son Jamie had insisted that he and Private Whittier return to camp to advise Captain Eaton of the state of affairs. After so many weeks of worry, he had finally held his son in the relative safety and abundance of his frigate at anchor in the Bay of Bomba, only to see him gallop off into the sunrise. At least, he thought, this time around he would have ample provisions. And he could not gainsay the pride he felt in his son's commitment to duty.

"Shall you be dining alone this morning, Captain? Or will Mr. Crabtree be joining you?"

Before Richard could answer, a faraway voice sounded through the open skylight.

"Sail ho!"

"Where away?" inquired the much louder voice of George Lee standing a few feet from the skylight on the quarterdeck directly above.

"Fine to nor'west, sir."

"Is she making for us?"

"That she is, sir. And I see one . . . two . . . three sets of sails, sir."

"Very well. I shall inform the captain."

"Belay that, Mr. Lee," Richard called up through the skylight. "The captain has heard the report and is coming on deck."

Richard shrugged on the undress uniform coat Simms held up for him. "Breakfast will have to wait, Sydney," he said as he collected his bicorne hat. "But I'll take along a cup of your coffee. No one brews it better."

"Thank you, Captain. I shall have breakfast for you whenever you desire it. Eggs, toast, bacon, and fried potatoes, cooked to your usual specifications." Simms handed his captain a cup of coffee. "And I shall prepare enough for two, just in case."

On the quarterdeck Richard returned the salutes of Lieutenant Lee, Lieutenant Meyers, and Midshipman Sterne. He took a sip of coffee, then shaded his eyes with his free hand and glanced aloft at the American ensign. Five knots from the east-northeast, he calculated the wind. A quick glance ashore revealed an empty beach strewn with green seaweed and edged by steep headlands except on the extreme eastern end, where a walkway of sorts provided a manageable pathway from the beach to high ground.

"Good morning, gentlemen," he said. "What do we have?"

"*Argus*, she looks to be, sir," Lee responded. "In company with *Hornet* and *Nautilus*. We'll have positive identification in a few minutes."

"I daresay you are correct, Mr. Lee," Richard said. "That being the case, all we need do now is await the arrival of General Eaton's army."

That happened two days later.

AT SIX BELLS in the forenoon watch, William Eaton, wearing a crisply pressed general's uniform, was piped aboard USS *Portsmouth*. Despite the trials and tribulations of his march across desert sands in the company of often unwilling and sometimes mutinous Arab allies, he appeared to be, as Agreen Crabtree later put it, in remarkably fine fiddle. As Agreen accompanied Eaton aft to meet the ships' officers and commanders gathered on the quarterdeck, boats from *Argus*, *Nautilus*, and *Hornet* were making for shore laden with fresh provisions for the army.

"I have brought with me from Syracuse seven thousand Spanish dollars," Isaac Hull informed Eaton after introductions were exchanged and the general was seated. "Commodore Barron has placed these funds at your disposal." As captain of the brig *Argus*, Isaac Hull served as co-commander with Richard Cutler in this expedition, just as they had done during the war with France in a raid on the island of Marie-Galante in the West Indies. The conversation paused while Sydney Simms served a dinner of mutton chops, fresh beans, and curried rice complemented by two bottles of Bordeaux.

When the table was in order, Eaton said, smiling, "That is most kind of him, Captain. I have certain . . . obligations due our Arab friends. 'Mercenaries' is hardly the word to describe these fellows. 'Bandits' serves better, 'extortionists' perhaps better still. The greater the perceived inconvenience or danger, the higher the wages they demand. I have had no such trouble with my European soldiers, even as their Arab allies were receiving higher payments or promises of payments. From that simple observation you may deduce your own conclusions about Arab versus Western culture. I can assure you, gentlemen, that these Arabs drew their own conclusions about us long ago. It grieves me no end, since I once admired the Arabic culture. I even taught myself several of its dialects and pestered my friend Pickering to appoint me consul to Tunis." He cut off a slab of mutton and chewed contemplatively before taking a sip of wine. "My Lord, this is delicious." He dabbed at his lips with a cloth napkin. "I haven't tasted such fine food in many months. My compliments to your steward, Captain Cutler. And to your son for agreeing to be my liaison officer, knowing full well the gastronomic sacrifice he was making."

Richard smiled. "Midshipmen don't normally eat this sort of fare, General. Unless they pay for it themselves, which few can do on a midshipman's wage. Except for the wine, which was drawn from my personal stores, this dinner is compliments of the United States Navy."

"As is your son," Eaton observed quite sincerely. "I predict he will go far in the service if that is his chosen profession. James is an exceptional young man. I would be hard-pressed to do without him. You must be very proud of him."

"His mother and I are both very proud of him," Richard said softly.

Lt. John Dent, the burly, dark-haired captain of the schooner *Nautilus*, asked into the ensuing silence, "General, apart from what you just said, how do you find our Arab allies? Specifically, how will they respond in battle? Can we rely on them?"

"You raise excellent questions, Lieutenant," Eaton replied. "Since I haven't had occasion to test them in battle, I can only speculate. However, along the march it was my great fortune to come upon a Bedouin tribe. They are local warriors, Tripolitans, and they despise Yusuf Karamanli. *Their* courage is not in question, and I have several hundred of them in my cavalry. I shall rely upon the ferocity of these Bedouins coupled with the discipline of the Europeans, the grit of our Marines, and the support of our Navy when I get to Derne. If I have those four elements, I could not care less how the Egyptians perform."

"As to naval support," Richard Cutler cautioned, "we may not be able to bring all our guns to bear at all times. I have studied the harbor at Derne, and I have interrogated the masters of captured merchantmen. The waters of the harbor are shallow, a fathom or two at best, for almost a quarter-mile from shore. My thought is to lighten *Nautilus* and *Hornet* as best we can and position them in close. *Argus* and *Portsmouth* can provide covering fire from farther out. Our guns won't be as accurate at that distance, but so be it."

"Agreed," Hull said without hesitation.

"Is that why," queried Lt. Samuel Evans, the bold-faced captain of *Hornet*, "the shore battery at Derne has only eight cannon facing seaward?"

Richard nodded. "Yes. The Tripolitans believe that Derne cannot be effectively attacked by sea."

"Then so be it, as you say, Captain Cutler." All eyes turned to General Eaton, who sat there smiling. "What you are telling us simply means we shall have to attack Derne by land, which has been my intention all along. For us to declare victory we must not just raze the town, we must take control of it." He held up his glass of wine as if in a silent toast to victory. "By the bye, I have a serious need of fieldpieces. I have Greek cannoneers in my army but no cannon for them to service. Might any of you have several to spare?"

Richard glanced at Hull, who said, "My understanding, General, is that *Constellation* is carrying fieldpieces for you. Unfortunately, it's been a fortnight since Commodore Barron or I have heard from Captain Campbell, so we must assume that he has been delayed. I had assumed you would make such a request, however, and I propose we offload several guns from one of our vessels." He shifted his gaze to *Hornet*'s captain. "May I suggest a pair of your brass 6-pounders, Sam? They are the lightest of the guns in our squadron, and as such we'd have the least difficulty getting them ashore and up a cliff, if need be. And offloading two of your guns would lighten your sloop. Of course, it would also reduce your number of guns to eight."

"Eight guns will suffice," Evans said.

"Well spoken, Lieutenant," Hull remarked. He glanced at Eaton. "Is this acceptable to you, General?"

"Most acceptable, Captain Hull," Eaton replied. "And thank *you* most cordially, Mr. Evans." His tone turned animated. "I've had some experience with brass 6-pounders, in the Northwest Territory while serving under General Wayne at the Battle of Fallen Timbers. You have heard of it? Well then, I can tell you that I should no more wish to be on the business end of one of those cannon than were the Shawnee and other tribes of the Western Confederacy. Those cannon won the day for us. I will be most pleased to deliver the same message here as I did there."

"When, exactly, do you intend to do that, General?"

"On the twenty-seventh, Lieutenant Dent, three days hence," Eaton replied. "Tomorrow, at the quickstep, we should reach Derne by late afternoon. That gives us the next day to reconnoiter, secure the cannon, and decide on our battle plan. I cannot finalize my plan until I have a chance to assess the town's defenses. But here is my thinking as of today, based on what Hamet Karamanli and others have told me about Derne . . ."

By THREE BELLS in the afternoon watch, massive cumulonimbus clouds were joining forces on the eastern horizon and the barometer was falling. Of greater concern to Josiah Smythe, there was a feel to the air and a look to the sea that augured wind, and a lot of it. Richard Cutler sensed the danger too and ordered Eaton rowed to the beach. He then signaled the other vessels in the squadron that he was making sail to put distance between *Portsmouth* and a lee shore. *Argus, Nautilus*, and *Hornet* acknowledged and followed in her wake once they had their boats aboard and secured to their chocks.

Ashore, the allied army moved inland to where the terrain was less rocky and more permeable. As they had since the first day of the march, Europeans and Arabs pitched their tents well apart from each other. Dawn the next morning broke warm and cloud-free after heavy rains and winds had pummeled the two campsites overnight. A quick breakfast of rice and beans, and the Marine drummer struck his familiar tattoo. Soldiers formed in ranks, and the army marched at double-time for much of the day. Late that afternoon their efforts were rewarded by the sight of high, undulating hills that Hamet confirmed marked the eastern boundary of the valley at Derne.

Eaton studied the crests of the hills. As best he could determine, and as scouts riding ahead soon confirmed, there were no enemy spotters stationed there.

"No doubt," Eaton commented that evening to Presley O'Bannon as they were about to review the next day's tactics, "the royal governor believes that Derne can no more be attacked by land than by sea."

"And why shouldn't he?" the Marine lieutenant responded. "What general in his right mind would march an army 450 miles across a harsh, barren desert to attack his town?"

"No general I know," Eaton replied with a laugh.

Early the next morning, Midshipman Cutler, Sergeant Campbell, and the two Greek army officers rode northward to a promontory that Jamie's father had recommended as the only location along the coast east of Derne where a 1,500-pound fieldpiece might be hauled up a twenty-foot cliff using man and horse power. Also to be hauled up: supplies of gunpowder, musket balls, flannel bags of grapeshot, and twenty round shot.

Eaton, Hamet Karamanli, and Lieutenant O'Bannon, meanwhile, climbed the highest hill on the eastern boundary. Lying flat on their bellies, they surveyed the town of Derne. What they saw below them surprised both Eaton and O'Bannon, despite what Hamet had previously told them. The valley—perhaps a mile and a half long and half a mile wide—was surrounded by hills on three sides and seemed even more fertile than the valley of the Eu ed Alli. To their right, against the harbor to the north, lay the town of five thousand citizens. To their left, from the town's southern limits to the hills in the far distance, stretched green fields of vegetables and fruit orchards. Eaton noted the lack of permanent walls around the town—Hamet had told them there weren't any because Derne had not been threatened by anyone in anyone's memory—but on the eastern edge of town, the one immediately below them, they noted a series of long stone buildings, one ending when the next began. The buildings formed a natural barrier and ended on a parallel with the most impressive building of them all, a majestic marble structure of ornate architecture with two minarets and tiers of grand terraces fringed with multicolored flora. On the two highest tiers—one facing northward, the other southward—two large cannon had been turned with tackle and handspikes to aim eastward.

"The governor's palace?" Eaton asked Hamet.

"Yes," Hamet confirmed. "Those cannon weren't there when I was governor."

"Thirty-four pounders," Eaton mused after sizing them up. "Ugly buggers, aren't they? We'd do well to steer clear of their sights."

O'Bannon indicated a building perhaps fifty feet in front of the palace by the harbor. "There lies the fort, sir," he said.

He was pointing at a fair-sized structure with a single rounded turret on its western side, above which fluttered the green-and-white flag of Tripoli. Jutting out in front of it and into the harbor waters lapping at its base was a platform housing a battery of eight medium-sized howitzers set within stone embrasures.

"That's the Navy's problem," Eaton said. He focused his attention on what lay directly below them: an open space fifty feet or so wide between the northern end of the long stone buildings and the eastern side of the harbor fortress. That gap was closing fast. Arab soldiers and citizenry were hard at work digging a ravine and erecting earthworks along the ravine's eastern edge. "We'll have a time breaching that," Eaton muttered to himself. "But breach it we must." He lifted his gaze beyond the ravine to the town of Derne, visible at that angle as a jumble of narrow streets meandering between limestone residences. Most of these were stylish, three-story affairs with grapevine-draped iron stairways leading from the street up to the front door.

"It's exactly as you described it, Hamet," Eaton said, peering through the glass. "I must say, this town has much to commend it. Pity we may have to demolish it." He shifted his glass to the southwest corner of the town, on the opposite side from where the long stone buildings began. "What is that structure over there? It looks like another fort."

"It's a castle," Hamet replied. "A very old castle. It's used mostly for storage. It's not heavily defended because it's not safe to walk on the upper floors. If we could take it, we could use the first floor as our base."

"I agree," Eaton said. He searched further. "Those earthworks to the south and west don't look as formidable as those below us. So the enemy must believe that if an attack comes, it will come from where we are now. That's where they're concentrating their forces and artillery."

"Consider, General," O'Bannon observed, a glass at his eye, "*why* they believe that. If we strike from the south or west, we'd have to charge from those hills"—he indicated the hills fringing the southern and western horizons—"across a mile of open ground. That would give the enemy, what, three or four rounds at us before we could answer with one. We'd suffer heavy losses, losses we cannot afford."

Eaton nodded slowly. "I daresay you're right, Lieutenant. So we attack from here. That will mean charging down a steep slope into the teeth of enemy fire. But I grant you, it's a far shorter distance to the town than from across those fields."

O'Bannon had another thought to contribute. "When we force our way into the town, we'll have to guard against ambush from every house on every street. Our spies report that many homes have had holes knocked through their walls. That makes every citizen of Derne a potential sniper. That could in fact be the enemy's fallback strategy: lure us in and then pick us off one by one."

Eaton grimaced. "You're full of good cheer this morning, aren't you, Lieutenant. But again I must agree with you. So we'll need to place our chances in the hands of God and in the heat of the moment. If the Navy can neutralize the shore batteries and if we can take the palace, perhaps that will convince the good people of Derne to switch loyalties and declare for Hamet. We may even persuade them to employ those sniper tactics against the governor's soldiers."

As Eaton and O'Bannon continued to contemplate the pros and cons, Hamet Karamanli spoke up. "General," he said in a decisive tone, "I have a different proposition."

"Oh? And what might that be?"

"I suggest we split our forces. You and your Europeans attack from here. My cavalry will attack from there." He pointed toward the southern hills. "On horseback, we will reach those defenses before the enemy can fire a second round. If at the same time you can blast your way through those earthworks below us, together we will cause enough confusion and fear to our enemy to give us victory."

Before answering Hamet's proposal, Eaton cast his gaze out to the distant horizon where he could just barely make out the royals of a naval squadron standing off and on the pirate coast, its presence invisible to anyone in the town below him. After too many moments of dead silence, Hamet asked sourly, "What is it, General? You do not trust me?"

Eaton looked squarely at him. "I trust you, Hamet," he replied. "If I didn't, I wouldn't be here. But I have a harder time trusting the officers who lead your cavalry. Sheik Mahomet has certain qualities I admire. Sheik el Tahib, however, has none. On this march he has treated me more as an enemy than an ally."

Hamet blinked. "You speak the truth, General," he said. "At least what your heart tells you is the truth. I realize that the ways of my people and my religion seem odd to you, perhaps even heretical. But understand: your Christian ways seem the same to us Muslims. Let us put all that aside, shall we? Let us not dwell on our differences. Let us dwell instead on what has kept us together across hundreds of miles of desert. As you say, we are here now. We have achieved what many believed impossible. Derne is our destiny, General, yours and mine. My soldiers understand this, and they are not cowards. They will fight—for me, for glory, for money—it does not matter what, they will fight. They will follow me—because *I* will be leading them into battle, not Sheik el Tahib. If Allah wills it, I will be first to die for my cause. At stake, for me, is not just my throne. I fight for that, of course, but I fight also for my people. And I fight for my family. Do not forget that my brother still holds my wife and children hostage in Tripoli."

As Hamet spoke, Eaton stole a glance at O'Bannon, who was staring wide-eyed at Hamet.

"You speak like a prince, Hamet," Eaton declared with admiration. "I am as impressed by your words as I am with your proposed battle plan." He did not mention that Hamet's plan was identical to the one he had discussed three days earlier on *Portsmouth*'s quarterdeck. "Before we proceed, however, I suggest we offer our enemy the opportunity to surrender. We shall send an offer to the governor and see how he responds."

Within the hour an unarmed Bedouin tribesman rode through the enemy defenses toward the governor's palace under a white flag. The message he carried was written by the hand of Gen. William Eaton and bore his signature and that of Hamet Karamanli. The message informed the royal governor that an allied army was assembled outside the town and was prepared to attack. Eaton urged the governor to surrender Derne to Hamet and accept him as the rightful bashaw of Tripoli.

Twenty minutes later, the Bedouin reached down from his horse and handed Eaton a sealed envelope. Eaton broke the seal and read:

> *Your head or mine.*
> —*Mustafa Bey, Governor*

Eaton tore the letter in two. "Gentlemen," he informed his officers, "we attack at dawn tomorrow."

• • •

AT 7:15 the next morning Eaton ordered a stack of red cedar logs set ablaze atop the highest peak on the bluffs east of Derne. It was the signal to the American squadron to launch their bombardment.

"Signal ashore, Richard," Agreen Crabtree told Richard as *Portsmouth*'s captain stepped up onto the quarterdeck from his cabin. As the ship's bell at the break of the forecastle chimed seven times and a quartermaster's mate called out the hour, Agreen handed Richard a glass and pointed at a distant puff of black smoke.

"I see it, Agee." Richard lowered the glass and glanced at the other vessels in the squadron. *Hornet* and *Nautilus* had seen the signal and were crowding on canvas. *Argus,* too, was adding sail.

Richard studied the shore battery. "Have the men eaten breakfast?" he inquired. He noted that the conspicuous toil going on to the left of the fortress for the past two days had ceased, and that soldiers there were armed and taking position within the ravine they had fashioned abaft the earthworks.

"They have."

"The guns are run out?"

"Both sides, as ordered."

"Very well. Inform Mr. Smythe that I want her brought in, but no closer than a half-mile off the beach. That will bring our guns well within range."

"A half mile, aye, Captain." Agreen strode the short distance to the helm to inform the ship's master, and then passed word for Peter Weeks, the boatswain.

As the squeal of boatswains' pipes drove sailors to their stations, Richard called out for the senior midshipman standing nearby at the ready.

Timothy Osborne snapped a smart salute. "Aye, Captain."

"Please pass word for Lieutenant Corbett."

"Aye, aye, sir."

Carl Corbett, captain of Marines, strode across the quarterdeck from where he had been inspecting the three 6-pounder guns on the leeward side. "You sent for me, Captain?"

"Yes, Mr. Corbett," Richard said. "I need to ensure that my orders of yesterday are fully understood. I want half our contingent of Marines standing by. You may select those to go in on the first wave. I will send in a second wave when and if I deem it necessary."

Corbett saluted. "I have made my selections, Captain, and my men are ready. If I may say so, sir, we are all itching to get into the fight."

Richard answered the salute. "Very well. Please carry on."

"Richard," Agreen cautioned sotto voce when the captain returned to the larboard railing, "I hope t' God you know what you're doin'. Commodore Barron made it crystal clear that no further ground forces are t' be committed here. Eaton has t' make do with what he has, and he knows it. If the battle goes foul for him, we're authorized to get him and the Marines out. That's it. No one else. All we can offer Eaton is naval support."

"That's precisely what I intend to offer him, Agee," Richard replied as *Portsmouth* swerved off the wind and picked up speed. "Naval support."

At 8:00, the start of the forenoon watch, the American squadron commenced fire on Derne. *Portsmouth*'s 12-pounder long guns erupted in a broadside, sending 144 pounds of hot metal screeching into the fort and palace. *Hornet,* with *Nautilus* close on her heels, tacked in closer to shore and concentrated her fire on the fort's seaward battery. After they had delivered their initial payload and were wearing ship to deliver a second, *Argus* pounded the northern reaches of the town with her own version of hell.

On the north-facing tier near the top of the governor's palace, the ominous black maw of a massive cannon flashed orange. A 34-pound ball shrieked over *Portsmouth*'s mizzen and plunged into the sea beyond. Through a glass, Richard noted its gun crew adjusting the quoin to aim lower.

"Mr. Osborne!"

"Sir!"

"Advise Mr. Meyers to take out that gun!"

"Aye, aye, sir!"

Moments later, Richard heard Meyers's directives belowdecks: "Fire as your guns bear! Make sure of it, captains!"

On a starboard tack, *Portsmouth*'s larboard battery opened fire on the palace. Gun after gun exploded, each gun captain patiently waiting until the top tier of the palace had been drawn into his sights. Every shot chomped a hungry bite. The third shot ripped through the round turret of a minaret, collapsing it like a child's toy hit by a rock. The eighth shot struck home, hammering into the base of the 34-pounder with an almighty clang heard far out to sea.

"Nice shot, Eric," Richard said softly.

Sailing on a close haul to southeastward, Captain Evans suddenly defied both the odds and his orders and slewed off the wind, sailing *Hornet* bow-on to within a hundred yards of the shore battery. To Richard, watching through a glass, it seemed a suicidal maneuver. *Hornet* was taking a horrific toll from enemy cannon and musket fire. Her forward sails were holed; lethal slivers of wood from her butchered railing and top-hamper flew up and out in all directions. One shot tore through her ensign halyard, severing it and sending the Stars and Stripes zigzagging down from on high. An officer Richard could not identify grabbed the bulky fifteen-foot-long flag before it hit the water and hauled it, foot by foot, up the mainmast ratlines as enemy musketry whipped and zinged around him. Seemingly oblivious to it all, he reached the masthead truck and, with a last mighty heave, tied the ensign securely to it. On his descent, a shot caught him in the thigh. Instinctively he reached out to the wound, a reflex that caused him to lose his grip on the shrouds and tumble headlong into the sea.

As *Hornet* presented her starboard broadside of four brass 6-pounders, a sailor on the larboard side tied a rope around his waist, knotted the other end around the mizzenmast bitts, and dove into the water. Swimming furiously to where the stricken officer was feebly thrashing about, he reached the spot just as the officer disappeared beneath the waves. The sailor jackknifed his body and splashed downward with a violent kick. Moments later he reemerged above the surface, his right arm wrapped across the officer's chest. The sailor managed to coax the officer onto his back just as eager hands aboard the sloop pulled hard in unison and hauled both men back aboard.

Richard let out a breath. "Sweet Jesus in heaven," he said to Agreen. "Both those men deserve a medal for what they just did." He swung his glass to shore, noting with satisfaction that one shot from *Hornet*'s broadside had upended a cannon. *Nautilus*, sailing fast to her aid, unleashed her guns into the confusion ashore and put another cannon out of action. Return fire from the shore battery became more sporadic as *Nautilus* covered *Hornet*, allowing the badly damaged sloop to come about and make good her escape.

Hornet's resolve, combined with the heroics of officer and sailor and the subsequent action by Lieutenant Dent, inspired the two larger naval vessels to their own heroic deed. Richard Cutler and Isaac Hull ignored their own orders and together sailed to within four cable lengths of the beach. First on one tack, then on the other, they brought their broadsides to bear on the fort and the palace behind it, pounding, pulverizing, pummeling the enemy until the enemy could take no more and fled.

"THEY'RE ABANDONING the fort!" James Cutler exclaimed. Try as he may, he could not maintain an officer's stiff upper lip. "And the palace, by God!"

Eaton, O'Bannon, and Cutler were scrutinizing the town from a high ridge directly above the earthworks built up along the northeast sector. Behind the officers, Sergeant Campbell stood at ease with his six Marines. Further behind stood ninety European mercenaries also at their ease. Below, to the right, on a small promontory jutting out from the ridge, Greek cannoneers made ready the one 6-pounder they had managed to haul up the cliff. It lay flat on a carriage without wheels, its muzzle aimed downward at the earthworks.

"So they have, Mr. Cutler," Eaton agreed. "So they have. The Navy has done its job. Now it's time to do ours." He swung his gaze southward and his smug disposition disintegrated. "Damn*nation*, Karamanli!" he cursed aloud. "Where *are* you? Bathing your sorry ass in an oasis?" He swung the glass back to the earthworks below them and did a mental count of the soldiers running from the fort and palace to the ravine. "There must be, what, fifty of them?" he asked O'Bannon, who had been doing the same sort of exercise.

"Closer to seventy or eighty, I would say."

"So adding them to the mix, they have almost a thousand in arms down there?"

O'Bannon nodded. "That would seem a fair estimate, General."

"A thousand of them to a hundred of us." Eaton continued to study the defenses through a glass, as though searching for a chink in a suit of armor into which he might thrust a blade. "Ten-to-one odds." He collapsed the spyglass. "I would say those odds were very much in our favor, were the enemy not so well entrenched. And had we allies we could depend on." He consulted his waistcoat watch. "Mr. Cutler!"

"Sir?"

"Ride over to Hamet. Find out why he is sitting on his hindquarters. Tell him to attack. *Order* him to attack! And Mr. Cutler?"

"Yes sir?"

"Forget all that nonsense you've learned about being an officer and a gentleman. Remember what I have told you time and time again, that the only way to get these goddamn Arabs to actually *do* anything is to shove the muzzle of a pistol against their forehead or a hot poker up their ass. Got it?"

"Yes, sir!"

The mile and a half to where Hamet's cavalry was supposed to be arrayed in battle formation behind the rolling hills fringing the southern horizon was tough going. Jamie's horse slid through the loose stones and pebbles, pocked here and there with treacherous hollows. About halfway there Jamie paused for a sip of water. He splashed some onto a handkerchief and was wiping his face and neck when he heard a great shout and the drumming of distant hooves. He turned toward the sound and watched in awe as streams of cavalry cascaded over the southern hills like Saladin's Saracens, their scimitars, muskets, and great green-and-white banners raised high. As they thundered past, Jamie noted the unmistakable markings of Bedouin tribesmen galloping out ahead in a frenzied surge behind their leader, a figure mounted on a steed as cloud-white as his robes, his scimitar pointing skyward at first and then arcing slowly downward until it pointed ahead at those who had usurped his throne.

Mesmerized by the sight of a full-fledged frontal assault of Arab against Arab, Jamie sat stock still in the saddle. Nothing he had witnessed on the march across Cyrenaica suggested that this well-coordinated charge was even remotely possible. Only when erratic gunfire broke out from behind the town's defenses did he tear his eyes away and coax his horse around.

He reached Eaton's position on foot, leading his horse, a moment before the Greek cannoneers fired on the earthworks below. Out to sea, the guns of the naval squadron fell silent. The entire north wall of the palace, save for the low central portions shielded by the fort, was rubble.

The 6-pounder shell struck the ground just in front of the earthworks, sending up a spray of sand and debris. A Greek gunner inserted the quoin one notch. The second shot hit the earthworks squarely, an iron fist pounding a pathway through.

"A few more shots like that and we can parade ourselves in," Eaton said happily as he scrutinized the southern defenses. What he observed was most encouraging. Hamet's cavalry was leaping over those defenses, forcing the defenders into a haphazard retreat. "Welcome back, Mr. Cutler," he said blithely to the midshipman beside him. "Now tell me, which was it?"

"Sir?" Jamie was bent forward, his hands on his knees, catching his breath

"Which was it? Cold steel or hot poker? Whichever it was, it was most persuasive."

"Neither, sir," Jamie said. "Mr. Karamanli launched his attack before I reached him."

Eaton smirked but kept his eyes on the promontory below. "I am aware of that, Mr. Cutler. I was watching you. I was being flippant." Then his face darkened. "*Shit!*"

"What is it, sir?" Jamie asked tentatively.

O'Bannon, standing next to Eaton, answered him. "It seems we've lost the use of our cannon, Mr. Cutler. Evidently one of the Greeks neglected to remove the rammer before firing. Wherever that rammer is now, it's of no use to us."

RICHARD CUTLER, half a mile out to sea, did not observe what happened to the rammer. Nor could he see from the quarterdeck what was happening in the town, although lookouts high up on the frigate's crosstrees reported that Hamet's Arabs had breached Derne's southern defenses and had taken the castle. They had not yet, however, advanced into the town. Enemy defenders had scattered and were either taking refuge in individual buildings or gathering at the south side of the governor's palace. The plan, Richard knew, was for Hamet and Eaton to join forces at that compound. But Hamet was apparently content to stay put and Eaton had not yet launched his attack.

"Why go t' what's left of the palace?" Agreen wondered aloud. He, Lee, and Meyers had joined their captain on the quarterdeck, and all four had their spyglasses trained on Derne. "T' protect the royal governor? It's no place for a last stand."

"Possibly," Richard mused, "assuming the royal governor is still in there. Which I doubt. And I doubt he's the one coordinating the town's defenses either. My money is on the commander of the reinforcements from Tripoli. He's obviously a man Yusuf trusts."

"What of General Eaton, sir?" George Lee asked. "Why isn't he attacking?"

"I don't know, Mr. Lee. I wish I did. Mr. Corbett!"

"Right behind you, sir."

Richard wheeled about. "Have Mr. Weeks call away the boats. Make ready the first wave of Marines."

Corbett saluted. "Aye, aye, sir."

"Mr. Meyers!"

"Sir!"

"Advise the lookouts to report any movement of any kind the moment it occurs.

"Aye, aye, sir!"

That last order was entirely unnecessary, and every officer aboard knew it. But every officer aboard *Portsmouth* and the other vessels in the squadron also knew that Richard Cutler was the only man among them who had a son ashore on the front line of battle.

"GENERAL, it's past time," O'Bannon cautioned. "We can't delay any longer. The enemy's number in the ravine is increasing by the minute. Ours is not. We either attack now or stand down."

"I didn't come all this distance to stand down," Eaton replied testily. He trained his glass a final time on the old castle in the southwest sector of the town. Hamet was in there, no doubt. He could see his white-robed cavalrymen on the lower ramparts and outside the walls. But he noted with mounting disgust that the soldiers were in no apparent hurry to heed a further call to arms. For the life of him, Eaton could not understand why Hamet was taking his sweet time capitalizing on his advantage. He did, however, understand the probable consequences of his one hundred soldiers going it alone. Dark fury boiled within him anew. To Hamet Karamanli, Eaton and his Christian soldiers were nothing more than sacrificial lambs being led to an altar. "Advise the men to fix bayonets, Mr. O'Bannon."

O'Bannon turned about. "Sergeant Campbell!"

"Sir!"

"We shall fix bayonets!"

"Sir!"

Campbell issued the order, and soldiers inserted the end of their musket barrels into the attachment loop of their bayonets and turned the double-edged blades firmly to the right, fixing them in place.

Eaton, wearing full undress uniform, mounted his horse. O'Bannon and Jamie mounted theirs. Eaton slid his saber from its sheath and wheeled his horse about to face his command. He raised his saber; "To honor and glory!" he shouted. "Follow me, my brave lads! Today, victory is ours!" He wheeled his horse back around and walked him to the crest of the ridge, then sliced down his saber.

"*Charge!*"

The Marine drummer pounded his drum, and Christian soldiers surged over the ridge. When the last of them had gone over, the young Marine tossed the drum aside, seized his musket, and ran after them.

Arabs in the ravine opened fire in a volley as random in aim as it was ineffectual. To Eaton's supreme satisfaction, as he lurched and pitched down the sandy slope, there appeared to be no officer down there trained in the art of staged firing—first from one squad, then from another while the first squad reloaded—that could inflict sustained fire upon a charging enemy. Better still, their undisciplined pattern of musketry suggested an enemy unnerved by the blood-curdling screams in many languages and the advancing line of glistening bayonets. By the time the Arabs reloaded, the allied force was more than halfway down the hill and picking up speed on ground becoming firmer and more level with each step.

The second round of enemy fire was as undisciplined as the first. But since it was discharged at a much closer range, it took its toll. One Marine fell, then another. Behind them, a score of mercenaries collapsed onto their knees or staggered forward before falling facedown on the rocky ground. Suddenly, directly ahead of Jamie Cutler, General Eaton jerked on the reins of his horse and grabbed hold of his left wrist. The horse's front legs buckled, throwing Eaton off. Jamie reined in, dismounted, and ran to where Eaton was struggling to get up. Americans and Europeans streamed past him, hard behind Lieutenant O'Bannon, now leading the charge.

"General, you're hit, sir!" Jamie said when he reached the general's side. He helped Eaton to a sitting position as the battle raged just a few yards away. The Christian soldiers surged relentlessly forward, pushing back their adversaries.

Eaton grimaced with pain. "It's my wrist," he said. Musket shot kicked up the ground around them, some shot ricocheting unpredictably. "But praise God I don't think it's serious." He held up his wrist for closer inspection. Surprisingly, there was little blood. "Look at that. Bastard went clean through it. There's a hole on either side."

"Here, sir, allow me." Jamie shook off his uniform coat and withdrew a small dirk at his belt. Holding his shirt out from his stomach, he sliced downward from his chest, cutting off a sizable strip of cotton cloth, which he wrapped tightly around the wound and secured with two double knots fashioned from pieces torn at the cloth's ends. "That should hold it for now, sir."

Eaton flexed his fingers and turned his wrist this way and that. "Excellent work, Mr. Cutler," he said. A chance shot from an enemy musket dug in dangerously close. "Your ship's surgeon would be proud. I have one final favor to ask: the use of your horse. Mine had the good sense to run off."

"She's yours, General."

"Thank you." Eaton found his hat, put a foot in a stirrup, and with effort swung himself aboard the roan. He looked down at Jamie and touched the front of his hat. "See you at the palace, Mr. Cutler."

"*Argus* IS SIGNALING, Captain."

Richard Cutler was pacing back and forth on the weather side of the quarterdeck. Lieutenant Crabtree was keeping pace step for step.

Richard stopped short. "How does the message read, Agee?"

"According t' Mr. Boyle," referring to the signal midshipman, "Captain Hull is inquirin' about your intentions."

"My intentions? By that I assume he means whether I intend to invite him to supper this evening."

Agreen's expression remained deadpan. "Could be. Or it could be he's wonderin' why the jolly boat and launch are swayed out, and why twenty Marines in full gear are standin' by on the weather deck."

"Ah. Perhaps you're right, Agee." Richard pondered his reply. "You may advise Mr. Boyle to advise Captain Hull that I am preparing for all contingencies."

Agreen grinned. "An excellent response, if I may say so, Captain."

The reply was hoisted up the signal halyard as excited shouts from lookouts brought every spyglass to bear on shore. A cluster of uniformed soldiers was advancing into Derne from the earthworks. Those Arab defenders willing and able to put up a fight were backing away step by step, parrying bayonet thrusts as best they could with their short-snubbed scimitars, seemingly to no avail. Many were gored where they stood by the vicious thrust of a bayonet, doubling over before the bloody blade was withdrawn in search of another victim. Arabs still heavily outnumbered Christians, but neither side seemed overly impressed by that margin. Close-quarter combat was quickly turning into a one-sided slaughter.

To the south, between the palace and the castle, another battle was raging, but the naval officers could not determine its course. It was apparently being waged street by street, and there were many buildings blocking their view.

"My. Crabtree," Richard said to his first lieutenant, "we shall reduce sail to tops'ls, royals, jib, and driver. Bring her in on a parallel course with the coast, three cable lengths out. We'll tow the boats behind. And I shall have the guns run out, both sides."

"Aye, Captain. Shall we beat to quarters?"

"I don't think that will be necessary. This is a precautionary measure only."

"Understood, Captain."

As Agreen Crabtree issued the orders to Josiah Smythe and Peter Weeks, Lieutenant Meyers and Lieutenant Lee stepped down the main hatchway to the gun deck, their station for action.

Three cable lengths—three-tenths of a sea mile. Richard would not have even considered sailing his ship in so close to shore in such treacherous waters had the wind not shifted to southward and strengthened to ten knots, a steady offshore lubber's breeze that could quickly carry them away from any danger. There was still a risk, of course. The wind could shift again. But Richard told himself that if he kept his sea senses alert, and if the leadsman in the fore-chains kept a sharp eye on the seabed, he would not be placing his ship in undue danger.

Under reduced sail *Portsmouth* glided along the coastline on a close haul near the spot where *Hornet* had earlier presented her broadside to the fort. No cannon, no musket, no weapon of any kind offered a challenge.

Suddenly Agreen touched Richard's arm. "There," he said, pointing. "Sweet Jesus, would you look at that."

He was indicating the fields west of Derne. Tripolitans were climbing, jumping, leaping over the town's defenses into those fields, then running pell-mell toward the presumed safety of the western hills. A few men carried weapons; most did not.

"They're giving us a target, Richard. Shall we respond?"

Richard watched the rout unfold before his eyes. Slowly he shook his head. "No, Agee. Leave them be. They're no longer a threat. And likely there are civilians in there among the soldiers. We have nothing to gain by killing them, and perhaps a lot to lose."

"Agreed," Agreen said, adding with a smile, "Maybe what's happening at the fort is more t' your liking. Have a gander."

Richard trained his glass on what remained of the shore battery. Both the battery and the fort immediately behind it were deserted except for three men charging up the ramparts. One of the three, praise God, was his son. And he looked to be all right, although his badly torn shirt gave pause. A second man Richard identified as Lt. Presley O'Bannon. The third man he could not readily make out, but by his sheer bulk he had to be Marine private William Whittier. Whoever he was, he was carrying something bulky, and he was the first through the open door. O'Bannon followed him in. Jamie gave *Portsmouth* an enthusiastic wave before he too disappeared inside.

"What the . . . ?"

"There's your answer, Agee," Richard said some moments later in a voice choked with emotion.

The two friends watched along with the rest of *Portsmouth*'s company as the flag of Tripoli slid down the flagpole that topped the fort's lone turret. In its place, hauled up by two Marines and a midshipman, rose a mass of cloth, its provenance uncertain as it pulsed its way upward in short spurts, slowly at first, then more purposefully, until its body caught the wind and unfurled with a snap revealing fifteen stars and fifteen stripes. The vision of victory rose higher and higher above the shores of Tripoli, impelled, so it seemed, by the hurrahs and huzzahs of a naval squadron at sea and an allied army on shore.

"There, before God, is your answer."

Epilogue

THE RAISING OF the American flag, however thunderous the acclaim that greeted it, did not end the battle for Derne. Two days later, reinforcements from Tripoli—seven hundred cavalry and three hundred foot-soldiers—charged onto the scene. They made ready their attack on the same high ground Hamet's force had used. General Eaton, in command at his headquarters at the battered fort by the harbor, put every available hand to work shoring up the town's defenses. A good number of Derne's citizens pitched in, eager to demonstrate either their support for Hamet or their contempt for his brother—or both. Fighting shoulder to shoulder, Hamet's Muslims and Eaton's Christians successfully repelled the attacks.

His situation grave, the royal governor of Derne first took refuge in a mosque. When Eaton threatened to march in and drag him out, the governor appealed to a higher authority: a prominent local sheik, who granted the governor safe haven in his harem. Eaton scoffed at the notion and trooped his Marines to the sheik's home, only to be warned not to step inside. The citizens of Derne were warming to Hamet, the sheik said. Should his ally, General Eaton, desecrate the ancient right of sanctuary in a harem, they would be offended and turn against him. He did not mention that before taking refuge in the harem, Mustifa Bey had made it known about town that he was offering a reward of six hundred dollars for Eaton's head and thirty dollars for the head of any other Christian dog.

Eaton granted the governor one day's grace. Late that night, the sheik slipped the governor past the guards, out of Derne, and into the custody of the royal forces encamped in the southern hills.

With Derne secure, Eaton prepared to move on Tripoli. "On to Tripoli!" became the battle cry of the allied army. But there were other forces in play.

[232]

When *Hornet* brought word of the victory at Derne to Samuel Barron in Syracuse, the commodore was no doubt relieved that he had already submitted his letter of resignation and was soon to give up command of the Mediterranean Squadron. Two weeks earlier, convinced at last by Tobias Lear that Eaton's expedition was nothing more than a pipe dream, Barron had sent Lear to Tripoli aboard the frigate *Essex*. His mission: to negotiate a peace treaty on behalf of the United States and to secure the release of *Philadelphia*'s crew as quickly as possible. When Commo. John Rodgers, eager to take up the fight, sailed in from Gibraltar several weeks later to assume command of the squadron, he found his hands tied. He along with everyone else had to await the outcome of the negotiations.

In Tripoli, Lear found a receptive audience. Word of the disaster at Derne had seeped like raw sewage into every nook and cranny of the bashaw's castle, and Yusuf and his Divan were concerned. The costs of this war were mounting by the day. So were the impatience and rancor of the masses and the specter of ultimate defeat. With the assistance of his foreign secretary acting in concert with the Spanish and Danish consuls in Tripoli, Yusuf orchestrated an offer. For a total sum of sixty thousand dollars—all of it ransom money, not a dollar in tribute—he would consent to peace, liberate his prisoners, and never again, as Allah was his witness, threaten the interests of the United States in the Mediterranean. Among other concessions: his personal guarantee of Hamet's safety and his promise to release Hamet's family as hostages, although not right away. Yusuf insisted on a three-year "cooling-off" period before his brother's wife and children would actually be set free. Lear made a counteroffer or two but generally accepted the proffered terms. The principals signed the agreement ending the war on June 10.

Lear immediately sent out formal dispatches announcing the treaty, including one carried by USS *Constellation* to Derne. He added a personal note to Eaton, in essence congratulating him for the stunning victory that finally had forced Yusuf Karamanli to the bargaining table.

Lear's dispatch disgusted Eaton, who viewed it as a sop from an inept career diplomat too incompetent to incorporate military strategy. But what infuriated him beyond measure was the accompanying dispatch from Commo. John Rodgers ordering Eaton to evacuate the Marines and Europeans from Derne, but no one else. In effect, Eaton was ordered to leave his Arab allies and the citizens of Derne to their fate. And he could well imagine what that fate would be.

Forced to obey a command that to his mind represented an insufferable breach of duty, honor, and decorum, Eaton fabricated an uprising along

Derne's southern defenses to draw Hamet's Arab soldiers away from the harbor. When they returned to headquarters, the Christians were gone. The next morning, when the citizens of Derne awoke to discover what had transpired during the night, those safely aboard *Constellation* could hear their mournful wails from a mile offshore.

Hamet Karamanli, graceful and pragmatic as always, accepted his fate and returned to Egypt. His mercenaries were never paid. Year after year, William Eaton lobbied Congress to grant Hamet an annual pension in recognition of services rendered to the United States. Year after year his appeals fell on deaf ears. As the drumbeat of war with England began to sound on the distant horizon, the First Barbary War faded from public memory.

MUCH HAS BEEN WRITTEN about the historical significance of the First Barbary War. The exploits of the U.S. Marines involved added to the luster of the Corps. The second line of the Marines' Hymn refers specifically to the Battle of Derne, and the ceremonial sword of the Marine Corps is to this day a replica of the Mameluke sword Hamet Karamanli presented to Lt. Presley O'Bannon for his valor and bravery. Gen. William Eaton's march across the desert is also legendary, and bears an uncanny semblance to the better-publicized exploits of British officer Thomas E. Lawrence in Arabia during World War I more than a century later.

But it was the U.S. Navy that took center stage in this conflict. In the Mediterranean, the U.S. Navy acted for the first time as a cohesive fighting force capable of formulating and implementing complex strategies while deployed thousands of miles from home waters. Its power was revealed in all its glory, and it was a power respected and revered even by such Royal Navy luminaries as Admiral Horatio Lord Nelson.

From such tests of courage are leaders born, and the First Barbary War produced its fair share: Edward Preble, of course, but also those young naval officers under his command whom he came to refer to affectionately as "my boys." Among them is Lt. Stephen Decatur, whose raid on *Philadelphia* is the stuff of legend. He returned home a true American hero for the ages. At the still-tender age of twenty-five he became the youngest American officer ever to achieve the rank of captain.

But perhaps first among the Barbary heroes is Lt. Richard Somers, captain of *Intrepid* during her final voyage. He and the brave volunteers who sailed with him are not forgotten. In 2004 the New Jersey legislature passed a resolution calling for the repatriation of the remains of Somers and his crew, buried since 1805 on the shores of Tripoli. In April 2011 a similar bill was introduced in Congress. Space to receive their remains has been reserved at Arlington National Cemetery.

In 1806 USS *Constitution* brought the Tripoli Monument from Italy, when it was fashioned, to the Washington Navy Yard. Inscribed on the thirty-foot white marble sculpture crowned by the American eagle are the names of the honored dead of the war, among them Richard Somers, James Decatur, Joseph Israel, and Henry Wadsworth (Longfellow's uncle). In 1860 that monument, the oldest military monument in the United States, was moved to the spot where it stands today, on Decatur Road near Preble Hall at the U.S. Naval Academy in Annapolis, Maryland.

Glossary

aback   In a position to catch the wind on the forward surface. A sail is aback when it is pressed against the mast by a headwind.

abaft   Toward the stern of a ship. Used relatively, as in "abaft the beam" of a vessel.

able seaman   A general term for a sailor with considerable experience in performing the basic tasks of sailing a ship.

after cabin   The cabin in the stern of the ship used by the captain, commodore, or admiral.

aide-de-camp   An officer acting as a confidential assistant to a senior officer.

alee or *leeward*   On or toward the sheltered side of a ship; away from the wind.

amidships   In or toward the middle of a vessel.

athwart   Across from side to side, transversely.

back   To turn a sail or a yard so that the wind blows directly on the front of a sail, thus slowing the ship's forward motion.

back and fill   To go backward and forward.

backstay   A long rope that supports a mast and counters forward pull.

ballast   Any heavy material placed in a ship's hold to improve her stability, such as pig iron, gravel, stones, or lead.

Barbary States   Morocco, Algiers, Tunis, and Tripoli. All except Morocco were under the nominal rule of the Ottoman sultan in Constantinople.

bark or *barque*   A three-masted vessel with the foremast and mainmast square-rigged, and the mizzenmast fore-and-aft rigged.

bar-shot   Shot consisting of two half cannonballs joined by an iron bar, used to damage the masts and rigging of enemy vessels.

before the mast   Term to describe common sailors, who were berthed in the forecastle, the part of the ship forward of the foremast.

before the wind   Sailing with the wind directly astern.

belay   To secure a running rope used to work the sails. Also, to disregard, as in "Belay that last order."

belaying pin   A fixed pin used on board ship to secure a rope fastened around it.

bend   To make fast. To bend on a sail means to make it fast to a yard or stay.

binnacle   A box that houses the compass, found on the deck of a ship near the helm.

boatswain   A petty officer in charge of a ship's equipment and crew, roughly the equivalent in rank to a sergeant in the army.

bollard   A short post on a ship or quay for securing a rope.

bower   The name of a ship's two largest anchors. The best-bower is carried on the starboard bow; the small-bower is carried on the larboard bow.

bowsprit   A spar running out from the bow of a ship, to which the forestays are fastened.

brace   A rope attached to the end of a yard, used to swing or trim the sail. To "brace up" means to bring the yards closer to fore-and-aft by hauling on the lee braces.

brail up   To haul up the foot or lower corners of a sail by means of the brails, small ropes fastened to the edges of sails to truss them up before furling.

brig   A two-masted square-rigged vessel having an additional fore-and-aft sail on the gaff and a boom on her mainmast.

Bristol-fashion   Shipshape.

broach-to   To veer or inadvertently to cause the ship to veer to windward, bringing her broadside to meet the wind and sea, a potentially dangerous situation, often the result of a ship being driven too hard.

buntline   A line for restraining the loose center of a sail when it is furled.

by the wind   As close as possible to the direction from which the wind is blowing.

cable   A strong, thick rope to which the ship's anchor is fastened. Also a unit of measure equaling approximately one-tenth of a sea mile, or two hundred yards.

cable-tier   A place in a hold where cables are stored.

camboose   A term of Dutch origin adopted by the early U.S. Navy to describe the wood-burning stove used in food preparation on a warship. Also, the general area of food preparation, now referred to as the galley.

canister shot or *case shot*   Many small iron balls packed in a cylindrical tin case that is fired from a cannon.

capstan   A broad, revolving cylinder with a vertical axis used for winding a rope or cable.

caravel-built Describing a vessel whose outer planks are flush and smooth, as opposed to a clinker-built vessel, whose outer planks overlap.

cartridge   A case made of paper, flannel, or metal that contains the charge of powder for a firearm.

catharpings   Small ropes that brace the shrouds of the lower masts.

cathead or *cat*   A horizontal beam at each side of a ship's bow used for raising and carrying an anchor.

chains or *chain-wale* or *channel*   A structure projecting horizontally from a ship's sides abreast of the masts that is used to widen the basis for the shrouds.

clap on   To add on, as in more sail or more hands on a line.

clewgarnet   Tackle used to clew up the courses or lower square sails when they are bring furled.

close-hauled   Sailing with sails hauled in as tight as possible, which allows the vessel to lie as close to the wind as possible.

commodore   A captain appointed as commander in chief of a squadron of ships or a station.

companion   An opening in a ship's deck leading below to a cabin via a companionway.

cordage   Cords or ropes, especially those in the rigging of a ship.

corvette or *corsair*   A warship with a flush deck and a single tier of guns.

course   The sail that hangs on the lowest yard of a square-rigged vessel.

crosstrees   A pair of horizontal struts attached to a ship's mast to spread the rigging, especially at the head of a topmast.

cutwater   The forward edge of the stem or prow that divides the water before it reaches the bow.

daisy-cutter   Another name for a swivel gun.

deadlight   A protective cover fitted over a porthole or window on a ship.

dead reckoning   The process of calculating position at sea by estimating the direction and distance traveled.

dogwatch   Either of two short watches on a ship (1600–1800 hours and 1800–2000 hours).

East Indiaman   A large and heavily armed merchant ship built by the various East India companies. Considered the ultimate sea vessels of their day in comfort and ornamentation.

ensign   The flag carried by a ship to indicate her nationality.

fathom   Six feet in depth or length.

fife rail   A rail around the mainmast of a ship that holds belaying pins.

flag lieutenant   An officer acting as an aide-de-camp to an admiral.

footrope   A rope beneath a yard for sailors to stand on while reefing or furling.

forecastle   The forward part of a ship below the deck, traditionally where the crew was quartered.

furl   To roll up and bind a sail neatly to its yard or boom.

gangway   On deep-waisted ships, a narrow platform from the quarterdeck to the forecastle. Also, a movable bridge linking a ship to the shore.

gig   A light, narrow ship's boat normally used by the commander.

grape or *grapeshot*   Small cast-iron balls, bound together by a canvas bag, that scatter like shotgun pellets when fired.

grapnel or *grappling hook*   A device with iron claws that is attached to a rope and used for dragging or grasping, such as holding two ships together.

grating   The open woodwork cover for the hatchway.

half-seas over   Drunk.

halyard   A rope or tackle used to raise or lower a sail.

hawser   A large rope used in warping and mooring.

heave to   To halt a ship by setting the sails to counteract each other, a tactic often employed to ride out a storm.

hull-down   Referring to another ship being so far away that only her masts and sails are visible above the horizon.

impress   To force to serve in the navy.

jack   The small flag flown from the jack-staff on the bowsprit of a vessel, such as the British Union Jack and Dutch Jack.

jolly boat   A clinker-built ship's boat, smaller than a cutter, used for small work.

keelhaul   To punish by dragging someone through the water from one side of the boat to the other, under the keel.

langrage   Case shot with jagged pieces of iron, useful in damaging rigging and sails and killing men on deck.

larboard   The left side of a ship, now called the port side.

lateen sail   A triangular sail set on a long yard at a forty-five-degree angle to the mast.

laudanum   An alcoholic solution of opium.

lee   The side of a ship, land mass, or rock that is sheltered from the wind.

leech   The free edges of a sail, such as the vertical edges of a square sail and the aft edge of a fore-and-aft sail.

lighter   A boat or barge used to ferry cargo to and from ships at anchor.

loblolly boy   An assistant who helps a ship's surgeon and his mates.

manger   A small triangular area in the bow of a warship in which animals are kept.

muster-book   The official log of a ship's company.

ordnance   Mounted guns, mortars, munitions, and the like.

orlop   The lowest deck on a sailing ship having at least three decks.

parole   Word of honor, especially the pledge made by a prisoner of war, agreeing not to try to escape or, if released, to abide by certain conditions.

petty officer   A naval officer with rank corresponding to that of a noncommissioned officer in the Army.

pig   An oblong mass of metal, usually of iron, often used as ballast in a ship.

poop   A short, raised aftermost deck found only on very large sailing ships. Also, a vessel is said to be "pooped" when a heavy sea breaks over her stern, as in a gale.

post captain   A rank in the Royal Navy indicating the receipt of a commission as officer in command of a post ship; that is, a rated ship having no less than 20 guns.

privateer   A privately owned armed ship with a government commission authorizing it to act as a warship.

prize   An enemy vessel and its cargo captured at sea by a warship or a privateer.

purser   An officer responsible for keeping the ship's accounts and issuing food and clothing.

quadrant   An instrument that measures the angle of heavenly bodies for use in navigation.

quarterdeck   That part of a ship's upper deck near the stern traditionally reserved for the ship's officers.

quay   A dock or landing place, usually built of stone.

queue   A plait of hair; a pigtail.

quoin   A wooden wedge with a handle at the thick end used to adjust the elevation of a gun.

ratlines   Small lines fastened horizontally to the shrouds of a vessels for climbing up and down the rigging.

reef   A horizontal portion of a sail that can be rolled or folded up to reduce the amount of canvas exposed to the wind; the act of so rolling a sail.

rig   The arrangement of a vessel's masts and sails. The two main categories are square-rigged and fore-and-aft rigged.

rode   A rope securing an anchor.

round shot   Balls of cast iron fired from smooth-bore cannon.

royal   A small sail hoisted above the topgallant that is used in light and favorable winds.

scupper   An opening in a ship's side that allows water to run from the deck into the sea.

sheet   A rope used to extend the sail or to alter its direction. To *sheet home* is to haul in a sheet until the foot of the sail is as straight and as taut as possible.

ship-rigged   Carrying square sails on all three masts.

shipwright   A person employed in the construction of ships.

shrouds   A set of ropes forming part of the standing rigging and supporting the mast and topmast.

slops   Ready-made clothing from the ship's stores, or slop-chests.

slow-match   A very slow burning fuse used to ignite the charge in a large gun.

stay   Part of the standing rigging, a rope that supports a mast.

staysail   A triangular fore-and-aft sail hoisted upon a stay.

stem   The curved upright bow timber of a vessel.

stern sheets   The rear of an open boat and the seats there.

studdingsail or *stunsail*   An extra sail set outside the square sails during a fair wind.

swivel-gun   A small cannon mounted on a swivel so that it can be fired in any direction.

tack   A sailing vessel's course relative to the direction of the wind and the position of her sails. On a "starboard tack," the wind is coming across the starboard side. Also, the corner to which a rope is fastened to secure the sail.

taffrail   The rail at the upper end of a ship's stern.

tampion   A wooden stopper for the muzzle of a gun.

tholepin or *thole*   One of a pair of pegs set in a gunwale of a boat to hold an oar in place.

three sheets to the wind   Very drunk.

top   A platform constructed at the head of each of the lower masts of a ship to extend the topmast shrouds. Also used as a lookout and fighting platform.

topgallant   The third mast, sail, or yard above the deck.

top-hamper   A ship's masts, sails, and rigging.

topsail   The second sail above the deck, set above the course or mainsail.

touchhole   A vent in the breech of a firearm through which the charge is ignited.

tumblehome   The inward inclination of a ship's upper sides that causes the upper deck to be narrower than the lower decks.

waist   The middle part of a ship's upper deck between the quarterdeck and the forecastle.

wardroom   The messroom on board ship for the commissioned officers and senior warrant officers.

watch   A fixed period of duty on a ship. Watches are traditionally four hours long except for the two dogwatches, which are two hours long.

wherry   A rowboat used to carry passengers.

windward   Facing the wind or on the side facing the wind. Contrast *leeward*.

xebec   A three-masted Arab corsair equipped with lateen sails. Larger xebecs had a square sail on the foremast.

yard   A cylindrical spar slung across a ship's mast from which a sail hangs.

yardarm   The outer extremity of a yard.

About the Author

William C. Hammond is a literary agent and business consultant who lives with his three sons in Minneapolis, Minnesota. A lifelong student of history and a longtime devotee of nautical fiction, he sails whenever possible on Lake Superior and off the coast of New England.

The **Naval Institute Press** is the book-publishing arm of the U.S. Naval Institute, a private, nonprofit, membership society for sea service professionals and others who share an interest in naval and maritime affairs. Established in 1873 at the U.S. Naval Academy in Annapolis, Maryland, where its offices remain today, the Naval Institute has members worldwide.

Members of the Naval Institute support the education programs of the society and receive the influential monthly magazine *Proceedings* or the colorful bimonthly magazine *Naval History* and discounts on fine nautical prints and on ship and aircraft photos. They also have access to the transcripts of the Institute's Oral History Program and get discounted admission to any of the Institute-sponsored seminars offered around the country.

The Naval Institute's book-publishing program, begun in 1898 with basic guides to naval practices, has broadened its scope to include books of more general interest. Now the Naval Institute Press publishes about seventy titles each year, ranging from how-to books on boating and navigation to battle histories, biographies, ship and aircraft guides, and novels. Institute members receive significant discounts on the Press's more than eight hundred books in print.

Full-time students are eligible for special half-price membership rates. Life memberships are also available.

For a free catalog describing Naval Institute Press books currently available, and for further information about joining the U.S. Naval Institute, please write to:

Member Services
U.S. Naval Institute
291 Wood Road
Annapolis, MD 21402-5034
Telephone: (800) 233-8764
Fax: (410) 571-1703
Web address: www.usni.org